AMBITION AND DESIRE

Aaron reached out to stroke a wisp of fiery hair back from Sophia's cheek. His fingers grazed her skin and a tremor ran down her spine as he whispered, "I've wanted you from the first moment I saw you. And now I want you more than ever. I want you to want me."

"No, Aaron . . ."

"I won't let you push me away, Sophia. You won't suffer for the passion between us, I promise you that. I've already opened doors for you that you would've found closed otherwise, and this is only the beginning. With my support—"

"I won't sell myself to you, Aaron."

"And I won't let you sacrifice me to your ambitions. That is what you're trying to do, isn't it?"

"No . . . yes . . ." Suddenly overwhelmed by conflicting desires, Sophia shook her head. What did she want? She wanted to feel Aaron's arms around her. She wanted to surrender to this aching need so new and so strong that Aaron raised it with a touch, with a glance. She wanted . . .

Suddenly she was in Aaron's arms, all her restraint slipping away . . .

ELAINE BARBIERI
TATTERED SILK

ZEBRA BOOKS
KENSINGTON PUBLISHING CORP.

Benji, only you and I really know . . .

ZEBRA BOOKS

are published by

Kensington Publishing Corp.
475 Park Avenue South
New York, NY 10016

Copyright © 1991 by Elaine Barbieri

First printing: September, 1991

Printed in the United States of America

Acknowledgments

Giacomo De Stefano, Museum Curator, Paterson Museum, Paterson, N.J.

Grace George, Tour Director, The Great Falls Historic District, Paterson, N.J.

Evelyn M. Hershey, The American Labor Museum, Botto House, Paterson, N.J.

E. "Bunny" Kuiken, Trustee, The American Labor Museum, Botto House, Paterson, N.J.

Steven J. Malzone, Paterson Historian

Josephine Robertson, Retired Silk Worker

Prologue

A warm breeze gusted through the bedroom window, stirring the sultry night air and bathing the perspired flesh of the lovers lying passionately entwined. Sophia's lips parted in a soft gasp and she arched her back, accepting their hungry joining. She clutched her lover close, glorying in each thrust, meeting and giving fully.

A sliver of moonlight slanted through the drawn shade of the room, touching her face with its silver light, and she heard a short intake of breath, a muttered curse, and then a fervent whisper.

"You're so beautiful, Sophia. I've never loved anyone the way I love you. I never will."

The words opened an old wound, stirring new pain, and she pleaded softly, "Hush . . . don't speak."

The loving rhythm abruptly stilled and Sophia heard strain in the deep voice that demanded harshly, "Tell me you love me, Sophia."

Sophia shook her head. No. Where there was once love, only passion remained.

"Sophia . . ."

The elation was dimming. Sophia sought to regain it with her soft whisper.

"I want you, *caro.*"

"Tell me you love me."

Filled with sadness, Sophia whispered, "You ask too much."

The kiss that met her lips was angry. It was touched with desperation, remorse, and pain. She returned it, aching with the reality that a part of her had gone cold, never to be touched by his kiss again.

His cheek was warm as it rested against hers. She felt the moistness of tears and she shuddered, her mind drumming, "Too late . . . too late . . ."

Emotions swelled, overwhelming in the frenzy of passion that followed. Gasping in the wake of shuddering culmination, Sophia felt the weight of her lover heavy against her. She felt his hands in her hair, caressing her, his lips against her ear as he whispered, "I'll make you love me again, Sophia. You know I will."

Silent, Sophia closed her eyes. Tears streaked from their corners into the fiery hair at her temples. Yes, she knew . . . many things . . .

Momentarily disoriented as she awakened later, Sophia realized the bed beside her was empty. She frowned into the shadows as the bedroom door clicked closed. She turned her head to the window to stare intently at the first gray light of dawn peeking through the blind.

Yes, she knew many things. And she remembered . . .

Chapter One

1901

Fiery tresses streaming against her shoulders, her expression determined, Sophia turned the corner onto Mill Street. She crossed the cobbled road without a thought to the clatter of looms resounding through the open windows of the mills lining the street, or to the attention that a young woman of such fragile beauty and unusual coloring received when abroad in early-morning streets commonly frequented by a dark-haired, olive-skinned throng.

"Buon giorno, Sophia!"

Sophia turned at a young man's passing greeting. *"Buon giorno,* Mario!"

Her smiling response was accompanied by a coy flutter of glorious blue eyes that sent a flush to the young man's cheeks, but Sophia did not pause to see that his gaze followed the sway of her hips as she turned up the hill. Passing without a glance the Franklin Mill, touted for producing the finest silk in the world, she continued on to the top, her pace steady as she passed a ridge of sharp, jutting rocks and a brief, heavily foliated patch preceded the view she sought.

A black wrought-iron railing came into sight on the walk ahead of her, and a familiar sense of awe assailed Sophia as the thunder of the great falls grew louder. Her heart pounding, she stepped up to the rail, exhilarated at witnessing again the power of the river as it careened over the precipice to crash into the deep cataract below. Mesmerized by the plummeting crystal currents of water, she gasped aloud as a rainbow appeared in the mist above the churning rapids. Her spirits soared. It was a sign.

This was Sophia's special place. It had been since her family had arrived in this new country years earlier and come to Paterson, the city of silk mills and hope. Her father had taken her to see the falls and told her in a whisper meant for her ears alone that dreams were like the rainbows at the foot of the falls, waiting for the right light to bring them to life. He had stroked her hair, pride bright in his eyes as he had added, "You'll make your own light someday, *figlia mia*. Papa knows."

Sophia followed the path of the rapids with her gaze, her smile growing as the rainbow expanded to touch the lacy foam with brightening color. The colors reached their zenith, then gradually faded into the mists from which they had come, but the brilliant hues remained alive in her mind.

A familiar mill whistle interrupted her thoughts, turning Sophia abruptly toward the sound. Reality intruded, bringing a frown to her face. Determined that she would not be slave to its raucous call much longer, Sophia started back in the direction from which she had come.

Breathless with anxiety, Rosalie Marone hurried across the empty mill yard toward Kingston Silk Mill. She was oblivious of the hot morning sun that beat down on her youthful shoulders and the sweet scent of wildflowers edging the dirt surface of the lot. The rhythmic clacking of the looms reverberated through the open windows of the great redbrick building in front of her, an indication that, within, work had already begun for the day. Her adolescent frame quaked nervously. The employees' entrance was deserted, and, looking behind her, she saw Angela Moretti still dogged her steps.

Rosalie's face tightened with anger. Angela's taunting had made them late for work, but she was suddenly determined

10

that she would not suffer the consequences in vain.

Turning abruptly, Rosalie confronted her tormentor. Her dark eyes narrowed and her cheeks flushed with hot color as she hissed into Angela's plump face, "You're a liar! Take back everything you said about Sophia or you'll be sorry!"

"I'm not a liar! Everybody knows why all the boys like Sophia. Even my mama said she's nothing but a—"

"I don't care what your mama said! *I* said, take it back!"

"No!"

Springing forward without warning, Rosalie threw herself against the heavier girl, knocking her to the ground. In a blur of movement, Rosalie straddled her tormentor's heaving chest, yanking her hair mercilessly as she ordered, "Take it back or I'll pull your hair out by the roots!"

"No! I won't! Let me go! You're hurting me!" Tears overflowed Angela's small, dark eyes as she sobbed, "I'm going to tell my brother!"

Trembling with rage, Rosalie pulled Angela's hair harder. "Take back everything you said or I'll—"

The remainder of Rosalie's threat went unspoken as she was jerked unexpectedly into the air by the back of her dress and deposited roughly on her feet. Unable to move, she watched as Joey Moretti then pulled his sister to her feet and turned back toward her, his expression livid. Fear closed Rosalie's throat as Joey towered threateningly over her, and she blinked at the fury in his eyes the moment before a deep voice commanded sharply from the rear.

"Get back to work, Joey!"

All eyes snapped toward Lyle Kingston where the young, stiff-faced supervisor stood a few feet away. Rosalie saw rebellion flare briefly in Joey's eyes the second before he clamped his teeth tightly shut, and, without spoken response, he shoved his sister back toward the mill. Kingston followed close behind them without a glance at Rosalie's sisters as they raced past him on their way toward her.

Sophia pinned Rosalie with her gaze the moment she reached her side, demanding, "What happened? Why were you fighting?"

Rosalie raised her chin defensively against her adored sister's anger. "It was Angela's fault. She . . . she said terrible things about you again. She said that you—"

"*Basta!* I told you to ignore everything the girls say about me. They're jealous because their brothers follow me around like puppies."

"But Angela said that you were—"

"I don't care what she said. She lied!"

Dusting off Rosalie's clothing and smoothing the hair back from her perspired cheeks, Sophia scolded, "Look at you! Fourteen years old is too old to fight on the ground like a child." Noting Rosalie's downcast gaze, Sophia paused, then raised her sister's chin to wink unexpectedly. "Don't worry. I'll fix Angela. I have Joey Moretti wrapped around my little finger. I'll make him squirm, and then I'll make sure he tells his *sorella grassa* to watch what she says about me from now on."

Turning toward Anna, who had stood sober and silent through the whole exchange, Sophia cautioned, "Not a word to Mama about this. *Capisce,* Anna?"

Anna hesitated, then nodded. Satisfied, Sophia smiled and linked her sisters' arms with hers as she pulled them back toward the mill.

Immensely relieved as she fell into step, Rosalie smiled. Sophia had said she would take care of everything, and Sophia always did what she said.

The slapping crack of the looms swelled to a din as Sophia ushered her sisters ahead of her into the mill. Lyle Kingston stood just inside the entrance and Sophia flashed the blond, unsmiling supervisor a deliberately provocative glance. "So, you're good for something after all, eh, nephew of the boss?" she commented in a voice meant for his ears alone as she passed.

Laughing at his frown, Sophia winked boldly, well aware as she walked toward her machine that she had irritated him even more. It amused her that Lyle Kingston's frown intimidated so many of her fellow workers, while it had so little effect on her.

Lyle Kingston's gaze followed her, and Sophia's smile broadened. She supposed some were intimidated by the sheer size of him, his superior height and broad, muscular shoulders that bespoke a life that had not been totally privileged. She suspected, however, that the full power of his presence lay in the sober, unyielding set of his chiseled features and in the penetrating stare of unusual honey-colored eyes that missed little on the mill floor and tolerated less. The "nephew of the boss" was very handsome in a fairhaired, Anglo-Saxon way that was far from the dark Mediterranean standards to which she was accustomed, but, strangely, it was the inner man, carefully concealed, to whom she was drawn.

She knew no more about Lyle Kingston than the other mill workers did, only that he was the adopted son of Matthew Kingston's only sister, but she sensed much. She had seen Matthew Kingston's resentment when Lyle Kingston arrived at his mill a month earlier to take on the duties of his deceased mill supervisor. She did not doubt the rumors that the elder Kingston had brought his "nephew" to the Paterson mill against his better judgment. Little had been expected of him because of those rumors, and Sophia had been inordinately pleased to see them all proved wrong.

Lyle Kingston did his job very well, but she somehow knew doing the job well was not enough for him. She had seen in his eyes from the first that he was ambitious. She had seen a harshness, a driving desire to prove himself, and she had sympathized with that need, for a similar, silent need drove her as well. That common need eliminated the distinction of station between them on her part, and she had not been able to resist the teasing winks and flirtatious smiles behind which a more serious nature lay unsuspected, and which had earned her a reputation that was not totally deserved.

Sophia smiled. But she was not a fool. She understood the motivations that drove Lyle Kingston and knew that his uncle's acceptance of him was too important to him to chance disapproval by showing an interest in any of the female employees of the mill—most especially her.

Sophia's smile dimmed. Only in that way did Lyle Kingston and she differ. She had come to realize that she would never earn the approval of some, and she had stopped trying.

Forcing away her unpleasant thoughts, Sophia was suddenly aware that the handsome blond supervisor's gaze still followed her. Surrendering to impulse, she added a subtle wiggle to the spontaneous sway of her hips, laughing softly.

Lyle Kingston swore under his breath as Sophia Marone strolled away, her sway deliberate. His unusual eyes moved into annoyed slits. Sophia Morone was a beauty, all right. A man couldn't help looking at her, and she knew it.

Lyle's irritation grew as the scuffle in the yard a few minutes earlier returned to mind. He had made an error in allowing the three Marone girls to reenter the mill without a reprimand similar to the one he had delivered to Joey and Angela Moretti. He didn't have to look at Joey Moretti to see that his lapse had been noted. Joey would reach an obvious conclusion that was partially true. He hadn't spoken more than a few words to Sophia Marone since he had arrived at the mill a month earlier, but he could not deny his attraction to her.

Lyle's gaze narrowed further. The brazen young Italian woman intrigued him because he knew there was more to her than met the eye. Her work was superior and her mind was sharp—although he doubted any of the young men she twisted around her finger gave any thought to her mind. He had seen the genuine warmth and respect between her sisters and her, and the complete absence of jealousy that normally marked relations between women. He also sensed—

Lyle's gaze unconsciously returned to Sophia as she reached her machine and gathered her hair in her hands. She posed artfully as she pinned the lustrous mass into a knot atop her head, her silhouette gracefully outlined against the brilliant sunlight streaming through the mill windows, and Lyle gave a low, spontaneous snort. Wise to the ways of women and the world, he knew that Sophia Marone knew he was watching her. He also knew that she was laughing.

Lyle squared his shoulders, his lips moving into a determined line as he added a silent postscript to that thought. She did *not* know, however, that he was one fellow she'd never succeed in attaching to her lead.

Still watching her a few moments later, Lyle unconsciously amended that last thought. No, Sophia Marone was too smart. She wouldn't even try.

"Eh, Joey, *che successo?*"

Snapped from his observance of Sophia Marone with a start, Joey's heavy features darkened as he snapped at the short, balding warper beside him, "Nothing's the matter with me! What's the matter with you?"

Vito Speroni pulled his pointed chin back against his wrinkled neck, raising his gray wiry eyebrows until they almost met the peak of the visor he wore low on his forehead. He looked pointedly at the silk thread dangling from Joey's fingers.

Joey flushed. He glanced guiltily at the creel and then at the warper's wheel in front of him, suddenly aware that of the dozens of bobbins of silk thread he had yet to line up according to the designer's pattern, he had not yet attached a single one. Speroni's short laugh infuriated him further as he continued coyly, "Eh? It's not me who's been staring at Sophia for the last five minutes with fire in his eyes."

Joey looked around him, noting the heads that jerked the other way as he did. Were he not so furious, he would be amused that so many grown men feared his temper while beautiful Sophia dismissed it and him so easily.

Joey's frustrated agitation increased. What was he doing wrong? Why did Sophia ignore him? He was considered handsome by most, was the oldest son and the pride of the Moretti family. Joey's lips tightened. But Sophia had eyes for the new superintendent. She was too much of a fool to see that the hard, unsmiling bastard who bore the Kingston name would never stoop to involve himself with her or any of the other women in the mill. She was too much of a fool to see that Joey Moretti was the man for her and that he could—

"Joey!"

Joey turned on the smaller man, his dark eyes snapping. "Why don't you mind your own business, eh, Vito? Or better yet, make a formal complaint about me and give me the chance I'm looking for to show Mr. Nephew of-the-boss who he's fooling with!"

All sign of amusement left Vito's thin face as he shook his head with true concern. "You're a smart fellow, Joey, but you're not acting smart now. You're making a mistake letting Sophia know how you feel. She's too smart for you."

"Too smart for me, eh?" Joey bristled.

"That's right, too smart. She'll be trouble for you."

Joey looked at the smaller fellow, his square jaw twitching. If Vito hadn't been his father's best friend before he passed away, if he didn't know that Vito meant well, if he didn't know that to fight in this place would put him out on the street for good, *and if he didn't know in his heart that Vito was right* . . .

Joey clamped his teeth tightly shut, determined. It made no difference what happened today anyway, because, in the end, Sophia would marry him. After she did, he would make sure she stopped her teasing ways. He would also make sure that she paid for every moment of embarrassment she had made him suffer.

But until then . . . Joey's stomach twisted into painful knots as Sophia posed for the nephew of the boss, pinning her lustrous hair to the top of her head . . . until then he would bite his tongue and wait.

* * *

16

Maria Marone floured the breadboard again, mumbling a low curse under her breath as she kneaded the dough with a practiced hand. The day had started poorly when she spilled a full pot of soup on her kitchen floor. It had taken her an endless time to clean up the mess and she had been behind with her work ever since.

Maria looked up at the clock on the wall, her thin lips twitching nervously. She glanced around her normally orderly kitchen, skimming the great black stove that had yet to be cleaned, the dishpan with dirty dishes still stacked inside, and the basket of laundry that had yet to be washed. She remembered the dress pattern she had cut out the previous night and the twitching increased. She had promised Mrs. Barlot that she would have the dress finished by the end of the week, but her work had fallen behind to the point where she doubted she would have any time at all to work on it that day.

Suddenly realizing that her hands were shaking, Maria straightened up, took a deep breath, and closed her eyes. It was foolishness to allow herself to become so upset. No one cared if her kitchen was not orderly, and no one would care if the bread was not baked before noon or if she left the laundry for another day. Only she would care.

But that was enough.

Maria opened her eyes, and as she did, caught a glimpse of the tight-faced woman reflected back at her from the small mirror on the nearby wall. Her first reaction was denial. That woman could not really be Maria Marone . . .

Maria turned and faced the mirror squarely. The woman who returned her assessing stare was still as thin as a girl and still carried her taller than average height erectly, but all resemblance to the young woman who had once been the beauty of the Provincia di Avellino stopped there. The brilliant red hair that she had inherited from Nonna Alvino—the hair she had knotted so carefully at the nape of her neck that morning—was now a dull gray. The startling blue of her eyes was faded and the sweet line of her lips was pinched and tight. A deep network of lines now covered the smooth, flawless skin that had once stirred whispered words of love that had shaken her young heart.

Maria raised her chin, forcing the return of the strong demeanor that had become customary with her, as a wave of emotion as bitter as gall overwhelmed her. Vanity was a curse! Her sainted mother had brought her to her senses many years ago, and Maria cursed her failure in not having been able to make Sophia recognize that wisdom as clearly as she.

Maria took a deep breath, consoling herself that in all other areas of her marriage she had performed well. She was a good, frugal woman. She took great care with Anthony and her daughters' earnings when they were placed in her hands each week in accordance with old-country custom. She spent wisely and only on necessities, without taking a penny out for herself. She contributed to the family income with the money she earned as a seamstress, and she did it proudly. Her family always had clean clothes to wear, supper waiting on the table when they returned from their labors, and a home that shone with cleanliness.

Maria's pale eyes flickered momentarily. And in the privacy of the marital bed that she shared with Anthony she was a dutiful if not passionate wife, who seldom refused her husband.

Sophia's face appeared unexpectedly before her eyes, and Maria felt a familiar knot tighten in the pit of her stomach. Sophia, her husband's favored child and the most willful of all her children, was the main cause of her anxiety. Her rebellion haunted Maria's quiet moments. Sophia no longer spoke freely of her foolish dreams, the ambitions that she knew would never come to be, but she knew her eldest daughter still harbored them in her mind. Maria briefly closed her eyes. She knew what it was to dream dreams that crumbled to dust. She knew the pain of it and the deep scars remaining. She feared Sophia's dreams because she feared her daughter would someday—

A sound in the doorway behind her caused Maria to turn sharply in its direction. Her face flushed with dismay at the

18

sight of a woman's oversize bulk shadowed against the morning sun. Marcella Negri, the most incorrigible gossip on Prospect Street . . .

Maria's greeting was forced. *"Buon giorno, Marcella. Avanti. Come sta?"*

Her polite invitation to enter issued, Maria gave the dough a nervous pat. Marcella would not miss the dishes in the sink or the clothes waiting to be washed.

Marcella opened the screen door wide to accommodate her generous proportions, smiling in a way that sent the hackles rising on Maria's neck as she entered and responded a trifle too sweetly, *"Bene, grazie,* Maria." Marcella's sharp eyes swept the room as she sat heavily on the nearest chair. "I see you're late with your work today." Marcella's head bobbed on fleshy shoulders that appeared to swallow her wrinkled neck. "So many clothes yet to wash . . . and dishes, too. If it were not so important, I would come back another time to talk to you, but I heard something a little while ago that you will want to know . . ."

Marcella paused, allowing her opening words to be absorbed completely before continuing. The false sympathy with which the woman spoke was a glaring warning of what was to come. Maria took a small step backward, waiting . . .

Chapter Two

The winder's hum droned steadily as Sophia worked in silence, her mind returning again and again to the scene of Rosalie and Angela Moretti's encounter earlier that morning. She recalled Joey Moretti's rough handling of her sister and nodded unconsciously. She would take care of Joey . . . and Angela, too. As for Angela's jealous lies, she had known telling Rosalie to ignore them was useless even as she said the words, for the baby of the family was not one to allow Sophia's name to be used in vain.

The spot of warmth inside her that was Sophia's love for her sisters spread to a golden glow. As angry as she had been to see Rosalie fighting, she had been unable to suppress her pride. Rosalie showed the promise of the strong young woman she would one day become, and she was thankful that Rosalie's strength did not threaten Mama or antagonize her in the way her own did, and that Mama had not been successful in undermining Rosalie's confidence in the same way she had undermined Anna's.

Suddenly realizing she would do neither her sisters nor herself any good by dwelling on things she could not change, Sophia looked out the window at the sun-drenched lot beyond. It was unseasonably warm for early June, and the day had gotten progressively brighter, in sharp contrast with the somber mill interior. Its glow beckoned to her. She knew that just beyond the door the sun-dappled waters of the lower raceway, fed by the great falls, ran past the mill on its headlong course into the Passaic River. She remembered the day her mother's harsh ridicule of her childish dreams had sent her to the solace of the falls, despite the price she knew she would pay for her temporary escape. She had made herself a promise then.

Promises, promises . . . Sophia shook her head with a rueful smile. She had gone home that night to face Mama's wrath, and even Papa had not been able to save her. A week later, Mama had seen to it that she started work after school in this same mill. Those dreams had never seemed more distant than when, at twelve, she became employed at the mill full-time.

A cooling breeze gusted through the window, loosening a fiery tendril against her brow. Sophia brushed it back unconsciously. Years had passed since then. She was seventeen now, quick, clever, and more determined than ever before.

And men were crazy for her! Sophia glanced heavenward with a short laugh. *Grazie a Dio* for their foolishness! It eased the way for her and made things bearable in this dull place where she had spent so many years of her life waiting.

Snapped back to reality by the appearance of a dangling end of silk thread on the winder in front of her, Sophia secured it with a skilled hand, appraising the swifts of hard silk that fed the whirling bobbins. The unrelenting din of looms at the far end of the floor overwhelmed the muffled hum of the winders, but her own machines had a distinctive sound that Sophia knew well.

She was good at her job. Forty ends on each side of two machines ran with little interruption under her watchful eye, but her skill was hard-won. Tucked vividly into memory were those first days when, at twelve, she feared the huge machine would conquer her. Also firmly impressed into memory was the resolution she had made then to have no one suspect she was afraid. She prided herself that five years later it was generally believed that Sophia Marone had never had an uncertain moment in her life.

Sophia followed a familiar path around her machines, her

nimble fingers flying at their task. She stood back a few moments later, a hand on the curve of her hip while she considered the jealous gossip that plagued her. A wry smile quirked the corner of her mouth. Ah, but it was so difficult being a beautiful peacock amidst so many plain, dull hens . . .

A flutter of movement across the aisle from her machines drew Sophia's attention from her amused thoughts to the winders where Anna worked. Snapped ends from two swifts had become entangled. A loose thread from a third threatened a difficult situation. Anna's movements became more clumsy with her growing panic, and Sophia felt a familiar despair.

Dear Anna . . . Mama's dominating influence had left its mark. At fifteen she was frightened of life and painfully unsure of herself. Paining Sophia even more deeply was her concern that with the best of intentions, her own interference at times like this weakened Anna's confidence.

The hurt of her sister's growing agitation causing a hard knot in her stomach, Sophia made a difficult decision. Steeling herself, she turned from the sight of her sister's distress and walked to the opposite side of her machine.

A familiar panic began building inside Anna. The hum of the winder seemed to escalate in her ears and her hands trembled as she struggled to untangle the knotted threads, her eyes shifting to yet another snapped end that appeared farther down the merciless machine. Taking the scissors from her pocket, she snipped the knot and secured the end to the bobbin, groaning aloud as the scissors slipped from her clumsy fingers. Retrieving it a moment later, she looked up to see the dangle of snapped ends had increased.

Anna looked around her, aware that the situation had become alarmingly familiar. She wondered how much longer her inefficiency would be tolerated in a mill where lost time meant lost money, and where there was always another young worker eager to take her place. A brief gust of warm air whipped a strand of dark hair against Anna's pale cheek, and she shuddered as if touched by an icy draft. She could not face Mama's anger if that happened. She was not as brave or clever as Sophia, or as bright and quick as Rosalie, but Mama had always said she was the most dependable of them all. Tears brimmed in Anna's eyes. She couldn't do anything right. She would be fired and she would have to go home to . . .

"These ends aren't your enemy, Anna."

Anna looked up at the sound of Sophia's voice, swallowing the tears that choked her throat as Sophia secured the ends that had so easily eluded her own hands and chided her lightly. "If not for these ends, we would have no job at all, would we? You mustn't be angry with them and frown when they try to escape you. You must treat them gently and smile as if they were precious lovers when you put them firmly in place."

"Sophia!" Anna's color returned in an embarrassed flush. She glanced around them, the panic of a few minutes earlier momentarily forgotten in her concern that Sophia's bold words might be overheard. "You shouldn't speak of such things! What would Mama say?"

Sophia laughed, pleased to have momentarily distracted her sister from her growing panic.

"There, that's the last of them." Snipping the ends of her winder's knot with a flourish minutes later, Sophia turned to see Anna frowning.

"You didn't tie a flat knot, Sophia. You know Mr. Kingston wants us to tie only flat knots."

Sophia shrugged. "Flat knots take too long."

"But—"

Sophia leaned forward to speak softly into her sister's wide, dark eyes. "Listen to me. I *never* tie flat knots, and the weavers *never* complain about the bobbins I wind."

"None of the men would complain about *you*, Sophia."

"They won't complain if you tie winder's knots instead of flat knots, either."

"But I don't look like you, Sophia."

23

Sophia raised her delicate shoulders in an exaggerated shrug. "So? If they have any complaints, send them to me."

"But—"

"Tie a winder's knot and smile, Anna."

Pleased to see Anna's lips curve slowly upward, Sophia returned to her machines. A sea of dangling ends met her eyes, and she groaned aloud.

"So you must take your own advice," Sophia muttered grimly under her breath. "Tie a winder's knot and smile . . ."

Lyle Kingston looked up from his desk, glancing through the glass panel of the superintendent's office that allowed a view of the mill floor. He was intensely aware of the closed connecting door to Matthew Kingston's office behind him. Uncle Matthew and his cousin, Paul, had been secreted behind that door since the departure of business acquaintances, Samuel Weiss, and his arrogant son, Aaron, a few hours earlier. That closed door was a personal affront that he resented almost as much as his unofficial status in the mill. The injustice of it all galled him.

Lyle's lips tightened. His bearing of the Kingston name was a farce, the sting of which had never faded. Had things been done according to Matthew Kingston's liking, the illegitimate son of an unfortunate young British girl would never have been adopted into his family. He could still remember vividly the argument that had progressed behind Aunt Julia's closed study door—the shouting, the anger in his uncle's deep voice, and the firmness with which Aunt Julia had challenged him the first night she had brought him to her home.

He remembered Matthew Kingston's words. "An impoverished old maid has no place taking in an orphan of questionable background—especially into a family as socially prominent as ours."

Furious, Uncle Matthew had emerged from the study a short time later, ignoring the sober seven-year-old boy sitting on the first step of the staircase as if he did not exist. Aunt Julia had not been strong enough to hold out against her older brother completely, however, and he remembered her sadness the day he was shipped off to boarding school shortly thereafter. A Kingston in name only, he taught his haughty schoolmates to respect him, if not to fully accept him, but it was not *their* acceptance he grew determined to acquire.

Aunt Julia's insistence had finally forced his uncle to bring him from the relative obscurity of his Honesdale mill to Paterson a month earlier, and he was wise enough to realize that the position vacated at the former superintendent's death wasn't the only reason.

Lyle gave a short, hard laugh. "Cousin" Paul had been a disappointment to his father from the first day he entered the mill, and Lyle knew he had been allowed to assume the position only because Paul had failed so miserably. He wondered how long it would take his uncle to admit that his quiet, likable cousin was not happy without an artist's brush in his hand and that he had no desire to fill his father's shoes.

Lyle paused and took a deep breath. Well, *he* had the desire and the ability to fill those expensive, handmade shoes of Matthew Kingston. He had worked toward that end his entire life, from the moment his uncle's deprecating sneer first touched him. He had no intention of allowing the Kingston name he carried or his hard work go to waste. Born into the world without a name and without a future, with his young mother's dying words his only legacy, he had long ago determined that he would not exit the world the same way.

Sophia Marone's bright-red hair came into view between the machines and Lyle's eyes narrowed. "Nephew of the boss . . ." It was the only title he could lay claim to since arriving at the mill, but it was only Sophia Marone, the bold little flirt that she was, who had the courage to address him by the label that most of the other workers just used behind his back.

25

"You must have more important things to do than stare at that Marone girl, Nephew." Lyle turned at the unexpected sound of his uncle's voice, his expression freezing as Matthew Kingston continued coldly. "I would've thought you had better sense than to entertain thoughts of that cheap baggage."

Meeting his uncle's criticism with a cool smile, Lyle responded, "I have the sense not to make unsubstantiated judgments of people, Uncle. I hope you'll at least give me credit for that."

His patrician face coloring at his nephew's indirect rebuke, Matthew Kingston responded, "You'll soon learn that I'll give you credit only where it's earned and due."

Noting his cousin's pained expression, Lyle did not respond. He watched in silence as his uncle and cousin left the office and walked toward the exit. The steel in his gaze gave silent emphasis to his dark thoughts as he opened the door and stepped back onto the mill floor.

Brilliant rays of late-afternoon sun kissed Sophia's skin with a golden hue as she leaned against the wooden fence outside the employees' entrance of Kingston Mill. One of the first to leave at the end of the day, she waited for her sisters to emerge while watching with a deceptively casual gaze as the workers streamed through the doorway.

A cooling breeze lifted hair lit by the sunlight into a glittering blaze of color from her shoulders. That same breeze molded her plain white blouse and dark skirt against gentle curves formerly concealed by the austerity of the garments' line. A familiar figure stepped through the mill doorway into the yard and Sophia openly averted her gaze as Joey Moretti approached her.

"Sophia . . ."

Sophia looked up coldly. Joey flushed and she restrained a smile at his discomfort. Joey was several years older than she, but in dealing with her, he was a child—a nasty, spoiled child who didn't fool her for a minute.

"What do you want, Joey?"

"You're not angry, are you, Sophia?"

"Angry?" Sophia looked pointedly at Angela, who watched them from a safe distance. "Why should I be angry?"

Joey followed the line of her gaze and frowned as he addressed his sister sharply. "What are you waiting for, Angela? Go home!"

Angela's full face became stubborn. "I'm waiting for you, Joey. I'm not going home until you do."

Joey took a threatening step toward his sister, his expression darkening. "I told you to go home. Do what I say!"

Startled into movement by her brother's anger, Angela took a few running steps backward. "I'm going to tell Mama on you, Joey. Mama doesn't want you bothering with *her*. Mama says she's . . ."

"Angela! Go home! Now!" Waiting only until his sister moved obediently toward the street, Joey turned back to Sophia, his expression pained. "She's jealous of you, Sophia, because she's fat and homely and you're so pretty."

"Go home to your mama, Joey."

"Sophia . . ." Joey's dark eyes filled with misery, and Sophia glimpsed victory on the horizon as he rasped, "You know how I feel about you. I don't care what my mama or anybody else says about you. I know the truth. You're beautiful and good and . . . and I love you."

"You *love* me?" Sophia's tone held just the right touch of ridicule. "Is that why you let your sister talk about me the way she does? Is that why you let her torment Rosalie and get her in trouble for defending me?"

"No, I—"

"You love me . . ." Sophia laughed again.

"I do love you, Sophia . . ."

Sophia shook her head.

"I *do*. I'll make sure Angela never talks about you again. I give you my word . . ."

Sophia did not respond. Instead, she looked deliberately past Joey's broad shoulders to the spot where Angela had retreated to observe them in safety. Joey followed her gaze, his expression hardening at the sight of his sister. Looking back at Sophia, he grasped her hand with an anxious whisper.

"I'll make her apologize, and then I'll make sure she never talks about you again. You'll forgive me then, won't you?"

Sophia shrugged.

"And you'll go to the picnic with me on Sunday."

Sophia shrugged again.

Joey smiled. He kissed her hand unexpectedly, then flushed when she withdrew it from his grasp without a word. He nodded soberly. "I'll make her apologize. You'll see."

Sophia watched with satisfaction as Joey walked back to his sister and gave her an angry shake before pulling her into step beside him. He was still haranguing her as they stepped out onto the street and slipped from sight.

Turning back to the mill, Sophia waved her sisters toward her as they peeked out from the mill doorway. She laughed as Rosalie ran as fast as her legs would carry her, gasping when she reached her side, "Did you fix Joey—and Angela, too?"

"I fixed Joey, and *Joey's* going to fix Angela. You won't have to worry about her anymore."

An uncomfortable sound from Anna turned Sophia toward her as she whispered soberly, "What's Joey going to do to her?"

Sophia remained patiently firm. "He's going to give her exactly what she deserves." Her expression softening, Sophia continued. "And you don't have to worry about Mama, Anna. It'll be all right now."

A protective swell rose inside Sophia at Anna's nod. How much her dear sisters needed her . . .

Their arms linked, they had not gone more than a few steps when Sophia noticed Lyle Kingston observing them a short distance away. She mentally paused, her satisfaction intensifying at the realization that the nephew of the boss had witnessed the entire exchange with Joey. Lyle Kingston knew what it meant to be talked about behind his back. He was a kindred spirit, a fellow soldier who could appreciate what it meant to win even the smallest battle in a war of jealous, whispered rumors.

With a smile, Sophia silently invited him to share her victory. His eyes narrowing, his gaze remaining fixed and hard, the nephew of the boss did not return her smile and Sophia's elation dimmed. Choosing to ignore his unexpected reaction, she told herself she didn't care, that if he chose not to smile at her, there were many others who would.

Responding to impulse as she came abreast of Lyle Kingston a moment later, Sophia turned toward him to comment with a flutter of extravagantly long lashes and a delicate shrug, "Joey's a fool for me, you know."

"Sophia!"

Ignoring Anna's shocked exclamation, Sophia continued innocently on her way.

Anthony Marone breathed a deep sigh of relief as his feet touched the wooden porch outside the rented, third-floor flat that was his home. Pausing, he turned to look at the sky, to breathe deeply of the clear air and the tantalizing aroma coming through the screened door of the kitchen a few feet away. The sun, slowly dropping below the horizon, tinted the fading blue of the sky with streaks of pinkish gold. He had worked with the master dyer for the greater part of the day to achieve a color that now paled in comparison with that breathtaking hue.

Sliding his hand into his pocket, Anthony fingered the silk remnant he had folded so carefully, suddenly unsure whether the scrap of material could bring a smile to Maria's once beautiful face. So little made his Maria smile these days.

A familiar sense of futility slowly unfolded within Anthony's mind. So much had changed since those years long ago when Maria and he were young. He remembered the small village where they were born, and the difficult day when he finally acknowledged his feelings for her to himself.

His love had seemed so hopeless, for his beautiful Maria had been taken under the wing of the countess who owned a summer château on the hill just beyond their homes. With the wealthy woman's guidance, Maria had learned to read and write and to perfect her talent as a seamstress until she was far above the average man in their village. And Anthony knew that there was no man more average than he.

With an unconscious smile, Anthony recalled the Anthony Marone of his youth, the amiable, happy fellow who followed the family trade as a potter. The son of Cesare Marone and the eldest of six children, he was congenial, not of necessity, but because it was his nature to seek the bright side of life and to find humor where others saw none. Never handsome, he was the shortest of his four brothers and muscularly built, with a thick head of curly black hair and a ready smile his only assets. He had had little success in hiding his feelings for Maria from his family, and when the time came for him to marry, he was stunned to find the marriage so easily arranged.

Anthony sighed. Maria had not loved him in the way he loved her at the time of their marriage, but she had been obedient to her family's wishes. When Sophia was born that first year, he had seen in his lovely child who so resembled her mother a way to more openly express the love that he kept so carefully controlled within him.

Ah, yes . . . then the steady downward spiral of fortunes in his home country and his ultimate decision to leave their home forever—to come to this new land that boasted equality of opportunity for all.

Pausing again in his thoughts, Anthony looked down on the niche he had carved for his family and himself in this new land. He saw a stone courtyard surrounded on three sides by three-story dwellings with open windows that allowed glimpses of sights and sounds similar to those in his own home. Laundry yet to be gathered flapped gently on a line that crisscrossed a small, grassy yard beyond as the gusting breeze stirred the smell of chicken coops in the rear. He knew that on hot summer days the smell of the chicken coops would compete with the odor of the red outhouse a respectable distance away and with the fragrance of grapes ripening on vines that he himself had planted.

Anthony also knew that each morning at five A.M. he would make his way out of the narrow alleyway presently shadowed in the late-afternoon sun, and he would walk toward the dye house of Martin Stein where he would labor for the next twelve hours of the day. He would return weary and thoughtful as he had today, realizing that he could hope for little more than he had now—a home that was clean and adequate, a stomach that had known little deprivation in recent years, and a day of rest on Sunday when he might drink a glass of home-made wine and prepare himself for the long labor of the six days that would follow.

A spot of sadness inside Anthony expanded to a familiar ache. Satisfied for himself, he only wished he could have offered Maria more.

Anthony's square-tipped fingers twitched spasmodically on the scrap of silk fabric in his hand. He withdrew it from his pocket. Inadequate gifts, these colorful scraps that he brought home to his wife and which she fashioned into patchwork quilts for those more wealthy than they to enjoy . . . meager gifts from a simple peasant to one who had once been a beautiful princess.

Anthony sighed and took off his cap to rub a strong, stubby hand against his head. The years had taken their toll on him as well. His black curly hair had deserted him, leaving a shiny pate in its place, and a face that had never been handsome was now marked with the ravages of hard labor and time until it was so similar to his father's that the resemblance was startling, even to himself.

An irrepressible smile turned up the corners of Anthony's lips at that last thought. But Papa had maintained until the day he died that he was the handsomest man in the village. Anthony was never quite certain if that claim was the result of poor eyesight or a sense of humor even greater than his own.

His smile growing, Anthony unconsciously stroked his

full, dark mustache. With each hair that fell from his head, he had cultivated a greater fullness to the masterpiece he wore beneath his strong nose. It was a source of pride to him—this joke he played on nature, and it gave him solace to know that time could change the outside of a man, but it could do little to the inside unless he allowed it. He was determined it would not—for himself, for Maria, and for his daughters.

His daughters . . . Anthony's dark eyes brightened as he turned toward the kitchen door. All different, all lovely, but Sophia . . .

Sophia's face appeared before his mind's eye and Anthony's spirits rose. So similar to the girl her mother had once been on the outside, Sophia was as different from her mother on the inside as night was from day. It was a silent source of pride to him that her indefatigable optimism and humor was his own blood holding true. He knew Maria would never truly understand Sophia for that reason. Nor would she understand the love he felt for his lovely, eldest daughter—because Maria had never truly understood the love he felt for her.

Anthony turned toward the kitchen door, walking slowly as he untied the sweat-stained handkerchief around his neck and rolled it into a ball in his hand. Hope stirred anew despite his weariness. Perhaps tonight, when the girls were abed, when Maria unbound her hair, slipped on her spotless white nightgown, and lay down beside him . . . perhaps when he took her into his arms, he would finally be able to make her understand how much he loved her—how much he had loved her all of his life.

The warmth of those thoughts still bright in his eyes, Anthony pulled open the screen door and walked into the kitchen. His greeting died on his lips at first sight of his wife's stiff face. The glow inside him faded as he closed the door behind him. Not bothering to advance into the room, he remained silent, waiting . . .

Julia Kingston stood at the window of her modest Broadway home, her pleasant features alight with anticipation. A small woman, she was also slight of stature to the point of frailty, with graying curls tightly framing a small, heart-shaped face and an ever-present pallor to finely lined cheeks. With a keen, penetrating stare, quick, precise movements, and the dark, finely tailored clothing from which she never deviated, she resembled a tiny, fragile bird, an analogy that was totally inaccurate when her heart and mind were united to turn her delicate spine to steel.

Anticipation flushing her cheeks with unaccustomed color, Julia ran white, fluttering hands little larger than a child's against her respectably bound hair, mentally chastising herself. She knew it was wrong to await Lyle's return from the mill each day with such pleasure. She told herself that his residence was merely a temporary situation until he was able to find himself suitable rooms, that he would be moving soon, and that she did herself a disservice by indulging these maternal feelings to which she had little right. But all sensible thoughts fell by the wayside when Lyle was again due home and her stubborn feet followed the familiar path to this window overlooking the street.

Julia smiled. But Lyle was such a dear young man, and he had worked so hard to fulfill the promise she had seen in his eyes that first time she had visited the orphanage so many years ago.

Julia's smile slowly faded. Father should never have given the total earnings of his life's work to Matthew so he might start the mill. That simple act had given Matthew unfair power over her life when Father had died shortly thereafter, leaving her destitute and dependent on Matthew. Her life had not been her own in the time since.

Frowning, Julia gave that thought further consideration. Of course, Papa could never have known that success would change Matthew from a brilliant, sympathetic young man with ambitions that had seemed far beyond him into a mature man whose snobbish arrogance and autocratic manner was almost beyond enduring. Nor could he have known that the only man she had ever loved would die three months before their wedding. She had never found a man to replace William in her life, but she had known the moment she saw Lyle in that group of orphans that he was destined to be the child that fate had denied her.

Lyle Clark had been the name Lyle had borne then, but Julia knew in her heart that Kingston was the only name he should truly bear. She had overridden Matthew's objections in adopting Lyle, fighting him tooth and nail and conceding partial victory to him only when she knew she must compromise or lose the dear boy. She had hated her brother then, for the weeks and months of Lyle's life he had stolen from her when he insisted on a boarding school too far away to allow Lyle weekly visits home. As much as she loved her nephew, Paul, it had been one of the greatest joys of the passing years to observe that the dear fellow had no interest at all in following his father into the silk mill.

Spontaneous pride surfaced, brightening Julia's small smile. On the other hand, she hadn't needed to tell Lyle where to direct his interest. Lyle's anger, greater each time Matthew looked at him with barely concealed scorn, had directed his path and forged a driving ambition.

A tall, familiar figure turned into sight on the corner, pushing all thought from Julia's mind. Her small features twitching with pleasure, she turned to call over her shoulder, "Maggie, Lyle's coming."

A low grunt from the direction of the kitchen was her housekeeper's only response.

Poised as motionlessly as a small, delicate bird, Julia watched Lyle approach.

"He's here, Maggie!"

Aunt Julia's thin voice carried through the open window as Lyle stepped onto the wide wooden porch. Aunt Julia met him at the door, her pale face alight with pleasure. He kissed the paper-thin skin of her cheek as she looked up sweetly into his eyes, his voice tinged with disapproval as he spoke.

"How long have you been waiting at the window for me, Aunt Julia? You know you mustn't tire yourself."

"Oh, pooh! I've had a weak heart all of my life. I've become accustomed to it and I've made my compromises. Besides, I've never felt better than I have since you came home a month ago."

Lyle curved his arm gently around his aunt's shoulders. Aunt Julia was a dear, loving woman for whom he had true affection, but she was not the beautiful young mother whom the world had treated so badly and whose bright face and glowing eyes were a vivid memory that would not fade from his mind.

The appearance of Maggie's broad, bustling figure raised his head to her dour expression. A tall, heavy Scottish woman, disciplined in manner and dress to an excessive degree, she had not changed a hair in appearance since the day he first saw her. He remembered when, as a child, he had briefly believed that stern demeanor meant disapproval, but he had long since discovered the reverse to be true. Ultimately, Maggie's acceptance and her strict, unorthodox manner of displaying affection was one of the first steps in the healing of childish wounds that had formerly bled so freely.

Assuming a dour expression that mimicked Maggie's too well not to bring an amused sparkle into his aunt's eye, Lyle commented, "I see Maggie's almost ready to serve dinner. I hope it's not mutton pies or haggis stew again."

Maggie raised a thick, stern brow, addressing him directly in the same manner in which she had always addressed him as a child. "Aye, and ye'll eat what I put on the table, laddie. Yer aunt's done just that for twenty-five years or more, and ye'll do the same."

Lyle's brown brows furrowed with mock belligerence. "Oh, I will?"

Flushing, Aunt Julia slapped his arm lightly. "You mustn't tease Maggie so, especially when she's gone to such great lengths to please you. She's worked all afternoon making a—"

"I've worked the afternoon long to please meself and none else, I'll have ye know." Maggie's tall figure jerked erect as she interjected without hesitation. "And it was me own sweet tooth that forced me into makin' the raspberry trifle for dessert—"

"Raspberry trifle . . ."

His favorite dessert. Lyle's throat tightened at the effort to which Maggie had gone in order to please him.

Maggie paused in midstep. Misunderstanding his sudden silence, she countered with forced indifference, "And I suppose I willna' mind if I must eat it all meself."

Recovering in time to salve her feelings, Lyle rewarded her with a rare smile. "Oh, no, you won't. Trifle is my compensation for all the haggis stew you've made me eat over the years."

Maggie shook her graying head with a thoughtful glance. "Aye, me haggis . . . Well, sit yerself down, for ye must wade through another bowl of the foul stuff if ye hopes to get yer dessert this night."

Maggie turned toward the kitchen as Lyle groaned appropriately. Seated at the head of the table opposite Aunt Julia a short time later, he looked up with surprise as Maggie placed a fragrant lamb roast directly in front of him, instructing, " 'Tis for the master of the house to carve."

Hesitant to pick up the blade that rested beside his hand, Lyle heard a soft sound opposite him. Looking up, he met Aunt Julia's small, moist eyes as she urged, "What are you waiting for, dear?"

With difficulty, Lyle picked up the knife.

"Not a word of it is true, Mama!"

Sophia's sharp defense against her mother's angry accusations flushed Maria's face a deep red. Trembling, Rosalie responded in spontaneous defense, "It wasn't Sophia's fault, Mama! I was the one who—"

"State zitto!" Halting Rosalie midsentence, Maria continued with growing heat. "I know whose fault it is that I must

36

listen to Marcella Negri report the disgraceful conduct of my daughters . . . that I must be humiliated by the behavior of my own flesh and blood!"

"But it wasn't Sophia's fault!" Rosalie interrupted bravely again, fearing more for Sophia than herself. Mama grew more incensed with each passing moment. It was always like this, each time there was trouble . . . Sophia's fault . . . *always* Sophia's fault . . .

Glancing at Anna who stood silently beside her, her face white with strain, Rosalie knew there would be no help there. She continued persistently. "Sophia wasn't even there when Angela and I started fighting, and when she came, she told me that I shouldn't have fought with Angela—that I should've ignored everything she said."

Mama nodded her head, unconvinced. "Sophia is innocent, eh? So tell me, what did Angela say that made you so angry?"

Rosalie hesitated in response, unwilling to repeat Angela's lies to her mother. "She said . . . she said . . ." Her mind went blank and she glanced toward Papa where he stood observing tensely. But he did not speak and Rosalie began to panic. "She said—"

"Rosalie was defending me when she fought with Angela Moretti."

Tears filled Rosalie's eyes at Sophia's interjection. She had tried to rescue Sophia from Mama, but it was again Sophia who had rescued *her*.

"But you're wrong if you think anything Angela said about me was true." Sophia's chin was high, her voice steady, and pride swelled inside Rosalie for her beautiful, brave sister. No one else, not even Papa, faced Mama so courageously.

"I am never wrong when it comes to you, Sophia." Maria's pale eyes became hot points of light as she stared into her daughter's unyielding expression. "I know you too well."

"No, Mama, you don't know me at all."

Maria took a threatening step forward, her voice low with warning. "You will not contradict me again, Sophia! *I* don't listen to *you*. *You* listen to *me!* I'm not the fool that you think me to be! I know everything! Joey Moretti is a fine young man, but you torment him by flaunting yourself in front of him. You don't care for your good name or for the good name of your family and your sisters! You care only for your foolish games and the enjoyment of the moment. With each day, each thoughtless action, you blacken our name more, and your chances of finding a husband grow more dim."

Disdain shone from Sophia's eyes. "I'm not interested in getting married."

"Oh, you're not!" Maria appeared to swell with fury. "And what are you interested in, eh? Hopeless dreams . . . senseless folly that will bring your sisters down with you when you fall? I tell you now, daughter of mine, I will never allow that to happen!"

Sophia's beautiful face grew cold. "And how will you stop it, Mama?"

"With the back of my hand!"

"I've felt the back of your hand before."

Her hand flying so swiftly that the blow could not be anticipated, Maria slapped Sophia sharply across the face.

"Maria!"

At her side in seconds, Anthony grasped his wife's arm, but she ignored his protest as she shook herself free. Her lips trembling, her nostrils quivering with rage, Maria hissed into her daughter's white face, "And so you feel it again!"

Sophia showed no reaction even as a red welt appeared on her smooth cheek, and she kept her silence as Maria continued hotly. "Now I'll tell you what you will do, and what you will *not* do. You will stay away from Joey Moretti, *capisce?* You will leave him alone! You will behave in a manner that will bring no further disgrace upon your family."

Sophia responded levelly, coldly impassive. "And if Joey Moretti won't stay away from me?"

"Sophia . . ." Papa's soft interjection turned her to his pained expression, to the plea in his eyes that went unspoken. A silent moment passed. An unfathomable emotion flickering across her brilliant eyes, Sophia then nodded. "All right, Mama. I'll leave Joey Moretti alone."

Maria allowed her burning stare to singe Sophia a moment longer, then she turned abruptly and walked out of the house. The sound of her step on the porch stairs snapped Papa into motion, and within moments he disappeared through the doorway behind her.

Sophia was still staring at the doorway when a sob broke from Rosalie's throat. Turning toward her, Sophia commented dryly, "So, you're crying? It was my face that Mama slapped, not yours."

Closing the distance between them, Rosalie threw her arms around Sophia's waist, hugging her close. Her heart filled with remorse, she choked, "It's my fault that Mama's angry with you. I'm sorry, Sophia."

As she separated herself from Rosalie's clinging arms, Sophia looked directly into her sister's red-rimmed eyes. "Don't be sorry, Rosalie," she said, "because the truth is that Mama needs no one to make her angry with me. That anger is with her always. Come now," Sophia implored, wiping away Rosalie's tears. "If Mama comes back and finds you crying, she'll get angry all over again."

Forcing her tears to halt, Rosalie watched as Sophia turned toward Anna. Touching Anna's trembling shoulder, Sophia whispered, "Anna . . ."

"Why must things always be this way, Sophia?"

The torment in Anna's voice brought a sadness to Sophia's face that touched Rosalie's troubled heart. She was saddened to the point of despair as Sophia slid an arm around Anna's shoulders and responded in a heartfelt whisper, *"Cara* Anna, I only wish I knew . . ."

His hands in his pockets, his broad shoulders hunched against the burden of his thoughts, Lyle walked briskly along Broadway. He had eaten supper and made his excuses to his aunt so he might escape for some solitude and sort out his mind.

He glanced up as he passed his uncle's mansion. As in all things, Uncle Matthew had not been satisfied until he left his mark for all to see, in this case by compromising the purity of the Greek revival structure with ornate balconies and unnecessary bric-a-brac that bespoke wealth more loudly than taste.

Lyle paused at that thought, Aunt Julia's words in conversation the previous hour returning. Clearly visible in his mind's eye was her distant expression as she had said in an almost wistful tone, "Your uncle Matthew wasn't always the man he is today, Lyle dear. He was once a dear boy who smiled easily and was kind and affectionate. He was several years younger than I, and I loved him so dearly then." Aunt Julia had sighed. "I'm not quite certain what happened to that darling young fellow. Perhaps it was his success in business . . . the great sums of money that he managed to accumulate, the power he wields in the industry . . . Perhaps he felt he must change to live up to a certain image. I don't know. Or perhaps it was his marriage." Aunt Julia had shrugged. "Edith isn't an easy woman. I think she's made Matthew pay dearly for her family's social status. Or perhaps . . ." She had shrugged her frail shoulders again. "But I suppose it is senseless to speculate, except to say that there's little left of the young man I once adored. That reality, my dear Lyle, is one of the greatest sadnesses of my life."

Lyle shifted uncomfortably and resumed his step. He had tried to comfort Aunt Julia then, but her words had been unsettling. They nagged at him, joining his discomfort at the image of Sophia Marone that had haunted him all evening long.

Brilliant red hair and flashing blue eyes returned again to his mind, and he silently acknowledged that he had never seen a lovelier sight than Sophia Marone bathed in golden sunlight as she had stood outside the mill that afternoon. But he hadn't been fool enough to believe that her casual pose was unaffected. It had been too perfectly set—the sun gleaming on her brilliant hair, glinting on the ivory clarity of her skin, glittering on the heavy, gold-tipped lashes that framed her glowing eyes. It hadn't been until he saw Joe Moretti emerge from the mill that he had realized the reason for her elaborate pose.

"Joey's a fool for me, you know."

Lyle's lips tightened. Sophia Marone was a brazen hussy, and he was beginning to believe that she wasn't as smart as he had originally thought. She couldn't be, or she would see that she was heading for trouble with that fellow.

Suddenly annoyed with himself, Lyle slipped his hands from his pockets and began walking with a more deliberate stride. What was wrong with him tonight, anyway? What did he care if his uncle Matthew had once been a "dear boy," when he was now an arrogant swine? What difference did it make to him if Sophia Marone finally found the trouble she appeared to be so diligently seeking? He had learned the hard way that "caring" was a mistake.

Lyle frowned. He had no time for beautiful redheaded women, no matter how intense the invasion of this particular woman in his mind. He gave a low snort, certain of the cure.

Turning the corner onto Main Street, Lyle spotted the familiar storefront he sought. Slipping into the narrow alley beside it, he emerged into the small courtyard beyond and knocked on the door there. The sound of a light step preceded the slitted opening of the door and a purring sound of delight as the door swung wide and a satin-clad female thrust her lush proportions tightly against him.

Warm, wet mouth . . . hot pulsing body . . . Lyle groaned under the heady warmth of Kitty's greeting as one hand tightened in her heavy gold hair and the other kneaded the soft flesh of her buttocks. Two staggering steps still tightly wound in each other's arms and Lyle pushed the door shut behind him, his disturbing thoughts forgotten.

Rosalie's steady, even breathing echoed in the darkness of the silent bedroom. Lying beside her in the bed the three sisters shared, Sophia took comfort in the sound. Anna slept

41

also, as quiet in sleep as she had remained throughout the long, silent meal that had followed their mother's explosive display.

Relieved to cast aside the unaffected facade she had maintained during the grueling ordeal, Sophia looked toward the window of their room and the shafts of silver moonlight slanting through the gaping shade. A floating curl of smoke filtered into the room, its acrid odor comfortingly familiar, and Sophia knew that Papa was on the porch, a small black cigar clenched in his teeth, as unable to sleep as she. She touched her palm to her face, felt the welt on her cheek, and her sadness turned to sudden anger.

Mama said that she had disgraced the family . . . that she would bring her sisters down with her when she fell . . . that she must leave Joey Moretti alone!

Sophia restrained the bitter laughter that swelled within her. Accusations . . . threats. Mama never stopped to assess the effect her ruthless tactics had on the rest of the family — on her sisters, who tried to defend her with the truth, and on Papa, who suffered for all of them.

Mama claimed she only did what she knew was best, but those words were nothing more than a cruel joke which cut more deeply than a knife, and at which she was forbidden to laugh.

Finally drifting off to sleep sometime later, the scent of her father's cigar still lingering, Sophia was left with the tormenting uncertainty of wondering on whom that joke had truly been played.

Chapter Three

The heavy overcast that dimmed the light of morning turned to pounding rain as the three Marone sisters emerged from the alleyway beside their home. Silently groaning, Rosalie raised the umbrella Mama had pushed into her hand minutes before, waiting until her sisters scrambled under it beside her to join the stream of workers already making their way toward the mills.

The rain grew heavier, drumming against the sidewalk, soaking their shoes and the hems of their dark skirts as Rosalie adjusted the umbrella downward in an attempt to avoid a gusting blast that sprayed her face.

"Rosalie, I'm getting wet!"

"I'm doing my best, Anna!"

"Here, give the umbrella to me."

Rosalie looked up with silent relief as Sophia took the umbrella out of her hand and held it higher. It was the first time Sophia had spoken that morning, since she had looked into the small mirror in their room and seen the purple bruise that marked her cheek. Rosalie forced away the tears that filled her dark eyes at her sister's humiliation. Sophia would not allow herself to cry, and neither would she.

Another gusting blast and the sisters' groaning chorus elicited a simultaneous burst of laughter, followed by

Sophia's wry, tension-relieving comment as they continued laboriously down the street amidst sidewalk congestion that grew greater with each step.

"What do you think, Anna? Are the raindrops tears for the mark that mars my beautiful face?" Digging her sister in the ribs with her elbow in an obvious effort to consign the previous discomfort to the past, she questioned with a quirk of her lips, "Or do you think that Sophia Marone is crazy to think that the skies cry for her when she doesn't even cry for herself?"

Responding to Sophia's frivolous question with unexpected sobriety, Anna shook her head. "No, you aren't crazy, Sophia, because I think that when you don't cry for yourself, others cry for you more."

Halting suddenly, forcing her sisters to do the same as she held the umbrella rigidly overhead, Sophia said with quiet intensity, "I want no one to cry for me, Anna—not you or Rosalie or Papa because . . ."

Suddenly conscious of the obstruction they were causing on the crowded sidewalk, Sophia grimaced. On the street a carriage passed, water beading on its polished exterior as it traveled briskly toward the mills, and Sophia continued determinedly, "because I'll be riding in a smart carriage like that one someday, wearing a silk gown and a big hat, and then Mama will see."

Rosalie's throat tightened. "Mama's sorry that she hit you, Sophia. I know she is."

Sophia shook her head. "No *piccolina,* she isn't, but Mama will do what she must, and so will I." Suddenly smiling, Sophia winked. "And there are so, so many things that I must yet do! Come on!"

Ignoring the puddles that littered the walk and the startled pedestrians around them, Sophia started off at a run. Laughing as her sisters screeched their complaints, she stopped, allowing them to gather under the umbrella once more. With a shake of her head, she resumed a modest pace in the stream that moved steadily onward, and Rosalie's heart filled to breaking for her beautiful, brave Sophia.

The stream of mill workers flowing toward the mills thickened, umbrellas lowered against the rain bouncing briskly. A flash of bright red hair and a trim female body caught Aaron Weiss's eye as his carriage moved rapidly forward, and he leaned spontaneously toward the window, his gaze intensifying. Another gust brought the sea of black umbrellas down against the wind and Aaron cursed under his breath, sliding back against the velour upholstery of his carriage as it turned onto Van Houten Street. He was certain that he had seen that Marone girl in the surging throng the moment before one quickly moving dark skirt became indistinguishable from the next. He gave a jaded laugh. But one skirt always became indistinguishable from the next sooner or later.

Resuming a comfortable position, Aaron shrugged. It made little difference anyway. He was not on his way to Kingston Mill to flirt with the help. He had an errand of a totally different nature to run.

Removing his smart black bowler from hid head with a sudden frown of disgust, Aaron placed it on the seat beside him and smoothed his dark, neatly trimmed hair. Aaron Weiss, the only son of Samuel Weiss and heir to the Weiss family silk fortune — a glorified errand boy! He was not happy with the meager use his father made of his considerable talents, but he supposed the situation could be worse. His name could have been Paul Kingston . . .

Never truly friendly with the Kingstons, Aaron knew his father would have declined the invitation to a meeting the previous day were the situation in the mills not cause for alarm. However, it was time for drastic measures, and Samuel Weiss was not one to sacrifice the well-being of his business for the sake of personal dislikes.

Unification . . . Aaron unconsciously nodded. He

agreed completely that there was no other way to beat workers who struck the mills at the drop of a hat with demands that would cut the mills' profits to shreds. A familiar annoyance ticked his smoothly shaved cheek. What right did employees have to demand an increase in pay when profits rose? What right did they have to fight the industrialization that was the normal path of progress?

Aaron's expression tightened. Picketing of the mills for inconsequential grievances, and the humiliation of workers refusing to join wildcat strikes, had become almost weekly occurrences. The highly skilled weavers and dyers from overseas who were the backbone of the industry were accustomed to protesting industrialization. They had needed only the recent arrival of socialists and anarchists on the scene to inflame the situation.

The police had proved useless, favoring the strikers against the mill owners, and that disturbing situation had been the main point under discussion during the previous night's dinner at the Kingston house. As for himself, he had been immediately opposed to Kingston's idea of a private police force to protect the mills from this type of anarchy, for he was certain that type of action would only worsen the situation. He had adamantly expressed that opinion to his father on the way home.

Aaron sighed. Kingston and many mill owners like him had already built a few plants in Pennsylvania where a less militant attitude prevailed, and where there was an endless supply of labor for unskilled jobs. Inexperienced workers of coal-mining towns were then hired where local authorities without divided loyalties were able to keep the women and children who constituted the work force under control. Kingston's Honesdale plant already handled a portion of the work that constituted the throwing activity of raw silk, and he knew the gradual shifting of that processing to the mill there would continue.

The problem wasn't that easily solved, however, for the mill owners were well aware that the heart of the silk industry lay in weaving and dyeing, and that Paterson's abundant and easily accessible supply of soft water, which lent itself perfectly to the production of the vibrant colors of silk that had made the city famous, could not be easily duplicated elsewhere. The city's long history of successful manufacture, its proximity to New York City's fashion center and port, and the communities of European master weavers and dyers who had made the city their home, made its position ideal.

Aaron again considered the situation in Kingston's mill, concluding with a wry twist of his lips that it held no greater threat than the situation in his father's mill, despite Matthew Kingston's protestations.

Aaron shook his head, still wondering how the small, frail sister of the vibrant, powerful Matthew Kingston had managed to convince her brother to install her adopted bastard son as mill supervisor. It was not as if Lyle Kingston were particularly likable. Admittedly, the fellow had the good sense to dress well and to carry himself proudly, despite his origins, and he doubtless presented a better appearance than his "cousin" and natural heir to the mills. Aaron shrugged. He supposed in those ways the private schools Matthew Kingston had insisted upon and financed over the years had done their job. But rumor had it that Lyle Kingston was not particularly popular in the mill, that his personality was cold and his attitude abrupt. It was not disputed, nonetheless, that during his short month of his employment there, he had demanded and received silent respect from his uncle and the workers alike for supervisory abilities learned the hard way at the Honesdale mill and others like it. Lyle Kingston ran a tight ship, where the Kingston heir before him had failed miserably.

However, other rumors about the fellow were rife within circles of the silk elite. They included whispers that Lyle Kingston was ambitious . . . too ambitious to suit the senior Kingston; that the senior Kingston would continue to use him as he presently used him, without the benefit of a formal position, allowing him only enough authority to be effective in his job; that although the two protagonists in this undeclared war of the Kingstons despised each other, they would continue their watchful coexistence as long as each considered it to his own personal advantage.

As for himself, Aaron was betting on the elder Kingston, who was in the position of power. His personal opinion of Lyle Kingston, based on brief exposures to his rather abrasive personality, was that he was exceedingly arrogant and that he had an exaggerated conception of his own worth. As far as Aaron was concerned, Matthew Kingston was right. The outside of a man might change, but the inside stayed the same. Lyle Kingston was a bastard, and a bastard he would always remain.

His mind drawn back to the present as his carriage negotiated the small bridge over the raceway that separated Kingston Mill from the street, Aaron peered out the window at the workers streaming across the muddy lot as the deluge continued. The carriage drew to a gradual halt and Aaron remained seated, deciding to await a lull in the downpour rather than risk compromising his impeccable appearance. He was absentmindedly watching the line of approaching workers when his interest became more fixed at the running approach of three women sharing an umbrella. Their dash toward the entrance to the mill allowed him another glimpse of brilliant red hair and a flashing smile. The acknowledgment tugging somewhere in the area of his loins surprised him.

Sophia Marone . . . That name had lingered somewhere in the back of Aaron's mind since he had first seen her a few weeks ago. He supposed he owed it to himself to find out if the stories about the sultry beauty were true.

He smiled. He only hoped they were.

The three young women slipped into the mill and Aaron sat back, his expression sobering. He despised being used to relay messages, but unlike Paul and Lyle Kingston, he knew that his menial tasks were only temporary. He had a great future in store which demanded no more than a little patience and continued support of his father's policies. A flash of gleaming red hair returned opportunely to mind, and Aaron consoled himself that he would make good use of the time in between.

Suddenly impatient, Aaron picked up his hat. Thrusting open the carriage door, he dashed toward the mill entrance.

Her head remaining steadfastly forward despite the nagging presence at her side, Sophia continued setting up her ends. Aware that the winders around her were already working at full speed, she moved faster, ignoring all else but the fine silk threads, only to feel Joey's hand grip her arm in an attempt to turn her to face him.

"I'm talking to you, Sophia. Why won't you look at me?"

"I told you I'm busy, Joey."

"Sophia . . ."

Agitated, Sophia fought to retain her patience. She didn't like being accosted by Joey the moment she entered the mill. She didn't like having him follow her to her machine like an annoying puppy dragging at her skirt. She didn't like knowing that the entire scene would be reported back to her mother with gusto by wagging tongues that had nothing better to do than to carry tales.

Her patience evaporated as Joey remained doggedly at her side, and she snapped, "Did it never occur to you that I don't look at you because I dont' want to look at you?"

Joey's lips tightened. "That isn't what you said yesterday. Yesterday you said that if Angela apologized—"

"Yesterday was yesterday and today is today."

"Angela won't bother you anymore. She's going to apologize."

"I don't care about Angela. It doesn't matter anymore. Just go away."

Sophia glanced toward the looms in the rear, noting that Lyle Kingston stood at the warping wheel Joey had left unattended. Beside him she saw Vito Speroni wave an accusing finger at her.

Sophia snapped, "The nephew of the boss is looking at you and he's looking at me. Do you want us both to lose our jobs? What will your mama say then?"

"I don't care what she says. I want to know what's wrong. Why you're angry and why you won't look at me."

"Ask your mama why I don't look at you, Joey!"

"Mama . . . ?"

Facing Joey fully for the first time, Sophia hissed, "Your mama, who has a long tongue that whispers into my mama's ear. Your mama, who tells my mama that you're a good boy and that I mustn't torment you any longer. So, I no longer torment you! Go away!"

Joey whitened at Sophia's anger. He searched her face for a sign of relenting, his expression slowly changing as his gaze came to rest on her bruised cheek.

"What happened to your face?"

"Nothing."

"I asked you—"

Suddenly beside them, Lyle Kingston stated flatly, "I don't care what you asked her, Moretti, and I have the feeling she doesn't, either. Get to work. If I find you where you shouldn't be one more time, you're out the door."

Sophia's heart began a rapid pounding as Joey returned Lyle's gaze with obvious heat. His small, even teeth clamped tightly shut, his jaw hardening, and Sophia's relief was intense as Joey turned abruptly, without response, and stomped back toward the rear. She turned back to her machine, only to hear the nephew of the boss state in the same cool tone, "I'll talk to you later."

Sophia looked up to see Lyle Kingston striding toward the mill entrance, his broad back blocking a clear view of the well-dressed man who stood just inside the doorway shaking the rain from his coat. She wondered what the nephew of the boss would have said had he not been called away.

Sophia shrugged. She was certain it would not be long before she found out.

The oversize windows that lined the dye-house walls echoed with the sound of the drumming rain, drawing Anthony Marone's eye to their grime-coated surface. He had reported for work an hour earlier, through a deluge that showed no sign of relenting. He had arrived soaked to the skin, but his personal discomfort caused him little concern. Foremost on his mind was his knowledge that his daughters were on their way to work even as he watched the downpour continue. He knew they had one umbrella between them, adequate protection even from a storm such as this in Maria's eyes, and his mind rebelled again against her unnecessary frugality, often carried to the extreme where it was no longer a virtue in his eyes. His sole consolation was his knowledge that his daughters were strong, healthy young women who would suffer little long-term effects from a soaking chill, but his gentle heart wished for more than feeble rationalization.

Allowing his gaze to drift down the brick walls surrounding him, Anthony assessed the rolls of silk fabric carefully racked nearby, awaiting the master dyer's touch; the endless skeins of hard silk soon to be dyed, piled on tables between the vats, and the great tubs stained from years of use, where dyes for the intense shades of silk for which the city had become world famous were mixed. On the floor where no provision was made for drainage, Anthony saw a combination of accumulated moisture and brackish overflow from the vats, and he silently acknowledged the generally accepted fact that the dye house was the dirtiest and most unhealthy place in the silk industry.

However, that reality bothered Anthony very little as he turned and made his way across the slippery shop floor, heavy wooden clogs marking his progress between the tubs with a peculiarly hollow sound. There were many dyers' helpers working alongside him who fought the conditions under which they all worked. They also fought a pay scale they considered inadequate, saying they were the forgotten men of the silk industry, but Anthony didn't attend meetings of disgruntled workers. He had little interest in strikes. He ignored the constant presence of steam and fumes which were suffocating in the summer and which often condensed and froze in the winter. He suffered without protest the painful effects of boiling chemicals that often peeled the skin from his hands and arms, and he adopted without complaint the uncomfortable wooden shoes they all wore to protect feet that were often soaked at the end of the day despite that meager precaution.

Working under the supervision of the master dyer, he never forgot that although many of the men who worked around him had come to the city as skilled and semiskilled labor, he had not. He knew he would be a happy man were it not for the conflict between his wife and daughter, which was so intense that it was tearing him apart.

An overwhelming wave of sadness drew tears to Anthony's dark eyes, and he brushed them away with the back of his arm as he cast a self-conscious glance around him. He had slept very little the previous night. The crack of Maria's hand as it struck Sophia's cheek still reverberated in his ears, and he knew the sound would not soon be forgotten. Maria had stormed out of the house immediately afterward, and he had caught up with her just as she reached the street. She had been infuriated, beyond speech, and, after a silent walk, they had returned home.

He had not had an opportunity to speak with Sophia in the time since, but the friction between mother and daughter was of long standing. He knew that the confrontation was not due to a single set of circumstances. He believed Sophia was innocent of the often vicious gossip circulating about her, that she had been wronged by her mother's attack and that she suffered her mother's lack of understanding and sympathy for the plight of a beautiful, intelligent young woman with too much to offer her meager circumstances in life. However, he also believed that, strangely enough, it was Maria who suffered most in these encounters.

For he had held Maria in his arms the previous night and felt her trembling. He had heard his wife's whimpering cries in sleep and he knew that there was a torment deep inside Maria that would not abate, a torment that flamed to fury at the challenge in Sophia's eyes.

Deep lines of frustration marked Anthony's face. He would talk to Sophia, but he knew he could say little to assuage her distress. He could not explain the complicated torment his wife endured in administering her motherly duties, because he didn't truly understand it himself. He only knew that he was certain Maria loved her daughters—*all* of them—and that she was doing what she felt was best for them.

Anthony also knew that *he* loved his daughters—all of them—but that he loved one of them more.

Turning at the sound of his name, Anthony acknowledged the summons of the master dyer. Brushing his hands unconsciously against the canvas apron tied securely around his waist, he attempted, temporarily, to put his disturbing thoughts behind him.

Standing inside the mill entrance shaking the rain from his clothing, Aaron watched Lyle Kingston approach. Kingston's broad shoulders were squared, his face set in a mask of formal courtesy that held little warmth. Uncertain of the true cause for the spontaneous animosity between them, Aaron knew only that he was annoyed. He regretted his impulsive dash into the building, feeling foolish now that he stood shaking himself like a bedraggled dog, especially knowing that his impulse had been triggered by thoughts of the redheaded baggage working briskly within his view.

The fact that the arrogant bastard who bore the Kingston name had been in fast conversation with the object of his aspiring attentions only moments previous and that the fellow had obviously just driven a dark-haired, fierce-looking employee away from her under duress was another point of agitation. He had been right from the first. The girl was trouble, and the last thing he needed was a problem with that Italian breed of knife-wielding, malevolent agitators of which that dark-haired fellow appeared to be a part.

Inhaling deeply, Aaron pulled himself erect. He unconsciously affected the haughty mien with which he greeted those inferior to his station as he accepted Lyle Kingston's outstretched hand.

"It's a hell of day out there, Kingston," he began without social preamble. "I hope Matthew has already arrived. I have a message from my father and I have no time to waste."

"Uncle Matthew and Paul are in the office, but I wasn't aware that they were expecting you this morning."

"Oh? Does Matthew usually keep you apprised of his daily calendar? I understood he was never one to take *employees* into his confidence."

Kingston's unusual eyes narrowed into slits that were just short of menacing as he responded coolly, "I suppose that's true, but times are changing in the mills, aren't they? I think we all have to face the fact, however uncomfortable it may be for some, that we have to change with them if we hope to survive." Not allowing time for response, Kingston motioned him casually forward. "Follow me. I'm sure you remember the way to Uncle Matthew's office, but I'll take you there anyway. Consider it a matter of courtesy from a member of the family."

Kingston strode down the narrow aisle between the machines, and Aaron's irritation soared as he was forced to follow obediently behind. Cheeky bastard! Matthew Kingston would do well to watch his back with this fellow stalking his tracks.

Still fuming as they reached the glass enclosure separating the offices from the mill floor, Aaron managed a brittle smile as Lyle Kingston turned toward him and opened the door.

"I'll tell Uncle Matthew and Paul that you're here."

"That won't be necessary." Matthew Kingston's voice turned their attention toward him as he appeared in his office doorway, frowning. He halted his nephew's advance into the outer office.

"There's greater need for you on the floor than there is in here, Lyle." Extending his hand toward Aaron, he smiled. "Come in, my boy. Paul and I have been waiting for you."

Accepting the elder Kingston's hand, Aaron all but laughed aloud. Preceding Matthew Kingston into the inner office, Aaron could not resist a backward glance. The bogus Kingston had turned obediently on his heel, consigned to the mill floor where he belonged!

Hah! The sight almost made his former aggravation worthwhile.

Turning as door clicked closed behind them, Aaron nodded briefly at Paul Kingston before beginning without a hint of apology, "I don't think you'll be happy to hear what I have to say, Matthew . . ."

Still fuming silently minutes later, Lyle wound his way along the narrow aisles of the mill floor, the memory of Weiss's supercilious sneer gnawing at his insides. There were many who were far more deserving of the name "bastard" than he.

Breathing deeply, Lyle attempted to rein his agitation under control. He had been subjected to that type of intolerance most of his life. As a child he had alleviated his anger with his fists, but he was only too aware that as an adult, the process of gaining satisfaction was far more involved and painstaking.

Lyle passed the tubs where hard silk was being soaked in preparation for throwing, his jaw twitching. A short time in the nearby wiz and the process would begin. He glanced up in further assessment of the floor. There were sixty looms in the rear, warping wheels that fed the looms, quilling machines where bobbins used inside the loom shuttle were meticulously wound. And row upon row of winders . . .

His finely chiseled features tight, Lyle inhaled another steadying breath. He had taken the confusion and conflict that had resulted from Paul's temporary supervision of the mill and restored it to efficient productivity in one short month. If he were allowed to initiate other innovative measures, he could further increase productivity without affecting the status of a single employee. Anger surged anew. He had much to offer his uncle, for his talent for this work was instinctive and boundless.

A voice sounding abruptly in the back of Lyle's mind halted his escalating anger. It reminded him that only two months earlier, the path to a position in his uncle's Paterson mill had seemed hopelessly blocked, and that he was now running the mill successfully, even if that success went temporarily unacknowledged. He had made progress, and he would make more. All he needed was time and patience.

In the meantime, though, what he needed was to do his job and do it well while he ignored slights from those who thought themselves above him. Aaron Weiss's haughty face returned to mind, and Lyle's jaw hardened. Weiss's time would come.

Finding himself beside the winders, Lyle watched the nimble-fingered workers in the execution of their work — women of all ages and sizes, with the Marone girls taking up the final tier of machines. Far superior to them all in ability was Sophia Marone, whose touch was as light as a butterfly's wing as it moved efficiently along the machine.

The events of earlier that morning returned to mind and

Lyle frowned. Sophia was looking for trouble when she toyed with that hot-blooded Joey Moretti, and it appeared she was too much of a fool to realize it. He could not allow her foolishness to continue, especially when it affected the performance of his employees.

A familiar knot tightened in his stomach as Lyle started deliberately toward her. It was his fervent wish that he didn't have to deal with this beautiful, apparently frivolous young woman to whom he was drawn despite himself. He was annoyed that he must.

His irritation more visible than he realized, Lyle approached Sophia coldly.

Aware of Lyle Kingston's approach, Sophia did not look up. Somehow needing the few seconds it took for him to reach her side, she averted her face. She had escaped the nephew of the boss's reprimand in the past. She knew she would not escape it now.

"Sophia . . ."

Sophia looked up from the whirling bobbins, meeting the hard eyes other mill workers had come to fear. Strangely, the tension inside her drained at the contact and a spontaneous warmth swelled inside her. She smiled, realizing moments earlier she had not felt a smile left in her.

"So, you've come back to speak to me as you promised. What do you want to talk about, nephew of the boss?"

Lyle Kingston's expression tightened. "You're wasting your time, Sophia. I'm not one of the fellows who trail at your heels. Your wiles won't work on me. You'll do well to remember that. And while you're at it, I suggest you also remember that the 'nephew of the boss' runs this mill, whether he has the formal title of supervisor or not."

Sophia looked into the gold eyes coldly holding hers, responding with an understanding that came from deep within her, "It is difficult, isn't it, to feel the strength inside you—to know that you're capable of so much, only to have

57

opportunity withheld from you because of circumstance? You don't have to remind me that you're the supervisor here. Unlike some others, I don't dispute your accomplishments. Nor do I deny your right to reprimand me now."

Lyle Kingston's eyes narrowed, and Sophia felt his distrust the moment before he responded sharply, "I don't need your permission to say what you should be smart enough to realize for yourself. You're risking your job here by tormenting Joey Moretti, but you—"

The familiarity of those critical words drove Sophia to instant fury.

"I torment Joey Moretti? Are you as blind as the rest of them, then? What of Joey Moretti's tormenting of me? How many times must I tell him that I want no part of him before he'll believe me? *He's* the fool, not I! His conceit is so great that he can't believe a woman could turn him down, and his family is so taken with his charms that they believe every woman is trying to steal him away from them!" Turning on Lyle squarely, Sophia hissed, "So I say, *futida* to them, and *futida* to you, nephew-of-the-boss!"

Sophia raised her chin, still flushed with anger. She noted the further hardening of Lyle's jaw as he regarded her intently, and the sudden tightening of his gaze as he focused on her cheek.

"What happened to your face?"

Startled at his question, Sophia gave a hard laugh. "Nothing! What do you care?"

His gold eyes holding hers with a heat that was almost threatening, Kingston repeated slowly, "What happened to your face?"

Suddenly aware that his anger was no longer directed at her, but at the person who had marked her, Sophia was momentarily stunned into silence. When she spoke, her voice was void of her former agitation.

"Nothing. It matters little."

Menace in the set of his broad shoulders, Lyle responded tightly, "That's where you're wrong."

His unexpected concern, however begrudging, brought tears to Sophia's eyes where threat had failed, and she averted her face. When she looked back a moment later, he was gone.

Intense anger and a fiercely protective swell drove Lyle toward the warping wheel of Joey Moretti with long, angry strides. Sophia was right. He knew what it was to defend himself against whispered innuendo and unjust conclusions. He had often borne the marks of battles in defense of his name, and he knew that although his physical wounds had long ago healed, the scars inside remained. Those scars had been ripped raw upon seeing the welt that marred Sophia's smooth cheek. His fury was instinctive, and his need for satisfaction intense.

Joey Moretti focused on his approach. He assumed a challenging stance, and Lyle felt his heart begin a heavy pumping. His fists tightly clenched, he was rapidly closing the distance between them when Matthew Kingston's voice sounded over the din of the floor, halting him abruptly in his tracks.

"Lyle—a moment with you, please."

Startled from the blood-red haze that had enveloped him, Lyle turned toward his uncle, silently aghast. What had he intended to do, damn it!

Sanity returning, Lyle walked toward the mill entrance where his uncle stood with Weiss and Paul flanking his sides. Weiss stared past him in the direction of Sophia Marone as he approached, and Lyle felt the heat inside him rise anew.

"Paul and I are leaving with Aaron. We'll be back before noon."

Nodding with a silent curse, Lyle offered no spoken response as the three dashed out the door. He stared after them for long moments, resentment and frustration lingering, even as he glanced back at Moretti and realized he

59

should be grateful that his uncle had inadvertently stopped him from making a monumental mistake.

Determined he would not make that same mistake again, Lyle turned abruptly and strode toward the office.

Watching as Lyle walked back to the office, Sophia heaved a silent sigh of relief. For a moment she had thought that he was going to confront—

Suddenly smiling at the absurdity of that thought, Sophia turned back to her machine only to have her attention drawn to the pinch-faced girl poised watchfully nearby. Certain as she was that the nosy little gossip would pass along whatever she had overheard at the first opportunity, Sophia glared as the girl stared annoyingly at her cheek. Unintimidated, her small eyes popping with feigned innocence, Jacqueline inquired, "What happened to your face, Sophia?"

Sophia stared back at her just as intently. "What happened to yours?"

Surprised, the girl shook her head. "Nothing happened to my face."

"Eh?" Sophia shrugged. "So, nothing happened to mine either."

Leaving the girl openmouthed, Sophia walked to the end of her machine and resumed her work.

Chapter Four

Matthew Kingston walked briskly down the staircase toward the foyer of his home. Morning sun shone through the leaded glass panels beside the weathered oak door, the multifaceted prisms reflecting a rainbow of colors that painted the walls in dazzling display. Immune to the sight, Matthew grimaced at the sound of church bells tolling in the distance, a reminder that this day of the Kingston Mill employee picnic was a day of rest during which he would have no rest at all.

At the foot of the staircase, he turned toward the breakfast room, his expression jaded as he glanced again toward the bright sunlight streaming through the spotless panes. With characteristic arrogance he paused at the foyer mirror, mumbling, "It knew better than to rain today."

Matthew smiled as he assessed his reflection with an appreciative eye. Silver threads were sprinkled liberally among the dark in his hair, and his aristocratic mien was touched by time, but he was still handsome. His skin did not sag, the fine line of his profile was still sharp and clear, and his carefully cultivated mustache added just the right touch of virile appeal. His physique was as trim as in his youth, a matter which he attended to with strict discipline, and his carriage was erect. His casual attire, the light jacket and trousers and the fine, monogrammed shirt he wore, was faultlessly tailored, as was his entire wardrobe, and he knew the light straw hat that he had purchased specifically for this occasion—for he did not intend to wear the abomination again—would be the final touch of informality to affect the image of congenial participation in this dreaded event that he chose to convey.

Edith and Paul were already seated at the table when he entered the morning room. He nodded in acknowledgment of their greetings, his gaze openly assessing their appearance.

"Do I pass inspection, dear?" Edith's endearment was delivered with a sarcastic twist to her lips as she rose gracefully from her chair and pirouetted for his approval.

Deciding that his wife's informal gray cotton sprigged with miniature embroidered rosebuds suited her pale countenance as well as the occasion, Matthew arched a well-shaped brow.

"I don't believe I like starting the day with cynicism, Edith. You know your apparel never meets with disapproval from me."

"That's nice, dear." Edith picked up her fork, "because we both know that it wouldn't make much difference if it did."

His lip twitching with annoyance, Matthew turned toward the sideboard. "I know that only too well."

Lifting the lid of each chafing dish in turn, Matthew picked critically at the breakfast offerings. During their twenty-eight years of marriage, Edith had never missed an opportunity to remind him that it was the Leighton name that had brought him the social acceptability that he so desired at the time of their marriage, and the Leighton money which provided the necessary funds when Kingston Mill floundered during its early years.

Uninhibited by her ordinary appearance, Edith carried herself even now, when the bloom of youth was fading, with the self-confidence and pride that had first attracted him to her. During their years together, she had been his rival, his mentor, his antagonist, and his ally. She laughed at his vanity, opposed him when she pleased, and, as irritating and unsettling as she could sometimes be, as plain and unhandsome she would always be, he supposed no other woman suited him more than she. The truth was, her self-assured arrogance outshone even his own — as unwarranted as it sometimes was — and the homely reflection of himself that he saw in her fascinated him.

Dismissing his introspection as soon as his plate was filled, Matthew turned back toward the table. Seating himself, he addressed his son with deliberate casualness.

"I suppose you'll dress for the picnic when you've finished breakfast."

Paul's gaze jumped to meet his, and Matthew had the feeling that for all his silence, his son was no more easily intimidated than his mother as he responded, "I am dressed, Father." Glancing down at his dark trousers and open-necked shirt, he shrugged. "This is a picnic, after all, not a gala ball."

Matthew's spine slowly stiffened. "Whatever the occasion, you have an image to uphold as my son. I expect you to maintain it."

"Matthew . . ."

Matthew's head jerked back toward his wife. "You know I'm right, Edith. I won't have my son mistaken for a common mill hand. Bearing my name, he's above that level."

"As usual, you allow yourself to become upset over nothing, Matthew."

"I do not!"

"I tell you —"

"Father, I suppose I haven't made myself clear." Interrupting, his pale face flushed at the angry exchange he had instigated between his parents, Paul continued. "Of course I'll wear a suitable jacket and tie and . . ." He glanced toward the foyer where two straw men's hats hung side by side. "And one of those things, too, if you think its necessary."

But it was too little, too late, as far as Matthew was concerned. Paul was a Leighton, a product of his mother's genes with his faded coloring, inadequate size, and light hair already thinning at the youthful age of twenty-four. Facing his son now, Matthew realized that Paul's narrow, pointed face was so similar to Edith's that he could retch. He wondered again at the caprice of fate that had given him such an unsuitable son. Pushing his untouched plate away from him, Matthew looked directly into his son's pale eyes.

"You're aware of the importance I place on this picnic, Paul. This year is particularly critical. The situation is such with labor in this city at this point in time that it's urgent that we make our employees feel valued and safe, although I admit that it'll be far from enjoyable to spend the day with noisy, perspiring immigrants who are making the best of the day at my expense."

"Father!"

"The truth is the truth, Paul."

His face flushing more darkly, Paul rose to his feet. "I'll attend the picnic, Father, because I know it's important to you, and also because, unlike you, I don't care to insult the people who are responsible for making the family business a success."

Matthew's face took on a hue similar to that of his son's as he also rose. "I'm the person who made the 'family business' a success, and no one else! And while I'm making things perfectly clear, I'll add that while I expect you to join in the festivities today, I also expect you to

64

maintain a distance from the common herd that is suitable to your position."

Paul's expression tightened with challenge. "How far is 'suitable,' Father?"

"As far as I tell you!" His anger barely held in check, Matthew continued in a softer tone. "I've neglected to give Lyle similar instructions on his conduct today. I'll rely on you to correct that oversight."

"You want me to tell Lyle to—"

"You'll speak to Lyle this morning as soon as you're finished here, and you'll tell him that I expect him to remember that he bears the Kingston name, and that he should act accordingly. Ignoring Paul's silence, Matthew continued. "I've seen the eye he has for that redheaded Marone girl, and I expect you to remind him that if he must find entertainment with women of that type, he should keep his distance from those at the mill. Tell him to stick with that tart he visits. What is her name anyway? Kitty, isn't it?"

"I don't know, Father, and neither do I care."

Allowing the silence between them to deepen after his son's succinct response, Matthew retorted, "That's the crux of the problem, isn't it, Paul? You don't care about any of this."

"I have no talent for mill business, Father. I've accepted that truth. When will you?"

"But you have a talent for that worthless daubing you devote so many hours to each day. You'll never make your fortune painting pictures, Paul!"

"And if I haven't set my sights on a monetary goal?"

"Easy words for a fellow whose father's fortune has smoothed the way for him all his life." Regarding his son's stiffened expression, Matthew continued. "The truth is difficult to face, isn't it? And while we're presently viewing things as they truly stand, I'll tell you now that as my heir, I expect you to fulfill your obligations."

Paul's expression became strained, but Matthew showed no mercy as he continued tightly. "Your aunt has foisted a pretender on me, and it's your reticence to assume your expected position in the mill that gives her hope. I will not have a *bastard* take my place. You owe me your allegiance in this, Paul."

"I don't owe you my entire life."

"Oh, don't you?"

Maintaining an unyielding facade as Paul turned abruptly and walked out of the room, Matthew glanced back at his wife. Also standing beside her chair, her eyes pools of pale ice, she offered softly, "Matthew, you're a despicable fool."

Left in the silence of her wake as Edith quietly exited the room, Matthew waited only a moment before seating himself and picking up his fork.

Urging Anna along beside her, Sophia turned the corner onto Mill Street. She crossed the cobbled road and glanced behind her at the gradually thickening throng surging toward the grounds behind the falls where the Kingston Mill annual picnic was to be held. At her other side, Rosalie easily matched her pace, and, glancing down into her bright, animated face, Sophia felt a surge of almost maternal pride.

"Do you think there'll be a band again this year, Sophia? I never heard anything more wonderful than those marches they played last year. I'm hungry. I was too excited to eat breakfast. What do you suppose they'll have to eat? Do you think we'll be able—"

"One question at a time, Rosalie, please!" Laughing aloud at her sister's enthusiasm, Sophia turned up the hill past Franklin Mill, laughing again as she continued. "Better yet are no questions at all. We'll soon see what Mr. Kingston has waiting for us this year."

Glancing again toward Anna, Sophia felt the bite of sharp comparison between her two beloved sisters. Rosalie was so full of life and eagerness, while Anna . . .

Sophia shook Anna's arm and smiled encouragingly as her sister's dark eyes looked up into hers. "Are you feeling all right, Anna? You're so quiet."

"I'm fine." Anna forced a smile before glancing back revealingly toward their mother and father, who walked behind at a more sedate pace. "It's just that I heard Papa talking to Mama this morning. She didn't want to come. She said—"

Sophia's smile momentarily dimmed. "I know what she said, but Mama won't have to worry. Joey will stay away from me because his mama will be watching, and Mrs. Moretti will keep her mouth shut because she won't want anyone to realize what a fool her son really is."

"Mama thinks that you—"

Sophia forced a smile. "I told you. I don't care what Mama thinks about me. I'm going to have fun today." Sophia gave Anna's arm an encouraging shake. "Aren't you?"

Anna's sober expression slowly warmed under the brilliance of Sophia's smile, and Sophia felt her spirits rise as her younger sister nodded with unexpected determination. "Yes, I am. I'm going to have a very good time."

Resolved that she would, Sophia grasped each sister by the hand and pulled the girls up the hill.

The roar of the falls was muffled by the crowd surging onto the picnic grounds as the sun steadily climbed the morning sky. Standing near the entrance to the wooded grove, a position he had occupied with Paul since his arrival, Lyle watched the families of the employees arrive, nodding in greeting as they streamed past—women in assorted dress, breathless, smiling, with children of all sizes and ages in tow, and men in their Sunday dress. He turned to look at Paul, amused at the straw hat resting awkwardly on his pale hair. Recognizing his uncle's hand there, Lyle knew Paul would dispense with that small concession as well as they would both dispense with the formality of jackets as soon as it was feasible.

Still watching the entrance, Lyle saw a small, fair-haired toddler escape his mother's scrutiny to join a dark-complexioned fellow in a puddle that had not totally dried from the rain of the previous few days. The howling as he was snatched away, the excited exclamations of the two young mothers in different foreign tongues, neither of which the other understood, was a comical picture forcing a clearer picture of the diverse origins from which the employees of Kingston Mill were drawn.

German, French, Italian, Jew, Slovak . . . Lyle shook his head. Yet all communicated well enough to work efficiently with each other during the long workday. It was after the workday was over that things changed, however, with each group slowly dispersing to neighborhood streets that rang with sounds of their native tongues and where, comfortable at last, they had very little interaction with each other.

Still watching, Lyle saw the French settling on one side of the grove, the German in a small cluster nearby, the Italians in another corner. Together, but separate. He was tempted to laugh. He wondered if Uncle Matthew knew that his thinking and the thinking of his immigrant workers ran on an ironically similar parallel. Glancing unconsciously at his cousin, the *legitimate* Kingston standing beside him, Lyle could not help but wonder where this separation according to origin left him.

Appearing to read his mind as he glanced up, Paul gave a short laugh, "Do you think Father gave the employees' their instructions this morning, too?"

Paul's total acceptance of him while his parents kept

him at an effective distance had been difficult for Lyle to understand in his youth. Stranger still was the affection and spontaneous understanding that had marked the relationship between Paul and Lyle from the first. It was only later Lyle realized that with totally different personalities and with totally different reasons for their lack of standing in Matthew Kingston's eyes, Paul and he were united by Matthew's disapproval. Lyle was tempted to laugh. If Uncle Matthew only knew of the bond he had forged . . .

Refuting the instructions Paul had dutifully relayed with a slight shrug of his shoulders, Lyle responded, "What orders?"

Paul's response was an amused smile.

Glancing around him, Lyle unconsciously surveyed the grounds again. The grove was beautiful and cool, with the massive trees overhead filtering out the growing humidity of the day. The sound of the river swollen by rain as it cascaded over the gaping falls a safe distance away was a soothing echo. He had to credit his uncle with the foresight to have gained permission to use this location, and for the organization of an affair which appeared to be running with unexpected efficiency. He surveyed again the fires where the first sausages of the day were already cooking, where peppers and potatoes were fragrantly roasting, and where long tables piled high with breads, vegetables, and every manner of food, tempted the palate. In another corner of the grove, barrels of beer, wine, and soft drinks with dripping spigots tempted the approaching hoard. Set a reasonable distance away, the uniformed band of Professor Morcanti, uncomfortably seated on wooden folding chairs, prepared to play.

"Your father seems to have spared no expense for the occasion."

"Father always puts on a lavish affair." Paul's smile dimmed. "It's too bad that he's such a hypocrite. But then, nothing for nothing is Father's motto. You wouldn't expect any different from him, would you? He wouldn't ever—"

Lyle turned toward his cousin as he abruptly stopped speaking. Startled by his expression, he followed the line of Paul's gaze, stopping abruptly as it came to rest on the three Marone sisters as they entered the grove.

A familiar knot twisted in Lyle's stomach as Paul commented softly, "She really *is* a beauty, isn't she, Lyle? There's a haunting quality to her, something that makes it difficult for a person to forget the way she—"

A hot, surging emotion to which Lyle refused to put a name forced him to interrupt his cousin's ramblings.

"I guess she's beautiful—if you like flashy women."

Paul turned sharply, the anger in his eyes fading as he abruptly laughed aloud. "I didn't mean Sophia! I meant her sister, Anna. Everybody overlooks her because she fades into Sophia's shadow, but there's something about her . . ."

"What's this?" Lyle raised his brow. "If Uncle Matthew heard you now . . ."

Paul shrugged, his thin face suddenly sober. "Anna's only a child, but I won't have to worry about what my father thinks much longer, in any case. I've been making plans, Lyle. I might as well tell you about them. I've applied to study under one of the greatest artists in France, Monsieur Gaston LeDeux. If I have half the talent that I think I have, he'll whip it into shape."

Speechless at his cousin's disclosure, Lyle was surprised to hear himself finally inquire, "Are you sure you want to do that, Paul? Are you sure you want to give up everything that's waiting for you here, in the mill? Your father is a difficult man. You can't be certain what he might do if you should eventually change your mind and want to come back."

Paul shrugged. "I'm not sure of anything right now, except that I have to try. You understand, don't you, Lyle?"

Nodding, his gaze intent on his cousin's earnest expression, Lyle was startled as a familiar voice sounded sweetly nearby, "Good morning, nephew of the boss. A good day for a picnic, no?"

Turning swiftly, Lyle was almost knocked breathless by the unexpected proximity of Sophia Marone's animated beauty. Annoyed at his reaction, he did no more than nod as she greeted Paul and continued past, her sisters in tow. He didn't realize he was staring after her until Paul nudged him sharply.

"You're going to have to watch that, Lyle. Father thinks you're interested in her. If you ever expect to gain his approval, she's the last one you should be looking at—"

Unwilling to listen to the words he didn't want to hear, Lyle cut his cousin off sharply.

"The truth is that I'll never get your father's approval—and what I do is none of his business."

Paul nodded. "Father said he would rather see you stick to your little whore—I think he said her name is Kitty."

"How did he know about Kitty? Lyle paused, his jaw tightening. "The bastard!"

Paul raised his brow with a quirk of his lips. "Funny, that's what Father calls you."

Lyle's expression darkened. "I don't think it's funny at all."

His pale face sobering, Paul offered lightly, "It's funnier than you think, Lyle, although I realize you're not in a position to enjoy the joke."

About to respond, Lyle found himself caught by the malevolent gaze of a tall, gray-haired woman who walked on the arm of a shorter, congenial-looking fellow with a magnificent black mustache. She looked away moments later, but the heat of her gaze remained as Paul whispered, "That's Maria Marone." And at Lyle's look of surprise, "Yeah, the mother of the three girls—a real witch, I hear, in more ways than one. And it looks like she's put the evil eye on you for looking at her daughter."

"Don't tell me that you believe in that 'evil eye' foolishness!"

Paul shook his head. "You never know about these 'Eye-talians.'" And then in a mocking tone, "Look, here comes Father's carriage. He's making a truly grand entrance, isn't he?"

Lyle muttered an appropriate response. His gaze followed Matthew Kingston's gleaming black carriage as it turned into the grove, but his mind returned to the revelations of his conversation with Paul. Strolling forward to extend the necessary greetings to his uncle and aunt, Lyle was not even tempted to smile.

Maria glanced back at Lyle Kingston and clutched her husband's arm.

"You see! I told you! The girl asks for trouble. Now she flaunts herself before the fellow who bears the Kingston name. Did you see how his eyes followed her? *Che scorno!*"

Anthony regarded his wife's anxiety wearily, then shook his head. "Maria, *cara mia*, there was a time when many eyes followed you the same way, including mine."

His words appearing to inflame Maria's concerns rather than allay them, Anthony felt his frustration soar. Continuing on without speaking until they reached a wooded copse nearby, Anthony abruptly drew his wife behind the closest tree and, taking her in his arms, kissed her soundly. Gasping, her face aflame, Maria glanced around them with embarrassment as her husband whispered, "Now let the wagging tongues call Anthony

Marone an old *buffone* for loving his wife with so much passion after all these many years—for then the gossip will be true."

Tears brimmed in Maria's light eyes. She was still staring at him when her face appeared to crumple and she slid her arms around him unexpectedly to kiss him warmly on the mouth in return. Her voice hoarse, she responded softly, "*Sì*, Anthony, for then the gossip will be very true indeed."

Taking his arm, Maria drew Anthony out into the open once more. She raised her chin as she walked quietly beside him to the nearest empty table and sat down.

The humid morning had slipped into a hot, sultry afternoon at the picnic grounds. Underneath the band of the captain's cap he wore pulled squarely down on his forehead, Professor Morcanti's brow was beaded with sweat. The underarms of his pale-blue uniform, elaborately decorated with gold buttons, braid, and epaulets, were darkly ringed. Deeply engrossed in the final chords of a series of rousing marches, he raised his baton, waving it with a wild flourish before bringing it down with dramatic emphasis on the final note.

A swell of applause turned him toward the appreciative picnickers with a smile. Bowing stiffly as he wiped a stained white handkerchief across his forehead and down both of his perspiration-streaked cheeks, he extended his arm toward his musicians in smiling acknowledgment before turning back to face them. Tapping the stand in front of him, the professor again raised his baton.

Lyle was incredulous. The band had been playing nonstop for an hour, uniforms buttoned to the neck and formal caps pushed down on their sweaty brows in a humid heat that was growing more unbearable by the moment. Around him, sitting at tables littered with emptied plates and full glasses and sprawled on blankets underneath the trees, satiated picnickers laughed, reprimanded squabbling children, and dozed from the sheer exhaustion of a day's gluttonous indulgence. Only the old professor and his tireless musicians appeared to have the energy to continue full-speed ahead.

A sudden chorus of laughter interrupted Lyle's thoughts, and he turned in the direction of the sound, his lips flattening into an unsmiling line. He had not really needed to turn to identify the person in the center of the group, for he knew that although the faces around her occasionally changed, Sophia remained its unaltered focus.

Lyle attempted to dispel the swell of unfamiliar emotions that plagued him with each thought of Sophia Marone. Why shouldn't she be at the center of that group of fawning young men? Radiant despite the pale-pink dress she wore that had seen far too many washdays to be considered in its prime, her flaming hair gathered informally back from her face with a ribbon that allowed the shimmering mass to cascade down her back in riotous disarray, her delicate features too vivacious and her moist lips too often returning sharp quips to her admirers for her behavior to be considered genteel, Sophia was a breath of fresh air on a sultry day, and a feast for the eye.

Lyle surveyed the company gathered around her. Although her sisters had recently wandered out of sight, they had been a part of the group most of the day, with the other young women gathered there only joining in a bid for a fair share of male attention. But without deliberate effort, Sophia still reigned supreme.

Noticeably absent from the group, however, Joey Moretti stared broodingly from the table he shared with his family a short distance away. Lyle gave a low grunt, uncomfortably uncertain what his reaction would be

74

if the fellow attempted to bother Sophia again.

Nearby, in a cluster of tables, Lyle saw that Sophia's parents sat with the family of warper Salvatore Grimaldi. Through the course of the day, Lyle had seen the affection with which Sophia joked with her father. He had seen her light the fellow's small black cigar with a teasing wink when they finished eating, and had watched her travel back and forth countless times to the wine barrel to fill her father's glass. He saw the pride in Anthony Marone's eyes, always brighter when he beheld his eldest daughter, and he saw the ready laughter and consistent humor that had been that homely peasant's only visible bequest to her.

It had taken only a brief second glance to see that Maria Marone was everything that her husband was not.

Behind him, quietly conversing at a table set a respectable distance away from the crowd and fervently wishing, Lyle was certain, that he was anyplace other than there, sat Uncle Matthew. Lyle's lips pulled into an unconscious sneer. Uncle Matthew's benevolent smile proved what a supremely fine actor he really was. Aunt Edith was less hypocritical, however, maintaining that same reserve she displayed to all, with only an occasional display of warmth when speaking to Paul.

A sudden raucous call from within the grove announced the beginning of the sack races, and Lyle could swear that he heard a unanimous groan of relief from the weary musicians as the Professor brought the music to a halt with a sweep of his baton.

Appearing from all quarters of the crowded grove, game masters called for participants in various languages, urging their people onward. The former lethargy of the grove slowly dispelled as lines began forming in the clearing, and Lyle waited only until informal cheering sections formed at the sidelines before turning to follow the winding path that led away from the crowd. He had done his

75

duty for the time being. Paul had already disappeared, leaving him to lend his appearance to the scene alone, and as far as he was concerned, Uncle Matthew could now leave his informal throne and descend among the masses to congratulate the winners himself. He was no longer available.

Lyle walked slowly on the dusty path. The thunder of falling water grew louder as a few children raced past him toward the games, and he knew that the view of the falls from the high, rocky cliffs bordering it, gradually coming into sight, would soon be emptied of revelers. He was grateful for the solitude he would be afforded. This unusual day had stirred so many emotions inside him, had opened up so many avenues of thought for which he was uncertain he was fully prepared, that he needed time to sort them out.

He had walked the bridge that spanned the chasm only once before, many years ago. It had been a strangely ablutionary experience that he did not wish to share with shouting and giggling teenagers.

The wooded area around him rapidly thinned as the roar of the falls grew louder, and Lyle grimaced as he saw the Cottage on the Cliff, a holiday spot that had become increasingly popular of late. Pleased to see the excitement in the grove had emptied that area as well, he continued toward the bridge. Relieved from the heat of the day by the first airborne mist that washed his cheek, Lyle was momentarily mesmerized by the roaring flow cascading over the edge of sheer rock as the falls came into full view. Two days of rain had swelled the river into rushing, muddied crystal that plummeted from a periphery sliced deep into towering rock. Standing stock-still, he stared down into the gorge below him where the water rebounded in a powerful spray at the base of the falls before sinking into the rapids. As he watched, a rainbow materialized abruptly above the foam.

"It's beautiful, isn't it?"

Lyle looked up at the sound of the familiar voice, surprised to see Sophia standing on the bridge. He wondered how he could have missed seeing her before.

Conflicting emotions assailing him, he moved spontaneously toward her, stopping only when he stood beside her at midspan. Silent, unsmiling, he was more intent on Sophia than on the spectacle flowing beneath their feet as he looked down into her equally serious, extraordinary beauty. Nature had embellished that beauty by dampening Sophia's gleaming tresses into curling spirals that lay against her back, tempting his touch; by dropping a gossamer veil of moisture on her creamy skin that his lips suddenly longed to taste; and by depositing gleaming droplets on the thick, gold-tipped lashes that framed startlingly blue eyes filled with his own intense reflection.

It was abruptly and undeniably clear to Lyle that as strongly as he wished it otherwise, his feelings for this unusual, incredibly lovely young woman were as complex as she herself. Causing him even more concern was the thought that those feelings were as intricately involved with the inner core of him as they were with the human side of him that was slowly succumbing to her physical allure.

Lyle swallowed thickly, his heart beginning a heavy pounding. His plans did not include becoming involved with any woman at this time, and at no time in his future did he envision exposing himself to the innate honesty and candor that he knew instinctively any relationship with this young woman would demand. But she was so close, and he knew that if he had the courage to try, he could read as much in those incredible eyes as she appeared to be able to read in his.

That thought sobered Lyle further, drowning out the sound of the rushing torrent beneath them as an insistent voice in the back of his mind filled the silence with the warning: *This is not wise . . .*

Hoots of laughter and strident shouts of encouragement echoed in the grove as the three-legged race continued. Standing on the sidelines, Rosalie covered her ears,
her face reddening as the fellows from their group called
out ribald remarks to the participants who were slipping
and stumbling toward the roughly drawn finish line. She
glanced toward the table where Mama and Papa sat in
deep conversation with the Grimaldis, relieved that they
paid no attention to the lively scene.

Uncovering her ears, she watched as Carlo and Nicholas, bragging so boldly only minutes before, fell to the
ground with a loud "Whuff!" The spectators roared with
laughter as they struggled to regain their feet, their faces
and clothes smeared with dirt, but their expressions determined. Jumping up and down, Rosalie covered her
lips with her fingertips in an effort to contain her excitement as they moved into contention once more by leaping over the sprawled figures of Enrico Penti and
Salvatore Rossi. She laughed aloud. They were such
fools, all of them, but they were so amusing. She glanced
around her, suddenly realizing that some of the other fellows standing on the sidelines beside her had disappeared. They were missing all the fun!

Turning, Rosalie spotted a small group gathered in a
stand of trees a short distance away. She paused, caught
by the solemnity of the listeners and the agitated hand
motions of the person holding their attention. The fellow
who was speaking was dark-complexioned. He wore a
jacket and open-necked shirt, and a cap pulled down low
on his forehead despite the heat of the afternoon. She did
not remember having seen him earlier in the day, and
she was fairly certain that he was not an employee of the
mill.

A prickle of apprehension moved down Rosalie's spine the moment before a sudden chorus of cheers turned her back to the finish line to see Carlo and Nicholas, as well as Enrico and Salvatore, lying in the dust, while two of the French weavers stood swaying triumphantly at the finish line. But the joy of the moment turned strangely cold as Rosalie turned around again to look at the fellows gathered in the trees behind her.

Without conscious volition, Rosalie started walking toward them, only to be stayed unexpectedly by a gentle touch on her arm as Anna warned, "Don't go over there, Rosalie. You'll get in trouble."

"What do you mean?" Rosalie directed another inquisitive glance at the group, noting the growing agitation on the part of the speaker. "What's going on, Anna?"

Anna's dark eyes were wide with apprehension. "That fellow, the one doing the talking, is Enrico Malatesta. He's from that socialist group. You know the one I mean — The Group for the Right to Existence. He's crazy, Rosalie! He's telling those fellows that no one really cares about them and their rights, and that if they aren't prepared to fight for better conditions, they're not going to get them. He said that this picnic is just a farce to lull everyone into thinking that Mr. Kingston values his employees and that they'll pay for this day in the end."

"Somebody should tell Mr. Kingston!"

"Shh!" Anna looked around them, anxious to see if they had been overheard. "Don't get involved, Rosalie. I heard Papa say that anybody who tries to go against these people suffers. They're vicious!"

"Oh, Anna . . ." Rosalie shook her head, her small, pert face concerned. Anna was always so frightened that she only wanted to stick her head in the sand. Sophia was so concerned with her problems with Mama and the things she wanted to do in life that she had little interest in the strikes that threatened their future. Rosalie hesitated, knowing that unlike her sister, she was not content to allow these events to happen around her without understanding them. She made a decision.

"I'm going over there to listen to what that fellow has to say, Anna."

"No!" Anna looked toward the table where Mama and Papa still sat. "Papa wants us to stay out of the labor troubles."

"I'm going to stay out of them. I'm just going to listen."

"Rosalie . . ."

"I'm going!"

Not waiting for her sister's response, Rosalie ignored the sack races forming behind her and started toward the group gathered in the trees. As Malatesta's agitated voice grew clearer, she felt excitement prickle along her spine. She was not a child any longer, even if everyone in the family seemed to think of her as one.

Walking to a spot where she stood unobserved, Rosalie listened.

Her eyes darting to the table where Mama and Papa sat unawares, then back to Rosalie as she stood a few feet from the impassioned socialist, Anna felt her heart begin an escalated beating. Her throat filled as she realized she was as helpless against Rosalie's unexpected rebellion as she was against Sophia's. Her chest heaved with suppressed emotion, and she pushed a strand of hair back from her cheek, glancing around her to see if anyone had noted her distress.

A loud simultaneous cheer announced the start of the sack races, and grateful for the diversion, Anna scampered off onto one of the many trails leading out of the cleared area around her. She took a deep breath and brushed a tear from her cheek as she slipped out of sight. Her pace remained steady, although she was uncertain where the path would take her, and it was only when the sounds behind her became safely muted that she slowed her step and sat abruptly on a boulder beside the trail. She breathed deeply once, twice, in an effort to gain control of her emotions. The peace of the glade had begun to take a soothing effect when she was suddenly startled by an unexpected voice.

"Are you all right, Anna?"

Jumping spontaneously to her feet, she blinked as Paul Kingston stepped fully into sight from around the sharp curve in front of her. She blinked again, stuttering, "Y-yes, I'm all right. I was just . . ."

Unable to face the pale eyes filled with concern, Anna lowered her chin, only to have Paul Kingston raise it again until she could no longer avoid his scrutiny.

"What happened, Anna. Who made you cry?"

"Nobody! I mean . . ." Anna took a deep breath and attempted a smile. "There's really nothing wrong. I'm just feeling . . . unhappy, that's all."

"Unhappy, at a picnic?" Paul Kingston's thin face creased into a gentle smile. "I thought my father had taken care of everything today, but I guess I was wrong."

"Oh, no! The picnic is wonderful! It's just that sometimes I feel . . ."

The realization suddenly returned that Paul Kingston was her employer's son, that he was merely being kind, and that like most other people, he had no real interest in her response, and she halted abruptly.

Paul Kingston waited, then urged softly, "Yes, you feel . . . ?"

Anna took a deep breath. "I don't know. I can't seem to do anything right, and even when I know I must do something, I can't decide what." Anna paused, honesty forcing her to add, "Or maybe I'm just too frightened to try."

Paul nodded. "I know how it is to be made to feel inadequate."

Anna shook her head, denying the sympathetic fellow's implication. "It isn't my sisters' faults! They can't help it if they're smarter than I am, and braver, and prettier . . ."

"You're the really beautiful one in your family, Anna."

Anna shook her head again. "No, I'm not!"

Paul Kingston smiled a warm smile that showed his white, even teeth and fleeting dimple. "Oh, yes, you are. You may not be as flamboyantly beautiful as Sophia, or as impishly pretty as Rosalie, but you have a soft, brooding beauty that's far more interesting."

Anna lowered her eyes. "Mama says I'm moody and too quiet. She says—"

"I don't think your mama sees you through the same eyes that I see you. Anna, look at me."

Accustomed to commands, Anna looked up to see a surprising uncertainty in Paul Kingston's expression the moment before he stated abruptly, "I'd like to sketch you, Anna. Would you sit for me?"

Anna's jaw dropped and her eyes widened. "Sketch *me?* But why?"

Paul shook his head. "I don't really know why, except that I have the feeling that painting your portrait would bring out the best in me. I'd like to give it a try."

Anna did not respond, and Paul's smile and tone became coaxing. "I have a sketching pad and an easel set up just around the curve in the path. The sunlight filters down through the trees there. It's a natural enhancement that could add just the lighting I'm looking for. I would be happy to pay you for—"

"Oh, I couldn't take money from you. Mama would think—" Anna swallowed, unwilling to relate the conclusion she feared her mama would reach if she told such an incredible story. Her heart beginning a rapid beating of another kind, Anna felt a slow anticipation building within her. Gathering her courage, she nodded.

"All right. If you want to paint my picture . . ." She hesitated, feeling foolish in repeating such an unbelievable request, "Then I'll be happy to sit for you." She hastened to add, "But you mustn't tell Mama—or anyone. I . . . I don't want them to laugh."

His expression became strangely sober and Paul Kingston nodded solemnly. "I don't want them to laugh, either, Anna." Taking her arm, Paul drew her with him around the curve in the trail. He motioned to a boulder where the sunlight shone unrestricted.

"Sit there. That's right. Look at me. Raise your chin and put your hands in your lap. That's right." And as she sat there obediently, Anna was filled with disbelief.

Lyle Kingston stood beside Sophia on the bridge, his massive size dwarfing her. But she knew the power of his presence was not limited to size alone. As the silence between them lengthened, her heart began a heavy pounding. The aura that surrounded him was touched with both danger and promise, and a part of her cried out to sample each, however briefly, even as another part of her felt the heat of his gaze and urged caution.

It occurred to her that she hadn't realized how handsome the nephew of the boss truly was. At close range his tawny gold hair and eyes seemed almost too beautiful for a man, but the hard line of his jaw and the touch of arrogance in his classic profile supported the grim determination often evident there in a way that bespoke a strength that could not be denied.

It was not the colors or textures of the man, however, that sent a shiver down Sophia's spine. It was the feeling that should he decide to try, those tawny eyes could see as clearly into her soul as she felt she could see into his. Growing stronger with every moment he remained by her side was the realization that although this sober, mysterious man had tried to refute this inexplicable bond that drew them together, the cracks in his defenses had spread until now, at this moment, she could almost hear the entire wall crumbling. The sound reverberated in her heart, leaving her strangely shaken.

In an unconscious effort to alleviate the intensity of the moment, Sophia glanced down at the water flowing beneath them. She sought to clarify her feelings for both herself and the man at her side as she spoke hesitantly.

"This was my favorite place when I was a child, you know. I saw my dreams in the rainbows at the foot of the falls, and I can still remember that first summer when the drought reduced the river to a trickle and the rainbows disappeared." Her laugh was self-derisive. "I felt betrayed."

Sophia looked up to meet Lyle Kingston's eyes, then glanced away again in an effort to relieve herself of the draining power of his gaze. Concentrating on the cascading torrents nearby, she continued. "But the waters flowed again, and so did my dreams, and that experience taught a lesson to the clever child that I was. I learned that I couldn't depend on rainbows to make my dreams come true. I've never forgotten that lesson."

Lyle spoke, his voice unexpectedly hushed as he reached out to touch a lock of hair on her shoulder. "What are your dreams, Sophia?"

"Ah, my dreams . . ." Sophia paused, momentarily uncertain how to respond. "They're deceptively simple. I want to escape the mills. I don't want to spend the rest of my life winding bobbins of silk thread and looking to a future where I'll marry and raise children to wind bobbins of silk thread after me." Looking up, seeking the understanding she felt instinctively she could receive from him alone, she was moved to whisper more intimately than before, "You see, there's something special inside

84

me, something I've always known was there. Since I was a child, I've seen a vision of myself in my mind as I'll someday be, and I know as surely as I stand beside you now that I'll someday have a wardrobe filled with dresses made from the silk that I now wind, and those same people who gossip about me now will bow their heads in greeting when I pass."

Sophia halted abruptly, her voice assuming an almost challenging tone. "Does that sound strange to you, nephew of the boss, coming from the daughter of a poor immigrant?"

"That's a very ambitious dream, Sophia."

Suddenly self-conscious, Sophia did not respond. She had not confided the full scope of her efforts to anyone, not even her sisters. She had passed off lightly the hours she had spent in the library, reading and studying. She had dismissed the hours she had spent looking in the windows of the exclusive stores around town as frivolous entertainment. And the sketches she labored over so diligently . . .

Feeling herself on uncertain ground, Sophia efficiently shifted the course of their conversation.

"I've told you my dreams, nephew of the boss, but I don't have to ask yours. I know what they are."

Unexpected annoyance touched Lyle Kingston's face, and Sophia felt him begin to withdraw as he responded caustically, "So, mind-reading is now included in your talents."

Sophia shook her head, glorious blue eyes melding with gold. "I don't need a special talent to know what you're thinking, *caro* nephew." The spontaneous endearment slipped from her lips without realization. "It's like reading my own mind."

Lyle's eyes narrowed, and when he spoke, she heard a note of cynicism in his tone. "Then you must know what I'm thinking now."

His challenge was no true challenge at all as Sophia responded, "Yes, I do. You're wondering why you should care at all what I say or do. The question is always in your eyes when you look at me, but it was stronger while you watched me in the grove today."

Lyle stiffened, his discomfort with her intuitiveness obvious. "I suppose I was watching you."

"And you were thinking—"

Lyle's expression tightened. "I was thinking that you were acting unwisely with those young fellows today."

"Oh, so?"

"You were asking for trouble, and you may yet get it. Moretti didn't take his eyes off you for a minute. When Francesco put his arm around you, Moretti almost—"

"Moretti, Moretti!" Sophia's temper flared. "I'm tired of hearing the name. I can't control Joey's behavior. I can only control my own, and I won't pander to the approval of others."

"What about your family?"

"My family?" Sophia paused, her anger fading as quickly as it had come. "They are very dear to me, but I've found that I must follow my own path because we're so different from each other." She gave a short laugh, amused at the thought that touched her mind. "If we were animals instead of people, my family and I, we'd be an assorted lot."

When he appeared to be confused by her words, Sophia elaborated with a smile. "Anna would be a wounded fawn, with those great dark eyes, needing so much. Rosalie would be a bright little squirrel, always working, always thinking and looking ahead. Papa would be the Papa Bear of the storybooks, jolly and harmless in appearance, but fiercely protective of his family—and inside so very, very strong and loving. And Mama . . ." Sophia paused, her smile dimming. "Mama would be Mama."

Lyle's eyes registered understanding of the wealth of meaning in those last few words. He asked the obvious question.

"What animal would you be, Sophia?"

Sophia's response was instantaneous. "A sly red fox, of course!"

Lyle nodded, then questioned unexpectedly, "What animal would I be?"

"Oh, dear nephew of the boss," Sophia shook her head, her humor fully returning, "You don't really want to know . . ."

Lyle laughed aloud at her unanticipated response, a smile of incredible beauty spreading across his lips, and Sophia's spirits soared. It was first time she had heard him laugh, or even smile with true mirth, and she felt privileged to have inspired the emotion.

Without conscious thought, Sophia raised her hand to touch her fingertips to his lips. She was filled with regret as the shudder that shook him stole his smile. Holding her gaze with his, he slid his arm around her, and a strange fire shot up her spine. His breath was warm against her cheek as he whispered, "You're very beautiful, Sophia."

Taking no pleasure in words she had heard so often before, Sophia didn't smile. She was impatient with small talk that would cloud the truths that needed to be spoken quickly, before the emotion of the moment assumed control.

"I know I'm beautiful, just as you must know that you're as beautiful as I. In that way, and in so many others, we're alike, isn't that so, *caro* nephew? You know what's inside you, too, that others can't see. You see your dreams just beyond your grasp, and they eat at you, just as mine eat at me. You burn with the desire to be more than you are, just as I do, and because we're so alike and because our dreams progress so slowly, we're drawn to each other." Sophia took a deep breath as her hand fell to Lyle's arm and she whispered, "I've felt the bond between us tug many times, and I've taken hope in knowing that there's finally someone who could understand all the things that go unspoken inside me." Sophia paused again, searching his gaze intently. "We've been given a gift in our meeting, but you've chosen to acknowledge only the physical attraction between us. Why do you fight the understanding that could give us both so much comfort?"

Caution warred with other feelings in the tawny eyes that held hers, as sudden realization reduced her voice to a tone barely audible above the river's roar, "Ah, yes, I know what you fear, *caro* nephew. You're afraid that this thing that draws us together could lead where neither of us can afford to follow."

A shudder shook Sophia and she sighed unconsciously. "But neither of us can afford to make that mistake, don't you see? It's because we understand each other's circumstances so well, because we're too wise, and because we both have so many things that we must do, that we know we can never allow ourselves to become more than friends."

Lyle's eyes searched hers. "The kind of friendship you talk about is hard, Sophia. It'll be especially difficult between us."

"Lyle . . . *caro* . . ." The warmth inside Sophia burned brightly, "But it will be so worthwhile . . ."

Acknowledgment of her whispered words was in the spasmodic tightening of Lyle's hand as it clutched hers, in the gentleness of his touch as he drew her closer. And it was in the incredibly sweet touch of his lips as they met hers gently with a lingering, bittersweet kiss.

Holding her close for long moments after their kiss had ended, Lyle whispered huskily against her hair, "All right, Sophia, friends . . ."

Regret was in Lyle's eyes and in his sigh as he drew back from her. The sentiment resounded inside Sophia, but she knew instinctively that one word had forged a commitment that would forever hold them fast. Turning to walk beside him, Sophia slid her arm through his and leaned warmly against his side as they started back across the bridge. When she looked up, Lyle's gaze was no longer veiled. She felt its warmth penetrate her soul and she knew that they, who read each other's hearts so well, need say no more at all.

Pulling back amidst the trees as the handsome couple on the bridge turned his way, Joey Moretti felt a deep fury rise inside him. So, he had been right all along! Sophia, fool that she was, had eyes for the nephew of the boss.

Tormenting himself as they drew closer, Joey recalled Sophia's gentle stroking of Lyle Kingston's lips, and he groaned, wishing it were he who had felt her touch. He remembered Kingston's hand had caressed her back, and he wished it were his arm that had held her fast. He remembered the ease with which Sophia allowed Kingston to draw her against him, the spontaneity of their kiss, and the knife of pain inside him cut deeper. He watched with growing jealousy the inexplicable understanding in the look they exchanged as they drew closer, walking arm in arm.

Joey briefly closed his eyes against the pain of it. It could not be so! Those glances were feigned for whatever reasons motivated each of them in turn. They were different, their worlds too far apart—his Sophia and that arrogant nephew of the boss! Joey nodded, taking comfort in that simple rationale, maintaining in his mind that Sophia and he were the same and that he would make Sophia realize that truth in the end.

Joey knew it would be so, because in the end, he also knew that he would have Sophia—or she would have no one at all.

Chapter Five

Concerned at his aunt's agitation, Lyle assessed her pallor and the faintly blue tinge to her lips as he spoke reassuringly.

"I won't be moving far, Aunt Julia. I'll be easy to reach if you need me."

Her breakfast untouched on the table in front of her, her distress apparent, Julia replied softly, "If you're going to be so close, why must you move at all, dear? Haven't you been comfortable here?"

"Of course I have." Lyle reached across the table, taking her dainty hand into his. He had dreaded making the announcement that he had found rooms of his own, and with good cause, it appeared. Aunt Julia was not taking it well. He continued gently. "The truth is that my residence here doesn't sit well with Uncle Matthew. He considers it an imposition on him since he supports you."

"He supports me with my own money—my *own* money that my father lent to him before he died! For that reason I have no compunctions about having Matthew support me, and I have no compunctions about using *my* money as I see fit. If that includes your living here—"

Regretting his aunt's distress, Lyle whispered with a smile, "You know there's only one way to look at things as far as Uncle Matthew is concerned. *His* way. I'm sorry."

"I'm sorry, too."

Lyle smiled in an attempt to draw a smile from her as well. "I need a place of my own anyway, Aunt Julia. Somewhere I can bring my friends."

"You could always bring your friends here, dear." Aunt Julia appeared genuinely surprised. "Didn't you realize your friends would always be welcome?"

"Aunt Julia . . ."

"Oh!" Aunt Julia's small eyes suddenly widened. "You mean women friends. I'm sorry. I should've realized . . ."

Lyle unconsciously shook his head. Aunt Julia, in her sweet, distracted way, always got directly to the point. But she was correct. He needed rooms of his own for meetings with a woman, although those meetings would not be the kind she imagined. Kitty still took care of his physical needs, and her quarters suited him well enough for that purpose. But then there was Sophia. A warmth moved inside him at the thought of her. They had maintained a casual relationship on the surface since the picnic several weeks earlier, but the barriers that had come down that day were gone forever. Without them, he had been amazed how clearly Sophia and he could communicate with a glance, how much could be said in short, inadequate conversations, how well he felt he had come to know her, without really knowing her at all.

But he wanted something more now. He wanted a place where Sophia and he could talk freely if they chose. Whatever thoughts he might temporarily entertain when Sophia's incredible eyes moved thoughtfully over his face with a touch that was almost physical, when her laughter raised his spirits, and when her empathy touched his heart, his intentions were sincere. Sophia was a friend. Never having allowed true friendship into his life before, he valued it too highly to betray it.

With particular warmth, Lyle recalled the morning Sophia slipped her precious packet from underneath her machine and showed him the surprisingly well-drawn fashion sketch she had worked on the previous night. He was not an expert, but he had been to enough silk expositions and silk fashion shows to know that her gift of style as well as the intricate particulars of accessory and trim—details of the trade that he had not expected her to comprehend—were instinctive. But he knew as well as Sophia that she had many hurdles yet to clear in the difficult field she had chosen, and he understood her frustration at the slow progress she was making.

If he had been ineffective in relieving her frustrations in that regard during the past few weeks, however, he had been successful in another. He had seen to it that Joey Moretti no longer bothered her by telling him flatly that he would do so at the expense of his job. The venom in that fellow's gaze had been a sight to see.

"Lyle . . . Lyle, dear."

Coming back to the present with a start, Lyle looked up apologetically. "Yes, I'm sorry, what did you say, Aunt Julia?"

"I said that if you should become serious with a woman, you *will* bring her to meet me, won't you?"

Lyle smiled, envisioning in his mind this fragile lady's reaction to Sophia's flamboyant beauty, her candor, her unbridled enthusiasm and quick tongue. Maybe someday.

"Yes, I will." Squeezing her hand again, Lyle pushed back his plate and stood up. "I'll be moving my things at the end of the week. I hope you'll come and visit me when I'm settled."

Aunt Julia's eyes brightened with pleasure. "I'll be delighted, but . . . you will extend a formal invitation, won't you? I wouldn't want to walk in on . . . I mean . . ."

Barely restraining a smile, Lyle leaned down to press a fleeting kiss against her cheek. "Of course."

In the hallway a few minutes later, Lyle reached for the doorknob as a bit of conversation behind him caught his ear.

"Lyle's moving out this weekend, Maggie. He says he needs a place of his own."

And Maggie's brief, knowing reply, "Aye. The laddie has himself a woman."

"You're making a mistake, Father."

Confronting his father in the opulent foyer of the family residence in order to spare his mother the agitation of a tableside disagreement, Aaron continued with visible resentment. "And I resent being asked to carry messages back and forth to Matthew Kingston like glorified office help."

Samuel Weiss's slow smile was almost a grimace. Openly favoring his right foot as he drew his slight frame up to its full, meager height, he responded irritably, "You don't like being an errand boy? Would you like me to step down now and let you run the mill? Is that what you want?"

Aaron's handsome face stiffened. His father stood a few inches shorter than he and was half as broad at the shoulder, but Samuel Weiss's formidability had no dependence on physical size. Aaron had learned early on that his father's sharp tongue could cut more deeply than a knife, and with incredible accuracy. That ability had grown more acute with the years, and although Aaron was now an adult, he still hesitated to challenge his father when he was in an aggressive state of mind.

Relentless, the elder Weiss pinned his son with a sharp, merciless gaze. "What do you want, Aaron? Tell me."

"I'm not challenging your authority, Father, but I'll repeat what I said before. You're making a mistake."

Samuel Weiss's cheek twitched revealingly underneath his graying beard, but an almost indiscernible flicker in his eye encouraged Aaron to continue. "Matthew Kingston is wrong, and I think you're wrong if you turn around to his way of thinking. He underestimates the intelligence of some of the activists in the city. The Knights of Labor, The Group for the Right to Existence, the Socialist Labor Party—they're all well organized anarchist groups. The rebellion instigated at Stein's Dye House is a perfect example."

The elder Weiss gave a righteous snort. "That was Stein's fault for hiring all the unskilled Italians turned away elsewhere. Many of them came from the worst and most dangerous element immigrating into the city. He was looking for cheap labor, but he got more than he bargained for."

"That's my point, Father. These men have begun proliferating in the industry. We aren't dealing with simple immigrants anymore who'll be lulled into forgetting their radical views with a picnic, a token raise, or a few promises. With the severe political upheaval presently underway in Italy, Paterson has become the center of international radicalism. The plan to incite the weavers and the dyers into organized rebellion was clearly stated in the latest issue of *La Questione Sociale."*

"I pay no attention to that propaganda."

"You should. We can't allow ourselves to give these people the ammunition they're seeking to turn the neutral workers against us."

His impatience all too visible, Samuel Weiss shook his head. "I'm not the fool you seem to think me to be, Aaron. I'm well aware of everything you've said."

"But you will be a fool if you let Matthew Kingston convince you to establish a private police force."

Samuel Weiss's small frame appeared to swell with anger. "I will not be preached to like a child by my own son! If you think I underestimate the intelligence of those with whom we're in conflict, I can only say you underestimate my intelligence as well."

Aaron paused in the face of his father's growing agitation, realizing he mimicked the behavior against which he warned his father. It would do him no good to raise his father's ire to a point where there was no possibility of continuing a rational discussion. In any case, he had never for a moment questioned his father's intelligence. Realizing those words needed to be vocalized, he smiled, uncomfortable voicing even an indirect apology.

"I wasn't questioning your intelligence, Father. It just looked to me as if you were being swept away by Matthew Kingston's enthusiasm. He's already convinced a few others to reverse their stand."

"The gout has affected my foot, Aaron, not my brain. You needn't worry that Kingston will convince me of anything. However, I do think it's important to keep the fellow *talking* rather than acting."

Aaron gave a short, startled laugh. "So, you're playing witht the arrogant fool!"

"I'm keeping him out of trouble while my private investigators work their way inside the organizations you mentioned. For the present, it suits my purpose just to keep one step ahead of these fellows."

Aaron shook his head, genuinely impressed. "I'm sorry, Father. I should've realized . . ."

His peculiarly keen eyes intent on his son's handsome face, Samuel Weiss nodded. "That's right, Aaron. You should've. While we're talking, and before your mother calls us in for breakfast, I think I should make another point clear to you. You're my only son and heir. Everything I've built, everything I've accomplished, has been for you and the family you'll one day have. If I'm hard on you, if you feel I hold you back, remember that I look forward to the day when you're ready to work beside me on equal terms."

"I'm ready now, Father."

"No. You think you are, but you aren't." Weiss shook his head. "There's something lacking in you, Aaron. There's a coldness, a lack of judgment or sensitivity — I'm not certain which — that makes me unwilling to trust your decisions completely. I suppose much of that is due to the privileged existence you've led, but I can't undo the past. I can only look to the future and hope that maturity will handle that deficiency."

Aaron's expression hardened at his father's unexpectedly critical judgment. His resentment forced a question he would otherwise have hesitated to ask. "How far in the future, Father? I'm getting tired of waiting."

Silent for long moments, Samuel stared at his son. He finally broke the silence between them with frustration rife in his tone. "You prove my point only too well with that statement. You're impatient and arrogant. Those two vices occasionally force you into unwise behavior that we can't afford, given the volatile situations we presently face."

The steel returned to Samuel's voice. "You'll have to wait until *I* feel you're ready, Aaron." Pausing for effect, Weiss concluded. "I hope we understand each other."

Annoyed to see the truth in his father's assessment, Aaron nodded.

Turning to look into the breakfast room, Samuel grimaced at his wife's annoyed expression. "Your mother will make me pay for keeping her waiting this morning, but I want to impress upon you that I'm relying on you to relay my message to Kingston and to keep the channels of communication open. You can be extremely charming when you wish to be, Aaron. It's one of your outstanding skills. I'm depending upon you."

Aaron nodded again, his brow rising as his father added unexpectedly, "You're looking dapper this morning. New suit? It's almost a shame to waste it on Matthew Kingston."

Turning without awaiting a reply, Samuel Weiss limped away, and Aaron was incredulous at his father's perceptivity. He hadn't worn this suit to impress Matthew Kingston, and it was obvious that his father knew it. Discomforted and annoyed, Aaron made the sudden decision that if his father had guessed his intentions, he didn't really care.

Taking a deep breath of heavy morning air as she emerged from the alleyway onto the street, Sophia turned toward her father, a step behind her.

"Ah, another hot day." She tucked her arm under his and smiled into his eyes. Opportunities to have her father all to herself had become too rare of late. She squeezed his arm. "Why don't you smile, Papa? You like the heat, no?"

Anthony raised his wiry brows and gave his daughter an assessing glance. "You tease your papa, eh, Sophia?"

Sophia nodded. "Sí, I tease my papa."

Matching her father's step with her own, Sophia surveyed the early-morning street and the brick-faced tenements rising above the awning storefronts lining the sidewalk. She saw the first signs of awakening in the raising of window shades and in the sharp cry of a child that was followed by a mother's heated admonition in rapid Italian. The aroma of baking bread from Tomasi's Bakery around the corner filled the air, and as she watched, a milk wagon turned onto the street, its wooden wheels resounding hollowly against the cobblestones with its plodding pace. She noted with amusement that the milkman busied himself in the rear of the wagon as the well-tutored horse halted automatically at a scheduled stop. She was amused. Now if the milkman could only manage to have the horse select the right containers . . .

Farther down the street a few men emerged from narrow alleyways between the buildings and turned in the direction of the dye houses where the earliest shifts began. Pausing as a striped cat skittered across their path and darted into a doorway nearby, Papa reached into his pocket and withdrew the stump of a small black cigar and clamped it between his teeth.

Sophia shook her head disapprovingly. "Papa, there isn't enough of that cigar left to make it worth lighting. Why don't you throw it away?" She frowned. "Didn't Mama give you money for cigars this week?"

Papa fished in his jacket pocket for a match, his eyes narrowing. "Your mama gave me money, and this cigar is good enough." Withdrawing a wooden match, Anthony struck it against the seat of his pants and, tilting his head back, carefully held it to the tip of the cigar.

"Hey, Anthony!" From the doorway of Scalla's Grocery Store, Martin Scalla cautioned jokingly as he rested his oversize fists on his hips, "You'd better watch yourself, Anthony, or you're gonna light your nose instead of your cigar!"

Sophia fought to maintain a sober facade as Anthony cast the fellow a look of disdain, calling back in reply, "What's the matter? You think my name is Scalla?" Turning back to Sophia as Scalla walked back into the store, smiling and shaking his head, Anthony winked. "That takes care of that *faccia brutta* for today."

Laughing, Sophia responded, "Mr. Scalla isn't ugly. He's a handsome man."

Anthony's wiry brows rose again. "But not as handsome as your papa, eh?"

Grinning broadly, Sophia squeezed her father's arm. Never quite certain if his vanity was feigned or genuine, she responded emphatically, "No, *never* as handsome as my papa."

Certain any day that started with the sun shining on her head and her hand tucked under her father's arm had to be a good one, Sophia was content to walk in silence. Things had changed so much in the past few weeks, and she was filled with hope. The turning point seemed to have been the day of the picnic, but she was uncertain why.

She thought back. The most noticeable difference seemed to be in Mama. Mama was more relaxed of late and not as inclined to jump to conclusions when Sophia returned a bit late from the library or from an errand. Mama had even complimented her on the work she had done on Mrs. Correnti's dress, a difficult project that Mama had turned over entirely to her the previous week. Although she was not quite certain how long this peaceful coexistence would last, Sophia was more relieved than she cared to admit.

And then there was Anna . . . Of late, the melancholy always evident in Anna's eyes was tempered with a quiet kind of pride she had never seen there before. It gave her hope for her timid sister.

As for Rosalie . . . Sophia shook her head. Too much interest in the crazy doings of the labor unions—too much concern about rights and wages and a shortened workday when, in truth, women were excluded from debate and refused a vote in the union that represented them. It was not wise, but Sophia could not subdue a surge of pride in her bright little sister. Rosalie would not be one to let life pass her by.

Lyle Kingston's image came before her mind's eye, and Sophia felt her heart warm. She had known from the beginning it could be as it was between them. It was as if they had known each other all their lives, so natural was the relationship between them, and she knew that the nephew of the boss felt the same.

Oh, but she was careful . . . She didn't permit the concern in his deep-gold eyes to touch her heart in a way that it could. She wouldn't let the soft timbre of his voice in a tone reserved for her alone affect her, or the touch of his long fingers against her arm escalate the beating of her heart as it so often threatened. She knew that to take a step in that direction would be to take a step too far.

They were friends, becoming closer each day. They could not afford to be more.

"Sophia . . ."

Sophia turned to see her father's dark eyes intent upon her face. "Yes, Papa?"

He patted her hand. "I'm glad you're going into work early today. I'm glad we have a chance to talk."

The curling smoke from the stunted stogie clenched between her father's teeth rose between them. Its acrid smell was one she would always associate with Papa and his whispered words of concern and understanding when the world seemed dark and unfriendly. Love for this short, homely fellow who had never failed her rose in her throat.

He continued haltingly. "Sophia . . . You are happy?" His gaze seeming to deepen, he pressed. "On the outside you smile, but on the inside . . . you are happy, *figlia mia?* Your mama is not too hard on you?"

Sophia shook her head. "No, Papa, everything is all right."

Anthony flushed. "Your mama doesn't care for things that a young girl cares for." He looked at her worn blouse

101

and skirt. "She doesn't see the need for pretty things that other girls your age have."

"I don't need pretty things, Papa."

"*Sí, tu sei una bella ragazza,*" he mused almost to himself. "But a beautiful girl should have pretty things, too." Reaching into his pocket, Anthony pulled out a worn leather purse.

"No, Papa, I don't want—"

"*Sí,* you take." Removing three carefully folded dollar bills, he pressed them into her hand. "Papa wants to see a pretty ribbon in your hair, or a lace handkerchief tucked in your sleeve—whatever you like. You buy for Papa."

"But Anna and Rosalie—"

"They will have their turn."

"Oh, Papa . . ."

Holding the bills tight in her hand, Sophia averted her face and continued walking, her throat too tight to speak. She knew what the money meant to Papa, who had so little to spare for himself, and she knew how long it had taken him to save this amount. She also knew it meant he wouldn't light the next cigar he put in his mouth, for when it was gone, there would be no money for more. She knew it meant that he would walk away when his friends gathered around the table for a game of briscola on Sunday, and he would pretend he was too tired to play boccie because he wouldn't have the money to wager on the results. She knew he would go without in countless small ways because of her and that the bills in her hand were another expression of the love her father had given her all of his life.

Silent as they reached Kingston Mill, Sophia slipped her hand out from under her father's arm. Giving his great mustache a playful tug, she said softly, "There's no other man in the city as handsome as you, Papa."

From the doorway of the mill a few moments later, Sophia watched the white smoke of her father's stogie swirl behind him as he continued down the street.

Flesh against flesh, heat against heat . . . Aaron groaned aloud as Wanda moved against his sweat-dampened body, her mouth burning a titillating trail that set him to quaking. Entwining his hands in her unbound hair, twisting strands the color of autumn gold until a sharp bite forced instant release, Aaron laughed aloud. He pulled her slender body up to cover his with a harsh whisper.

"No, you won't get rid of me so early today, my pet. We're going to spend some time together, you and I, and we're going to love it."

With a quick roll, he was atop her, looking down into the unusual sloe eyes and exotic features that had first enticed him into this uncommon whore's bed. He remembered the first time he saw her at a party at one of his clubs almost a year earlier. She had come in with the rest of the women, but he had immediately singled her out. His patronage in the time since had allowed her to progress to a select clientele which she entertained at her own quarters in a pleasant neighborhood. The dear girl that she was, Wanda expressed her appreciation in the most entertainingly intimate ways.

Winding his hands in the heavy silk of her hair once more, Aaron laughed as excitement lit a flame in the dark eyes looking up into his. "You like your work, don't you, darling?" he whispered. He nodded knowingly. "As a matter of fact, you love it . . ."

Unable to resist the allure of dark eyes that devoured him, of creamy flesh that welcomed him, of the red lips separated and waiting, Aaron crushed his mouth onto hers, grinding deeper and harder until the bitter taste of blood met his tongue. Ripping his mouth from hers, his heart pounding, Aaron cupped her full breasts with his hands, covering the erect nipples with his hungry mouth, biting, tantalizing until Wanda's low moans of pleasure reached a fevered pitch.

Halting abruptly, Aaron heard the groan of frustration that escaped her lips and he drew back. Lifting himself off her, he rolled back against the pillow beside her, enjoying the fury that mounted in the quiet whore's eyes as he gripped her arms, holding off her attempted mounting.

"You want me, don't you, my sweet little witch . . ." Not waiting for her reply he tormented, "You like the feel of my body against yours. If I were a different sort, I have the feeling that I could visit here at will, without giving any payment at all. Isn't that right, my pretty little harlot?"

Sloe eyes filled with passion flickered at his use of the humiliating term, and he whispered softly, "I want to hear you say it, dear Wanda. I want to hear you say you want me."

Wanda's full lips trembled, parting with reluctance to rasp, "I want you."

"Louder . . ."

"I want you, Aaron."

"How much?"

"Very much . . . very, very—"

"All right—now."

Releasing her, Aaron watched as a flush of embarrassed hunger covered the girl's fair skin in the moment before she slid herself atop him. He heard her soft sound of anticipation the moment before she pleasured him in a way no other woman did so well. This sweet little whore worshipped him, and he wanted . . . he wanted . . .

But it was too late as the wave of ecstasy sweeping over him obliterated conscious thought. Weak and gasping moments later, satiated as only this earnest little trollop could sate him, he felt her slip her arms around him. He waited for her to speak the words that he knew instinctively she spoke to no other.

He was almost asleep when he felt her lips against his ear and heard her say, "I love you, Aaron."

And it amused him then, as always, knowing in his heart that she meant every word.

With an emotion strangely akin to jealousy Lyle watched from the window of the office as Sophia entered the mill. He had seen her approaching with her father, musing as he had many times before at the closeness between the short, homely fellow and his beautiful daughter. He had only to see Sophia's expression when she spoke about her father to know what the old man meant to her, and the tightness inside him grew.

Lyle heard the warning bell that sounded in his mind. The friendship between Sophia and him was only of short duration, but he was already getting possessive of her. These were unfamiliar emotions which he recognized as unwise and foreign to his makeup. But however uncomfortable he was with them, he was somehow powerless against them.

Sophia entered the mill, surprising him by walking directly toward her machine. In the weeks since the picnic, she usually came to the office looking for him when she arrived early, knowing that it was safe to seek him out before the other workers arrived. Observing more carefully through the glass enclosure, he noted that Sophia kept her back to him.

Suddenly suspicious, Lyle opened the door and started

105

toward her. He was within a few feet of her when she turned abruptly at his approach. Astonished to see that she was crying, Lyle was suddenly furious.

Closing the remaining distance between them in a few quick steps, he gripped her shoulders, forcing her face up to his. "What happened? Did your father make you cry?" His voice softened. "Sophia, tell me what happened."

Sophia gave a short laugh as she brushed the tears from her cheeks. "It's only that my papa is too good to me."

"Too *good?*" Lyle's hands dropped to his sides. "What are you talking about?"

Opening up the hand she held clenched at her side, Sophia showed him the carefully folded bills, her eyes filling again as she said hoarsely, "See what he gave me . . ."

Lyle stared at her hand, responding flatly, "Three dollars."

Sophia's chin rose defensively at his tone. "It's more than money. It's love."

Lyle was suddenly annoyed. "It's three dollars, and it's your own money. Your mother takes everything you earn the minute you walk through the door at the end of the week. You've told me so yourself."

"That's the way it is!" Sophia grew defensive. "I can't change tradition." Suddenly turning her back on him, Sophia ordered gruffly, "Go away! I don't want to speak to you anymore. You're a fool."

"Sophia . . ."

"Go away!"

"I'm sorry."

"You're not!"

"Yes, I am." Again gripping her shoulders, Lyle turned Sophia around to face him. Where there were tears before, he saw only anger and he gave a short laugh. "Well, at least you've stopped crying."

Sophia's brows knitted as she responded softly, "Why are you such a fool sometimes, Lyle? Can't you recognize love when you see it? Is it because you've been shown so little love in *your* life?"

Lyle shifted uncomfortably. Sophia's assessment was too close to the mark for comfort. He wasn't familiar with the kind of love Sophia spoke about, nor did he understand the fiercely strong bonding in her family, despite individual friction, or the sentimentality which he dared challenge only at the risk of losing her friendship.

Unwilling to contemplate that thought, Lyle offered softly in response, "Maybe you're right." And then with a smile he couldn't resist, "And maybe you're not. What are you going to do with the money? Save it or—"

"Save it? No!" Sophia's eyes were suddenly bright, her anger of a few minutes earlier forgotten as she continued. "I've given the matter much thought. I've done as much as I can on my own. I'm going to buy a sketching pad and pencils, and when I have something presentable to show, I'm going to find work in a fashion salon where I'll be able to learn more."

Uncertain if he was ready for her response, Lyle pressed, "And then?"

Sophia slipped the carefully folded bills into the deep pocket of her skirt and smiled. "Who knows? I've learned that I must take one step at a time or the path will overwhelm me."

A sound at the entrance announced the arrival of Jacqueline Moreau and her brother, and Lyle cursed under his breath as the girl looked directly at them with a knowing smile. Exchanging an annoyed glance with Sophia, he turned back toward his office. He was tired of aborted conversations. He wanted to know Sophia better—to fully understand her. Somewhere in the back of his mind was the feeling that if he came to know Sophia more completely, he would come to know himself better as well.

Lyle considered that thought again as he approached his office door. He then seriously wondered if the latter intimate acquaintance was one that he would be better off without.

"Hurry up, Harry! We're not out for a leisurely ride."

Ignoring his driver's grunt of acknowledgment and the crack of the whip that propelled the carriage to a faster pace, Aaron drew his watch out of his pocket again and frowned. He was annoyed at his own tardiness. He had not expected to doze in Wanda's bed until midmorning. Wanda had suffered for the lapse, and rightfully so, for he knew she had deliberately allowed him to stay longer than he should. That tendency had grown stronger in Wanda as the duration of their association lengthened, and he alternated between pleasure and disgust with the little harlot's infatuation with him.

Of course, that infatuation had its compensations. A smile briefly relieved Aaron's frown. Wanda was an accommodating little piece. All his friends agreed, but he knew from their outspoken discussions of her services that she reserved special treatment for him whenever he visited her. That pleased him and allowed him a feeling of power over her that often, as in cases such as today when he was feeling particularly inadequate about the conduct of his life, was just the medicine he needed.

Aaron paused on that thought, admitting to himself that he behaved badly on those occasions, but he consoled himself that Wanda seemed to achieve a particular satisfaction in pleasing him then.

Removing his bowler, Aaron ran a cursory palm against the surface of his smoothly combed hair, straightened his collar and tie, and stretched out his legs to run his fingers along the crease in his trousers. He had dressed too quickly to be entirely comfortable with his appearance, and he disliked the feeling. But then, he disliked being sent to Kingston Mill, he disliked dealing with Lyle Kingston, however briefly, and he disliked the thought that he would have to pander to Matthew Kingston's inflated opinion of himself in order to follow his father's orders.

The rattle of the small bridge spanning the raceway abruptly raised Aaron's head, alerting him to his arrival on the grounds of Kingston Mill. Carefully replacing his hat on his head and a smile on his face as the carriage drew to a halt, he pushed open the door and instructed briefly, "Wait for me, Harry."

Aaron paused in the doorway of the mill. The overwhelming din allowed him a few moments to survey the premises without his presence being noted, and Aaron was determined to make the best of it. His gaze darted between the machines. Where had he last seen that red-headed tart?

A flash of bright hair turned Aaron in the right direction the moment before Sophia Marone came into full view, and Aaron stifled a gasp at the sight of her. Damn, she was an incredible beauty with that flaming hair and creamy skin! Those extraordinary eyes . . .

Enthralled, Aaron was not ready for the unexpected voice at his elbow that turned him toward Lyle Kingston's tight expression.

"My uncle has been expecting you. Follow me."

"No, thanks." Inwardly seething at the bastard's gall, Aaron added flatly, "I can find my way. But don't go far. I'm going to ask your uncle for a tour of his processing

109

from start to finish. I'm sure you're the *employee* best suited to the service."

Not bothering to reply, Kingston turned and walked away.

A slow flush rising to his face, Aaron cursed low under his breath and turned toward the office. A bastard the fellow was born, and a bastard he would always be.

The noon hour was approaching, heralded by the grumble of Sophia's stomach as she adjusted yet another tangled skein. She was impatient for the day to end. Unconsciously patting the three dollars in her pocket, she smiled. She would make good use of her father's gift, and when she did—

"I want to stop here, Kingston." An unfamiliar voice drew Sophia from her thoughts, and she turned spontaneously toward the sound. A handsome, well-dressed fellow standing at the end of the aisle walked toward her. He smiled unexpectedly, even, white teeth contrasting with breathtaking effect against the smooth tone of his skin as eyes like black velvet boldly assessed her from head to toe.

His insulting manner effectively negated the impact of his smile and Sophia drew back. Her irritation climbing, she questioned with acid sweetness, "So . . . do you like what you see?"

Appearing intrigued, the fellow turned toward Lyle who stood rigidly behind him.

"Introduce me to this young woman, Kingston. I'd like to ask her some questions."

A glance at Lyle revealed a telltale flush, a tense tick in his cheek, and tightly concealed fury that set his eyes ablaze. Recognizing that he was one step short of mayhem and suspecting the reason, Sophia responded spontaneously to the disaster she felt impending. Her smile deliberately bold, she responded in Lyle's stead.

"Excuse me, sir, but I'm busy. I have no time to talk today. Some other time, eh?"

Without allowing the gentleman an opportunity for reply, Sophia walked around to the other side of the machine. She was working briskly when she heard a step behind her and turned to the fellow's devastating smile and smooth response.

"I'm sorry, too. I look forward to seeing you again."

Gone a moment later, he left her with a clear memory of his handsome, smiling face, the image of Lyle's tightly balled fists as he stared at the fellow's retreating back, and the promise of all that had obviously gone unsaid between the two men. She was suddenly certain that whoever he was, she hadn't seen the last of him.

Chapter Six

"No, Sophia, we couldn't do that!" Anna glanced toward Rosalie for support, then turned back to Sophia with eyes wide with anxiety. "Mama will find out."

Sophia frowned with disgust as the three sisters turned the corner onto Prospect Street. She had had a difficult day at the mill, and she was tired. The weight of the summer air was overwhelming, a heavy blanket that could not be shed, making effort difficult and work a nightmare. Complicating matters, the skeins furnished to her that morning had been poorly wound and the thread brittle. Snapped ends had continued to plague her most of the day, trying her patience and testing her skill. Weighing on her mind and complicating the difficulty of her effort was the thought of the beautiful sketching pad and pencils she had purchased a week earlier, and the lone sketch she had been able to complete in the time since. Frustration was driving her mad.

She needed a place to work. Night hours at the library were limited, inhibiting her progress, but Lyle had generously offered her use of his rooms to work if she could only get her sisters to cooperate. She tried again.

"Mama won't find out. She doesn't go to church and you know she doesn't speak to Father McCall. She doesn't like him."

"But Sophia—" Anna's eyes widened further. "It's sacrilegious to lie about going to church! Aren't you afraid God will punish you?"

"I'm afraid of nothing, Anna!" Sophia's patience was nearing its end as their home came into sight and the problem remained unsettled. "No, that's wrong. I'm afraid that opportunity will pass me by while I waste time arguing and waiting. I told you and Rosalie how important it is for me to complete the sketches I need. You know Mama. I can't work at home. But I tell you now that I will do this—with or without your help, even if I must go—"

"Don't worry, we'll do it, Sophia."

Anna turned sharply toward Rosalie at her unexpected interjection. She was about to protest when Rosalie offered brightly, "We'll just tell Mama that we're going to make a novena, and she won't say another word. She'll assume we're all going together, so we won't really be lying. As long as we all come home together, she'll never know the difference."

"But—"

"We'll volunteer to help Father McCall clean the church afterward." Rosalie turned to Sophia, proud of her innovative thought. "That will even give you more time."

"Clean the church?" Anna grimaced.

"Anna, don't be lazy. Sophia would do it for you."

"But—"

Unable to bear Anna's discomfort a moment longer, Sophia addressed her softly, understanding in her tone where there had been only irritation before.

"Anna, I know how you feel. You don't want to lie to Mama, but you won't really be lying. You don't want to do this because you worry about me being in *caro* Lyle's rooms, but I'll be safe there. You're afraid that I'm facing disappointment in trying to accomplish something that's beyond me, but I'm not. I'll finish these sketches

113

and I'll get a position where I can learn more. I'll *wear* silk someday, and I promise you that when I do, you and Rosalie will wear silk, too."

Her eyes clouding, Anna whispered, "I . . . I don't care if I never wear silk, Sophia."

Pausing, Sophia returned, "Anna, *mia cara sorella,* but *I* care."

Holding Sophia's intense gaze with her own for long, silent moments, Anna whispered, "All right, I'll do it."

"Brava, brava, Anna!" Her exuberance exceeding all bounds, Sophia danced her sister around the sidewalk in a quick step, the heat of the day forgotten. "You'll see, we'll —"

"Sophia?" Mama's voice calling from the window above the sidewalk raised Sophia's head with a snap. *"Cosa succede?"*

"Nothing's the matter, Mama. We're coming right up."

Turning toward the alleyway, Sophia waited only until she was out of Mama's sight before she rolled her eyes and whispered to Anna with a wink, "Too late to change your mind. You gave me your word."

"Sí . . . too late . . ."

Anna's dour expression inspired a simultaneous burst of laughter that united the sisters where all else had seemed to fail. Relieved from the suffocating weight of frustration, Sophia threw her arms around her sisters' shoulders with spontaneous delight as they walked into the yard.

On the street outside Lyle's small, comfortable quarters, the heat of the day had begun to cool and daylight waned. The cobbled streets echoed with the rattle of carriages traveling at a more sedate pace as they moved toward home, and strolling couples conversed, relaxed as

114

evening approached. Inside Lyle's rooms, however, the conversation progressed as heatedly as before.

"*Caro* Lyle, you must not be stubborn! Do as I say. I can cure your headache."

Silence followed Sophia's emphatic statement and Lyle could do no more than stare. He was not feeling well. His head had been pounding for three days, and the pain had reached the point where it nauseated him. The doctor's powders had had no effect, and he was at his wit's end. Sophia had appeared at his door unexpectedly a short time earlier, sketching pad and pencils in hand. She had been unable to visit his rooms in the past, although he had extended the invitation many times, and at present he was truly uncertain what unnerved him more, the pain in his head or this beauteous woman who became more perplexing with each passing moment.

The silence of his bachelor quarters grew prolonged until Lyle finally exploded with an exasperated, "Damn it, Sophia, you don't really expect me to participate in this . . . this ridiculous witchcraft, do you?"

"Witchcraft!" Sophia shook her head in emphatic denial. "No, no, it's not witchcraft. Neither is it ridiculous."

Sophia's great blue eyes were bright with confidence, her perfect features drawn into a serious mask that threatened his sanity, and Lyle mentally groaned. He had created his own hell.

"*Caro* Lyle, are you listening?"

"Yes, I'm listening!"

"Then come, let me prove it to you."

Pulling him across the room, back to the stool where she had already attempted to seat him twice before, Sophia pushed him down, ordering firmly, "Sit! Don't get up this time, and let me explain."

Sliding her fingers into his heavy gold hair, Sophia gently massaged the crown of his head as she began patiently, "There is much jealousy and bad feeling about you in the mill and someone has given you the evil eye — *Malocchio*. That's why your head hurts, why the pain won't stop. It's fortunate that I know the cure for this sickness."

Lyle steeled himself against the almost indecent pleasure of Sophia's fingertips moving against his scalp. It seemed he had been trying to deny the pleasure Sophia gave him in one way or another since the first time he saw her. It was a losing battle, but it was not one he was yet willing to surrender.

Closing his eyes, Lyle mumbled, "Bad feeling about me in the mill I can understand. I was never very popular there, but jealousy? No. There isn't a person in the mill who's jealous of my position, such as it is."

"Lyle . . ." Sophia's tone was threaded with strain as she tilted his face up to hers, coaxing him to open his eyes. "Your *position* doesn't stir the jealousy of others. It's your friendship with me that makes them jealous."

"My friendship with you?"

Sophia smiled. "You didn't think Joey would forgive so easily, did you? Or that his mama would forget her son suffers because of you?"

Lyle stiffened as a familiar anger rose. "He'll learn what it really means to suffer if he bothers you again."

"Ah. See? Is your head pounding harder?"

Lyle's annoyance increased. Was she always right?

Leaning down, Sophia unexpectedly kissed his cheek, cooing softly, *"Povero caro* Lyle. Don't worry. I can cure the evil eye. Nonna Alvino taught me how to do it at the stroke of midnight the Christmas before we left the old country. It's the only time the ritual for *Malocchio* can be passed on. She said she knew my mama would never teach it to me and that as the eldest daughter of the fam-

116

ily, it was something that I should know. I was very young, but I'll never forget it."

Reaching into her pocket, Sophia withdrew a scarred pocket knife.

Lyle could feel his eyes bulge.

"Not to worry." Sophia soothed him softly, then flicked out the gleaming blade.

Lyle leaped to his feet, only to have Sophia command again, "Sit!"

Dropping back to the stool, Lyle closed his eyes. He snapped them open wide again when Sophia said, "All right. Here we go."

Reaching toward the table she had prepared earlier, Sophia poured water into a saucer, then sprinkled oil on the surface. Her eyes widened as she clucked noisily and lowered the saucer for his perusal. "See the eyes that follow you? We must dispel them."

Lyle frowned. He saw nothing but drops of oil floating on water. He was incredulous at himself as he remained seated while Sophia passed the saucer over his head three times, chanting, *"Occhio contro occhio, portare via gelosia e scappare occhio."*

The small black-handled knife struck the floor beside his feet and Lyle jumped, only to feel Sophia's hand on his shoulder hold him in place as she spit three times toward the blade.

A weak smile touched Lyle's lips as Sophia walked to the window and emptied the saucer over the ledge. He did not resist when she returned to his side, refilled the saucer, and began again.

Beyond protest a short time later as he sat with his elbows resting on his knees, his hands cupping his chin, Lyle almost groaned aloud when the blade hit the floor for the third time.

Back at his side after her third trip to the window to

117

empty the saucer, Sophia touched his shoulder. "Lyle, look at me."

Lyle looked up. Sophia was so beautiful. He thought all witches were supposed to be ugly.

"Your headache is gone?"

Lyle blinked.

"Well?"

Lyle nodded, incredulous. The headache that had all but destroyed his sanity for three days had disappeared!

He had not yet spoken a word when Sophia cocked her head saucily and winked, her sweeping eyelashes batting her cheeks as she said casually, "I can cure sties, too, and the mumps, and—"

"No more . . . no more . . ." Suddenly laughing, Lyle stood up and pulled Sophia into his arms and hugged her tight. The warmth of her touched him in many ways as he drew back a moment later to kiss her hard on the lips. Firmly denying stronger feelings, he snapped her apart from him to stare into her eyes with mock sobriety as he ordered, "Never . . . *never* let me doubt you again."

Her eyes dancing, Sophia nodded soberly in return. "No, never again."

Sophia ran toward her sisters where they stood anxiously awaiting her on the street corner a short time later. Taking their hands, she pulled them along beside her without stopping.

"Hurry. We're late."

Panting as she struggled to match Sophia's pace, Rosalie inquired worriedly, "What happened?"

Sophia smiled cryptically. "I was called upon to perform an act of mercy."

Ignoring her sisters' surprised confusion, Sophia halted further questions with a quick wink as she pulled them

118

along behind her.

"That redheaded girl looks familiar."

Samuel Weiss's comment turned Aaron toward his father with surprise as their carriage moved briskly along the darkened street. They were later than usual in leaving for the Hamilton Club, having run an errand along the way, but Aaron had not realized how opportune the deviation in their regular route would prove.

He had noticed Sophia Marone immediately. It had been impossible to miss her as she ran effortlessly along the street despite the weight of the evening air, that glorious red hair streaming behind her. His heart had leaped at the sight of her, and he had silently cursed his inexplicable fascination with the common little tart.

But then, their first and last encounter in the mill had been unforgettable. He had not expected that the girl would have so much spirit, that she would put him in his place with a haughty lift of her chin and a few short words. Neither had he expected that she would dismiss him. He had not accepted that dismissal with the calm that he now viewed it, and it had, in fact, only been his pride that had forced him to walk away from her with a smile.

In the time since, he had deliberately ignored persistent thoughts of Sophia Marone. However, he had only needed to see her tonight to realize that she was a far easier piece than she pretended to be.

Aaron's lip twitched with agitation. He knew who lived in the house she had left so hastily. He also knew that he'd be damned before he'd let Lyle Kingston, bastard that he was, play free and easy with a woman he wanted.

"I know who she is . . ." His father spoke again, and

119

Aaron turned back to face him, concealing his inner aggravation. "She's that woman who works for Kingston—the one whose reputation suits her rather flamboyant looks."

"Sophia Marone . . ."

Samuel Weiss's gray brows rose assessingly. "So you know her name."

"A name like hers travels bachelor circles quickly, Father."

The elder Weiss appeared thoughtful. "I suppose so, but I would've thought that a fellow who wanted to impress his uncle with his intelligence and judgment would think twice before becoming involved with an employee. She comes from a very common family, if rumor is correct, from the type of background where a man might find himself in more trouble than it's worth if he's found consorting with one of their 'virgins.' "

"Father, I had no idea you were so well attuned to the fodder of the gossip mill." Aaron could not suppress a laugh. "But I wouldn't worry about Lyle Kingston." Aaron raised his brow. "You were referring to him, weren't you?" Not waiting for his father's response, Aaron continued. "Because the truth is, the bastard Kingston will never be accepted by his 'uncle.' Believe me . . . I know Matthew Kingston. He despises the pretender."

Staring his son directly in the eye, Samuel Weiss warned softly, "It's my feeling there's more to Lyle Kingston than either you or his uncle credit. He's an intelligent, well-educated fellow, and he has a sober determination—"

"And an arrogance that will keep his uncle and him apart until the day he dies!" A familiar anger rising, Aaron shrugged. "I don't want to talk about Lyle Kingston. He disturbs my appetite and I have no intention of letting him spoil the evening."

120

Appearing amused, the elder Weiss shrugged. "All this rancor . . . You wouldn't be jealous of him, would you, Son?"

"Jealous?" Aaron's temper flared. "The fellow has nothing I want. Tarts like the Marone girl are easy to come by."

"Some are easier than others. But the canon I referred to a while ago—about a young man who hopes to instill confidence in his intelligence and judgment—refers to any fellow in Lyle Kingston's position, whether he's an adopted bastard or a legal heir."

Aaron's smoothly shaven cheek twitched. "You know as well as I do that some women are born for the amusement of men, Father. And there are some of us who are of an age where challenge whets the appetite."

Samuel's small eyes narrowed into sharp pinpoints of light. "I suppose it's time to put generalities aside in this conversation, Aaron, because I can see generalities serve your purpose only too well. So I'll say it right out. Stay away from that woman. She's a common sort who'll drag you down to her level if you become involved with her. We have enough trouble with Italian agitators already. We don't want to give them any more ammunition for their cause with our own stupidity."

Aaron flushed. He disliked being told what to do, and he disliked even less his father's uncanny ability to read his mind. Startling him even further, the elder Weiss continued with his penetrating stare. "Unfortunately, at this point in time I know you better than you know yourself, Aaron. You can make what you want of that statement, but I assure you that it's true. So I'll warn you again, stay away from that woman, because if you become involved with her and things go badly, you won't be able to come to me."

121

Samuel paused for effect, then continued with a tightening of his jaw and a rise of his chin. "Do you understand me, Aaron?"

Aaron smiled stiffly. "I understand you very well." Glancing out the window as the Hamilton Club came into view, Aaron silently applauded their opportune arrival as he adjusted his evening clothes and placed his black silk topper square on his handsome brow. He stepped down out of the carriage in front of the impressive stone structure, his father's warning ringing in his ears.

So, the old man knew him better than he knew himself . . . Perhaps, but if he did, his father also knew that with that warning, he had sealed his son's course of action. Aaron's lips tightened into a determined line. He wanted Sophia Marone and he was now more bent on getting her than ever.

Turning, Aaron closed the carriage door with a decisive snap. He'd get her, too. He always got what he wanted, sooner or later.

The light was long gone, but Paul still labored. Squinting at the canvas in front of him, he grunted, glanced around him, then walked to the nearby table and adjusted the lamp. Back at his easel a moment later, he attempted to suppress his elation as he took slow, backward steps, staring at the face he had captured so perfectly with his brush. An overstuffed footstool bumped the back of his calves and he sat abruptly on the padded seat.

He had captured Anna's features perfectly — the large, round eyes, high cheekbones, and small mouth. The time he had taken to pose her that day in the grove had not been wasted. Her position, staring off into the distance just left of center, allowed him to take advantage of her profile, a bit strong for some, but to his mind a perfect balance for those outstanding eyes and magnificent brows. He had caught the slope of her shoulder and the lay of her hair against it. He had caught the colors, the textures. He had caught it all—including the soul. It was the best work he had ever done.

But Paul was not smiling. He would complete the painting by the end of the month at his present rate of progress, but his problems would not be over.

"I don't think I recognize the girl, Paul."

Jumping with a start at the sound of his mother's voice, Paul turned to see his father standing silently behind her at the door. Silently cursing, realizing he had caused this visit by neglecting to appear for dinner, he forced a smile.

"I don't think you know her, Mother. She's lovely, isn't she?"

"On the other hand, *I* find her vaguely familiar." Stepping forward, Matthew perused the painting with a critical eye. "It seems that the younger generation of males bearing the Kingston name has a fascination for Italian women."

"Father, I—"

"That *is* that younger Marone girl who works for me, isn't it, Paul? The one who's borderline in her job—not particularly competent?"

Feeling his spine stiffening, Paul forced a smile. "I'm glad you recognized Anna, Father. I suppose that means I've done a credible job of capturing her likeness on canvas."

"I suppose that also means my son is more a fool than I imagined!"

"Matthew!"

"Never mind, Mother." Paul's smile grew stiffer as he turned back to his father. "I should think you'd be re-

123

lieved, even if you thought me to be involved with a mill worker—and an Italian at that. You've silently questioned my masculinity for years, haven't you, Father?"

Edith Kingston's face paled as she glanced uncomfortably between them. "Matthew, tell Paul he's wrong!"

Matthew remained silent and Paul gave a sardonic laugh. "I hope you're ready for another disappointment, Father, because the truth is that I'm not involved with Anna Marone, and I don't intend to become involved with her. She's a child—sweet and innocent, and those are two of the qualities I wanted to capture in my portrait. She also has a haunting beauty quite unlike any I've ever seen before."

Matthew's back stiffened at his son's open defiance. His response was acidic.

"You believe you've painted another Mona Lisa, is that it, Paul?"

His father's sarcasm drawing blood, Paul responded, "I haven't quite managed to accomplish work of that caliber, but you may be sure I'll continue to try. I know you wouldn't expect any less of a Kingston."

"Don't push me too far, Paul."

Matthew's anger mounted visibly, and Paul felt a perverse satisfaction temper his own. His mother's mounting agitation was another matter, however, and unwilling to allow her distress to continue, he walked toward her and slid his arm around her shoulders.

"Mother, I'm sorry. I sometimes forget—"

"You forget," Matthew interrupted heatedly, "that you live under my roof, eat at my table, and that in times of uncertainty such as those which we are now enduring in the silk industry, you owe me—"

"You're repeating yourself, Matthew!" Interrupting her husband without compunction, Edith raised her chin, meeting his eyes with familiar dissension. "Let me remind you again that half of all you own is mine by law—for which I must thank the foresight of my father in having settled that technicality legally before we wed. I also remind you that this carriage house is part of *my* portion of our properties, and I have chosen to give it to Paul for his use. We are, therefore, trespassing, and suffer his good will in order to remain."

"Edith, this is ridicul—"

"You've outstayed your welcome, Matthew, and I think you should leave Paul to his work. As for myself . . ." Turning back to her son, Edith continued. "I regret having interfered with your creativity and—"

"Creativity! Nonsense!"

"Matthew . . ." Edith's voice dripped with ice. "Please leave."

"My son needs to hear the truth! He's wasting valuable time that should be spent on more important things, things that really matter, things that will—"

"*Leave*, Matthew." Edith's face became inordinately flushed. "Now!"

Holding his wife's frigid gaze for interminable seconds, Matthew turned abruptly, slamming the door viciously behind him. The silent room rang with the sound as Paul forced a smile.

"He's right, you know. I do have a responsibility to you and Father."

"Dear Paul." The ice in Edith's gaze melted as she continued softly. "I did you a great disservice, having such strong genes, you know. The truth is that you're too much of a Leighton for your father to countenance."

"I know."

"I suppose I've done you another disservice as well by openly supporting your artistic ability. It seems that by believing in you so strongly, I've destroyed any possibility for closeness between you and your father."

Paul kissed his mother's cheek gently. "No you didn't. I don't want to be like him, Mother. I never did, and I'll always be grateful for your support." Addressing the anxiety in her eyes that went unexpressed, Paul continued. "As for my interest in women, you needn't have any fears. It's a matter of priorities. I want to get my direction in life straightened out before I involve someone else in it and I—"

"Paul . . ." Edith waved her hand in an attempt to stop him. "You don't have to make any explanations to me."

"I don't, but Father's worried because I'm not seeing a woman, and I don't want his suspicions to cloud your mind. Please don't worry on that score."

"I never did". Edith paused. "Perhaps that's why your absorption in this portrait worried me, because I felt your feelings for the girl might be personal. I know I disappoint you in saying that, but you're far more generous than I am with respect to the class of people employed in our mills. I was raised to believe—"

"Anna Marone is a child, Mother. When the portrait is completed you'll see that she's too timid and too innocent to cast her thoughts in the direction you and Father seem to be thinking. But there's a luminous quality about her that's as delicate as a candle's flickering flame. The glow is almost imperceptible at times, and at others it flares with brilliance in those pools of emotion through which she sees the world. I want to capture that full luminescence on canvas."

Edith hesitated. Her eyes moving with begrudging understanding over her beloved son's intense expression, she finally whispered, "If you must, I suppose you must."

"Darling Mother." Paul smiled. "If you could only instill some of that tolerance for my decisions into your husband . . ."

Edith turned soberly toward the door. She looked up at

him as he fell into step beside her. "I conceded defeat in that attempt long ago, dear. I suppose we'll have to make do with the man your father is, and continue to fight him every step of the way." Edith smiled unexpectedly. "To be truthful, if your father were anything else but difficult, I think I'd be at a loss in handling him."

Carefully escorting her down the steps, Paul responded spontaneously, "You're never at a loss, Mother."

"You think not?" She shrugged. "Perhaps." Edith paused again, her gaze direct as she questioned, "Well, are you ready to face your father again when we step inside the house, dear? He's abominable when his feathers are ruffled, you know."

"And only a woman as strong as you could love him."

Edith considered that thought as she slipped her hand under her son's arm and proceeded across the darkened yard. "Truthfully, in all our years of marriage, I've never quite been able to determine how great a part love plays in my feelings for your father." She hesitated again. "I would feel safe in saying that your father feels the same. So you see, dear, neither of your parents possesses true credentials for giving advice on your private life. I recognized that long ago, but I'm afraid your father will admit to shortcomings in no area of his life."

"One of his greatest charms . . ."

"Charm is your father's stock in trade, although he's insincere. I'm grateful you're not like him in that way — or, thankfully, like me, for I'm a cold person."

"Mother—"

"Not with you, dear." Edith patted her son's arm. "Never with you. And I tell you now, although the words may not need be said, that whatever course you decide to follow, I'll stand behind you."

"And if I decide to divorce myself from the mill entirely?"

Edith paused, her gaze pained. "My dear, I hope you'll consider that step very carefully."

"And if I decide to do it?"

Edith's discomfort became more apparent. "It's your decision."

"Mother . . ." Paul covered his mother's hand with his own as he spoke with sudden earnestness. "Lyle is everything that I should be at the mill. He's—"

"He's a bastard, Paul."

Ice returned unexpectedly to Edith's pale eyes, freezing Paul's response, as she continued. "He'll always be a bastard with no right to the Kingston name. Nothing will ever change that in your father's eyes or mine. I'm sorry."

A wealth of regret in his simple response, Paul whispered, "I'm sorry, too" as they stepped into the house and closed out the night behind them.

Maria Marone plucked nervously at her dress as she looked up at the doorway again, then at the clock on the kitchen wall. Anthony was late in returning from work. Too many hours . . . too much work in heat that drained his energy. She did not like it, but Anthony wanted so much for his family.

Maria walked to the door and looked out into the shadowed yard. Barely visible in the darkness were the grapevines Anthony had planted there years earlier. Later in the season Anthony would pick his grapes and he would carry them down into the cellar to make his wine.

Maria's lips tightened. Then the complaints would begin. Josephine Amatti on the first floor would complain of the gnats that the crushed fruit drew, and her daughter would complain of the smell, wrinkling her big nose and protesting, "*Puzzo, puzzo,* Maria!" until she felt she would go mad.

Maria grimaced, knowing the sum she so diligently saved grew too slowly to spare them another year of such complaints. But the sum grew, nevertheless, and she was certain that the time was not far off when her diligence would be rewarded. Anthony would have a home of his own, with his own patch of ground behind it. There he would build an arbor that would support his vines and provide a shady retreat in the hot days of summer. He would plant fig trees as his father had before him, looking forward to a time when he would reserve the best of the treasured fruit for the grandchildren he would someday have — again, as his father had before him.

Maria paused, her expression hardening. Anthony deserved that much for the good life he had given them, for all that he had done — and for all that had been done to him . . .

Maria looked, at the clock again, frowning. Her daughters were late in returning from novena, but she was glad. She needed a few minutes alone with Anthony. The visitor she had had that afternoon was unexpected. In the time since her visitor's departure, she had carefully reviewed their discussion and had felt the weight of years being lifted from her shoulders. So much now depended upon —

The sound of a familiar heavy step on the staircase relieved Maria's frown and she walked quickly to the stove to stir the food warming there. She had made Anthony his favorite meal. He would be pleased and he would be relaxed, and then they would talk.

Anthony reached the door, and Maria looked up, smiling.

Chapter Seven

"Get out of my way!"

Ignoring the protests of several of the employees standing in observance, Lyle thrust the loom-fixer aside and crouched beside the loom. His frustration was evident in the tense lines of his face as he stared at the maze of belts and wheels that had been performing so poorly over the past week. He was at the end of his tether and unable to ignore the suspicion that there was a plan afoot to slow production in the mill.

Lyle shot the annoyed mechanic a sharp glance. He was not the fool these men obviously thought him to be. He knew that agitators were active outside the mill every day, that they accosted the workers upon entering and leaving with their malicious brand of venom. He was also aware that a socialist agitator had actually had the gall to slip onto the grounds the day of the picnic to incite workers who had come there for a day of relaxation and enjoyment.

Doubling of loom assignments in some mills had stirred unanimous protest among the workers in the city. Employees wanted assurances that they would not be producing themselves out of work with their increased performance. They wanted guarantees.

Guarantees? Lyle almost laughed. He had discovered a hard truth long ago. There were no guarantees.

His shirt adhering to his broad back with perspiration, his even features screwed into a grimace of disgust, Lyle studied the machinery more closely. The truth was that he didn't have the answers to any of the workers' questions. He was kept very carefully apart from that area of management by his "uncle." As far as Matthew Kingston was concerned, questions and answers were not his province. Production was.

Lyle shot a sharp glance toward the emotionless face of the loom-fixer standing nearby. He had been after Rinaldi for days to find the cause of the machinery slowdown, but it had been no use. The looms ran, as did the other machines, and Rinaldi claimed to have done his job to the best of his ability. Collusion—that's what it was. If there was something wrong with these looms, and the other machinery on the floor that all seemed to be suffering from the same summer malaise, this highly skilled mechanic was not about to find it.

Lyle's frustration rose. The drop in productivity would soon backfire into his own face. He had not wanted to shut down the looms, but it was time for drastic measures. His light brows knit into a frown as Lyle studied the maze of belts and wheels that drove the complicated machinery. He was familiar enough with them to see that there was no apparent damage, no problem that he could pinpoint with the naked eye.

Lyle shifted closer. He traced the wheels with his fingertips, searching—and froze. He rubbed his forefinger and thumb together, his jaw tightening. He ran his finger along one belt, then another, then turned to glance up at the men standing around him. Drawing himself to his feet, he glared at Rinaldi before moving on to check the next loom.

Turning when he reached the end of aisle, his examination complete, he stated flatly, "Soap."

"Soap?" An innocent shrug was Rinaldi's response.

"Yes, soap!"

131

Lyle met Joey Moretti's barely concealed amusement where he stood in the center of the group of workers observing his inspection. Lyle's anger soared as he forced himself to address the group as a whole.

"Soaping the belts so they'll slip and make the machinery run more slowly is an old trick. I suppose it's my fault that I didn't suspect it sooner, but I'm telling you now, tricks like this won't slip past me again. You can be sure that I'll go directly from here to the winders and check to see if the bobbins have been oiled to slow production, too, and—"

"Make sure you check *all* the winders, Mr. Boss." Joey's interjection turned Lyle to his sneer. "Or won't you check on the winders of your 'friends?' "

"I have no friends on the floor—just employees! Keep that in mind, Moretti! And I'm not too stupid to realize that although this dirty work was done by a few, it was done with the knowledge of many, so I'm warning you . . . If this happens again, you'll all suffer! Now get these machines cleaned up!"

Turning without another word, Lyle stomped toward the office, his eye on the inner door behind which Matthew Kingston sat in privileged seclusion. It was time to wake up his dear uncle to a fact of life on the floor of his mill. It was time to let him know that functioning as he was, without true authority and without being privy to the intentions of management, he could not perform to the full extent of his ability. It was time to tell his uncle that he was tired of the game he was playing and he would not play it any longer.

The small groups standing in conversation after Lyle Kingston's angry announcement slowly disbursed to their respective machines. Observing from the doorway where

132

she had gone to catch a cooling breeze while the examination of the machines progressed, Sophia heard an unexpected voice in her ear.

"It looks like your nephew of the boss bites off more than he can chew."

The glass-paneled door slammed shut behind Lyle's bristling figure as Sophia turned to Joey Moretti's sneer. Joey stood so close that his warm body scent filled her nostrils and she fought an instinctive revulsion. Refusing to take a step backward that could be misconstrued as retreat, Sophia remained stationary as he continued. "You've attached yourself to a fellow who won't be with us much longer. His uncle is looking for an excuse to be rid of him."

"Is that why you talked Enrico and Giovanni into soaping the belts, so you could get rid of him more quickly?" Sophia laughed aloud. "You're more a fool than I thought you were. You've not only risked the livelihood of yourself and your two friends, but you've made the nephew of the boss appear more clever in his uncle's eyes by discovering your little trick."

"No, Sophia, no." Joey's dark eyes took on an unexpectedly earnest gleam. "If I'm a fool, I'm a fool only for you. You don't realize who really cares for you. It isn't the nephew of the boss who offers you marriage, who offers you his name, and who wants to take care of you the rest of your life."

"I don't want someone to take care of me! I can take care of myself."

"I can take care of you better, Sophia. I can love you and make you—"

"Stop!" Her stomach churning with loathing, Sophia shook her head. "I don't need a husband."

"That's not what your mama says."

Sophia froze. Joey's florid face slipped into wily lines

133

that disclosed more than his last, brief sentence revealed, and Sophia felt a slow apprehension assume control. Mama had acted strangely the previous night when Anna, Rosalie, and she had returned from novena—and Papa had seemed disturbed. Suspicion forced a harsh response.

"How do you know what my mama says?"

It was Joey's turn to laugh, and Sophia's stomach twisted at the sound as he looked deeply into her eyes. "Your mama and my mama have become good friends. Our families will soon be joined, Sophia—*cara mia.*"

The repugnance his words inspired drained the color from Sophia's face, forcing a single, scathing word of reply.

"Never!"

Fury replacing the softness of a moment before, Joey grabbed her arm roughly. "Never? We shall see!"

His gaze jerking unexpectedly toward the office, Joey muttered a curse under his breath. Releasing her, he turned toward the rear of the floor. Sophia sensed the reason for his abrupt retreat and started for her machine as well, only to be halted by the sound of Lyle's clipped question.

"Was Moretti bothering you again?"

Sophia turned to Lyle's tense expression. She shrugged. "Joey is a fool. I don't let fools bother me."

Lyle's eyes narrowed. "I asked you a question."

"*Sí,* and I've answered it."

Sophia was about to turn away when Lyle grated unexpectedly, "Do I have to check your machine to see if the bobbins were oiled, Sophia?"

Holding his gaze stiffly for a moment, Sophia turned and walked away. As she reached her machine she raised her chin, knowing the question would go unanswered because it should never have been asked at all.

134

Anthony wiped a sweaty arm across his forehead, squinting as perspiration ran into his eyes and down the side of his face. He glanced toward the dye-shop windows and grimaced at the sun beating steadily against the grimy panes. Steam rose from the dye box at which he worked, heightening his discomfort as the temperature soared. He looked around him. Groups of men had gathered to talk in the temporary absence of the boss. They conversed angrily, and he knew the subject they discussed. Strike.

Looking back to the vat in front of him, Anthony stirred the cloudy liquid, unwilling to join their number. The demands were of long standing, and he knew them by heart. The dyers were concerned at being required to increase the number of dye boxes for which they were responsible. The expansion of the industry and the demand for the special services of the master dyers had caused Martin Stein to add boxes without increasing the number of full-fledged dyers. Quality was threatened. True artisans, they wanted control over their product.

The pattern of work was also an issue—rushed work and extended hours that were followed by idle, unpaid days. A demand for standard payment, work or play, was seriously being considered. Behind all these demands was the activists' assurance that dyeing was unlikely to migrate elsewhere because of Paterson's mysteriously special water, so conducive to stylishly vivid colors, as well as Paterson's concentration of skilled labor. Many believed those assurances, but Anthony did not.

The heat intensified, and Anthony breathed deeply. He remembered only too clearly stories of Stein's response to previous strikes in earlier years, his angry denunciations of "Schweinhund" to all the strikers, and his long-term refusal to take his employees back, except as nonunionists. Anthony did not want these problems, especially now, when his home life was again ready to be plunged into turmoil.

The previous night returned to Anthony's mind, and he recalled his pleasure at Maria's smiling welcome when he arrived home. The house had been quiet with his daughters at novena, and he had been unexpectedly pleased at the thought of some time alone with his wife.

Strange, that in all his years of marriage he had not realized how crafty Maria could be. It had disappointed him and caused him to look back to examine his own behavior to see if he had forced her to adopt this dishonest approach when discussion of their eldest daughter was involved. As usual, he found himself wanting, and for that reason he had gathered his wife into his arms and considered more seriously the issue she raised.

The incredulity of it was with him still—that Carmela Moretti should pay Maria a call to discuss the betrothal of Sophia to her eldest son, Joey.

Were it not so serious, Anthony knew he would be tempted to laugh. Gone were the accusations against Sophia of having tantalized her son. Forgotten were the jealous rumors that persisted about his beautiful daughter, rumors Carmela herself had been so active in spreading. Sophia was now an angel in the woman's eyes, a beautiful angel who was suited so well to her handsome, sainted son.

The pity of it all was in Maria's response to Carmela's suggestion. She had been elated at the prospect of putting to rest rumors and bitter disputes of the past. He could still feel Maria's hands on his arms as she had gripped them so earnestly. He could still see the hope that shone so brightly in her face, and could still hear the sincerity of her pleas:

"Joey Moretti is a good boy, a handsome boy. He is

ambitious and he has money saved. He loves Sophia, and he will give her a good life."

His response that Sophia did not love Joey—in fact did not like him very much at all—was countered by Maria's sober response.

"You remember, Anthony, that I felt much the same when our families brought us together." Her face flushed when she whispered, "I was unhappy because I did not love you at all."

His throat had grown thick then, as he remembered how much he had loved Maria and how happy the day of their wedding had been for him. He had drawn Maria closer, and when her head fell against his shoulder, he had rested his cheek against it with the question he had hardly dared to ask.

"Maria—do you love me now?"

Her hoarse response had stolen his ability to respond. "*Sí*, Anthony. I love you more than I believed I ever could."

Those words had left him powerless against Maria's pleas. He had been unable to dispel the hope in her eyes, a light he had not seen there for many years, and for that reason he had agreed to consider Carmela Moretti's proposition.

But that was last night. The light of day, however, had left him incredulous at his promise. Barter Sophia away because of his love for her mother? How could he have considered it for a moment?

Ashamed, Anthony sighed. Whatever had possessed him last night, he was now committed to having the subject broached to Sophia. Anthony felt his tension rising. He knew what that meant. It meant an argument and it meant resumption of the state of undeclared war between Sophia and her mother. As in all wars, the embattled would not be the only casualties. Loved ones would suffer again, too. Anna, who had miraculously begun emerging from her shell; Rosalie, who had begun drawing closer to her mother; and himself, so torn between the two most important women in his life.

Turning, Anthony looked at the clock on the wall. It was growing late and the discourse between the dyers and their helpers was slowing their work. They would work late again tonight, and he worried that Maria would speak to Sophia before he arrived home. He should have told her to wait, but he had not. He should have told Maria he wanted to prepare Sophia for the proposal. He should have—

Drawn from his thoughts by a rough hand on his shoulder, Anthony turned to Carlo Francci's tense expression as the fellow demanded, "What about you, Anthony? You don't speak at all when we talk about strike. Are you with us or against us?"

A flush of color unrelated to the temperature of the shop rose to Anthony's sweaty face. His heavy features moved into uncharacteristically angry lines as he responded with quiet menace, "Remove your hand."

The sudden drop of Francci's jaw was almost comical, but Anthony was not inclined to laugh. Instead, he continued in a level tone. "I am unskilled and I have no place in the arguments of skilled labor. I have loyalties to those who employ me and to the men who work beside me, so I will tell you now, for all time. First—never lay your hand on me again. Second—I am neither with you or against you. I will stand with the majority and abide by their decision."

Turning back to his work, Anthony did not see the startled faces of his co-workers, or Francci's shrug as he walked back to the group standing nearby. Bright before Anthony's mind's eye was Sophia's beautiful face, and in his heart were his deep regrets.

* * *

"No, I'll have none of it!"

Her brilliant eyes wide with astonished fury, Sophia faced her mother across the small, neatly prepared kitchen table. "You didn't really believe I would consider marrying Joey Moretti even for a moment, did you?" Sophia shook her head, incredulous. "It was only a month ago that you told me never to 'flaunt myself in front of him again!"

"That's in the past. Carmela says she never believed what people say about you."

"Mama Moretti is a liar!"

"*Silenzio!*" Maria's pale face tightened. "You will listen to me and you will do as I say!"

"I will not!" Sophia jumped up from her chair, the impetus of her action sending the chair backward to slap against the floor, but Sophia expressed no regrets. "I won't marry Joey Moretti. I won't even discuss marrying him."

"You will!" Standing as well, leaving her two younger daughters seated and silent through the angry exchange, Maria walked to her daughter's side. "Sit!" When Sophia remained standing, she warned, "I will not tell you again!"

Trembling with rage, Sophia continued to stand as she whispered, "If Papa was here you wouldn't press me to marry Joey."

"Your papa has approved the match!"

"You lie!"

The impact of Maria's hand against Sophia's cheek cracked loudly in the silence, but Sophia showed no reaction to her mother's blow as she awaited her next move.

"So, you are silent at last!" Maria's eyes glittered with anger. "My eldest daughter is a fool! She thinks that a

139

flirting wink and a toss of her hip will gain her her dreams. They will not! She does not know that in the way of the world, beauty is used and cast aside, and that little true value is placed on a hank of bright hair or a glimpse of fair, smooth skin—aside from the night's pleasure it is worth. Beauty is fleeting! It will desert you! As your mother, I won't allow you to sacrifice your future for dreams that will never become reality! You're fortunate that Joey Moretti still wants you. He has told his mother that he loves you. You're well matched, you two, for in admitting that he loves you, Joey admits he is as much a fool as you. But he is a young, handsome fool who is hardworking and who will give you a good future."

"I want no part of a future with Joey Moretti."

"*I* will make that decision!"

Protest screaming in every inch of her body, Sophia kept her silence. She had already decided what she must do.

Watching her mother carefully, Sophia saw the gleam of victory in her pale eyes, but she suppressed her spontaneous response. She would allow her mother to savor a victory she had not won, and she would speak to Papa when he returned. Papa wouldn't turn against her, and tomorrow she would tell Joey Moretti—

Maria moved unexpectedly and Sophia took a spontaneous step backward that was not missed by her mother's sharp eye. Maria raised a narrow, arched brow. "Pick up your chair and sit. You will eat."

"I'm not hungry."

"You will eat! And then you will do your work and go to bed."

An unexpected sound from Rosalie turned all eyes in her direction as she bit her lip, then whispered, "But the novena . . ." Rosalie glanced at her sisters, then turned back to her mother with a plea in her voice. "We can't break the novena. Father McCall will wonder where we are and he'll send someone here to see what happened to us."

Maria's eyes veiled at the mention of Father McCall's name, and Sophia suppressed a growing smile. Clever Rosalie . . .

Hesitating only a moment longer, Maria addressed Sophia again. "You will go to novena with your sisters, and you will pray that God will forgive you for the vanity that makes you behave so badly. You will pray that Joey Moretti will not lose his desire for you, for there are few others who will offer for you if he should."

Sophia remained standing, silent protests echoing in her mind. Suddenly realizing she need to sacrifice the present to gain the future, Sophia settled into her chair. She picked up her spoon, with each mouthful she ate, her determination growing. She had told Lyle that time was running short, but she had not realized how very short indeed. She knew she must now make each hour count.

Mama turned back to the stove, and Sophia gave Rosalie a quick wink. Her face flushing, Rosalie looked down at her plate, and Sophia suppressed the smile that teased her lips despite the throbbing that had begun in her cheek.

The fine line of Sophia's lips firmed. That slap was an indirect present from Joey Moretti. She would thank him for it tomorrow.

Walking to the magnificent wardrobe that stretched almost the full length of his bedroom wall, Aaron selected a jacket, slipped it onto his shoulders, and shrugged it into place.

141

The opulence of his bedroom suite, the massive, ornately carved mahogany furniture, the fine Oriental rug under his feet, and the elegant satin bedcover on which discarded clothing was thoughtlessly tossed, was far from Aaron's busy mind as he silently retraced his steps. A cooling breeze wafted through the open window of his room, and he savored the relief it provided as he reached the mirror and assessed his appearance again. He smiled, knowing that he looked his best, but his immaculate appearance that evening was not accidental.

Earlier in the evening, he had driven the maid to the point of distraction, discarding one shirt after another until he found one laundered to his satisfaction. He had then dismissed her, powdered his shoulders and chest — a precaution he always took in the heavy heat of summer so he would remain dry and unwrinkled as long as possible — and slipped on his shirt. Carefully inspecting the crease in his trousers, he had then drawn them up over his long, muscular legs and secured them around his waist.

Aaron continued smug appraisal of his reflection. He was proud of his physical assets — a well-muscled chest sprinkled with enough black hair to appear masculine without appearing beastlike, his tight stomach, and flat hips. He had been told many times in intimate encounters that he was far more than adequate in other areas as well, and he was fairly certain that there was not a single woman of sound mind that would be left unimpressed by what she saw when she looked at him, either undressed or fully clothed.

Aaron paused at that thought, adding a silent, necessary postscript. No woman could fail to be impressed, with the possible exception of Sophia Marone.

A frown marred the perfection of Aaron's well-drawn features as the flame-haired vixen reappeared before his mind's eye. He was determined that he would do whatever he must in order to get that haughty little piece. He had been praised for his charm by the most difficult of taskmasters, his own father, and he intended to wield that weapon with a heavy hand.

Reaching for his hat, Aaron placed it carefully on his head, then smiled again at his reflection in the glass before turning toward the door. He negotiated the staircase with a rapid step. His hand was on the knob of the front door when his father's voice alerted him to his unexpected appearance in the living-room doorway.

Samuel Weiss studied him, his small eyes taking in each detail of his son's appearance. "You're looking well. Going out, I see."

Aaron replied cautiously, "I have an engagement with a very lovely lady. If you'll excuse me, I don't want to be late."

Seated in his carriage moments later, Aaron instructed briefly, "Ellison Street, Harry."

Lyle paced, covering the distance between the lumpy settee and the corner table that marked the dining area of his quarters. Through the doorway to his left was a compact kitchen that amply served his needs, and to his right was a bedroom that accommodated a bed, chest, and scarred dresser without an inch to spare. He glanced toward the windows which Aunt Julia had insisted should be sparkling before he moved in, and his agitation increased as the impending darkness met his eye. It was growing late.

Uncertain of the true reason for his disquiet, Lyle retraced his steps to the table where Sophia's sketches lay carefully piled. He leafed through them unconsciously. Sophia's raw talent was instantly recognizable, as was the

143

improvement in the sketches themselves since he had first seen her work. Sophia had ability and a strong desire to succeed. She needed only opportunity and she would realize her ambitions. Like himself. However, he had learned the hard way that opportunity was elusive, no matter how diligently sought.

Carefully replacing the sheets in their proper order, Lyle ran a hand through his heavy gold hair in a gesture that revealed his increasing agitation. He had had a terrible day. His frustration had increased after he had recognized the cause for the machinery slowdown at the mill. Sick of having his uncle's policies cripple his ability to handle the floor, he had stormed into the office and had it out with him then and there. Paul had been present and had spoken in his behalf, but little was accomplished, with the exception of a promise from Matthew to include him in future discussions of mill strategy that pertained directly to employee relations. The memory of Uncle Matthew's frigid expression was with him still, and Lyle was well aware that even that limited concession would not have been made were it not for the good of the mill.

Lyle resumed his unconscious pacing as Sophia's face loomed before his mind's eye. He recalled the tight line of her lips as she walked back toward her machine that morning, and he realized his agitation was due only in part to his uncle's reticence. Sophia had not answered the question he had asked her in the mill earlier that day, but if she came tonight, he was determined that she would.

A knock at the door interrupted Lyle's thoughts and he turned toward it, his heart beginning a sudden pounding. A moment later he drew the door open, rage of another kind suddenly overwhelming his mind at his first sight of Sophia.

Waiting only until he closed the door behind Sophia,

144

Lyle questioned sharply, "Who marked your face?"

Sophia raised her chin, anger sparking in her eyes at his tone. "I didn't come here to be questioned!"

"I want an answer, Sophia!"

Sophia did not reply.

Agitation assumed control as Lyle grasped her arms, holding her fast. "Was it Moretti? Did he touch you . . . because if he did—"

Sophia was suddenly laughing, but Lyle was struck by the lack of joy in the sound as she raised her brows with mock innocence. "Do you really think that Joey—my future husband—would do this?"

"Your future husband!"

Her beautiful eyes filling unexpectedly, Sophia raised her chin. "Sí, my mother's choice—but never mine."

"But I thought—"

"What did you think, Lyle? Did you think, as I did, that Mama Moretti would oppose her son's choice until her dying day? If so, you're as big a fool as I am in underestimating Joey's persuasive powers. It seems that he's convinced his mother I'm the only woman who can make him happy! As such, I've been transfigured in Carmela Moretti's eyes. My mother was so pleased at the thought of having me taken off her hands that she couldn't wait to tell me of my good fortune."

A lone tear escaped Sophia's brimming eyes, and she brushed it angrily away.

"Surely you don't intend to marry Moretti . . ."

"Never." Sophia's response was a whispered oath.

Lyle stroked Sophia's cheek, his frown deepening as his fingertips touched the bruise on her flawless skin. The ache inside him expanded to an almost physical pain. "How can you stay at home and suffer this treatment, Sophia? Why don't you leave—take a room somewhere. You can support yourself. If you need help, I'll—"

"I can't."

"Why?"

"You wouldn't understand."

"*I* wouldn't understand?"

Sophia's lips moved into a shadow of a smile for the first time when she saw his irritation. She hesitated, seeking the right words. "We're alike in so many ways, you and I, so much so that we often think each other's thoughts and share each other's dreams. We're different only in the matter of family."

Lyle could feel himself stiffening. "You're telling me that I wouldn't be able to understand how it is with a family because I have no true family of my own, because my mother—"

Slipping her hand across his lips, Sophia halted Lyle's bitter words with a distressed plea. "No, I didn't mean that. Let me explain." Sophia paused again, her brow furrowing. "You weren't raised the same way I was, *caro* Lyle. 'Nothing replaces blood' is a saying that's been inbred in me. It means that I owe a debt to those of my own blood, to my family. It's a debt of allegiance that means wherever I go, whatever I do, I'm tied to them with an invisible cord. Other things may change, but that remains, never to be altered."

"That's nonsense! You're talking about a debt that can never be paid! Will you sacrifice your life to that debt? Will you spend your life wanting—"

"No . . . no, I won't." Sophia caressed him with her gaze, obviously disturbed at his agitation. "Don't upset yourself."

"What are you saying, then?"

Sophia's expression softened. "Lyle, please try to understand. The debt of allegiance is a debt of love. It's especially strong between my father and me. From the earliest time that I can remember, my father has loved

146

me and believed in me. I could never leave his house in anger, because he would bleed with the pain of it — and I would bleed, too."

"You talk about your father, but what about you? Would you marry Moretti if your father told you to marry him?"

"My father would never do that."

"Are you so sure?" Uncertain of his reasoning, Lyle pressed relentlessly, "Would your mother have proposed this match without his approval?"

Sophia paused again. "Papa would never ask me to marry against my wishes."

"If he did . . . ?"

Anger flashed in Sophia's eyes. "I've already answered that question!"

Lyle stiffened at Sophia's tone. The ache deep inside him that had begun the moment Sophia had refused to answer his question in the mill that morning grew to a living anguish. Friendship with this beautiful, complex young woman was even more difficult than he had thought it would be. It cut and burned and churned him up inside in so many ways, while it appeared to leave her unscathed. He didn't like it. He didn't like knowing he was vulnerable as he had never been vulnerable before. He didn't like the subtle shifting of his priorities that had begun putting Sophia's interests above his own. An instinct for survival developed during a lifetime of uncertainty forced his spontaneous defense.

"So understanding family is beyond me." Lyle saw the flicker in Sophia's eyes at the bitterness in his voice. "You know, you almost had me convinced. I was beginning to believe we shared a special gift, but that gift has turned out to be a heavier burden than I care to carry." Hours of frustration erupting in an abrupt snap, he continued harshly. "And I'm telling you now that I won't suffer your anguish if you leave me powerless to act against it. You ask too much—more than I'm willing to give." Myriad emotions assaulting him, Lyle pushed Sophia away. His voice was lifeless as he stated flatly, "This isn't working out. Go home, Sophia."

"Lyle . . ."

Lyle steeled himself against the plea in Sophia's eyes as he forced himself to turn away. "Go home."

"No."

Sophia's slender arms slipped around his waist from behind and Lyle briefly closed his eyes against the warmth of her pressed against his back as she whispered, "I'm sorry. I didn't mean to upset you. Let me finish what I wanted to say. Please, turn around." The distress in Sophia's voice was more powerful than words as she repeated, "Please."

The single tear that trailed down Sophia's cheek as he turned back to her dissolved the last of his restraint, and Lyle slid his arms around her. He drew her close, his anger draining. The warm comfort of her was bittersweet as he breathed deeply in an attempt at control.

Sophia . . . Sophia . . . Lyle rocked her comfortingly, his mind in chaos as his body sang with the matchless pleasure of holding her in his arms. This beautiful young woman confused and agitated him, but the sheer power of other emotions she had awakened inside him was his true torment. She had brought to life a part of him that had previously lain dormant, a compulsive, possessive part of him, and his mind cried out for caution. He knew that if he was smart, he would separate himself from her before it was too late . . . before—

Unwilling to finish that last thought, uncertain if he could let Sophia go if he tried, Lyle drew her with him as he took a few backward steps toward the settee behind him. He sat and pulled her down onto his lap. He held her gently, his throat thick as he looked into her sober face.

"I'm sorry, too." Lyle attempted a smile, intensely conscious of Sophia's sweet breath as it fanned his face, of the warm lips only inches from his. "You were right all along, you know. I *can* look into your eyes and see myself reflected inside you, but the problem is that I'm not certain if that's good or bad for either one of us." Slowly drowning in those solemn azure depths, Lyle continued. "But I do know that all this means something you don't seem to realize, Sophia. It means that when someone cuts you, the blade slashes me, too. And when someone strikes you, I feel the pain. I've never turned the other cheek for myself, and I can't do it for you."

Sophia swallowed with visible effort, then forced a smile. "But you're worrying needlessly about me. I'm not floundering. I have a plan."

Unexpected tenderness swelled inside Lyle at the earnestness reflected on Sophia's exquisite face. He stroked a curling tendril of bright hair back from her cheek as she continued. "I'm going to talk to Papa. He'll settle things with Mama and the Morettis, and if he can't settle it to the satisfaction of all, he'll at least give me time."

A creeping disquiet began filtering into Lyle's brief calm. "Time to do what?"

"Time to finish my sketches and to find a new position. Once I'm out of the mills, Mama will see that I've started on another path."

"Your mother will be satisfied then?"

Sophia paused, her expression stiffening. "She'll have to be."

And if she isn't?"

"She'll have to be," Sophia repeated determindedly. "Everything will be all right. I know it will."

Closing the matter off from further discussion, Sophia

149

leaned her head against his shoulder, but Lyle was not easy with her response, nor with the realization that this strong, stubborn young woman inched more deeply into his heart with every breath she breathed.

Slave to the conflicting emotions warring inside him, Lyle drew Sophia closer. He knew she took comfort from being in his arms. She trusted him and had opened her heart to him in a way she had to no other man, but the nagging disquiet still remaining inside him demanded an answer.

Lyle's fingers tightened in the flowing silk of Sophia's hair as a former tension gradually returned. He took a steadying breath and asked abruptly, "Sophia, I want to know. Did you know about the slowdown in the mill?"

The quiet intimacy of the moment was shattered as Sophia stiffened and sat up. Feeling himself stiffen as well, Lyle pressed, "Did you know the belts on the looms had been soaped?" Sophia attempted to draw herself to her feet, but Lyle held her fast. She pulled back from him as he pressed insistently, "Did you?"

Sophia's brilliant eyes met his levelly. "Do you really think there's any way that I could *not* have known?"

The strength drained from Lyle's limbs. "You knew . . . yet you let it all go on day after day without telling me?"

"Would you make an informer out of me because of our friendship?"

"Friendship?" Lyle stared at her, incredulous. "What kind of friend are you? You knew how dire the situation was and how hard I've worked to make a success of my job, yet you let it all continue, day after day, when you could have stopped it with a word."

"I had faith in you. I knew you'd discover the problem for yourself."

"You also knew how dangerous the slowdown was to

150

my position at the mill and what it would mean to me if I was replaced."

"It wouldn't have come to that."

"And if it had?"

Sophia paused, her eyes misting as she responded incredulously, "Think what you're saying, Lyle! Think what you would've had me do! Can't you be satisfied that I took no part in the scheme? I didn't allow the bobbins on my or my sisters' machines to be oiled, but I couldn't inform on my fellow workers. You have no right to expect or ask that of me."

"I ask only what I would expect of friendship."

Sophia rose abruptly to her feet. "You ask too much! I won't *spy* for anyone!"

Anger flushed Lyle's face as he stood rigidly beside her. "You're right, I don't understand! You said we're alike, that we're close in so many ways that we can read each other's thoughts and feel each other's anguish. Well, if you felt mine, you had a poor way of showing it—by looking the other way when it mattered the most."

"Lyle, think what you're saying! Think of the barriers you're putting between us."

"The barriers *I'm* putting between us? Let me ask you—would you have turned your back on the dirty work that was done if your father was supervisor of the mill?"

Sophia hesitated momentarily. "It's not the same thing."

"Isn't it? Why? Because your father understands you in a way no one else does? Because he supports you and believes in you? Because the feelings between you are so special? I thought that described the feelings between us, too. What's the difference there? The bond of blood?"

"Lyle . . ."

"Is that it, Sophia? Because if it is, it's something I can't overcome and I won't even try." Pausing, furious with himself, with Sophia, and with countless circumstances he could not change, Lyle demanded, "Tell me! I want the truth!"

The knife of pain inside Lyle cut deeply as he stared down into Sophia's whitening countenance. He saw her hesitation and the trembling of her lips. He saw her weigh his words, and he saw the futility of protest gradually become accepted in her eyes. When she finally replied, her voice was filled with sadness.

"It seems you're right, Lyle. Some things can't be changed, no matter how strongly our hearts tug and strain toward each other, no matter how deeply the pain cuts."

"Sophia . . ."

"What else is there to say?" Taking her pad and pencils from the nearby table, Sophia clutched them tight against her. Searching his face a moment longer in silence, Sophia raised herself unexpectedly on her toes to press a light kiss against his lips. Her voice was a grating whisper.

"I will miss you."

Her eyes brimming, Sophia opened the door and fled before Lyle could catch his breath—before he was able to understand what had truly happened . . . before he realized that Sophia had just said good-bye.

Sophia dashed down the staircase toward the entrance to the street. The moist night air brushed her cheeks as she stepped out onto the sidewalk and Sophia breathed deeply, willing away the tears. In the last few hours her world had come tumbling down around her. Her home was a battleground from which she could not escape without shedding the blood of those she loved, and her sole sanctuary, the comfort of the friend on whom she had come to rely, was no longer available to her.

Unsure of her destination as she began walking rapidly, Sophia was certain of only one thing. She must forget the anguish she had glimpsed in Lyle's eyes as she left him. She must put it all behind her. She must—

Colliding unexpectedly with a man who stepped out of a doorway in front of her, Sophia gasped aloud as her pad flew from her hands, scattering sketches and pencils on the sidewalk around them. Paying little attention to the strong hands that attempted to steady her, she dropped to her knees to gather the precious sheets. She did not look at the man who crouched beside her in an attempt to help until he spoke in an unexpectedly familiar voice.

"I'm sorry! Are you all right?"

Looking up, Sophia recognized the arrogant mill owner's son, Aaron Weiss, as he added with surprise, "It's Sophia Marone, isn't it?"

Sophia reached for a sheet lying close by, only to have the fellow pick it up in her stead. She attempted to snatch it from his hand.

"I don't need your help!"

"But surely I can—"

"Give that to me!"

Her anxiety appearing to whet his interest, Weiss raised the sketch higher, out of her reach, as he perused it. He stood up abruptly and held it closer to the streetlight. His frown was accusing when he addressed her again.

"Where did you get this?"

Sophia strained to snatch the sketch from his hand, but the effort proved useless as Weiss demanded, "I asked you where you got this sketch."

"It's mine! Give it to me!"

"Yours?" Weiss's gaze was speculative. "You're telling me *you* drew this?"

153

"I'm telling you nothing, because it's none of your business." Kneeling, Sophia gathered up the remainder of her belongings and drew herself to her feet as Aaron questioned unexpectedly, "You have more of these sketches?"

Sophia was beginning to tremble. She had suffered enough inquisition that day. She would suffer no more from a pampered rich man's son who had never known an insecure day in his life. Realizing she could not force Aaron Weiss to surrender the sheet he stubbornly withheld, Sophia made a sudden decision. She turned away from him abruptly, only to have Weiss's hand close on her arm as she took her first step.

"Wait, please!"

"Let go of me."

Weiss was momentarily hesitant. All trace of arrogance disappeared from his handsome features, but Sophia was unaffected by his practiced charm as he smiled, "You do remember me, don't you? We met in Kingston Mill. My name is Aaron Weiss."

"I know who you are."

Her response obviously not what he expected, Weiss faltered, "I . . . I didn't mean to accuse you of anything. I was just interested in this sketch."

Sophia's smile was cold, despite its beauty. "Since you're so *interested* in it, you may keep it with my compliments."

Jerking her arm from his grip, Sophia ignored the fellow's grunt of surprise as she turned and walked rapidly away from him. Her feet fairly flying as she turned the corner of the street, she did not look back to see that the spoiled rich man's son was still standing where she had left him, staring after her as she disappeared from sight.

Chapter Eight

Edith entered the library of her home. Oblivious to the well-coordinated luxury of custom-made leather furniture and walls of leather-bound volumes, the sound of her step muted by the fine Persian rug under her feet, she walked toward the massive mahogany desk that dominated the far end of the room. She paused beside it, staring out the window to its rear, onto the garden beyond. Distracted as she was, she did not see the rose gardens in full bloom, or the bricked path that led to a secluded bower beneath a graceful willow tree — scenes of indolent beauty tended by an obedient gardener. Instead, she saw only the small carriage house to the rear of the yard, the second floor of which had become the focus of Paul's existence after she had turned it over to him a year earlier.

Her smooth face drawing into a frown, Edith searched the top drawer of the desk, then the second. She paused when she found the letter from her sister that she remembered having placed there days earlier. She slid the pink, scented sheets out of the envelope, the spark of an idea leaping into full-fledged flame. Paul had confided his desire to study under Monsieur LeDeux in Paris that morning. His enthusiasm was dampened, however, as a result of the heavy burden of guilt that Matthew had placed on his shoulders.

Edith's lips twitched with annoyance. Matthew was well aware of the closeness between herself and their son. He resented it, but he had not been above using it to his advantage in an attempt to get his son to comply with his wishes.

Edith raised her chin with renewed determination, her hand tightening on the letter in her hand. Drastic situations need be fought with drastic measures. Matthew would oppose her idea, but she would have her way in the end. She had no doubt that Lyle would find the proposition she intended offering him appealing. He would perhaps be flattered. Edith shrugged unconsciously. In truth, she didn't care what Lyle or anyone else thought, as long as Paul was happy and was allowed to follow the course of his life without interference.

Edith turned toward the door. Matthew was due home early today. They would have a quiet lunch together and she would broach her idea. Then it would be quiet no longer.

The sun shone unrestricted on Main Street as the traffic of midmorning grew greater. Delivery wagons, passenger carriages, and streetcars moved briskly on the cobbled street, passing an endless row of awninged storefronts that formed the main shopping district of the city. Aaron squinted into the distance, searching signs displayed from every nook and cranny above the sweeping awnings. He glanced at the storefront of Quackenbush and Sons's Hardware Store, one of the better establishments in town, and nodded to the senior Quackenbush in passing. He had no time for amenities.

Amending that thought as he stepped around two strolling matrons, Aaron tipped his hat to the younger of the two in acknowledgment of the spark of interest he saw in her eye as he passed. His erect carriage and purposeful stride belied the sleepless night he had passed after his encounter with Sophia Marone the previous evening. Were he not so proud, Aaron knew he would have been able to laugh at the joke that simple young woman had made of his elaborate plans.

Fool that he was, he had expected no problem at all in his intention to lie in wait for the redheaded little snip and to intercept her before she could reach her lover's quarters. He had expected to overwhelm her with his charm and convince her to spend the evening with him instead. He had believed that a young woman of her low station in life would be flattered by the invitation.

However, everything had gone wrong from the start. He had arrived at Lyle Kingston's residence a moment too late to catch Sophia Marone before she slipped out of sight through the doorway to Kingston's flat. Cursing, more disappointed than he cared to admit and uncertain what it was about the Marone girl that made him so desperate to have her, he had stood in the shadows nearby, determined to wait until she emerged again. He had not expected that her visit to Kingston would be so short — that she would emerge with tears in her eyes and with fashion sketches of unexpected quality.

His first thought upon seeing them had been that Kingston had stolen the sketches somewhere so the girl might pass them off as her own. It had taken only one glance at the girl's face, however, to reveal that the idea was absurd.

Aaron recalled the bungled conversation that followed, during which he had allowed Sophia Marone to lead their exchange far from the lines he originally intended. He remembered the pride in those brilliant eyes and in the rise of that delicate chin. And he remembered his humiliation when Sophia Marone left him standing on the street, staring at her departing back.

Later, in the privacy of his room, he had carefully

studied the sketch she left behind. Years spent in his father's jacquard room, where he had contributed to the sketching and desig: ng of the jacquard patterns that had made his father's mill famous, had lent him a keen appreciation of the talent for design. Sophia Marone's sketch, as rough as it was, had startled him with its quality. Upon closer examination of the sketch, her talent became even more impressive, and Aaron found himself wondering how many more surprises the little twit concealed behind that bold manner and beautiful face.

Aaron remembered the desolation he had glimpsed briefly in Sophia Marone's eyes, the manner in which she had clutched those sketches as she rushed out onto the street. Kingston and she had had a falling out. Benefit ing from his vast experience with women, he knew that the little tart was now as vulnerable as she would ever be — that if he wanted her, he would have to work quickly.

The realization that he wanted Sophia Marone more than he had ever wanted another woman both annoyed and titillated him. Those incredible eyes returned again to his mind and Aaron cursed under his breath. Their clarity, their depth of color, and the spirit shining there had been only too clear even in the meager street light the previous evening. It occurred to him that Kingston had probably promised her more than he could deliver. *He* would not make the same mistake.

His jaw tightening, Aaron slapped the envelope he carried against his thigh, knowing the sketch within was the key. He had set his mind on getting Sophia Marone, and he would succeed. Walking more quickly, he negotiated the few turns that brought Colt Street into sight. A few minutes later, affixing a smile on his lips that was his charming best, Aaron walked into the elite boutique of Madame Celeste Tourneau.

* * *

The din of the mill seemed inordinately deafening as Sophia worked along the winder, her fingers moving among the fine silk threads. The sound reverberated over and again inside her head, keeping time with the throbbing ache there. She paused to brush a wayward strand of hair from her cheek and glanced toward the sun shining on the lot outside the window in an attempt to escape her tumultuous thoughts. An almost irresistible urge to flee to the wonder of the falls rose inside her. She needed the peace of that place desperately, now that her life had degenerated into such bitter turmoil.

It had only taken one glance for Joey to read the response to his proposal on her face that morning, and as far as she was concerned the matter was settled, but her feelings for Lyle were not so easily reconciled. A painful formality now existed between them, but she was unable to forget the moment when the glow in Lyle's golden eyes went suddenly cold. She ached with the pain of it, uncertain how their sympathetic exchange had suddenly turned to unyielding conflict. She still found it difficult to believe that Lyle, who read her heart as well as she read his, had severed their friendship even as she sat intimately close to him, as she tasted his warm breath on her lips. The sense of betrayal was with her still.

Her problems had intensified when she stepped through the door of her home upon returning later. It had not been necessary for Mama or her to speak a word, so heavy was the tension in the brightly lit kitchen as Papa spoke.

"Do you want to marry Joey Moretti, Sophia?"

She remembered the weight of her father's sober gaze as she answered flatly.

"No."

Her father had dismissed her then, but the heated discussion that followed had not escaped her ears as her sisters and she lay abed in their room. Her first glimpse of her mother's face in the morning revealed only too clearly that all was not over and done.

Pausing, Sophia watched the bobbins whirl the shimmering threads. Their spinning was dizzying, and she closed her eyes, with sheer strength of will summoning to mind the vision of frothing currents of water tumbling into a deep chasm. She heard the thunderous sound, she felt the spray on her face, and peering closer, she saw rainbows in the mist. The colors brightened, beckoning her. Their iridescent hues glowed, warming her. She was transfused with their brilliance.

Sophia opened her eyes, returning to a reality that was no longer so cold, for the colors that were with her still.

"Are you insane?" Aghast, Matthew stared incredulously at his wife, his muscular frame appearing to swell with the vehemence of his response. "The answer is no!"

Unaffected by his ire, Edith faced her husband calmly. He had returned home at midday as planned, intending to devote the remainder of the afternoon to financial matters that needed to be settled outside the mill. She had prepared well for this encounter, choosing a gown of a pale dusty blue which her husband favored for the air of delicacy it lent her fair coloring and choosing an extravagant scent that she knew her husband unconsciously associated with power and success. Greeting him in her usual reserved manner, she had waited until luncheon was served before broaching her plan. His response had been swift and predictable, and Edith could not have been more pleased, despite his vehement resistance.

Raising her chin with a hint of disdain calculated to raise his ire, Edith countered, "I didn't breach this subject with you to obtain your approval, Matthew. I've already made my decision."

"I won't have it, Edith!" Matthew's well-trimmed mustache twitched revealingly. "How can you consider for a moment diluting Leighton blood with the blood of a bastard? Your sister can't be that desperate to find her daughter a husband that she'll consent to such a scheme!"

"My sister is a widow who relies on my judgment. She sees spinsterhood in Hope's future. She wants grandchildren, and she loves her daughter enough to want her to know the fulfillment of marriage.

"Fulfillment . . ."

Matthew's scoffing response raised a flush to Edith's cheek as she replied, "Not everyone is as dissatisfied with marriage as you appear to be, Matthew."

"I will not have you clouding the issue with personal issues, Edith! You don't fool me, you know. Your intention isn't to find a husband for your sister's homely daughter. Your intention, for whatever reason you've made this abrupt turnabout, is to make Lyle more acceptable to me with the dowry that would come with the match, and with the Leighton bloodline adding luster to any progeny he may produce. But it won't work! I'll never accept him in place of my son."

Edith's pale eyes hardened. She paused, agitated by his last remark. "Paul is a jewel—a talented, sensitive person who is special in every way. Do you really think I would expect to install the son of an immigrant British whore in his stead! Damn you, Matthew! Your stupidity is sometimes beyond bearing!"

"What is your intention then, may I ask?" Matthew drummed his fingers tensely on the pristine tablecloth, his poached salmon forgotten. "Are you expecting the fellow to perform the services of a stud?"

"Don't be vulgar, Matthew!"

"What, then?"

"It's my intention to make him more acceptable in the eyes of society."

"Why?"

"So that when you begin training him to take over control of the mill—"

"Never!"

"—he'll be accepted more easily by our peers."

"Never, I say! I would rather see the mill burn to the ground!"

"Don't be stubborn, Matthew!"

Matthew jumped to his feet. Slapping his napkin down on the table, his chest heaving, he warned, "You go too far, Edith. Our *son* will take over the responsibility of the mill when I feel he's ready."

"He will not—not immediately, anyway." Drawing herself to her feet, Edith approached her husband. Her eyes held his as she came to stand unexpectedly close. She deliberately allowed her slender body to brush his, measuring her husband's response as he assessed her. She swayed lightly toward him, and struggled to restrain a smile as a familiar light entered his eye. "We must give Paul time. If we appear to accept Lyle, Paul will feel free to follow through with his artistic studies."

"Damn it, Edith! That's the last thing I want him to do!"

"The sooner Paul is satisfied that he's gone as far as he can go in the art world, the sooner he'll settle down to the rigors of the everyday world."

Matthew's eyes narrowed. "What are you saying?"

"I'm saying you can train Lyle to carry on for you, and when Paul realizes that his true future lies in silk, he can return and the business will be his."

Matthew paused, then countered, "Even if I agreed to this preposterous scheme, what about Lyle? He's a proud sort and Hope isn't a very appealing woman. He may not consent to it."

"Lyle is ambitious. If Hope is a condition of his advancement, he'll agree."

162

"And when we no longer need him—what then?"

"He'll have served his purpose."

Matthew appeared suspicious even as his hand slipped to the small of Edith's back to press her closer. "It won't be as easy as you think. It's difficult enough that my sister adopted the wily bastard. If this all comes about, he'll then be your niece's husband and the father of her children."

"Matthew, dear, Lyle can always work for Paul."

"And if he doesn't want to take second place to Paul?"

"Will he have a choice?"

Matthew's eyes narrowed further. Edith felt them study her and she met his gaze boldly, her heart pounding with the pure sexual attraction her husband exuded when intrigued. He appealed to her most then, as he studied each line of her face, each fleeting expression, admiration and respect growing in his eyes—not for her beauty, which was nil, but for her intelligence, cunning, and the impeccable breeding obvious in every word she spoke, in every step she took.

Maintaining her pose of strict challenge, Edith was gratified to see the telltale signs of Matthew's mounting physical passion—the occasional tracing of his lower lip with the tip of his tongue, the quiver of his nostrils, the flush to his cheek, and the growing possessiveness of the hand that stroked her back.

Her own desire rising as well, Edith also knew that the physical act of lovemaking was never better between them than when she had challenged Matthew successfully and he sought to subjugate her with the sheer mastery of his sexual prowess. She also knew that passion would seal their pact more firmly than an oath.

Sliding her arms up to encircle her husband's neck, Edith whispered, "Paul is on an errand that will take most of the afternoon, and I have no particular plans—except for one." Drawing her husband's head down, Edith met his mouth with hers. Her lips separated, and she felt a surge of true passion as Matthew's tongue slid into her mouth and his arms crushed her slenderness against him. Separating herself from him moments later, she turned back to the table, attempting to ignore Matthew's sensual caress of her breasts, and the hot kisses he rained against the back of her neck. Instead, she reached for the small silver bell on the table, rang it, and called out in her genteel voice.

"Mabel, Mr. Kingston and I won't be accepting visitors this afternoon."

Turning back to her husband, Edith felt her heart give a little leap as he pulled her into his arms again and kissed her full on the mouth with an ardor that had long marked their intimate encounters. The rise of his manhood was hard against her as he suddenly separated himself from her and started toward the staircase, pulling her along behind him.

Later, as she lay beneath her husband's sated, perspired frame, Edith smiled, sated and perspired as well. Matthew, shrewd as he was, had no inkling that he had been outsmarted again.

Sophia's graceful hands flew at their task, setting up the ends as the workday ended. Glancing around her, she saw that many of the other warpers were already making their way toward the door and Sophia's agitation increased. Her concentration had been off the entire day, adding to the problem of poorly wound skeins that tangled at the bat of an eye. The result had been a horrendously difficult day when she was not physically up to the challenge.

Well aware that the casual observer would not guess her inner turmoil, Sophia maintained her calm facade, her agitation increasing as a glance to the rear revealed that Joey lingered at the warpers' wheel as the other warpers filed toward the door. Sophia worked faster. She would not allow Joey the opportunity he sought to get her alone.

Shutting off her last machine, Sophia walked quickly toward the door. She almost laughed as Joey snapped into motion, too late to reach her as she slipped out into the sunshine of late afternoon.

Relief shot adrenaline through her veins as Sophia reached her sisters' side and grasped their hands.

"Come quickly! Joey's behind me, and I'm not in the mood to deal with him."

The hasty steps of the three young women thudded against the short wooden bridge spanning the raceway a few moments later, only to come to an abrupt halt at the unexpected appearance of Anthony Marone waiting on the sidewalk.

Anthony addressed Rosalie and Anna. "I must talk to Sophia. You will walk ahead, but not too far. I don't want Mama to know that I've taken an hour off from my shift."

Sophia slipped her hand under her father's arm as her sisters obediently complied. Matching her steps to his as they crossed the street, Sophia was aware of her father's intense discomfort as he finally spoke.

"I'm sorry, *figlia mia*." Anthony began uncertainly as his dark eyes searched Sophia's face. "I thought only to make a compromise with your mother when she spoke of Joey Moretti's offer of marriage. Your mother was so certain it was best for you. I told her that she could speak to you, but I didn't expect to be delayed in returning home, and I didn't think—"

Unable to bear her father's distress, Sophia interrupted softly. "Everything will be all right, Papa. Joey knows I won't marry him."

Joey picked that moment to walk past them and An-

165

thony frowned at the heat in the angry young man's gaze. "I don't like the look of that fellow." His expression darkened further. "He's not good enough for my beautiful Sophia."

His unexpected anger under control as they reached the corner of the street, Anthony covered Sophia's hand with his. He patted it gently, the calluses on his palm rough against her skin as he looked directly into her eyes.

"Your mama means well, but she fears what she does not understand."

Sophia leaned forward to kiss her father's cheek. His great mustache ticked her and she smiled. Anthony's distress lightened visibly.

"*Sí, figlia mia,* smile. Your papa must go back to work now, but he'll always be there if you need him."

"Thank you, Papa."

Sophia watched her father walk back down the street moments later, a new aspect of her dire circumstances emerging. With each day that her future remained uncertain, the weight increased on Papa's already heavily burdened shoulders.

Catching up with her sisters, Sophia turned toward home, knowing that much depended on the next few evenings to come.

The lengthening shadows had fallen into twilight as Aaron peered out the window of his carriage, feeling unexpectedly foolish. He released a short, impatient breath, wondering for the hundredth time what he was doing covertly watching Sophia Marone's home, waiting for her to emerge like a sinister character in a cheap melodrama.

Aaron shifted impatiently. He had been unable to get the redheaded witch out of his mind the entire day. Each time her beautiful face returned to mind, he had become more certain of the desperation he had glimpsed briefly in her eyes the previous evening. He could not ignore the feeling that cautious persistence would be rewarded.

His gaze fixed on the alley beside the building where Sophia resided, Aaron felt his heart leap as Sophia suddenly emerged onto the street. Sophia's two younger sisters stepped out unexpectedly beside her, and Aaron muttered a curse. Were the sisters never separated?

The exchange of glances between the sisters and the unexpected haste with which they started toward the opposite corner interrupted Aaron's thoughts. Tapping the ceiling of the carriage, Aaron instructed sharply, "Follow the three women, Harry, but be sure to keep a safe distance behind. I don't want them to see us."

Too engrossed in his thoughts to wonder at Harry's reaction to his stealth, Aaron drew back into the shadows of the carriage. Becoming anxious as the girls turned the corner out of sight, Aaron urged, "Don't lose them, Harry! Hurry up!"

The carriage snapped into an accelerated pace as they turned onto Market Street, and Aaron gasped aloud as his driver barely avoided collision with a carriage parked unseen around the curve. Seizing the wall strap to steady himself, Aaron was about to shout in protest when his view of the three Marone sisters walking rapidly down the street forced restraint. He was as tense as a spring when the two sisters suddenly turned in another direction and Sophia continued on alone.

"Follow the redheaded woman, Harry!"

A knot of unreasonable jealousy twisted inside Aaron. It was obvious Sophia Marone had plans that did not include her sisters. He was determined to find out what they were.

Sophia's pace finally slowed as she approached Church Street. As he watched intently, she gave a last, cursory glance around her before slipping out of sight through a nearby doorway.

Aaron's jaw dropped with surprise. Momentarily unable to react, he finally managed a confused whisper.

"The library?"

Aaron sat back against the velour upholstery as his carriage drew to a halt. He was unwilling to speculate any further.

Sophia paused in the foyer of the library to catch her breath. She brushed a wayward strand of hair back from her face and smoothed her dress as she prepared to step into sight. The massive, multifloored brick building, the former residence of a wealthy Paterson family which had been enlarged to accommodate the city's vast collection of books, was familiar to her.

The grandeur of the site, both within and without, remained despite its conversion, and Sophia remembered being awed into speechlessness when she first entered the building as a child. However, that sense of wonder had soon dimmed under the unrelenting scrutiny of Mr. Horace Little.

Sophia's first step into sight proved that this night would be no exception as the overweight librarian's nasal tones sounded clearly on the silence of the room.

"So, back again, Miss Marone?"

Sophia nodded, unwilling to enter into a verbal exchange with the man. She didn't like the way his small eyes dissected her. The perspiration that rose to his brow as his gaze lingered, and the manner in which he licked his thick lips set her stomach to churning. Mr. Little's dislike of her had been obvious from the day she stepped through the doorway of the library years earlier. His attitude toward her had worsened as she had matured, however, and it did not take her long to realize that the reputation that dogged her had reached his ears. Her dismissal of the man's few cautious advances had left him resentful and with a strong desire for retribution.

Sophia started toward the table in the rear of the room that was mercifully hidden from clear view of the librarian's desk, only to have Mr. Little halt her again with a sharp reminder.

"We close promptly at eight, Miss Marone."

Sophia nodded briefly, heaving a sigh of relief when out of the man's sight. Grateful to find herself alone in the secluded corner of the room, she approached the bookcase against the rear wall. She cast a last cautious glance around her before sliding her hand into the narrow space between the shelf and the wall to withdraw the precious sheets and pencils secreted there the previous day.

Seated at a nearby table a moment later, Sophia closed her eyes in an effort to regain her composure. She told herself that Horace Little would not find the excuse he actively sought to ban her from the library — that she would finish her sketches and find a suitable position before Mama made life impossible at home.

Opening her eyes again, Sophia was suddenly ashamed of her weakness. She must keep foremost in her mind that she was Sophia Marone, that she could not submit to ordinary fears if she was to accomplish *un*ordinary goals. She must allow the world to see only the part of Sophia Marone that she wished it to see, with the intimate core of her — the part of her shared only once before — again held in secret.

Dismissing the image of Lyle's face as it appeared before her mind, Sophia also dismissed the loneliness that had replaced the warmth of him in her heart. Determined, she picked up her pencil and started to work.

The familiar Kingston mansion drew into sight as Lyle

turned the corner of the street, and the sense of disquiet with which he had accepted Aunt Edith's hasty, unexpected invitation to dinner surged to full-blooming suspicion. He was not certain what to expect, but he knew that anything was better than staying at home, reliving those moments when Sophia had walked out of his life the previous evening.

His spirits again sinking, Lyle sought to dispel the image of Sophia that had haunted him since the door of his apartment clicked closed behind her. He had spent the night alternating between berating himself for forcing the confrontation and congratulating himself for having put to an end an association that from the first had demanded more than he was prepared to give.

Lyle took a deep, steadying breath. The truth was that he had been jealous of the loyalties that Sophia placed above her feelings for him. He had wanted to be first with Sophia, but in asking that, strangely enough, he had asked for more than *Sophia* was willing to give.

Lyle smiled sadly. Sophia was so much wiser than he. She had recognized the direction in which they were heading and she had immediately made her decision. It gave him little satisfaction to know that she, too, suffered at the separation between them. He ached, knowing that while she had been rarely out of his sight at the mill during the day, she could have been on the other end of the earth, so final was the distance she had put between them.

Cursing the fate that had brought Sophia and him together, only to force them apart, Lyle stared at the Kingston mansion as he neared the imposing structure. His direction in life had been determined long before he met Sophia. It was as much a part of him as the old resentments that loomed again as Aunt Edith returned to mind. Those resentments ran deep, for he could not remember that cold woman ever showing a spark of warmth for him in any of the many encounters that had taken place over the years. He recalled feeling the chill of her pale eyes as a child and the disapproval she masked with indifference. And he remembered his solemn vow that he would one day see acceptance in its place.

Lyle climbed the front steps, the thought suddenly striking him as he approached the door that no one would understand his feelings at this moment better than Sophia. His sudden longing for her was a squeezing knot deep inside him as the front door opened unexpectedly to the sight of Paul's embarrassed smile. Accepting the hand his cousin extended toward him in greeting, Lyle stepped over the threshold, his brow rising in an unspoken inquiry to which Paul responded without hesitation.

"I'm sorry, Lyle. I want you to know from the outset that I opposed this scheme."

"Scheme?"

"Scheme—for lack of a better word. I can't stay for dinner, but I wanted to warn you to keep your sense of humor tonight, Cousin. You're going to need it."

Urging him toward the sitting room, Paul called out in a voice rife with forced conviviality, "Lyle has arrived, Mother."

"Paul, dear." Aunt Edith rose from her chair and smiled indulgently. "It wasn't really necessary to bellow from the hall. We heard Lyle arrive as well as you did."

Recognizing Paul's action as a deliberate ploy to distract attention from him, Lyle gave the room a covert glance. Uncle Matthew occupied a chair in the far corner, appearing unexpectedly uncomfortable, and other than his aunt, his cousin, and himself, he saw only one other person. Muriel Moray, a thinner, paler version of her sister Edith, smiled nervously at him. Aunt Julia was conspicuously absent from the family gathering, and Lyle had the feeling that her exclusion was a carefully planned lapse.

As if attuned to his thoughts, Edith offered pleasantly, "We're pleased you were able to have dinner with us tonight, Lyle." She turned toward her husband with a rise of her brow that was more effective than a command. "Aren't we, Matthew?"

Rising on cue, Matthew extended his hand toward Lyle with a mumbled greeting. Appearing satisfied, Edith continued. "You do remember my sister, Mrs. Moray, don't you, Lyle?" Aunt Edith took his elbow and escorted him toward the nervous woman and Lyle subdued his surprise, suddenly realizing that his aunt had never before touched him of her own accord.

Lyle took the quiet woman's hand and murmured an appropriate response. He was surprised to find her hand cold despite the warmth of the night, and his suspicions grew as Edith took his arm again and guided him toward the window. "It's been many years, but I'm sure you remember my niece, Hope."

Lyle looked up, startled. He hadn't noticed the young woman who stood as quiet and still as a shadow, almost hidden by the heavy window hangings. Hope Moray watched him with narrowed eyes that were less than friendly, and it was immediately obvious as he greeted her with a formal smile that the woman was not much different from the girl he had first seen as a child of seven—homely, distressingly thin, and woefully lacking in social graces.

Edith glanced back toward the doorway where Paul remained watching. Her smile warmed. "I do wish you would reconsider and stay for dinner, dear."

"Paul said he can't stay, Edith. Leave it at that."

Matthew's sharp interjection turned Edith toward her husband with a frown, allowing Lyle to catch his cousin's eye again. At the amused twitch of Paul's lips, Lyle had the sudden feeling that this would be a night to remember.

The strokes of Sophia's pencil were unnaturally loud in the silence of the library as the image she sought continued to elude her. She had redrawn the same sketch several times since arriving, and a glance at the clock on the library wall revealed that she had accomplished nothing more in the thirty minutes she had been there than to ruin several sheets of valuable paper.

Sophia wiped the perspiration from her brow with the back of her hand, her concentration intense. She had experienced few problems with the designs completed so far. An afternoon dress with sweeping lines had seemed to flow from the tip of her pencil with ease. Sketches for a home gown and a graceful summer dress were also completed. She had even designed a lounge gown employing detailed silk appliqués. However, designing a gown for a formal occasion so foreign to her own social sphere left her at a distinct loss.

Sophia stared intently at the ball gown lightly sketched on the sheet before her, her concentration intensifying as a dancing couple slowly materialized in her mind. The image grew clearer, taking on life, and Sophia's heart began a heady pounding as she started to draw the sweeping gown the sophisticated socialite wore. The gown was lovely, of a shimmering vermilion silk similar to a scrap Papa had brought home a few nights previous. The low neckline, threaded with black velvet ribbon, hung gracefully from the shoulders, ending in balloon sleeves of white silk so fine as to be almost transparent. The bodice was close-fitting and threaded with the same black velvet ribbon stretching downward to end in black bows midway on the trained skirt. The crowning glory of the garment, however, was the hemline, edged so generously in a broad band of shirred white silk as to create a floating cloud that hovered just above the floor as the couple swirled to the steps of the dance. A bobbing black plume attached to the upward sweep of the hair, long white evening gloves with countless buttons, dark stockings, and dancing shoes with a graceful heel completed the stunning ensemble.

The gown Sophia saw so clearly in her mind took rapid shape on the paper in front of her. Clumsy in her haste to capture it completely before it faded from mind, she reached for a colored pencil, only to knock it to the floor. Grunting her displeasure, she stood up abruptly in an attempt to retrieve it, unexpectedly coming face-to-face with the person who had been standing behind her, staring over her shoulder.

Sophia gasped, her anger at Aaron Weiss's unexpected intrusion into her privacy forestalled by the incredulity in his expression as he whispered, "That design is brilliant! If I hadn't watched you draw it line for line, I wouldn't have believed it was yours."

Sophia stared icily at Aaron Weiss, sarcasm heavy in her reply. "Incredible, isn't it, that someone as *common* as I could conceive something so beautiful?" Satisfied at the embarrassed flush that rose to the fellow's face, she continued. "I hope you don't expect me to give up this sketch as easily as I did the other one last night, Mr. Weiss. I warn you. I won't."

Extreme discomfiture flashed across the wealthy young man's handsome face as he attempted a smile.

"My behavior last night was unforgivable. My only excuse is that I didn't expect to run into you on the street, and your sketch surprised me." Aaron searched her expression for a sign of softening. Seeing little change, he continued, his eyes surprisingly earnest. "I'm not very good at apologies, but I hope you'll believe me when I say that I truly regret the nature of our exchanges in the past. I'd like to change the poor impression you must have of me."

Sophia's eyes narrowed. "What difference does it

174

make what impression I have of you, Mr. Weiss?"

"Because I'd like to get to know you better."

Sophia's smile became caustic as his intentions became suddenly clear. "So, my reputation is more widespread than I dreamed." Her smile faded. "You're wasting your time, Mr. Weiss."

Sophia attempted to turn back to the table, only to have Weiss grasp her hands unexpectedly.

"Wait, please."

"Let me go."

"I want to help you."

"I don't need anyone's help."

"But I can—"

In a blur of movement too quick to immediately comprehend, Sophia was struck free of Aaron Weiss's grip and thrust backward against the bookcase to her rear. Recovering her balance in time to see Joey facing the taller man with obvious rage, Sophia rasped, "What are you doing, Joey? Get out of here before Mr. Little calls the police!"

"Do you think I care what that fat one does?" Joey's eyes were wild. "Carlo told me he saw you come here. It's my right to protect my future wife!"

"Wife!" Aaron turned incredulously toward Sophia. "You couldn't possibly intend to marry this fool! He's—"

Joey's swinging blow caught Aaron without warning, sending him staggering backward. Sophia's heart leaped as Weiss's back struck the bookcase behind him with a loud crack. She turned at the sound of approaching footsteps as the two men squared off menacingly.

"What's going on back there?" Appearing around the corner of the stacks, Horace Little glanced between the two men, then turned triumphantly toward Sophia. "I knew his would happen sooner or later!" Little's color heightened. "A woman like you has no place in a library. You make trouble wherever you go. I want all of

175

you out of here immediately or I'll call the police!"

Her heart pounding furiously, Sophia struggled to retain a calm facade. "I didn't do anything wrong." She motioned toward the table where her sketches lay. "I was working."

"Work? These?" Joey motioned scathingly toward the table beside him, hatred in his eyes. "You come here to waste time drawing pictures?" The venom in Joey's expression swelled as he swept the sheets off the table and crushed them purposefully in his fists. Victory shone in his gaze as Sophia gasped aloud.

"You damned fool!" Moving unexpectedly, Aaron caught Joey on the jaw with an unexpected blow that knocked him to the floor. Retrieving the balled sheets, Aaron paid as little attention to the fallen man as he did to the rocking bookcase behind him from which books spilled helter-skelter. Instead, he placed the wrinkled sheets in Sophia's hands, true regret in his eyes as he whispered, "I'm sorry."

"Hooligans!" Waving his arms wildly, his jowled cheeks flapping with supreme agitation, Little screeched, "Look what you did! Get out of here, all of you!"

The futility of protest obvious, Sophia gathered her things from the table. She turned toward the door, only to be halted by Little's rough hand on her arm as he hissed, "Oh, no, you don't!" His fingers bit painfully into her flesh as he pointed at Joey, who sat groggily on the floor. "Take *him* with you when you go!"

"If you're wise, you'll unhand Miss Marone."

Little turned with a start at the threat in Aaron's tone. His rounded chin rose haughtily. "How dare you address me in that tone of voice in my own library! Do you know who I am?"

Aaron's eyes were cold. "Do you know who *I* am?"

Little was incensed. "I neither know nor care who you are!"

"My name is Aaron Weiss."

Little's small eyes widened and his face paled. His Adam's apple bobbed almost comically before he finally managed, "My apologies to you, Mr. Weiss. Your father is one of our most valued patrons. However, I must still insist that Miss Marone and her friend leave. Their behavior is insufferable by any standards. Neither of them will be tolerated in this library again."

A small smile touched Aaron's lips. "Must I remind you that *I'm* the person who knocked this fellow down?"

"Provoked beyond endurance, I have no doubt."

Aaron's expression darkened. "You will apologize to Miss Marone."

"No." Little's rotund body appeared to swell with indignation. "She's a common young woman."

Aaron turned toward Sophia with an obvious effort at control. "Allow me to escort you to the street, Sophia. When Mr. Little is *replaced*—"

Unwilling to allow the situation to worsen with threats, Sophia turned abruptly toward the door. She was intensely aware of the light pressure of Aaron Weiss's hand on her elbow as he walked beside her.

Appearing a step behind them as they emerged onto the street, Joey commanded, "I'll take you home, Sophia."

Sophia's eyes fluttered briefly closed. She could not take much more. Her jaw firm moments later, she stated flatly, "I don't need an escort."

"I said, I'll take you home!"

Sophia's anger soared. "You will *not* take me home. I'm not going anywhere with you, Joey. *Capisce?*"

Joey's aggressive step toward her was halted by the warning rife in Aaron's voice as he interrupted. "If you're smart you'll stop right where you are! You've gotten away with too much already, and you're not going to get away with any more. I'm personally acquainted with Matthew Kingston. One word from me, and you'll find yourself without a job tomorrow morning. Another word from me in the right circles, and there won't be a mill in the city that'll hire you." Weiss paused, allowing the portent of his words to register in Joey's furious mind before continuing. "So I'm telling you now, for the last time, get out of here."

Joey glanced back at Sophia, his anger turning hard and cold with unspoken promise as Aaron's voice cut like a knife into the sudden silence. "One more thing. If you make trouble for Miss Marone in any way, either at work or at home, I'll make sure that you suffer the consequences."

Joey hesitated only a moment longer, his gaze bitter, before turning away. The heat in his final glance lingered in Sophia's mind as he turned out of sight.

"May I escort you home, Sophia?"

Frowning, Sophia looked up at Aaron Weiss. She was confused by his unexpected efforts in her behalf and more shaken than she wished to reveal by the horrendous scene which had just transpired. Aware that she was not due to meet Anna and Rosalie for another hour, she shook her head. "I can't go home yet."

Unexpected compassion appeared in Weiss's dark eyes. "May I take you somewhere else, then?"

Sophia did not respond. She had nowhere to go—no one to turn to. Her sketches were ruined . . .

"May I take you for a ride, perhaps? My carriage is on the corner."

Sophia turned to look at the gleaming black carriage toward which Aaron Weiss motioned.

"Sophia . . ." The disturbed note in Aaron Weiss's voice turned her back to him as he continued. "That fellow's out of sight, but I wouldn't put it past him to be waiting for you in the dark somewhere. For the sake of my peace of mind, please . . ."

Silent, Sophia studied Aaron Weiss's handsome face.

178

His eyes were intense, glittering pools of concern. She read an unexpected sincerity there, where she had seen only a self-confident arrogance before. She didn't fool herself that he was all that he pretended to be, but she was suddenly too tired to care.

"All right, I'll ride with you."

Sophia was seated beside Aaron Weiss in the carriage as it moved down the street at a sedate pace when Aaron spoke again.

"I'd like to see the rest of your sketches, Sophia."

Sophia was not of a mood for games. "Why?"

"Why?" Aaron studied her silently for a long moment, and Sophia was intensely aware of his dark eyes moving over her face. He was considering the question carefully, and she experienced again a sense of surprise that this wealthy, arrogant man should be so concerned with her impression of him. He finally responded, "Because you're sitting beside me as my guest in this carriage, and I've come to realize that there's more to Sophia Marone than meets the eye. I'd like to know more. You have an incredible talent, as rough as it is—"

"As rough as it is?" Sophia's lips tightened.

Aaron took her hands into his unexpectedly. He was so close that she could see the dark pupils within the blackness of his eyes and could feel his intensity. She read a true fervor in those eyes, and startling her even more, a glimmer of respect that had been totally absent before. She paused to consider it, the male scent he wore touching her senses. It was the same expensive scent that had lingered long after he departed the mill that last time, and it occurred to her that although this handsome man smelled better than many of the women she knew, there was nothing feminine about him—that, indeed, the opposite was true, and she need be cautious for the sake of all she was and all she hoped to be.

Aaron's grip on her hands tightened as he responded

179

unexpectedly, "There're some things that need be said if we're to proceed with any honesty between us, Sophia." Aaron paused, looking at her with an intensity that sent confusing, almost debilitating, tremors down Sophia's spine. The heat of his gaze was mesmerizing as he continued slowly. "I was intrigued by you the first time I saw you, but you made it plain that you wanted nothing to do with me. That was a new experience for me that made me more determined than ever to get to know you." Aaron paused again. His gaze flickered before he proceeded determinedly, "There's no other way to say it. The truth is that I was waiting for you outside Lyle Kingston's flat when I ran into you last night, and that I followed you to the library tonight."

Sophia recoiled spontaneously, snatching back her hands.

"Please let me finish, Sophia." Something in his tone held her immobile as he continued. "I was confused by you. You weren't what I expected you to be when I spoke to you in the mill, and then when I saw your sketch, I realized that I had underestimated you in more ways than I realized. I behaved like the cad that I'm certain you thought me to be in wresting that sketch away from you, and when you left me standing on the street with it in my hand, I felt like a fool. I was determined to change your opinion of me. I wanted to impress you, so . . ." Aaron took a deep breath and plunged on, "So I took the sketch to Madame Tourneau for her opinion."

"You didn't!" Dismay bringing her close to tears, Sophia shook her head in unconscious denial. "It wasn't ready to be shown yet! You've ruined any chance I could've had with her!"

"Madame Tourneau liked it."

Sophia's jaw dropped with surprise, allowing Aaron the opportunity he intended. "I persuaded her to let me bring you in to talk to her about employment in her salon. That is what you want, isn't it?"

A long silent moment passed before Sophia spoke again.

"Why are you suddenly so interested in helping me?"

"Your talent—"

"My talent? Did you follow me to Lyle's house because of my talent? Did you follow me tonight for the same reason?"

Aaron stiffened. "I followed you because I wanted to get to know you, and—"

"And?"

Aaron's gaze remained steady. "And because I've always been determined to get what I want, one way or the other."

The fellow's blatant audacity left Sophia trembling with rage. "So, the truth at last, just when I was trying to convince myself that you meant what you said about wanting to help me."

"I did mean what I said." For an unknown reason, Aaron's discomfiture touched her as he continued earnestly. "I meant every word."

Sophia shook her head, her smile caustic. "What do you really want, Mr. Weiss?"

Weiss paused. "I want you to call me Aaron . . . and I want to be your friend."

"Friend?" Sophia laughed aloud, a sound totally void of mirth, and Aaron frowned at the vehemence of her reaction in the moment before she responded emphatically, "No. I've had enough of friendships."

"I want to help you."

Sophia's smile was brittle. "You're very clever, aren't you, *Aaron*. You hope to tease me with the prize just beyond my reach, but there's something you haven't taken into account. You see, I've spent every day of my life working toward that prize. I'll get it, with or without you."

"But I can make it easier for you . . . faster!"

Sophia's smile hardened. "Ah, but the payment you would ask in return . . ."

"If I said I want nothing from you, would you believe me?"

Sophia's reply was unhesitant. "No."

"If I said I wanted only what you were willing to give freely, would you believe me then?"

Sophia paused, acutely aware of his nearness and the growing heat of his gaze. She slowly shook her head. "I'm not sure."

"Would you believe me if I told you that I respect everything you've managed to accomplish, and that I want to help you succeed in doing what you've worked so hard to do? Would you believe me if I told you that you've made me more aware of my privileged existence than I've ever been before, and that by helping you take this last step, I'll be achieving something for myself as well?"

Almost overwhelmed by the powerful physical presence of this enigmatic man who stared intently into her eyes, Sophia managed a shaky laugh. "And would you believe, my dear fellow, that you're pushing believability a bit too far?"

Unable to suppress a smile at her frankness, Aaron pressed earnestly. "Will you let me help you, Sophia—just because I want to help you?"

Openly studying Aaron Weiss, Sophia saw hope dawn in the dark eyes that studied her intently in return. She responded slowly.

"I suppose I owe you something for rescuing me to-night, whatever your motives. I was too spent to deal with Joey, and the truth is that I'm too spent now to deny that I would welcome the help you offer."

Aaron released a tense breath, his relief apparent. "I'll speak to Madame Tourneau again tomorrow."

Unwilling to chance her voice, Sophia nodded. She turned her attention back to the crushed sketches on the seat beside her. The sound of the horse's hooves against the cobbled street reverberated in the silence as she looked down at them, her mind racing. So engrossed was she that she did not see the intensity with which Aaron regarded her bent head. She did not see him devour her with his gaze, nor did she see the cold triumph that grew in his smile.

Chapter Nine

The previous evening at the Kingston mansion behind him, Lyle sat at his desk, staring toward the mill entrance as the first mill workers filtered through the door. Carlo Rinaldi—always among the first, Gino Scalzone—muttering to himself, Jacque Montepelier—his eyes shifty. Lyle halted in his thoughts, watching Montepelier until he turned out of sight behind the machines. Something was going on . . .

Lyle cursed under his breath. He had warned his uncle that the doubling of loom assignments was an issue that had been fought from its inception. He had told him that the weavers were organized and the subject should be broached carefully if he wanted to avoid trouble, but, as usual, Uncle Matthew refused to listen. From the expressions of some of the weavers, it seemed word had somehow leaked about Uncle Matthew's intention to follow the lead of some of the other mills in implementing the new policy tomorrow.

Angela Moretti and her brother Joey walked through the entrance, interrupting Lyle's train of thought. Lyle's stomach clenched as Joey turned to look at him unexpectedly. His hands balled into fists as the fellow held contact with his gaze for long seconds, sneering openly before turning his back and heading toward his machine. The instinctive desire to wipe that look from Moretti's face in the same way he had removed similar sneers from similar faces in his youth was never stronger. However, he could not afford to indulge his anger in direct confrontation, especially now, with trouble pending in the mill, and with the previous night's surprising dinner with his aunt and uncle still fresh in his mind.

Hope Moray's unsmiling face returned to mind, and Lyle could not suppress the spontaneous swell of pity that rose inside him, despite the frigidity with which the plain young woman had treated him. In different ways, they both were less than they should be in Aunt Edith's eyes, and it appeared that Aunt Edith had plans for the two misfits of the family.

Standing, Lyle walked to the cabinet behind him and withdrew the file he sought. His jaw hardened. Aunt Edith's plan repelled him; however, he knew his aunt too well to believe the plan could be as simple as it appeared. He had determined during the long night just past that he would allow the devious woman to indulge her little games for as long as it suited him, for the truth was, he had little to lose and much to gain if his cooperation drew him deeper into the family business. And he knew his determination was such that he would win out in the end.

Walking back to his desk with a darkening frown, Lyle slapped down the file and looked up again at the mill entrance. He was well aware, as he looked intently through the glass at the thickening stream of workers, that his sleeplessness the previous night was not due to the unexpected turn in his relationship with his aunt and uncle. His heart jumped to a rapid beat as Sophia entered amidst the dark-haired throng, and Lyle suddenly realized that he had been hungry for the sight of her almost to the point of physical discomfort.

Intensely aware of the danger in that weakness, Lyle watched Sophia weave her way through the aisles toward her machines. Another voice in his mind interrupted his thoughts, nagging viciously that he had forced a separation between them just when Sophia needed him most. His conflicting thoughts raged as Sophia turned toward him unexpectedly. The sudden impact of her direct gaze left him defenseless. She did not smile. Motionless, waiting, Lyle felt his heart sink as Sophia slowly turned away.

"Sophia . . ."

Sophia jumped at the sound of Joey's voice beside her. She glanced spontaneously toward the office where Lyle had stood a moment earlier, grateful to see his attention diverted as Matthew Kingston stepped out of the inner office. She sighed with relief, only to utter a startled protest as Joey pulled her roughly out of sight of the glass enclosure.

"Puttana . . ."

"Watch what you say, Joey!"

Joey laughed harshly as he motioned toward the office with a twist of his head. "That fellow in there doesn't know yet that you've found someone to replace him. He'll soon find out, and then I will laugh."

"Get away from me!"

"I'll go." Joey's expression darkened. "I'll turn my back on you, but I tell you now that you'll be the one who regrets this moment someday, knowing that you could have been lying in my arms instead of—"

"Never!" Revulsion flushing her face with heat, Sophia repeated, "Never!"

His passion poorly concealed, Joey rasped, "Face of an angel and heart of a devil. Your own will claim you in the end!"

Joey disappeared into the next aisle as abruptly as he had appeared. Sophia attempted to dismiss the hatred of his words, telling herself as she resumed her work moments later that she felt no regrets, but she knew those words to be untrue.

Glancing up from the whirling bobbins in front of her, Sophia looked toward the office once more. She saw Lyle's blond head bent over the file on his desk. She saw the stretch of his broad shoulders under the white shirt he wore and she remembered the comfort she had felt in his embrace. He glanced up momentarily and she saw the flash of honey-colored eyes that warmed to molten gold when he smiled. She remembered the beauty of that rare smile. She remembered tracing it with her fingertips that day on the bridge above the falls, and she remembered the shudder that had shaken him when she did. She remembered wishing then that things were different, that they could both shake off the world and follow where the spontaneous warmth between them would lead. And she remembered telling him then that she knew they could never be more than friends.

The ache inside Sophia deepened. She missed the closeness her *caro* Lyle and she had shared. She missed talking to him. She missed his gentle touch, the sweet, clean scent of him, and the comfort of his arms when it seemed the world had turned against her. She missed the feeling that he understood better than anyone else the needs that drove her because similar needs drove him as well. And despite the differences that had driven them apart, Sophia consoled herself that he still cared. She knew he did, because *she* still cared as well. Their souls had touched. That could not be undone, and she suffered the weight of a bond that held fast, despite the attempt to sever it.

Stiffening as a foreign image intruded into her thoughts, Sophia knew that she could not expect the same of Aaron Weiss. Charming Aaron, with his wealth and influence and his desire to impress her, could not be trusted. Desperation had forced a liaison she would not have considered a few weeks earlier. She was wary of it and of the handsome mill owner's spoiled son, and she wondered what the evening to come would truly bring.

Matthew Kingston pulled the office door shut behind him and strode across the mill floor toward the exit. Lyle contemplated his uncle's well-tailored back with a hard smile. The forced conviviality of the previous evening was gone. His uncle had been barely civil upon arriving at the mill that morning, confirming Lyle's conclusion that the unexpected dinner invitation had been orchestrated by Aunt Edith and that his wife's change of attitude, whether false or true, had rubbed his uncle raw. He had not bothered to mention the subject of doubling loom assignments again. His uncle was adamant. It would go into effect tomorrow.

A sound at the inner office door turned Lyle toward it as Paul stepped into sight, his expression tense. In answer to Lyle's unspoken inquiry, Paul responded, "Father and I are going to a meeting at the Hamilton Club. His mood is foul this morning, Lyle. What did you do to him last night?"

Lyle shrugged. "Nothing at all. Your mother did most of the talking."

"That's the trouble, then." Paul appeared concerned. "I love my mother, Lyle, but I know her better than most . . . so please understand when I warn you that she's up to something."

"I know."

"She can twist my father around her little finger when she feels it worth the effort." At Lyle's surprise, Paul shrugged. "How do you think I've managed to survive all these years?"

Lyle scrutinized his cousin intensely. "Do you still intend to go to Paris to study, Paul?"

"Yes."

"Does your mother know."

"Yes."

Lyle nodded. "Thanks for your honesty, Paul."

Paul hesitated. "You *do* know that I'm the only member of my family that you can count on being truly honest with you."

"Yes, I know."

"I'm sorry, Lyle. I don't know why you put up with all of it."

"I do."

Giving Lyle's cryptic statement only a moment's thought, Paul turned toward the door with a grimace. "Father's waiting."

Lyle nodded. Yes, Uncle Matthew was waiting . . .

Night had fallen. The small jacquard room at the rear of the general offices of Weiss Mill was lit as brightly as day although the mill was empty and still. Sophia had arrived there moments earlier with Aaron, still uncomfortable with the memory of her sisters surprised glances when they saw the Weiss carriage waiting in the prearranged spot as they turned the corner. Upset as she had been the previous night, she had confided only the necessary details to them. She had been at a loss to explain her instinctive feeling that time had become her enemy, that she was suddenly more alone than she had ever been despite Aaron's offer of help, and that she must move quickly or her dreams would fade like the rainbows in the mist at the foot of the falls, never to become reality.

Sophia paused in her thoughts, assessing the wild disorder of the jacquard room as Aaron busied himself at a nearby table. Books, pattern sketches, and miscellaneous bolts of silk were strewn about, accumulating in tottering piles on corner desks. Colored inks and pens, chalks, and crayons were carelessly tossed into metal trays stacked nearby, and jacquard cards, the final product of the hours of specialized work done at the drawing table where she sat, lay in a careless heap on a stand near the door. She had silently despaired of the confusion at first, only to discover that Aaron was completely at home in the chaos, and that this chaos was deceiving.

Sophia considered that thought again. The room was like Aaron Weiss—not exactly as it appeared and difficult to fathom. She had not been prepared for the professional side of the unpredictable fellow which emerged as they stepped through the door. She had not expected the spoiled son of Samuel Weiss to be so knowledgeable.

Watching as Aaron collected various sketching materials from the stacked trays, Sophia realized that there was another change in Aaron as well. The fashionable, arrogant man whose conceited insensitivity had so repulsed her in their earlier meetings had disappeared. Another fellow had emerged in his stead, a serious young man who had shed his meticulously tailored jacket upon entering the room, who had loosened his tie and rolled up his sleeves with complete disregard for appearance. This man, with his heavy dark hair ruffled in a way that lent an unexpected vulnerability to his impressive presence, was appealing in a way the other was not. It struck her as he turned unexpectedly in her direction that he was incredibly handsome. She knew that the other Aaron Weiss was well aware of that fact, but about this fellow who looked at her so directly with eyes as dark as black velvet, she wondered . . .

The electric light above Sophia's head reflected in her glimmering tresses, igniting their fire anew as Aaron looked up from the cluttered trays in front of him. Aaron's heart began a heady pounding as the beautiful witch looked at him thoughtfully, her incredibly fine features drawn as if by a master's hand. She looked away to concentrate on the abused sketches lying on the drawing board in front of her, but Aaron's gaze lingered on her mouth. He could almost taste it.

A shudder chased down Aaron's spine. He was rapidly becoming obsessed with Sophia Marone. He recalled the restlessness with which he had passed the day, the rise of his anticipation as evening came, the sharpening of his senses the moment Sophia and her sisters turned the corner of Prospect Street into sight. He had almost laughed at the suspicion Sophia's sisters displayed toward him, those plain little wrens who were kin to an extravagantly beautiful bird of paradise who wanted more from life than she had been given.

The silence of the jacquard room grew pronounced, and Aaron felt a familiar heat rise inside him. He despised this game of cat-and-mouse he was forced to play, even as he consoled himself that this "courtship" was necessary. Sophia was too clever to give what she had to offer without gaining the most she could in return. However, Aaron consoled himself that as clever as she was, Sophia was merely a novice in a game where he was a proven master.

Aaron restrained a smile, silently congratulating himself on his earnest "confession" the previous evening. It had been a stroke of genius. He had taken a chance in revealing so much to Sophia, but he had needed to do something to offset her first impression of him. He had needed to put her off balance with his sincerity. And he had done it so well.

Still staring at Sophia's bent head, Aaron restrained a gasp as she moved unexpectedly. Her hair parted, exposing the creamy nape of her neck, and Aaron's heart pounded harder as he imagined trailing his lips against that white skin. He wanted to hear her soft moans of pleasure, to feel her turn in his arms to welcome him.

191

He wanted . . .

Aaron closed his eyes briefly in an attempt to control the sudden leap of his emotions. He wanted Sophia Marone badly. He would not be satisfied until the suspicion in her eyes was replaced by passion and her self-possessed arrogance replaced by pleading hunger. He wanted to feel her under him, subservient to him. He wanted to possess her completely. He wanted to forget that she had loved a bastard before him and that she might be thinking of him even now.

Uncomfortable with his thoughts, Aaron averted his gaze. He despised this unexpected jealousy that Sophia incited. It diluted the power he had always enjoyed wielding in his amorous liaisons and he was humiliated by his vulnerability to the persistent gnawings of such a demeaning emotion. He had been with many women—women of quality far above this common immigrant girl, but he had never been so affected.

Sophia looked up again, frowning as she said abruptly, "I'll never finish redrawing these sketches in time to show them to Madame Tourneau tomorrow."

"We'll finish." Aaron selected the paper he sought from the shelf over his head and walked to her side. His expression sober, he leafed through the wrinkled sketches, finally choosing the amber lounge gown that he had so clearly imagined Sophia wearing. He flattened the sketch over the screen on a lighted box nearby and secured the paper atop it. The sketch was clearly visible underneath as he positioned the paper carefully and traced a few strokes of the design before looking back up at Sophia.

"I'll trace the sketches, which will give you time to finish up the finer details. You don't have to worry about the quality of my work. I've had professional training, so I'm more than capable of reproducing rough outlines. If we work together, we'll have plenty of time to finish. As for setting up a meeting with Madame Tourneau so quickly, I've learned that striking while the iron is hot is an axiom that's unwise to ignore."

Sophia observed him silently, her doubts obvious, and Aaron's annoyance surged. He suddenly realized that dealing with this young woman was going to be a lesson in forbearance that he would not particularly enjoy. If he were not certain he could achieve his ends no other way . . .

Carefully assessing the result of his work a short time later, Aaron ran his manicured fingers through his hair, unconsciously adding a new depth of disorder to his ruffled appearance. Uncomfortable in the heat of the airless room, he unbuttoned his collar and rolled up his shirtsleeves further. Looking up unexpectedly, he caught Sophia watching him. He noted with surprise that a small smile played at the corners of her tempting lips. Suddenly conscious of his disheveled appearance, Aaron stiffened.

"Did I do something to amuse you, Sophia?"

Sophia's smile broadened, stealing his breath with its beauty as she responded, "Not really. It's just that I find I'm a bit more comfortable with you now that you no longer look prettier than I do."

Sophia's smile coaxed one from him in return, despite her audacious remark, and Aaron was abruptly certain that the ravishing Sophia was going to make this game he played more entertaining than he had ever hoped it could be.

"You must tell me the truth, Lyle."

Aunt Julia stood rigidly just inside the door of Lyle's flat, refusing to take another step as Lyle closed the door behind her. Aware that his aunt's supreme agitation was demonstrated as clearly by her unannounced arrival at his door at such a late hour as it was by the trembling of

193

her frail frame, Lyle took her elbow with concern.

"Please sit down, Aunt Julia. I'll make some tea."

"I don't want tea, Lyle. I want an answer." Julia's tone was clipped and impatient, and it was suddenly obvious to Lyle that his aunt's trembling had no relation to her delicate condition. Aunt Julia wasn't weak. She was furious.

"Please don't upset yourself, Aunt Julia. I really found it quite amusing that Aunt Edith should think to bring the two misfits of the family together."

"So it *is* true!" Aunt Julia's pale lips twitched. Her minute frame appeared to swell with intensity as she rasped, "How *dare* Matthew do such a thing! How *dare* he call you to his house to parade Edith's niece in front of you like a brood mare being offered up for stud!"

"Aunt Julia!" His aunt's bluntness was startling. It was so out of character for her that Lyle would have been tempted to laugh had her trembling not increased to an alarming degree. Slipping his arm around her shoulders, Lyle ushered her toward the settee. Seated beside her, he took her hand. "I suppose Aunt Edith thought I'd be flattered to be considered worthy of a Leighton. Before yesterday, I'd have thought Aunt Edith would've preferred to shoot the filly rather than offer her to me."

"It isn't amusing, Lyle." Aunt Julia remained rigid, her expression unsmiling. "This is by far the worst of a long line of insults my brother has made you suffer, but this time he's gone too far."

"If it's any consolation to you, Aunt Julia, I think Uncle Matthew is uncomfortable with the situation."

"He should be. He'll be more uncomfortable after I've finished speaking to him."

"Please, Aunt Julia." Truly concerned, Lyle attempted to allay his aunt's anger with a smile. "I've thought the whole thing over and decided to let Aunt Edith play out her game."

"I'm sorry, Lyle." Rising to her feet, Aunt Julia spoke in a voice that allowed no quarter. "I won't be so easily satisfied."

Aunt Julia paused, her expression reflecting a sudden remorse that was unexpected as he stood beside her. Looking intently into his eyes, she whispered, "I'm so sorry for having let you down all these years, Lyle. I haven't done well by you, but I give you my word, you won't suffer in the end."

Sliding his arms around Julia with spontaneous warmth, Lyle hugged her briefly. "You don't have to promise me anything, Aunt Julia. You've always given me your best. No one could ask for more."

"You're deserving of more, Lyle. Much more."

Lyle smiled. "You're prejudiced."

"And you're too generous with an old woman who hasn't lived up to her responsibilities as she should." When Lyle began to protest again, Julia shook her head and stepped back, her head high. "I'll be leaving now. Please don't trouble yourself about me. I'm fine."

Stopping him as he attempted to accompany her out through the doorway, Julia smiled. "No, please. Maggie's waiting for me in the carriage. You needn't be concerned."

Lyle watched from his doorway as his aunt walked down the staircase toward the entrance to the street. Upset by her distress, he remained staring at the closed door for long moments after she had pulled it closed behind her.

His view obscured, Lyle did not see Maggie step down onto the curb to assist her mistress up into the carriage. Nor did he see the anger that tightened Julia's lips as she whispered in response to the inquisitive rise of her maid's brow, "Yes, it's true, Maggie. Every word of it!"

As he turned back to his rooms and closed the door behind him, Lyle did not hear the determination ring in his aunt's voice as she looked up at her driver and commanded sharply, "Take me to my brother . . . now!"

Aaron was uncomfortable with the unexpected silence in his carriage as it turned onto Market Street for the second time that evening. It was a silence that had grown more pronounced with each block that brought Sophia nearer to her home, and he was uncertain as to the cause.

The evening had gone well. Working side by side, they had duplicated all but one of her ruined sketches. He had been stunned at Sophia's quick grasp of the few techniques of execution he had showed her, and although her efforts were far from expert, he knew they would impress even the sophisticated Madame Tourneau.

Aaron turned again to Sophia's profile etched against the streetlight shining through the window of the carriage. A familiar hunger stirred inside him. She was exquisite, possessed of a beauty that thrived on close scrutiny. He had never seen skin as clear and smooth as Sophia's, nor had he ever seen such perfection of feature. Her eyes were so clear that the brilliance was almost translucent. They were set to perfection above cheekbones that were flawlessly sculpted, and the subtle impudence of her nose suited her well without intruding into the graceful symmetry of her face. And her mouth . . .

The carriage drew to a halt and Sophia moved toward the door. Staying her, Aaron held her arm firmly but gently, careful to conceal his sudden anxiety.

"Sophia, wait. Is something wrong? You look upset."

"No, no . . ." Sophia shook her head, her frown deepening. "I was just thinking about tomorrow." Sophia paused. "It'll be difficult for me to get away from the mill in the morning if things don't go as expected. And even if I do, Madame Tourneau might not like the rest of my work."

Suddenly realizing that Sophia didn't truly understand the influence the Weiss name wielded, Aaron also realized that it was perhaps better if she did not. "Don't worry about tomorrow," he responded simply. "Everything will be all right."

Helping her down from the carriage moments later, Aaron watched as Sophia joined her sisters where they stood expectantly on the corner. He waited until they turned out of sight before getting back in his carriage, feeling suddenly disconcerted. He checked his watch. The evening was still young and Harry was awaiting his direction. Suddenly aware of the long empty hours ahead of him while he would be tormented by Sophia's image and his obsessive desire for her, he swore under his breath and instructed, "Wanda's house, Harry."

They had gone no more than a block when Aaron cursed again and tapped the roof of the carriage.

"Forget it, Harry. Take me home."

Aaron settled back against the seat, frowning. Why was he going home when he could be spending the remainder of the evening being entertained by the endlessly inventive Wanda? Aaron paused to consider his own confusing behavior. He supposed the answer was simple. He was not of a mood to appease his hunger with common fare when there was a magnificent feast in the offing.

The silence behind the closed doors of Matthew Kingston's study was ominous as Edith paused, her hand on the knob. Unable to rationalize her reluctance to intrude, Edith reviewed the events of the previous few minutes, her shock still acute.

It had been a quiet evening. Relaxed, taking their tea in the parlor as was their usual custom, Matthew and she were unprepared for Julia's abrupt entrance as she suddenly appeared in the doorway of the room, their protesting maid beside her. The look about Julia's small eyes had been as startling as her unannounced appearance. Edith remembered rising to extend a welcome, only to have Julia snap in a barely recognizable voice, "I wish to speak to Matthew alone."

Communicating with his diminutive sister in a way that was a complete mystery to her, Matthew had stated flatly, "I don't wish to discuss it, Julia!"

"You *will* discuss it, Matthew!" The adamancy in Julia's soft response had stunned Edith as the small woman challenged, "You will discuss it—now!"

Matthew had then shocked her by ordering, "Stay here, Edith. My sister obviously won't be satisfied until she's had her say. We'll go into the study."

The door closed behind them a few minutes later and in the ensuing moments, Edith's shock had yielded to outrage.

Edith's slender frame grew rigid. How dare Matthew ban her from a room in her own house! How dare he exclude her from a discussion that obviously concerned family! Most infuriating of all, how dare Julia, an indigent relative who had relied on their charity most of her life, take command of a situation in a home that was not her own!

Trembling with righteous fury, Edith pushed open the study door.

The tense discussion between brother and sister came to an abrupt halt as their eyes turned toward her with mutual impatience.

"Please leave us alone, Edith. This discussion is a private affair between Julia and me."

Edith's pale face twitched. "This is *my* house. I go *where* I please in it, *when* I please."

Matthew's expression, suddenly unyieldingly austere, set Edith back a step even before he commanded sharply,

"Get out, Edith."

Edith hesitated a moment longer.

"I said, get out!"

The door closed behind Edith with a hard snap that rang in the silence that followed, but Matthew was immune to the harsh vibrations as he faced his sister's resolute stance. Julia's burning stare impaled him as she spoke in a tone that did not rise above a hiss.

"I've put up with everything you've done over the years, Matthew. I've swallowed the mockery you made of our father's wishes, and I've allowed myself to remain beholden to your charity, all the while knowing full well that my rightful inheritance was the sum you claimed as your own when you married your wealthy wife. I did that because you were my brother, my only living relative, and I loved you."

The glitter of tears in Julia's small eyes hardened as she continued with no lessening of emotion, "I allowed you to dictate the course of my life, to direct it into channels that you felt would reflect well on the image you wished the Kingston name to project, because I respected you and all you wished to achieve."

Julia's small hands slowly clenched into fists. Her voice gradually grew in volume, shaking with fury as she rasped, "When I took Lyle into my home, I allowed your rage to cower me. I allowed you to convince me that boarding school would be best for a dear, angry, orphaned boy who needed love more than the education you touted would be his salvation. I allowed you to make me send him away! And when he returned, a grown man, handsome, educated, and intelligent beyond your wildest expectations, I allowed you to push him aside!"

"I did not push him aside! He works as my mill supervisor."

"Only because you had no recourse—because you needed him! But now this . . . this scheme, this humiliation—!"

"Do you realize what you're saying, Julia?" Matthew interrupted harshly. "Hope Moray comes from Leighton stock!"

"Hope Moray is a colorless snob of mediocre intelligence who isn't worthy of Lyle!"

"Marriage with a Moray will make Lyle socially acceptable! When Paul goes to France to study . . ." Matthew began breathing more heavily, revealing the stress of his words, "then perhaps I'll train him to work with me, and eventually—"

" 'Eventually?' " Julia's discerning eye did not fail her. "Liar! You hope to mislead Lyle . . . to use him while you need him . . . to make him think that because he married a Moray, he could eventually follow you. Then when Paul returns—"

"That's right!" Matthew's eyes widened with fury, spittle spraying from his lips as he rasped, "Lyle will never assume the reins of Kingston Mill! He's a bastard!"

"He's a Kingston!"

"He's a bastard!"

"Matthew, he's your *son!*"

His livid color draining abruptly, Matthew took a step backward. He shook his head adamantly. "He's not my son. He's the son of an immigrant British whore."

"He's the son of you and your former mistress."

"He is not! His mother slept with many men, even while I supported her and she swore fidelity to me! I found her with a man in the very bed we shared! I threw her out and she had the audacity to come to me later and claim that she carried my child."

"Lyle *is* your child."

"He is not! I will never believe that he is!" Matthew slowly straightened, his expression hardening.

"Have you told Lyle this lie? Is that why he dogs my steps, mimicking me, shaping himself in my image?"

"It isn't a lie. It's a sad truth of which Lyle is unaware—a secret his mother carried to her grave. If you see yourself in Lyle, it's merely your own blood holding true."

"Lyle is not my son!" Struggling to regain his composure, Matthew continued. "Paul is my son. He's the only son I'll ever have, and if you tell Lyle this lie that you perpetuate, I promise you that I'll drive him off. I'll see that he's banned from the mills. I'll—"

"While we're delivering ultimatums, Matthew," Julia interrupted softly, her slight frame as erect as a statue, "I warn you now that I'll stand for your despicable treatment of Lyle no longer. If you try to implement any of the loathsome practices you've just mentioned, I'll shout the truth of Lyle's birthright from the housetops." Halting for emphasis, Julia whispered, "But the first person I'll tell will be *Edith*."

The spasmodic jerk of Matthew's cleanly shaven cheek revealed the impact of her statement as she continued. "You know what her reaction will be. She'll never forgive you for displacing *her* son as your firstborn. Need I tell you what her next move will be—proud, haughty Edith, who shares ownership of the mill with you?"

Matthew paused to scrutinize his sister's deceptively fragile appearance. He smiled tightly. "So, you're a Kingston after all, Julia."

"I am. And so is Lyle."

Matthew's expression turned abruptly hard. "Lyle is *not* my son."

"He is."

"I told you, I'll never believe that."

"You won't allow yourself to believe it."

Matthew's expression was suddenly weary. "What do you want from me, Julia?"

201

Julia paused at her brother's unexpectedly passive tone, her mien unchanging. "Sadly, I don't expect you to claim Lyle as your son at this point in time, but that's your loss. However, I do expect you to treat him fairly and with honesty. No more lies. No more deceit."

"Is that all?"

Julia hesitated, studying her brother's face. "I suppose that's very little for a sister to ask of her brother. But I somehow fear it to be beyond you."

"Damn you, Julia!"

"Do I have your word?"

Matthew paused, hesitant.

"Do I?"

"Yes."

Julia continued to stare at him, prompting Matthew's sudden, vehement response. "Yes! I told you, yes! What more do you want me to say?"

Julia did not flinch in the face of Matthew's fury. Undaunted, she spoke in a voice that did not waver. "I beg you not to dismiss our discussion here today, Matthew, for the sake of all involved."

Turning, Julia drew open the door. Silent as a shadow she stepped into the hallway, leaving Matthew in the reverberations of her wake.

"Do you like Mr. Weiss, Sophia?" Rosalie spoke in a whisper as the gleaming carriage from which Sophia had alighted moments earlier slipped from their sight on the darkened street. Sophia turned, the shadow of the streetlamp holding her face in dark relief, cheating Rosalie of the opportunity she sought to assess her sister's reaction as she spoke.

"You're worried about me, Rosalie?"

Aware that Sophia had not answered her question, Rosalie urged, "Do you?"

Sophia's step slowed as her sister's keen stare remained intent on her face. "I don't know. Aaron Weiss is a clever one. I have a feeling I see only what he allows me to see." Sophia shrugged. "Sometimes I like what I see, and sometimes I don't—"

"I don't like the way he looks at you." Anna interrupted unexpectedly. "He doesn't look at you the way other men do. Alfredo, Guiseppi, even Joey—they watch the way you walk, they look at your hips, they look at your face and hair. They smile at you or are angry at you, but they admire you. This one is different."

Sophia's smile did not reach her eyes. "My new 'friend' is a man who likes playing games with women because he's so successful at them."

Rosalie's eyes widened and she swallowed with obvious anxiety. "But . . . but does he hope to play with you the same way?"

Sophia nodded. "I have no doubt that he does. Mr. Aaron Weiss thinks himself to be far more clever than I am, but he isn't. He doesn't know that I've played similar games many times, and that I'm as much an expert as he."

"But you aren't an expert, Sophia. You haven't even kissed a man yet!" Rosalie paused in afterthought, "Have you?"

Sophia raised her brows. "Little sisters shouldn't ask so many questions."

"But you haven't kissed as many men as Aaron Weiss!"

"I don't think Mr. Weiss cares to kiss men."

"Oh, Sophia, you know what I mean . . ."

Sophia's momentary levity faded. "Yes, I know what you mean, Rosalie, and you mustn't worry. Aaron Weiss hopes to overwhelm me with his charm, but I'm not the fool he thinks me to be."

Rosalie was confused. "Why do you bother with him then?"

"Because he can help me." A new note entered Sophia's voice, ringing a warning bell in Rosalie's mind as Sophia continued. "We worked well together tonight, and we finished days of work in one night because he was able to show me things he learned in school, things that I couldn't learn from books. He said he'll take me to meet Madame Tourneau tomorrow so I can get a position in her salon."

Rosalie's bright eyes pinned her. "Do you believe him?"

Sophia hesitated, then responded, "I believe him because he believes his patience will earn him a *special* reward."

"Sophia!"

Sophia shrugged. "Don't worry, Rosalie. Aaron Weiss isn't as smart as he thinks he is."

Their conversation ceased as they neared the alleyway that led to the rear yard of their home. Sophia was suddenly grateful for the interruption in their exchange as she paused to allow her sisters to precede her. Following behind them, she affixed a confident expression on her face, the shield she often used when she became uncomfortably aware that her bravado rang far from true.

Chapter Ten

"It's true, Mama." Excitement crept into Rosalie's eyes as her mother turned toward the breakfast table, kettle in hand. "I heard Joey and Vito talking yesterday. They said Mr. Kingston is pressing his employees too hard and the union is organizing in protest. They said that Mr. Kingston is planning to have the weavers double up on loom assignments so his profits will rise, but that we'll all find ourselves out of a job if we let him get away with it. They said if the announcement is made this morning, they're going to strike."

Maria assessed her daughters' expressions as the newly risen sun brightened her kitchen, reflecting its glare on the oilcloth tablecover she had scrubbed so diligently that morning. The possibility of a strike frightened her for the strain it would put on the small sum she had saved with such difficulty over the years. Adept at concealing her fears, Maria responded harshly, "Vito Speroni is a *buffone.*"

Feeling the weight of Sophia's stare, Maria turned sharply in her direction. The words her eldest daughter dared not speak were reflected clearly in her eyes. Maria countered them without hesitation.

"Joey Moretti is misguided by Vito."

Maria paused as Sophia glanced away. This reluctance for argument was new in Sophia. Hardly a word had been spoken between them since Anthony had officially refused

Joey Moretti's offer of marriage, but Sophia did not fool her mother. Sophia felt no remorse. She felt only a perverted sense of victory in having driven Joey Moretti away.

That thought raising her ire, Maria addressed her daughters harshly. "You will keep out of union affairs, *capisce?* Strikes aren't the business of women. The men run the union. They make the decisions and it is they who should strike. You'll stay in the mill and work."

"Oh, Mama, we can't do that!" Rosalie was aghast, distress evident in her bright eyes. "The workers don't stand a chance of winning if we don't all stand together!"

"But . . . but what if Mr. Kingston fires us for walking off the job?" Anna spoke with uncertainty. "What will we do then?"

"He can't fire us all, Anna."

Sophia's first voluntary statement turned Maria toward her eldest daughter angrily. "You will do as I say—all of you! You'll stay behind to work until the last person has left the floor. Then everyone will see that you weren't to blame for the trouble."

"But, Mama—"

"You will do as I say, Rosalie!"

Rosalie's lowered chin signaled her obedience, halting the rapid rise of Maria's agitation. She observed her daughters' silence as they pushed themselves away from the table and prepared to leave. Momentarily regretting her harshness, Maria turned to the stove and the paper sack waiting there.

"I've given each of you some grapes from your papa's vines with your lunch," she offered in a softer tone as she placed the sack in Anna's hands. "You must enjoy them now, because Papa will soon make the wine and there'll be no more."

"*Grazie*, Mama."

"*Grazie*, Mama."

206

Maria waited. Prolonging the silence, Sophia walked to the door.

"Thank you, Mama."

Ah, so Sophia relents . . . Maria's expression stiffened. She was not deceived. Sophia was up to something.

Her daughters' footsteps echoed on the wooden stairs as they descended toward the yard, and apprehension rose within Maria. Sophia had so far escaped unscathed from her escapades. But if she was not carefully watched, the time would come when . . .

Refusing to face the conclusion of that thought, Maria turned resolutely back to her work.

"Look at them out there, Lyle!" Paul motioned unconsciously toward the crowd of workers rapidly forming on the floor as the machines ran temporarily ignored. "They're daring us to go out there and break it up."

Lyle was acutely aware that Paul's use of the word "us" was merely a formality. It was the job of the mill supervisor to halt this type of activity, but Lyle's hesitation had little to do with his unofficial status.

Still staring at the group, Lyle mumbled, "I told your father that he had to handle the situation more diplomatically. He played right into the hands of the agitators, and I wouldn't be surprised if this same thing is going on in every mill that's declared the intention to double loom assignments this morning. Look at Moretti. He's right in the middle of it. He can't wait for me to stick my head out of the office."

Unconsciously searching the winder aisles, Lyle was relieved to see Sophia working along her machine. A quick glance revealed that her sisters were still working also. He wasn't concerned about Anna. As timid as she was, she would avoid problems—but not Rosalie. She was a clever little girl who followed the activities of the unions devotedly. She had more spirit than was sometimes wise, and he knew that if Rosalie became involved in the fray, Sophia would be right behind her. He didn't want that. He didn't want to make another difficult choice.

"You're going to have to do something, Lyle." Paul glanced back at the inner office door. You don't want Father coming out here and seeing this."

Lyle returned Paul's look in silence. No, he didn't. As brilliant a businessman as Matthew Kingston had proved to be, he was a disaster at managing men. The mill picnic aside, Uncle Matthew stayed as far away from his mill workers as possible. It was a class distinction that his uncle perpetuated with his bearing, his glance, and his tone of voice. Lyle knew that attitude would only serve to inflame the workers.

Annoyed to be forced into entering the situation before he felt it was wise, Lyle slowly drew himself to his feet. A few more minutes and the dissenters in the group would have had time to make their objections known. He had few friends on the floor, but he knew that he had earned the respect of the majority. With the dissenters as his base of support, he believed he would then be able to talk the men back to work.

Lyle surveyed the group again. Joey Moretti and his incendiary element had not yet finished speaking. He needed a little more time.

A sound at the inner office door turned Paul toward him with unexpected intensity. "If Father gets out there now, the workers will be out on the street in a minute. Damn it, Lyle, I'll be ready to leave for France soon, but if the mill's in trouble, I'll be stuck here until it's all cleared up! Do something—anything!"

Not waiting for Lyle's reply, Paul met his father at the inner office door as it opened. Turning him back with a few short words, he shut the door behind him.

Lyle looked back at the mill floor as the door clicked closed. His gaze intent on the agitated group, he drew himself to his feet.

Angry protests increased from the agitated group that grew larger by the minute, and Sophia's heart began a steady pounding. Most vocal of all was Joey, his complaints calculated to inflame. She heard the thread of truth in his words, but she could not make herself believe Joey's zeal was entirely inspired by the unfair practices of mill management. The hatred in his eyes was too intense.

Glancing behind her, Sophia saw Lyle step out onto the mill floor. Clad as he was in a simple shirt and trousers in deference to the heat of the summer morning, he could have been mistaken for a mill hand, were it not for his unconscious bearing. She knew he would be tested this day, as well as she, and her heart fluttered as he approached the angry workers. His jaw hardened, and she felt his anxieties. At another angry shout, his face turned to stone. Lyle was resolute, but he had little chance in this situation today. She suffered in knowing that he sensed it before he began.

"Damn it, Harry! Can't you go any faster!"

Aaron's agitated voice rang in the carriage, but his effort was wasted as the midmorning traffic on the congested street slowed to a halt.

Drumming his fingers impatiently on the padded armrest, his stomach twisting into tight knots, Aaron looked out the window, straining to see where the impediment in their progress lay. He saw to his disgust that the intersection of Main and Van Houten Streets was littered with shattered watermelons, the lush pink interiors splattered across the ground where a produce wagon had obviously come into contact with a van of the Mills Furniture Company.

Aaron squinted at the two drivers, his disposition odious. He had spent a miserable night and had awakened surprisingly tense. His tension had grown as he had accompanied his father to the mill as usual, only to find himself watching the clock with an intense interest that had raised his father's head in his direction several times before he had finally made an excuse to leave.

Aaron checked his pocket watch again, frowning darkly. He had no doubt his presence at Sophia's side would guarantee her a position in Madame Tourneau's salon, but he had become more concerned as the previous night had worn on just what that position would be. Aaron straightened his back and raised his chin. After all, Sophia was his protégée, and she had true talent. He had not realized its true extent until the previous evening. However, he was also aware that she needed experience and time to grow, and it was suddenly more important to him than he cared to admit that she be given the opportunity she sought.

Leaning forward, Aaron looked out the window again. The drivers of the two damaged wagons were conversing heatedly in the street, oblivious to the gradually lengthening lines of traffic backing up in four directions. A sickening feeling squeezed tight in his stomach. He did not want to be late. Muttering an appropriate curse, Aaron forced himself to sit back against the seat again.

Long minutes passed as the temperature in the stationary carriage climbed. Aaron's handsome face twitched. He was intensely aware that his dark jacket was beginning to adhere damply to his back, and that the knife-sharp crease in his trousers had dulled. A bead of perspiration slipped from under the brim of his bowler to roll down his cheek, and his temper soared to the danger point.

Shifting his position, Aaron looked toward the intersection again. The gaudy painting of the Passaic Falls in all its gushing glory emblazoned on the side of ungainly furniture wagon was an affront to his artistic sensibilities, increasing his irritation as the drivers argued on. As he watched, the fellows separated in obvious anger and walked back to their respective wagons where they each stood, arms folded, refusing to budge.

Aaron's patience snapped in a blaze of red, blinding color. Rising from his seat as if propelled, he leaned out the carriage window and yelled, "Get those goddamned wagons out of the street!"

All heads snapped in his direction, and Aaron felt his face redden. Falling back to his seat, he raised his hand to his brow, shocked at his own bourgeois conduct. What was wrong with him?

Aaron's hand dropped back to the seat beside him, his fingertips grazing the canvas case lying there, and the knot in his stomach tightened further. Annoyed at his own agitation, Aaron mentally railed. Damn it all, what difference did it make if he was late in picking up Sophia? She would wait. As for the sketches he had so carefully placed in the case the previous night, they were mere pieces of paper, a ploy to ensnare the woman he had designated as his next conquest—a means to an end. So, why was he so damned nervous? Why had he allowed the upcoming interview to gain outlandish proportions in his mind? Why was each moment spent in this motionless carriage stretching into an endless eternity?

Suddenly springing forward again as if launched, Aaron leaned out the carriage window, the veins in his neck bulging as he shouted, "I said, get those goddamned wagons out of the street!"

Looking up, Aaron caught his driver's shocked stare.

Beyond thoughts of decorum, he ordered sharply, "Drive around those idiots, Harry!"

His face beaded with perspiration under the unrelenting rays of the sun, Harry looked at him as if he had two heads. "Sir, the street is completely blocked!"

Unaware of the man's dismay, Aaron shouted, "Then drive over them, damn it!"

"Sir?"

Disgusted with his driver, with himself, and with the whole situation, Aaron flopped back again against the seat. He withdrew his watch from his waistcoat pocket and groaned. Making a sudden decision, Aaron grasped the handle of the canvas bag beside him and pushed open the carriage door. Stepping down onto the street he glared at Harry without speaking a word, then turned to make his way toward the intersection.

Aware of the curious glances of bystanders as he marched past the hopelessly jammed traffic, Aaron kept his head high. Intent on the drivers of the two damaged wagons, he paused briefly in passing, his shouted comment clear and succinct.

"Dimwits!"

Suddenly aware that he had yet a distance to walk if he were to keep his rendezvous, Aaron consoled himself that the canvas bag in his hand had remained untouched, and that all would soon be well.

He was walking at a breathless pace when he realized incredulously that he, Aaron Weiss, was doing all this just for the sake of a woman.

"We're tired of talking. It's time for action!"

The voice of Vito Speroni rose above the noise of the mill floor, interrupting the flow of Lyle's commanding argument. A chorus of adamant voices seconded Vito's shout, signaling the start of rhythmic chanting in the rear.

"Strike. Strike. Strike."

The drumming chant grew louder, and Lyle read his defeat on the same faces of those who had appeared to be listening intently to him only moments before. He knew instinctively that the time for reason had passed and passion had assumed control.

The excited workers disbursed as if by silent command, and the roar of the looms slowed to a halt. The whine of the winders remained. He looked up in time to see Sophia switch off her machines, and then there was silence.

"You see, Mr. Nephew of the Boss?" Suddenly at Lyle's elbow, Joey Moretti sneered. "Even the *puttana* turns her back on you now. But that was to be expected, no? She has herself a new man—one who can do more for her than you or I." Joey laughed aloud, waiting until Sophia and her sisters walked out through the doorway before following behind them.

"Lyle! What's going on here?"

Lyle turned slowly. He met his uncle's livid expression with a tight smile.

"That should be fairly obvious, Uncle. You're temporarily out of business."

Sophia stepped into the sunlight of midmorning, her heart pounding. Joey strode past her sisters and her from behind as if they did not exist and Sophia pulled her sisters aside.

"So now everyone sees that we were the last to leave and Mama will be satisfied."

Rosalie nodded, intent on a group forming in the corner of the yard. Her eyes widened.

"Look, Sophia! Someone on the street has placards. They're going to picket! I'm going to help them!"

"Wait."

Halting Rosalie's enthusiastic step, Sophia whispered, "I want Anna to go with you, and I want you to stay with the pickets until I get back. If anyone asks, tell them I'm in another part of the yard."

"Where're you going, Sophia!" Anna's dark eyes were alarmed. "Mama doesn't want you to get involved in the strike. It's too dangerous."

"Involved in the strike?" Sophia shook her head. "No." Her lips tightened. "The strike is a waste of time. Mr. Kingston will get what he wants in the end. I have other plans."

"Where are you going?"

Unwilling to answer, Sophia responded simply, "I'll return as quickly as I can."

"But—"

"Go, both of you!"

Waiting only until her sisters started hesitantly across the yard, Sophia turned into the milling crowd and worked her way toward the raceway bridge. A few steps onto the street and she saw Aaron standing in a nearby doorway, his tall, fashionable figure in vivid contrast with the working-class crowd that milled in the street. She smiled when she saw the canvas case he carried.

Working her way covertly to his side, Sophia accepted the hand he extended toward her as he pulled her into the doorway beside him and drew her back out of sight. Her heart fluttered unexpectedly at his nearness, and she was intensely conscious of the man behind his warm gaze as he whispered, "My carriage has been held up in an accident. We're going to have to walk. Do you mind?"

Uncertain if her breathlessness was due to her haste or the sudden realization that Aaron's lips were only inches from hers, Sophia shook her head.

Lowering his head unexpectedly, Aaron brushed her lips with his.

"For luck."

Sophia's lips parted in response, but no sound emerged as Aaron gripped her hand and draw her out with him onto the street.

The small office located at the rear of the exclusive salon of Celeste Tourneau was silent except for the sound of the diminutive Frenchwoman's fingers drumming the border of the fashion sketch that lay on the table in front of her. Madame's well-tended but aging face moved into lines of concentration as she appraised the sketch with a critical eye, cocking her head to study it from yet another angle. Dressed in a soft gray color that matched her hair and eyes too perfectly for coincidence, she gave the appearance of a fashionable gray dove, quiet and uncertain as it looked at the world around it.

But appearances were deceiving.

Madame Tourneau shifted the sketch so she might study it in comparison with the others in the portfolio. Her expression was discerning. She was a woman of the world who was not easily fooled and who was proud of her instinct. Her instinct had told her that the sketch Aaron Weiss had brought to her a few days earlier was more important to the charming, reportedly shallow young man, the son of one of her best customers, than he cared to admit. She had been surprised by the purity of line that the rough sketch offered, and she agreed to see the woman who drew it. However, she had not been prepared for these additional designs, nor for the commonly dressed, startlingly lovely red-haired young woman who stood beside Aaron Weiss, observing her closely. Celeste turned directly to the young woman, her scrutiny intense.

"You have an unusual sense of style, Mademoiselle

215

Marone. These sketches are unpolished, but they show considerable promise."

The young woman's eyes flashed proudly, and Celeste was struck with the vibrancy of her beauty as Sophia replied, "I've worked with silk for many years, and I've developed a feel for its flow. These are the first of my 'Seasons of Silk' designs. One day women will clamor for them."

Celeste raised her narrow, well-shaped brows. "You're very confident of your success, mademoiselle. So what do you want from me?"

The young woman did not flinch under her direct question. Instead, she responded candidly, her marvelous face sober. "I have a vision, madame, but I'm young and lacking in the experience to follow it through. I would like to work for you because I have much to contribute here and because there's much I can learn from the finest couturiere in the silk city."

"Aha!" Celeste smiled. She looked at Aaron Weiss where he stood silent through the exchange. He strove to appear indifferent, but Celeste knew better. She had seen the way his eyes dwelled on the girl with a mixture of fascination, concern, and outright lust. She had seen many smitten men in her time, and this fellow was among one of the worst afflicted. She could not resist a teasing wink as he looked at her.

"Your protégée flatters me! She has been coached by an expert!"

"My words and my work are my own, madame."

Celeste turned at the sharpness of young woman's response. The girl was firebrand, not unlike herself when she was young.

Celeste paused before she spoke stiffly in response. "I don't need anyone to design for me, mademoiselle. My customers prefer my designs."

216

The girl blinked revealingly.

"However . . ." Celeste motioned the young woman forward. "If you will step into the light . . . yes, that's it . . . Walk toward the door, if you please." The young woman obliged warily and a smile gradually grew on Celeste's narrow lips. "I can see that you need no instruction to hold your chin high, or to walk proudly. Brava, mademoiselle."

Celeste's thoughts went unspoken that the slight Italian woman would be a ravishing beauty when properly attired, and that the male patronage of her salon would undoubtedly increase should she decide to use her services.

Celeste darted a glance toward the handsome Aaron Weiss, who watched silently. The man's thoughts were written all over his face, and Celeste was touched with envy. It had been many years since a young man had looked at her in that way, especially a young man as wealthy and handsome as Aaron Weiss. But she also knew that Aaron's reputation was vile when it came to women, that his social sphere was far above this young woman's and boded poorly for his intentions, and that he would not have bothered to help the girl if he didn't feel it would be worth his while. Did this outspoken young woman know what was in store for her?

One glance at Sophia's proud face and Celeste's smile broadened. It would be interesting to see how these two managed with each other.

Her decision made, Celeste offered with affected hesitance, "As I've already said, mademoiselle, my customers have become fond of my own particular style of design. However, I'm in need of a mannequin, someone who will display my fashions at their very best. I've learned through long practice that women spend more freely when a gown takes life before their eyes on the form of a beautiful woman. As for the men . . ." Celeste laughed aloud. "They forget that their wives are obese and homely and imagine

217

the gown will make them as beautiful as the mannequin who shows it."

Celeste's smile faded. "Unfortunately, the young woman who has performed these services for my salon in the past has informed me that she is with child." A twist of Madame's lips revealed her impatience with the function of womanhood that she considered demeaning. "Already her waist has begun widening. She will have to be replaced and you'll do quite well for that position if you are of a mind to accept it."

The response to her offer came unexpectedly from Aaron Weiss, and Celeste raised her brow with surprise at his tight tone of voice.

"Sophia isn't interested in working as a mannequin, madame."

"On the contrary, madame, I'm very interested."

Sophia flashed Weiss a glance that snapped his lips closed with annoyance. Ah, so young Weiss was jealous and fit to burst at the thought of others ogling his pet! Celeste silently applauded the fiery little mademoiselle's spirit. She would not be dictated to by young Weiss.

Celeste concealed her amusement behind a businesslike mien. *"Bon.* I am pleased. I think we'll do well together. As for your weekly compensation, I can afford to pay no more than five dollars a week."

"Five dollars!"

Madame Celeste raised a haughty brow at Sophia's shocked protest. She paused, considering. "All right, six dollars, but not a penny more!"

Sophia paused, then swallowed visibly. "Six will be fine, madame."

Celeste darted a look at the silent Aaron Weiss. He was fuming. Even if she did not feel the girl would enhance the reputation of her establishment in many ways, Celeste had the feeling she would have employed her just for the pleasure

218

of following the affairs of these two very handsome and very strong-minded young people at close range.

"*Oui*, mademoiselle, you will do very nicely. Of course, I'll expect you to sew for me and perform other services for my customers when you're not involved in your regular duties." Waiting only for Sophia's nod of agreement, Celeste continued. "As for your designs . . ." Celeste shrugged. "We'll display them, if you like, to gauge reaction to them. If they are appreciated, we'll then see . . ."

Sophia Marone's glorious blue eyes shone with pleasure. "Thank you, madame. When would you like me to start?"

"Tomorrow will do."

"Tomorrow?" The girl hesitated only momentarily. "Of course."

Walking to the front of her establishment minutes later, nodding graciously as she passed smiling customers, Celeste watched through the salon window as the beauteous Sophia Marone took Aaron Weiss's arm and stepped up into the carriage that had drawn up to wait. She controlled the urge to laugh aloud. She had the feeling that in hiring this young woman, she had added some spice to the feast of life, and she looked forward to consuming it with enjoyment.

"You've made a mistake in accepting that position, Sophia."

Sophia turned toward Aaron as the carriage snapped into motion, her jubilation dimming at his obvious disapproval. Annoyed at the damper he attempted to put on her jubilant spirits, she raised her chin rebelliously.

"Have I?"

"Yes, you have!" Aaron removed his hat and slapped it down onto the seat beside him to rake an anxious hand through his dark hair. The motion was one that Sophia recognized as characteristic of him when agitated, and she realized with surprise that this cool, haughty fellow was genuinely upset.

"Be so good as to tell me why, please."

"Isn't it obvious?" Aaron's smooth cheek ticked. "Madame Tourneau has no intention of using your designs. She merely wants to use you to draw more customers into her salon."

"I don't know what you mean."

Aaron gave an angry snort. "It seems you aren't as smart as you think you are, Sophia. You're a beautiful woman and Madame Tourneau is clever. She was quite open about a mannequin's value in her salon, but there are some things she didn't tell you. She didn't say how demeaning the position would be. She didn't tell you that you would spend your day parading at the whim of her customers, turning this way and that at their direction. She didn't mention the male customers who visit her salon exclusively because she offers them this service and because some feel they have the freedom to examine the merchandise they intend to purchase very closely, to occasionally feel the textures . . ."

Sophia raised her chin a notch higher at Aaron's intimation. Her eyes narrowed. "You seem very familiar with the services of Madame's salon. May I assume you're speaking from personal experience?"

Aaron's lips tightened. "You may assume whatever you want."

"And that's where we differ, Aaron." Sophia's tone was acidic. "You may *not* assume whatever you want about me. You may *not* assume that I hold myself so cheaply that I would allow anyone liberties for the sake of my employment. You may *not* assume that I've taken this position for any other reason than to benefit from Madame's experience as a couturiere. And you may *not* assume that the as-

220

sistance you've given me allows you to dictate to me in any way!"

"I'm not dictating to you!"

Aaron took a deep, steadying breath and Sophia saw the effort he expended in holding his patience. She wondered at the intensity of his emotion and at the reason for the continued forbearance which she suspected was foreign to his character.

Aaron tried again. "I don't want you to make a mistake."

"I won't."

Aaron nodded. Sophia felt the heat of his gaze and the emotions he rigidly suppressed as he took her hand into his. "Sophia, I think we all make mistakes. I've made many, but I'll tell you now that I don't intend making any mistakes with you."

The unexpected change in Aaron's attitude gave Sophia a moment's pause. Uncertain of her feelings, she watched him raise her hand to his lips. Her heart began a slow pounding as his mouth lingered there with the skill of a practiced lover and she wondered at the many women whose hands he had kissed in this same way. With that sobering thought, Sophia responded evenly in return, "We are two with one purpose then, Aaron, because *I* don't intend making any mistakes with *you*."

The double entendre in her words was not lost on Aaron as Sophia slowly withdrew her hand from his and the carriage continued briskly along the street.

"How could you let this happen?" Matthew Kingston faced Lyle accusingly, his voice echoing in the unnatural silence of the mill floor. Outside the door, pickets marched adamantly, and a few paces beyond, a crowd of agitated workers still milled as the noon hour approached. Incensed, Matthew added hotly, "You

221

should have handled this situation before it went this far."

"Father, you're not being fair."

Turning sharply toward Paul, Matthew snapped, "Stay out of this! I removed you from supervisory duties with the thought that your cousin could handle them more efficiently than you, but I can see I expected too much. It seems Lyle is no more respected in the position of supervisor than you were!"

"Am I to consider myself the supervisor of this mill, Uncle? I wasn't sure." Lyle faced Matthew with a deceptively casual smile. "And neither is anyone else who works for you."

"You know damned well that you're the supervisor here! You're just trying to make excuses for your ineptitude."

"I may be many things, Uncle, but I'm not inept!" His rising anger barely in control, Lyle gestured toward the picket line outside the mill door. "I warned you this would happen, but you wouldn't hear it. I told you things should be handled differently, but you were afraid to surrender the reins as much as an inch. You'd rather see the mill go down the drain than let yourself believe I could possibly be right."

Lyle stared at his uncle's stiff face. "What's the matter, Uncle? No defense against the truth?"

Livid, Matthew snapped, "I don't have to defend myself to you! And I don't have to stand here and listen to you berate me and hold yourself exempt from fault in this debacle!"

"Even if it's the truth?"

"The truth as you wish to see it!" Visibly struggling to hold himself under control, Matthew drew himself rigidly erect. "Not only are you a bastard, but you're a bluffer and a fraud, Lyle Clark!"

"My name is Lyle Kingston."

"Your name is Lyle *Clark!* You've never been a true

222

Kingston, and you never will be, no matter how hard you strive!"

Pure unadulterated hatred rose inside Lyle as he studied his uncle in momentary silence. Matthew Kingston's handsome, mature face was blotched with a fury that matched his own, but Lyle maintained his reason, refusing to surrender to the emotion of the moment.

"So I'm a fraud and a bluffer. Are you sure of that?"

"I'm as sure of that as I ever was of anything in my life."

"Sure enough to make a very solemn wager?"

Matthew's cheek ticked revealingly and his light eyes narrowed. "What do you mean?"

"Let's put our cards on the table." A sneer lurking around his lips, Lyle stated flatly, "You've hated me since Aunt Julia first brought me into the family and you're incensed at having a bastard bear the Kingston name. You'd like nothing better than to be rid of me for good, but for some reason, you've been unwilling to take that final step. Every underhanded plot you've ever made against me has failed, including that last pitiful insult of flaunting poor Hope in front of my face."

His gaze intensifying, Lyle continued softly. "The only problem is that we're both tiring of the game, Uncle, and it's time to settle it once and for all, so I have a proposition to make you."

Matthew raised his chin, the persistent tick in his cheek betraying his emotion as he rasped, "Don't push me too far, Lyle . . ."

"Hear me out. You said I'm a bluffer and a fraud. I say you're wrong. I say that I can run this mill as well as you ever did—even better, and my proposition is this. Let Paul go to Paris to study for two years with your blessings, because the truth of it is that he's going, with or without them. And let me manage the mill without interference during that time."

Matthew gave a sharp laugh. "You're insane!"

"Am I? If you turn the management of the mill over to me for two years, I'm telling you that I can settle this strike without long-lasting effects and any others that might occur and that I can manage the implementation of the changes you want with more success than any of the other mills that undertake the same procedures." Lyle's eyes narrowed. "I'm telling you that in two years' time the profits of Kingston Mill under my supervision will match any of the others in Paterson, and surpass most. Of course, if I succeed, I'll also expect you to grant me a reasonable percentage of the profits, with an eye toward greater responsibility should Paul decide not to return to the business."

His face distorted with suppressed fury, Matthew sneered, "Oh, is that *all* you want? And if you fail?"

Lyle paused. "Dear Uncle, then I'll step out of your life forever."

"Lyle, don't be a fool!" Grabbing his arm roughly, Paul turned Lyle to his whitened face. "Paterson is facing its most difficult years in the silk industry. You'll be met with situations over which you'll have little control. Damn it, you know the way politics are shifting! More communist agitators are coming into the city every day! Are you really willing to accept responsibility for the tide of change that's presently sweeping the industry?"

"Tide of change . . ." Matthew scoffed. "You're a fool, Paul."

"No, you're the fool, Uncle! You've underestimated Paul and me all of our lives."

"I've underestimated no one!"

"This is your chance to prove it, Uncle." Lyle's smile was taunting. "You have nothing to lose, you know. You'll be here to oversee everything I do, so there's little chance that the situation will get out of hand. Two years will give Paul time to determine his direction, but he'll be free to come back to work with you if I fall flat on my face as you think I will."

My son will always have first choice in this mill—no matter what you achieve here!"

Lyle laughed aloud. "So you think I might succeed after all!"

"Never!"

"You're wrong, and you don't have the spine to stand behind your own beliefs."

"Bastard!"

"So you've said many times, Uncle."

"Damn you!" Close to apoplectic, Matthew held himself rigidly silent for long seconds before exploding. "All right, it's done then! I'll take your offer, with one provision. When you fail and are forced to leave, you will make it plain to your aunt Julia that this proposition was yours from its inception."

"If I fail . . ."

"You will! Are we agreed?"

"Agreed."

Matthew's smile was cold. "You've done me a greater favor than you could ever realize, 'Nephew.' I'll go home now and leave you to handle this . . ." he gestured to the persistent picket line outside the door, "by yourself, since you're so much better equipped to handle it than I." Turning to his sober-faced son, Matthew said harshly, "Get your bags packed, Paul. Your cousin is sending you merrily on your way to Paris, and you can thank *him* for it, not me. And while you're at it, you can say your final good-byes to him, because he won't be here when you return."

Turning with a snap, Matthew walked out the door, pushed his way through the picketers, and stepped up into his waiting carriage.

In the silence of his father's wake, Paul turned abruptly toward his cousin, incredulous.

"Do you realize what you've done? Whatever possessed you?" Paul's expression grew pained. "Whether Father admits it or not, the changes brewing in the industry won't be easily settled. The mills are in for trouble and you can rest assured that Father will see that you take the blame for every problem that arises."

Suddenly realizing he had no response, Lyle returned Paul's stare soberly. "I don't really know why I picked today to face your father down, Paul." Finding his gaze wandering to the lot outside the door for sign of Sophia's fiery tresses among the dark-haired crowd, Lyle continued more softly. "Or maybe I do. Maybe I'm tired of waiting for your father to dismiss his prejudices and see me for what I'm worth. Maybe I'm tired of sacrificing the present with thoughts to a future that might never materialize. Or maybe I've just taken all I can stand."

Paul shook his head. "I can't understand why you put yourself through all this. If I were you, I'd have turned my back on this place as soon as I came of age and never come back."

Lyle paused to consider Paul's statement. "Maybe you would have, but I doubt it. Your father hasn't been able to shame, threaten, or cajole you into forsaking what you feel you're really meant to do, has he?"

Paul's sudden smile was wry. "And now he's sending me off with his blessings because of you." His smile faded. "I'd feel better about it if I didn't think you were going to lose out in the end."

"I'm not going to fail." Lyle's deep voice was resolute. "Whatever course the industry takes, I'm going to make your father eat his words."

Intensely sober, Paul surveyed his cousin's expression. Lyle's gold eyes were hard, and his expression was unyielding. There was an indefinable quality there . . . He gave an unexpected laugh.

"Damned if I don't believe you."

Placing his hand on Paul's shoulder, Lyle suddenly smiled. "I'm glad of that." Shifting his gaze to the pickets outside the door, Lyle took a deep breath. "Well, the first step is always the hardest. Would you like to take it with me?"

"What are you going to do?"

"Watch and see."

Together, they stepped out into the yard.

Not turning back to watch the shiny black carriage as it drove on down the street, Sophia walked quickly across the raceway bridge, her eyes on the pickets marching in a circle in front of the mill entrance. Chanting loudly, her face wreathed in smiles, Rosalie waved her placard enthusiastically as she walked. Behind her, Anna mouthed the slogans with limited zeal as she stared at the shorter of the two young Kingstons standing nearby in deep conversation with strikers.

Sophia paused, frowning. Anna's gaze was unguarded and far too revealing as she stared wistfully at Paul Kingston's back. Sophia's jubilation dimmed. Oh, no, Anna . . .

As if attuned to her sister's thoughts, Anna glanced up. Unwilling to let her sister know her secret had been revealed, Sophia started toward her at a run. She grasped her sisters' arms as she reached them.

"Let someone else take those signs now. I have something to tell you."

Waiting only until the placards had been placed in other willing hands, Sophia drew her sisters aside. She looked cautiously around her then turned back to them, her eyes glowing.

227

"I'm finished at the mill."

"Oh, Sophia—"

Interrupting Anna's anxious reaction, Rosalie whispered in a rush, "What are you talking about, Sophia? What happened?"

"Madame Tourneau hired me! I start work in her salon tomorrow!"

"Tomorrow!"

"Mama won't let you do it, Sophia!"

Sophia's beautiful face hardened at Anna's interjection. "She has no choice, Anna."

Ignoring Anna's qualms, Sophia glanced toward the entrance of the mill and the men still conversing there. Lyle and Paul were talking to Jacques Montepelier and Gino Scalzone, and she realized Lyle had not been fooled for a moment into thinking that hotheads like Vito and Joey, no matter how vocal, were capable of directing so well organized a strike. Jacques and Gino were familiar with the problems of industrialization in the old country and were old hands at protest. She was proud of Lyle's instinct, but it was obvious that he was making little progress with the two adamant weavers. As she watched, the conversation ended abruptly and Paul and Lyle walked back into the mill.

Sophia turned to her sisters. "Wait here. I'll be right back."

"But Sophia . . ."

Sophia frowned, "Wait. *Capisce?*"

The angry shouts of the pickets turned Lyle toward Sophia as she paused in the doorway of the mill moments later. He approached her, concern eliminating the former stiffness between them as he drew her inside.

"Sophia, what are you doing here?" He looked out into the yard where the pickets continued to heckle angrily. "Don't you realize the chance you're taking walking past those pickets? Emotions are running too high for you to—"

"I must talk to you."

Lyle halted abruptly at her tone. Studying her expression briefly in silence, he then took her arm as he turned back to his cousin. "We're going into the office for a few minutes, Paul."

Lyle turned to her the moment he closed the office door behind them. "What's wrong, Sophia?"

Sophia took a deep, steadying breath with the realization that all the harsh words spoken between them had been thrust aside by her short expression of need. She was suddenly sure that would never change.

Lyle gripped her shoulder. "Has something happened?"

"Yes, but nothing is wrong. Everything is right." And then realizing the strike had created the opposite situation for him, Sophia took a step closer. Resting her palm against his chest, she felt the heavy pounding of his heart and realized that her own heart pounded as well as she whispered, "I've spoken to Madame Tourneau. She likes my sketches and has offered me a position in her salon. I start working for her tomorrow."

Lyle's face went still. When he finally spoke his smile was forced. "I'm happy for you, Sophia. It's what you wanted."

"It's only the first step. I have a long way yet to go."

The silence that followed was strained as Sophia's feelings vacillated between elation and regret. She knew instinctively that Lyle felt the same even as he raised a hand to her cheek, his expression hesitant.

"I know there are a lot of things I should say, Sophia. I should tell you how proud I am of you and that I know you'll do well because you have something special inside you, but I have too many regrets right now to say anything else except that I'm sorry. I let you down. I said things I didn't mean."

"No, you were right."

"I behaved like a jealous fool when I had no right to be jealous."

"I have no right to the feelings I have for you either, *caro* Lyle, but I feel them anyway." An emotion too intense to be ignored rose inside her as Sophia whispered, "Even while we were estranged from each other, my heart cried out to yours and you were closer to me in so many ways than anyone else. Anger has no place between us, because when all is said and done, I wish all the good things for you that I know you wish for me."

Lyle paused, then whispered, "So, you do read my mind, after all."

Sophia's smile was bittersweet. "I told you so, didn't I?"

"Then tell me what I'm thinking now."

Reading all she needed to know in the amber eyes holding hers, Sophia responded with a certainty that was innate, "You're thinking that you love me, even though you wish you didn't, and that a part of your heart will always belong to me although you know there are too many things that will keep us apart. And you read in my eyes that I understand."

Amber turned to burning gold as Lyle's gaze fell to Sophia's lips. She felt its scorching heat as Lyle whispered, "What else do you see?"

Sophia's voice dropped to a ragged whisper. "I see that you wish things could be different, and that you cry inside because when I leave the mill, I'll slip farther away from you."

Lyle's hand slid into the hair at her temple and Sophia felt his anguish as he caressed the throbbing pulse there. She shared the hunger he dared not acknowledge as his whisper tore at her heart.

"You see so much, Sophia. Do you also see that I want very much to kiss you—if only to say good-bye? I've never *really* kissed you, you know. Will you let me?"

A shudder shook Sophia's already trembling frame. That same desire was strong inside her as well as she responded earnestly, "Yes, please do."

Unwilling to sacrifice any portion of the precious moment, Sophia watched as Lyle's face descended slowly toward hers. She saw glittering flecks stir to life in the gold of his eyes as he drew closer. She saw the flare of his nostrils as his breathing quickened and she saw his lips part in anticipation as they neared hers. She heard his breath catch as her lips parted as well, and she saw his smooth skin flush as he muttered an indistinguishable oath the moment before their lips met with mutual longing and his arms closed tight around her.

The sweet taste of Lyle was warmly familiar, but the passion was new as Sophia slid her arms around him, accepting his kiss, indulging it with an aching awe. She traced the strong column of his neck with her fingertips as his mouth pressed deeper into hers. She felt the honey-gold of his hair against her palms as the beauty between them consumed her, as it raised her on fragile, fluttering wings to bond them in a way they had not been bonded before. She felt all that could and would not be, the wonder and the pain of it bringing hot tears to her eyes as Lyle finally tore his mouth from hers. His breathing ragged, his torment clearly visible, Lyle whispered, "Sophia, I wish—"

Sophia pressed her fingertips against his lips, halting his words as she whispered, "Useless wishes and senseless regrets are not for us."

Lyle's gaze consumed her. "For the first time I'm not so sure of that. I'm not sure of anything right now."

Sharing his uncertainty as well as his need, Sophia whispered in a shaken voice, "But unsure as you are, you know you'll do what you must. Isn't that so, my *caro* Lyle?"

Reflected in Lyle's tormented gaze was the war that raged inside him, and Sophia held her breath. At his begrudging nod a moment later, she released it to whisper in return. "And so must I."

Drawing her back into his arms, Lyle clutched her intimately close against the hard wall of his body, and Sophia indulged the bittersweet joy of the moment. She felt his breath against her hair as he whispered, "If you ever need me—"

"I know."

"Sophia, I—"

"I know . . . I know."

Forcing herself to withdraw from him, Sophia attempted a smile. *"Ciao, carissimo."*

Slipping back through the mill entrance into the yard moments later, Sophia did not hear the taunting calls or feel the anger of her fellow workers. Lingering on her lips was the warmth of Lyle's kiss and in her mind rang the echo of all that would go forever unspoken between them.

The sun had slipped past the horizon. Fading shafts of red and gold glowed against the darkening sky as Sophia slipped through the kitchen doorway and started down the steps to the yard. Behind her she heard Rosalie speaking to Anna with forced gaiety and she knew her dear sister sought to distract Mama from her departure. She smiled at her sister's ploy. Her sisters had waited expectantly during the long, uncomfortable meal for an announcement from her that had not come. She knew they had immediately realized where she was going when she slipped out the door.

Standing in the yard, Sophia cast a quick glance behind her before walking toward the open door to the cellar. She took the final six steps down with flying feet and followed the narrow stone corridor to the spot where the light from a single lantern warded off the darkness. She paused there. The pungent smell of wine grapes and cigar smoke met her nostrils, blending with the ever-present odor of mildew as she stood in the doorway of the small room, unobserved. The damp stone walls and dirt floor were familiar, the site of her father's yearly rendezvous with the fruit of his vines, and she watched as he dumped another basket of the fragrant fruit into the press. Smoke from the small stogie her father clenched tightly between his teeth encircled his head like a lacy halo as he slowly forced the press tighter, and she recalled standing beside him as a child, reaching out to catch the draining juice as Papa scolded with a smile.

Familiar scents, warm memories, and love were Papa's gifts to her, along with the understanding and approval that had never failed her. Remembering all this, Sophia finally spoke.

"Papa . . ."

Anthony jumped with a start and turned toward her with a shake of his head. "Sophia! What are you doing down here?" He waved his hand at the fruit gnats that hovered around his perspired pate and laughed. "You don't run away from the smell of my wine and call me *pazzo* like Josephine Amatti?" He pointed at the floor above his head and rolled his eyes.

Sophia laughed aloud, then whispered behind her hand, "Josephine is the one who's crazy."

Anthony paused to consider that thought, then nodded. "You're right, *figlia mia*. Josephine is crazy. The grapes smell good and the bugs don't bite me, and so I make my wine. Now, what's my beautiful daughter doing down here in this place that's fit only for old men and ripe grapes?"

Sophia's smile dimmed and Anthony straightened up. His gaze sobered. "Is it your mama?" He shook his head.

"She doesn't understand about strikes. I'll explain to her that you can't go back to work before the others or it will be dangerous. She will—"

"No, Papa." Sophia took a few steps closer, her father's concern for her softening her anxiety. "I just wanted to talk to you about something."

Placing the basket on the floor, the wine forgotten, Anthony frowned. "What's wrong, *figlia mia?* Tell your papa."

Sophia took a deep breath. "I gave up my job at the mill today."

Anthony went suddenly still. *"Non capisco.* What do you mean?"

"I have another job, Papa." Excitement creeping into her voice, Sophia continued. "I went to see Madame Tourneau at the Tourneau Dress Salon. You know, Papa, the big dress shop where all the rich ladies go. I showed her drawings I made of silk gowns and I told her that I wanted to learn from her. She hired me, Papa! I start work tomorrow!"

Anthony nodded, his dark eyes studying her. "Your mama knows?"

"No. I wanted to tell you first."

Anthony nodded again. *"Sì,* you did right. What will you do in this place?"

"I'll help sew the dresses and I'll be a mannequin. Madame says I'll bring new customers into the shop because I'm beautiful and her customers will like looking at me."

"Hmmm . . . Your mama won't want to hear that."

Sophia shrugged. "Then I won't tell her."

"Good." Anthony frowned. "This Madame will pay you well?"

"Six dollars a week!"

Anthony's heavy brows rose with surprise. "You earned only four dollars at the mill!" A smile twitched at his lips. "Your mama will be happy with that, but she won't be happy that you did all this without her permission."

"I know, but if I had asked her permission, she would've been angry and she would've said that I was aiming too high." Placing her hand on her father's hairy forearm, Sophia whispered, "I'll be wearing silk just as I said I would, Papa, and someday the dresses will belong to me!"

Anthony paused in response, his eyes strangely bright. "Sì, figlia mia, I know." Pausing again, he continued. "Don't worry. I'll go with you to talk to your mama. Everything will be all right."

Sophia's love for her father filled her to overflowing. "Thank you, Papa."

But it was obvious that Anthony was not at ease with his thoughts. He hesitated, seeking the right words. Sophia watched the working of anxiety on his homely, well-loved face as he cautioned softly, "Sophia . . . the people who come to these fancy stores aren't like us. You must be careful."

Sophia averted her gaze, guilt plaguing her at the part she had neglected to mention that Aaron Weiss had played in the affair. Her father's calloused fingertips raised her chin moments later.

"Figlia mia, Papa didn't mean to make you sad. Papa knows you're different from Anna and Rosalie. There is something special inside you. Mama knows, too, and she fears for you because of it. You must forgive her for her sharpness. She only wants to protect you."

Managing a smile, Sophia promised softly, "I'll make you proud of me, Papa. You'll see."

"Ah, Sophia . . ." Anthony smiled in return. "Your papa is already proud of you." His smile became wry. "But with your mama there's work to be done." Abruptly turning to wipe his hands on a rag lying nearby, Anthony then winked. "Come, we'll tell her the good news about the six dollars. That will make her happy. The rest will come

235

later."

Gratitude and love for her father swelling anew, Sophia hugged him tightly. The warmth of his arms closing briefly around her in return brought tears to her eyes as she whispered, "What would I do without you, Papa?"

"Figlia bella," Anthony's dark eyes held hers. "What would your papa do without you?"

The love in that short sentence filling her, Sophia turned toward the stairs. Unbidden, Aaron Weiss's handsome face flashed before her eyes and Sophia swallowed against the guilt of her silence.

Chapter Eleven

"*Oui*, Madame Pennington, I believe we have several gowns that will suit you very well. Sophia, you will come out here, please."

Prepared, awaiting her cue, Sophia emerged from the rear room of the salon. Clothed in purple silk from the daring neckline of her gown to her ankles, her upswept hair in startling contrast to the regal color, she walked swiftly. Halting in front of Madame, she turned to the buxom, dark-haired matron standing beside her and smiled.

"Turn around for Madame Pennington, Sophia. That's right. Thank you."

Whirling gracefully, Sophia listened intently as Madame addressed her customer in a subdued tone.

"This gown is a sample—just completed. The shade is perfect for a woman of your coloring and mature figure. The charity ball is only three weeks away, but since you are a favored patron, we will make a special effort to make it up for you in time."

Mrs. Pennington was obviously impressed, but she hesitated, her narrow lips pursed thoughtfully. Sophia paused, waiting. She had learned much in the first week of her employment. About Madame Tourneau she had learned that the clever couturiere was an excellent businesswoman who knew her customers' preferences and idiosyncracies well. She knew that Madame Tourneau would not countenance hesitation when she sensed a sale within reach, and that her devious mind was capable of formulating endless ways to deal with uncertainty. About herself Sophia had learned as soon as the first silk gown slipped down over her shoulders that her skin was born for its touch. She had also learned that there was limited satisfaction in being clothed in silk when neither the design nor the garment was her own.

Sophia paused, her thoughts coming inevitably to Aaron Weiss who had been so much a part of her first week at the salon. About Aaron Weiss she had learned that behind his sophisticated exterior was an intelligent man whose quick mind was a constant challenge, whose charm was a dangerous, debilitating weapon of which she must be wary, and whose dark eyes were increasingly effective in melting the cold core of resistance to him that she hoped to maintain.

Aware that Mrs. Pennington still hesitated, Sophia whirled gracefully again as the door opened and another customer entered. A short, well-dressed gentleman paused inside the doorway and Sophia frowned. Mr. Allistair Marks, wealthy and indulged owner of one of the most notorious dye houses in the city, had come into the salon with his wife on the second day of Sophia's employment. His eyes had devoured her behind his wife's plump back, and the few whispered comments he had made as she showed several gowns had set her stomach to churning. She understood from Madame's comments afterward that Mr. Marks had been one of the favorites of her former mannequin, Estelle, and Sophia had felt her fury rise at his presumption. The truth of Aaron's warning had returned to her then, and she had raised her chin, refusing to be deterred from her goal by the likes of swine such as Allistair Marks.

238

Madame interrupted her thoughts, and it did not take Sophia long to realize that there was a new game that must be played.

"Madame Pennington is undecided, Sophia." Madame Tourneau's smile was professional. "I'll show her some of our sketches while you change into the green velvet. But first . . ." Madame Tourneau's smile broadened pointedly. "Monsieur Marks has just entered. He would doubtless enjoy a closer glimpse, if you please. His taste is beyond question, which is the reason his wife allows him to purchase most of her gowns for her. I suspect he is looking for the perfect garment for his wife when they attend the charity ball. Quickly now."

Walking obediently toward the front of the salon where the wealthy businessman waited, Sophia was keenly aware that the man's heated gaze consumed her, dwelling on the white skin of her exposed shoulders and the rise of her breasts above the gathered silk of her bodice. Her lips curled with distaste, but she forced a smile that she hoped did not reveal the full extent of her revulsion as she greeted him with as professional a tone as she could muster.

"Madame has asked me to show you this gown, Mr. Marks." Sophia pivoted on her heel. "It's new . . . Madame's own creation, recently finished."

Allistair Marks leered. "It's lovely. Come closer, Sophia. The details of Madame's creations are a true mark of her genius."

Sophia gritted her teeth tighter, intensely conscious of the man's eager hands twitching at his sides. A scathing response rose in her throat, but she subdued it with supreme strength of will, aware that she need choose her words wisely.

Her smile fixed, Sophia took the necessary step closer and turned again, only to feel Mr. Marks's damp hand close around her arm as she turned back toward him. His face flushed, he licked his lips anxiously as his gaze swept her. Focusing on the rise of her bosom for extended moments, he then looked up, his thoughts obnoxiously apparent.

"The style is lovely, my dear, and so are you. You're a treat for the eyes, but the workmanship on this gown . . ." He looked back again to the bodice of the garment. "See here . . . this seam is pulled too tightly, is it not?"

Reaching boldly toward the spot indicated just below the exposed flesh at her neckline, Marks's intention was obvious in the split second before a deep voice cautioned, "That seam looks fine to me, Allistair. I suggest you leave it alone."

Assuming a possessive stance beside Sophia, Aaron extended his hand to the startled businessman in greeting, the tight lines of his face contradicting his friendly words, "Nice to see you again, Allistair." Marks accepted his hand with reservation and Aaron continued with an acid smile. "I see you've met Sophia. She's my protégée, you know, a true jewel that I'm pleased to have been able to help put in the right setting at last. You seem to like this gown she's showing, but if you don't mind my saying so, I don't think Mildred would look well in this color."

Uncertain how to react, Sophia glanced toward Madame as the astute Frenchwoman followed the progress of the conversation between the two men with narrowed eyes. Her stomach jumped as Aaron continued, in a softer tone rank with menace. "I'm sure Sophia will be happy to show you some of Madame's other gowns. However, I think I should warn you that Sophia shows only Madame's finest garments — garments of delicate material that don't bear *handling* well. You do understand, don't you, Allistair?"

His full mustache twitching, Marks finally spoke through a forced smile. "Yes, I think I understand. Look, but don't touch . . . a familiar admonition." Turning back to Sophia, Marks dipped his head courteously. "My apologies, my dear. It seems you've already found a benevolent, as well as possessive benefactor. I envy him. But in the event this fickle fellow's interest should wane—"

"It won't."

Ignoring Aaron's prompt interjection, Marks continued smoothly. "I would hope in that event you'll think of me. I can be a very generous man."

Her disgust concealed behind a careful smile, Sophia inquired sweetly, "As generous as you are to your wife, Mr. Marks?"

Marks laughed, unembarrassed. "Far more generous, I would say."

Uncertain if she was more angry with Aaron for the impression he had conveyed or by Marks himself, Sophia was about to tell the nauseating Mr. Marks exactly what she thought of his conclusion that she could be bought at any price when she was halted unexpectedly by Madame's opportune appearance at her elbow.

"If you will forgive me . . ." Addressing Marks directly, Madame drew Sophia a cautious few steps back. "Madame Pennington has decided to purchase this gown after all. I'm so sorry to disappoint you, monsieur, but I have a lovely green velvet that Sophia will be delighted to show you." Her gaze pointed, she urged Sophia toward the rear of the store. "If you please, Sophia."

Reluctantly following Madame's bidding, Sophia emerged again into the salon several changes later, inwardly fuming. Allistair Marks had assumed a comfortable chair where he ordered repeated turns and sweeps in front of him with each gown she showed. Seated a few feet away,

Aaron glowered moodily, his handsome face tight with anger as Marks put her through her paces, and Sophia was uncertain which of the men she resented more.

The restrictions her employment placed on her tongue never more vexing, Sophia was circulating among the other customers when Marks turned to Madame Tourneau with a few short words and rose from his seat. Nodding at her with a smile, he then turned and left the salon abruptly.

Responding to Madame's summons, intensely aware of Aaron's gaze as it followed her, Sophia walked to Madame's side. She was prepared for the worst when Madame smiled.

"You've done well this morning, Sophia. Monsieur Marks has purchased two of the gowns you showed him and has complimented me on my choice of mannequins. He is very impressed."

"Mr. Marks is a pig."

Celeste laughed aloud, unexpectedly amused. "A succinct and accurate assessment, but he's such a *wealthy* pig. Unfortunately, we tradesmen don't have the privilege of choosing our customers according to our personal standards." Madame's gaze settled pointedly on her. *"Comprendezvous, mademoiselle?"*

Waiting only for Sophia's short nod of acquiescence, Madame again smiled.

"Bon. And now, *ma chère,* as for the patient Monsieur Weiss . . ." Following Madame's gaze, Sophia was as startled as she to find that Aaron had left without a word. She was unexpectedly disturbed by Madame's dry comment, "Ah, so all patience sooner or later comes to an end."

The sound of the door opening again drew Madame's gaze toward the two matrons who paused in the doorway. Her shrewd eyes narrowed. "Quickly, Sophia—the ecru

242

gown with the full sleeves. Mrs. Wentworth dislikes bright colors, and Mrs. Anders never fails to follow her lead."

Heading toward the back room as Madame walked toward her waiting customers with a smile of welcome, Sophia felt the strain of the long morning's work. Aaron's silent perusal and the obvious agitation that drew his handsome features into dark lines had affected her strangely. She still had not recovered from the conflicting feelings he stirred with his heady glances, but she was not a fool. Aaron Weiss could not be trusted. She recognized the danger in his attentions and despised the spontaneous excitement he evoked within her.

Sophia raised her chin as the seamstress in the rear room moved to help with yet another change. Aaron Weiss was a threat she could not afford, and she was determined to keep that thought foremost in her mind.

The light of late afternoon was blinding as Sophia emerged onto the street and pulled the salon door closed behind her. Again clothed in the simple dark skirt and white blouse provided by Madame Tourneau for her employees, her blazing curls bound in a careless knot atop her head, she paused momentarily as an unexpected summons turned her toward Aaron's approach.

Smiling and eager, this Aaron Weiss was in startling contrast to the angry, moody Aaron who had guarded her like a begrudging watchdog that morning until Allistair Marks left the salon. Neither did this fellow bear any resemblance to the haughty, aloof Aaron Weiss who had so repulsed her their first meeting. She wondered at the many facets of this man's personality, intensely aware of the danger of her growing attraction to him.

Aaron's smile faltered momentarily at her frown. "I've

243

been waiting for you, Sophia. My carriage is over there."

Sophia did not return his smile. "I prefer to walk today." She attempted to turn away, only to have Aaron stay her with a light touch on her arm.

"Are you angry with me, Sophia?"

Sophia fought to control her reaction to his obvious distress as she forced a candid reply. "I suppose I am. You've obviously jumped to some conclusions that I dislike." Sophia paused, but was determined to continue. "I didn't make any promises to you when I accepted your help."

There were a few silent moments before Aaron gave a short, unexpected laugh. "Is that what you think—that I helped you get the position with Madame Tourneau because I expected your favors in return?" Aaron laughed again. "I gave up hopes of buying you the first time we met."

"Oh?" Momentarily nonplussed by his outspokenness, Sophia raised her brows questioningly. "That isn't what you led Mr. Marks to believe today."

Angry color flooded Aaron's face at the mention of Allistair Marks. "What did you expect me to do, damn it! When I walked in the door the damned lecher had his hands all over you!"

Sophia was outraged. "He didn't!"

"I was merely trying to protect you."

"I don't need your protection!"

Aaron paused, his jaw working tensely before he unexpectedly took her hand. She was startled to find his hand trembling as he spoke with an obvious attempt at control. "Please, Sophia. I don't want to fight with you."

The anguish in his voice tore at Sophia's resistance, removing the intended sharpness from her tone as she whispered in return, "What *do* you want from me, Aaron?"

"I want to talk to you."

Sophia struggled to remain aloof from his appeal. "We are talking."

"We aren't talking, Sophia. We're arguing about inconsequential things that shouldn't come between us. I want to really talk to you. I want to get to know you better, and I want you to get to know me."

"Why?"

"Because I care for you." Aaron's hand tightened on hers and she could feel as well as hear the intensity of emotions he suppressed as he added, "I care very much."

"I've been busy. I haven't had time—"

"You're not busy now."

"I have to go home."

"Have dinner with me."

"I can't. My mother wouldn't understand."

Aaron was momentarily silent. "Will you let me take you home, then?"

"Aaron . . ."

"Please."

Suddenly conscious of the stares their intense conversation was drawing from passersby, Sophia abruptly nodded. A devastating smile lit Aaron's face, and Sophia cautioned herself again against the danger of this man's appeal.

The carriage snapped into motion and Aaron was stunned at the intensity of his emotions as he looked at Sophia's profile etched against the passing streets. At a complete loss, Aaron felt the rise of anxiety. Things were not going as he had planned. Instead of drawing them together as he had thought, Sophia's employment at the salon had somehow put a distance between them that increased every day. His frustration had mounted daily and, contrary to his strictly controlled dealings with women in the past, he had begun behaving unwisely. He was losing control of the situation and was annoyed with himself and furious with Sophia because of it.

Aaron briefly closed his eyes in an attempt at the control that had all but deserted him. He wanted this woman desperately. She fascinated him, tempted him, challenged him at every turn. He sensed ecstasy beyond his wildest dreams was just beyond his reach, threatening him with a lifetime of regrets should he err.

Those thoughts sobering, Aaron faced Sophia solemnly as she turned toward him. Her glittering blue eyes were tinged with unexpected regret as they searched his face. When she spoke, she took him off guard with her unexpected candor.

"I'm sorry, Aaron. I haven't been fair with you, I suppose." Sophia paused, then continued with obvious determination. "I haven't been completely honest with you and I've misled you because of it." Her smile was apologetic, but her glorious eyes were direct. "You were attracted to me because the gossip about me intrigued you, isn't that right?" Sophia continued without waiting for a response, "But I'm not what you've been led to believe, and I've waited most of my life for the opportunity I have now, and I don't intend to let it pass me by. I have no time for a casual affair."

"Sophia . . ." Aching with the restraint forced on his emotions, Aaron suddenly realized he was more earnest than he had ever been in his life. "Please believe me when I tell you that all I want right now is for us to come to know each other better so you'll believe me when I tell you that my feelings for you are stronger than any I've ever felt before. I told you from the beginning that I don't want anything from you that you aren't willing to give freely. I meant that, but I didn't mean that I'd let you go easily—without a fight."

Sophia's expression became pained. "You don't understand, Aaron. I've set priorities."

Aaron paused in responding. "You're right, I *don't* understand, but I want to."

Sophia shook her head. "You couldn't."

"I can."

Sophia's eyes were sudden, intense pinpoints of light that sent shivers down Aaron's spine as she whispered, "No, you can't! Your future was planned for you the day you were born! How could you understand that an image of the woman I could one day be has been with me since I was a child—that it haunts me? How could you understand what I feel when my mother tells me that I'm a fool and that my vain pride will be my downfall and I'll never be anything more than I am now? How could you understand that every obstacle I encounter makes me more determined?"

Sophia's unexpected fervor raised a passion of his own as Aaron replied from the bottom of his heart, "You may not believe I can understand how you feel, Sophia, but you must know that I believe in you. Because I believe in you, because I care for you, I want to help you."

"I don't need—"

"You think you don't need my help anymore—I know." Aaron swallowed with difficulty, his next words coming hard. "But it's not a matter of need Sophia, not for me. It's a matter of wanting. I *want* to help you. I *want* to be with you. Sophia, I *care* for you."

"If you really care for me you'll respect my feelings and leave me alone."

"It's because I care so much for you that I can't."

Sophia's brilliant eyes challenged his. "A man who really cared would put my feelings before his own."

"A man who cares for you as much as I do would do

anything to prove it to you. That's all I'm asking, Sophia, for you to give me a chance to prove to you how I feel. Will you do that?"

No response.

"Sophia . . ." Aaron's voice dropped a notch lower. "Please . . ."

Silence again.

An unexpected voice from atop the carriage snapped Aaron's head upward. Suddenly realizing that the carriage had drawn to a halt, Aaron responded, "What do you want, Harry?"

"We've arrived at the corner of Prospect Street, sir. Did you want me to proceed or do you want to let the lady off here?"

Sophia was stiffening and Aaron could feel her mentally withdrawing. He felt a sudden urge to shout his frustration. Instead, he pleaded, "Sophia, have dinner with me."

Sophia shook her head. "No . . . I can't."

"Sophia . . ."

A moment later Sophia was out on the street walking toward her home. Following her with an avid gaze, Aaron's sense of loss was so complete that he suddenly realized he was prepared to sacrifice his precious pride, surrender his ego, do anything he must. He would beg . . . crawl on his knees . . . but he would have her in the end.

"You're quiet tonight, Sophia. Is something wrong?"

Sophia looked up from the table, suddenly realizing that her food lay uneaten as she toyed with her fork. Mama assessed her preoccupation as Papa looked worriedly between her and her sisters and her. She forced a smile.

"I'm fine, Papa. I was thinking of the work that I didn't finish for Madame today. I was barely able to touch the needle because of my other duties."

"Already you fall behind in your work?" Mama gave a low snort. "Soon you'll be back with your sisters on the picket line."

Stung by her mother's comments, Sophia raised her chin in challenge. "Madame is very satisfied with my work."

"Oh?" Maria's eyes narrowed assessingly. "Then why do you worry? You have other worries perhaps . . . other things that you plan and won't reveal to your mama until they're already done—"

"Maria, *lascia le esta!*" Anthony interrupted his wife sharply, his dark brows furrowed. "If Sophia hadn't found this position, you'd be without any income from your daughters during this strike." Maria's mein darkened and Anthony nodded. "Ah, you wouldn't like that, would you? You should be grateful that Sophia looks to improve herself. She's a good example to Anna and Rosalie."

"A good example?" Maria snapped to her feet, incensed. "You see only what you want to see in Sophia. Some day you'll regret spoiling her as you do."

"That's enough, Maria!" Anthony stiffened. "I do what I must to offset your excesses."

Tears rose in Maria's pale eyes at her husband's gruffness, and Sophia looked down at her plate as her mother turned to the sink. She was confused at the feelings Aaron's pleas had raised within her. The pain in his dark eyes touched her, despite her caution."

Mama turned back to the table and Sophia felt the nudge of conscience at sight of her red-rimmed eyes. She heard a low sound of discomfort from the chair beside hers the moment before Rosalie spoke.

"I heard Vito talking to Jacques Montepelier today.

249

Jacques said Lyle Kingston has been working day and night toward a settlement. He said that Lyle Kingston is determined to convince his uncle to make an adjustment that will make the situation livable for the weavers. He said he's hopeful the strike will soon be over because he's heard that Lyle Kingston will take over full management of the mill after Paul Kingston leaves."

Anna's gasp turned the attention of all at the table to her sudden whitening as she whispered, "Paul Kingston is leaving? You didn't tell me that, Rosalie. Where is he going?"

"To France to study. Vito said he's going to wait until the strike is settled because he doesn't want to leave his cousin alone during the difficulties he's facing."

Grateful as always for Rosalie's ingenuity in turning the conversation to easier channels, Sophia was suddenly caught by the torment on Anna's young face. She reached under the table to squeeze her sister's hand, only to hear her mother's bitter response.

"The wealthy have no difficulties and they have no conscience! They know money will buy them whatever they want or need. They hold the upper hand, and it will be no different with the strike. The Kingstons will win out in the end."

"You're bitter tonight, Maria." Papa's coarse features tightened as he slowly drew himself to his feet. "I've had a difficult day, and I have little patience left for bitterness. I'm going into the cellar to finish my work."

The silence that followed Papa's departure went unbroken for long moments before the scrape of chairs against the floor signaled the formal end of the meal. Working beside her mother and sisters until the dishes and pans had been washed and the kitchen restored to order, Sophia struggled with the image of Aaron Weiss that haunted her thoughts. She thought of Papa downstairs, making his wine, but she knew she could not talk to him about her confusion. Nor could she talk to Rosalie or Anna.

Grateful when the last dish had been returned to the rack and the last pan stored, Sophia walked out onto the porch. She looked up at the first stars of night twinkling in the sky overhead, envying them the serenity of that endless expanse where there was no conflict and where there were no decisions to be made. She imagined herself wrapped in that dark velvet, with the glittering stars adorning her hair and sparkling on her ears. She reveled in her fantasy, smiling.

"What are you doing, Sophia?"

Sophia turned toward Rosalie. "I was just standing here and thinking."

"Anna is upset. She went to our room."

"I know."

"It's Paul Kingston. She . . . cares about him. She doesn't want him to go away. She thinks she'll never see him again."

"I know."

"If Mama knew . . ."

Sophia turned sharply. "Mama mustn't ever know. She would shame Anna."

Rosalie nodded, suddenly raising eyes too wise for her years to Sophia's intense expression. "I'm good at keeping secrets, Sophia. I'll keep Anna's secret, and I'll always keep yours. You know that, don't you?"

Tears sprang to Sophia's eyes as she took an abrupt step forward and hugged Rosalie tight. "Yes, I know. I'll remember."

Rosalie disappeared back into the house and Sophia resumed her position at the railing, her eyes raised to the sky above her. Lyle's face appeared before her mind's eye and Sophia sighed. She wished she could talk to him,

251

but she knew that was impossible. She had declared her independence from him and pride stood in her way, even if the progress of their lives was not leading them in different directions.

Sophia flushed. She knew what Lyle thought of Aaron Weiss, and she sensed he was right, but . . .

Briefly closing her eyes, Sophia longed for the safety of Lyle's arms, for his comforting voice in her ear, only to have Aaron's image appear before her mind's eye, his dark eyes pleading.

"Sophia, come inside. I have something for you to do."

Sophia turned at the sound of her mother's voice. Mama was still angry. It would not be easy dealing with her tonight.

"Sophia, *subito!*"

Strengthening her forbearance, Sophia complied.

The evening sky was dark against the open mill windows, the silence seeming somehow unnatural as Lyle turned from his desk and walked toward the files behind him. The pickets had left for the day and Uncle Matthew and Paul had followed a short time later, granting him the solitude to work undisturbed, for which he was inordinately grateful. Lyle glanced at the clock on the wall and grimaced. It was almost nine, but he was determined that he wouldn't leave until he concluded the project he had started.

Feeling a familiar rise of frustration, Lyle ran an anxious hand through his heavy gold hair and unbuttoned his shirt another notch. The night air hung heavily in the room, increasing his discomfort as he searched the production sheets for the particular figures he sought. Despite the agreement struck the previous week, his uncle had not allowed him full rein in handling the strike. He had submitted to his uncle's demands, aware that Paul was still on the scene and their agreement was not officially in place, but it had not been easy. Stubborn, unyielding on every important point, Uncle Matthew had driven the strikers back to their picket lines time and again, prolonging the strike unnecessarily when Lyle was certain a token concession would already have brought the anxious men back to their machines.

Lyle's frustration soared. Every proposition he had made to date had been branded unworkable, impractical, or unrealistic, but tonight he was determined to prove his uncle wrong. He was certain that the figures would support his claim that a token bonus granted to those weavers who doubled their loom assignments voluntarily could be easily supported, and that the inducement of an additional bonus for production beyond a reasonable quota would not lower mill profits, but would, in the long run, increase them. He would prove—

The echo of familiar steps raised Lyle's head from the file in front of him with a frown. He closed his eyes briefly at the sight of his uncle walking stiffly toward him, Paul trailing disgustedly at his rear.

Paul's voice was rank with apology as the office door swung open.

"I'm sorry, Lyle. I tried to convince Father that he'd merely be in the way coming here tonight, but he insisted."

"I have no difficulty speaking for myself, Paul!" His mood obviously foul, Matthew turned back to Lyle, his eyes narrowing as he looked at the folder in his nephew's hand. "What do you have there?" He gave a short laugh. "Production figures? That should be simple. Our production is zero—nothing. We're at a standstill and will remain there until we've beaten these damned radicals at their own game!"

"This strike isn't presently being run by radicals, Uncle. It's being run by men who're fighting to protect their futures. That seems to be a point you're unwilling to accept, but it's true. There's no way these men are going to accept industrial progress without struggle unless you make some concessions along the way."

"Concessions!" Matthew Kingston was irate. "I *own* this mill and *I* make the decisions."

"And the weavers are skilled laborers. Your mill can't function without them! They're asking you for the respect due them and compensation for the loss of jobs they see in the future. They're reasonable men. They'll respond reasonably if you'll give them a chance."

"You're a poor judge of character, Lyle." Matthew sneered. "It's undoubtedly a flaw that can be traced to your genes."

"Father!"

"Don't interrupt, Paul! It's time my nephew learned to face his deficiencies."

Lyle forced a smile. He was wise to his uncle's game. The crafty fellow was desperate to escape the bargain he had struck the previous week, but Lyle was not about to be driven out by mere words when he was so close to victory. His smile broadened. "My deficiencies are all in your mind, Uncle. You choose to believe them because—"

"Because I know them to be true! You're a poor judge of character, of situations, and it appears of women, too."

Lyle's smile faded and Matthew gave a short laugh, pressing his point with obvious enjoyment. "Tell me, Lyle, where's that red-haired piece of baggage of whom you were so fond? I haven't seen her walking the picket lines, and I haven't seen her supporting you, either. She seems to have disappeared at the first sign of trouble."

254

Lyle's control slipped dramatically at his uncle's denigrating reference to Sophia. Bristling, he sought a subdued tone in reply.

"If you're referring to Sophia Marone, she's found a better job where she can expand upon her talents."

"Talents?" Matthew's short laugh was harsh. "Yes, I suppose Aaron Weiss has discovered her true talents. He's had much experience in that regard."

His anger rising, Lyle spoke in instinctive defense. "Whatever rumors you've heard, Uncle, I can tell you that Sophia worked hard to get her job with Madame Tourneau."

Matthew's laughter raised the hackles on Lyle's spine. "Really? That isn't what Allistair Marks told me this afternoon. The old fool was nearly forced to fisticuffs with Weiss when he began sniffing around the girl. Weiss warned him to stay away from her in full view of that Frenchwoman and her patrons. And the red-haired witch enjoyed every minute of it!"

"You're lying!"

"Am I?" Matthew appeared pleased. "Did you really think that tart cared for you? She was using you, just as those strikers are using you. And you're too much of a fool to realize it!"

"Father, you're not being fair! You're repeating gossip. You don't know that Sophia—"

"Keep out of this, Paul!" Matthew turned toward his son with a snarl. "Your weakness for that Italian trash's sister has warped your viewpoint."

"And your prejudice has warped yours!" His fury barely under control, Lyle faced his uncle squarely, his fists balled. "I've accepted your unfair criticisms of me, Uncle, but I don't intend to stand here and let you malign a friend."

"So, the red-haired tart is a 'friend' . . ." Matthew's ex-

255

pression hardened. "Well, she's Aaron's friend now, and I'm certain he'll use that 'friendship' to best advantage."

Barely maintaining control, Lyle withheld reply. He saw the satisfaction that curled his uncle's lip at his agitation and he knew his uncle sensed victory within his grasp. Determined to deny him that satisfaction, Lyle forced a smile with sheer strength of will.

"It won't work, Uncle. I know what you're up to, but you're not going to aggravate me into walking out on our bargain. When Paul leaves, *I* take over management of the mill and nothing you say will drive me away before I've made you admit that you've been wrong in everything you've ever said or thought about me."

"That will be the day!"

Choosing not to respond, Lyle withdrew the production file from the drawer and turned to his desk. "If you'll excuse me, I have work to do." He looked up at Matthew, his determination unmistakable. "I'll be ready in the morning to back up my newest proposal with figures. I guarantee that you'll be unable to deny its workability—that is, if you're capable of an unprejudiced evaluation."

Silence reigned for long, tense moments, finally broken by Matthew's low, furious tone.

"You dare to challenge my judgment?"

Choosing to neglect direct response, Lyle countered, "If my proposal is offered to the strikers tomorrow, the mill will be functioning at full capacity by the end of the week."

"You're wrong! These agitators are out for blood this time!"

Lyle paused, his gaze moving over his uncle's patrician features. The flush of rage deepened the lines of strain there, aging him before Lyle's eyes. His own anger suddenly paling, Lyle shrugged. "We'll see, won't we,

256

Uncle?"

Lyle was working at his desk when the slam of the entrance door signaled the exit of his uncle and cousin. Only then did Lyle raise his head from the figures in front of him. Staring silently into the shadows of the mill floor, he saw again the bright-haired image that had not been far from his mind during the furious pace of the past week.

Could it be true?

Giving a short laugh, Lyle shook his head. Rumors followed Sophia wherever she went. She was too smart and too determined to be fooled by the likes of Aaron Weiss. He need have no concerns there.

Lyle looked back down at the figures in front of him. On the other hand, his lifelong ambition hung precariously on the progress he would make with the strikers in the next few days. Like Sophia, he was too smart to be forced into an unwise position. And like Sophia, he would not allow this opportunity to escape him.

Chapter Twelve

The image of the previous night returned before Sophia's mind's eye. She was wrapped in the dark velvet of the night sky. Glittering stars adorned her dress and ears and sparkled in her hair. The vision, as vividly clear in the back room of Madame's salon as it had been the previous night, flowed spontaneously from the pencil she held in her hand onto the sheet of paper on the table in front of her, and her excitement grew. She rubbed charcoal into the sketched folds to simulate the black silk that would comprise the finished garment and pressed white chalk into the tiny sketched stars, simulating the sparkle of silver beads and black jets that would make up the celestial field decorating the skirt and daring décolletage. She colored the mannequin's hair a fiery red like her own, liberally disbursing the same sparkling stars there and at the lobes of her ears.

Not yet satisfied, Sophia sketched the escort at her side, her heart beginning a heady pounding as the male figure took on startling familiarity. His broad shoulders were soon covered in an evening coat with reveres trimmed with the same material as her gown. His chest-hugging waistcoat was of the same black silk, a narrow strip of which ran down the leg of the close-fitting trousers. His matching attire complete, she filled in the color of the phantom figure's hair. Dark.

"Sophia, you are there?"

Madame Tourneau's voice returned Sophia to the present with a startling snap. Looking up at the clock on the wall of the salon's rear room, she realized her lunch period was over although her sandwich lay uneaten on the table beside her hand.

"Sophia?"

"Yes, madame."

"The blue day gown, if you please." She could almost hear Madame smile. "Madame Hurtfield has a preference for blue."

Her sketch forgotten, Sophia stepped out onto the floor a few moments later, her hand rising to the upward sweep of her hair as she strolled forward in the day gown of a fragile batiste that was almost too light for the waning season. She smiled and turned for the woman, concentrating on the manner Madame took with her customer.

"As you see, it is a deceivingly simple dress, but a true treasure. I'm still showing it to a favored few customers who I know will appreciate its delicacy during this extended summer."

Sophia almost laughed. Madame was so clever as she continued to discuss the merits of her dress, beguiling the woman with a steady stream of cautious compliments.

The sound of the salon door opening turned Sophia in its direction. Her heart jumped and her step faltered at Aaron's appearance, but she was somehow unable to smile as he came to stand directly at her side. Strangely, neither could she speak, but Madame Tourneau was not similarly indisposed.

"Ah, Monsieur Weiss! You are becoming a frequent visitor of my establishment. What may I do for you?"

The aging couturiere placed a manicured hand on Aaron's sleeve, claiming his attention, and Sophia found herself both amused and annoyed at the Frenchwoman's appreciative eye. Struggling to regain her composure,

Sophia realized she should not have been surprised. Madame enjoyed beauty and clarity of line, and she knew that there was not a single flaw in Aaron's total physical symmetry. About the inner man, however, Sophia found she still had strong reservations, despite his stirring words the previous day.

As if reading her thoughts, Aaron glanced at her, his gaze dropping to her mouth, and Sophia was again breathless. A strong desire to flee almost overwhelmed her as Madame turned momentarily to her customer and Aaron whispered, "I didn't sleep at all last night for thinking about you, Sophia. We must talk."

Not up to her usual quick exchange, Sophia shook her head. She could not afford to confess that she had suffered similarly, only to finally fall asleep and dream of a battle between a handsome, golden-haired protector and an equally handsome but sinister dark-haired devil that she could not seem to resist.

Back after having left her customer with a mound of sketches to ponder, Madame Tourneau spoke sweetly into the silence between them.

"Your visits are always a pleasure, Monsieur Weiss, but I'm afraid I can't spare Sophia for more than a few minutes this afternoon." Celeste waved a graceful hand, indicating the customers who busied themselves at the shelves and racks of accessories. "As you can see, my poor shop is very busy and Sophia's services are needed."

"Yes, I can see, madame." A trace of the haughty Aaron Weiss of old flickered across his face the moment before he forced a smile. "But you won't suffer for the time I spend here. My mother has asked my opinion as to which of Paterson's couturieres she should recommend to the Silk Association Council for several projects. I'm considering recommending Madame Tourneau."

Madame nodded, her expression guarded. "I would very much appreciate your recommendation, Monsieur

Weiss." She then smiled. "Just a few moments more, Sophia, then the burgundy silk, if you please."

"Of course, madame."

"Do you have any objections if I accompany Sophia to the back room for a few moments, madame? It's a personal matter that can be disposed of quickly."

Waiting only for Madame's nod, Aaron walked beside Sophia, ignoring the two startled seamstresses as he entered the back room and drew the curtain closed behind him. Not bothering to speak as he turned toward Sophia, he cupped her face in his hands and covered her mouth with his.

Caught unawares, Sophia was drawn into Aaron's kiss, held captive by her own unexpected response. She was breathless, transfixed, as Aaron drew back moments later and whispered, "I'll be waiting for you after you're done working."

"Sophia!"

Madame Tourneau's voice, drawing closer, shattered the emotion of the moment, restoring sanity to Sophia's bemused mind. She replied unsteadily, "Y-yes, madame. I'll be right there."

Turning, Aaron walked back out into the salon, but not before Sophia saw the reluctance with which he parted from her, and not before she saw all that went unspoken in his solemn gaze.

Suddenly realizing that the two silent seamstresses were staring, Sophia raised her chin.

"Madame wants me to show Madame Hurtfield the burgundy silk."

Sophia closed her eyes and took a steadying breath as the gown slipped down over her shoulders. Prepared to step out into the salon moments later, she forced aside her raging uncertainties with a professional smile.

* * *

"Strike . . . strike . . . strike . . . strike . . ."

Appearing insensitive to the glaring sun that beat down on their heads, the ragged picket line circled in front of the mill entrance in repetition of the scene that had been played over and over since the strike began a week earlier.

Lyle stood just inside the mill entrance, intensely aware of Matthew Kingston standing stiffly behind him as the chant continued. Glancing back at his uncle, Lyle saw the beads of perspiration that stood out on his forehead, but Lyle was suddenly certain that the heat had little to do with his uncle's discomfort. The truth was that it was damned hard for Matthew Kingston to believe that he could be wrong.

Jacques Montepelier and his group were now studying the proposal Lyle had submitted to his uncle the first thing that morning. The feasibility of the proposal had been indisputable, backed up as it was with figures from the mill's production sheets, and Matthew had been unable to dismiss it. Lyle knew it would be one of the blackest days of his uncle's life if the union accepted it.

Lyle could not suppress a smile. He knew they would . . .

Appearing in the doorway on cue, Montepelier was sober, his expression noncommittal. His heart assuming a ragged beat, Lyle stepped forward, aware that his uncle stood a step to his rear as the fellow spoke briefly.

"This is a fair proposal. I'll take it to the membership and we'll vote on it tonight."

Lyle nodded, his response equally concise. "Good."

Waiting only until the man had disappeared back through the doorway out of sight, Lyle turned to Matthew. "Well, what do you think now, Uncle?"

Matthew sneered. "I think that you're overly optimistic. They'll turn it down just like they've turned down every other reasonable proposal we've made this week."

It was Lyle's turn to sneer. "We haven't made any other reasonable proposals this week, Uncle—only demands. They'll accept this offer, all right."

"Damned cocky . . ." Suddenly too furious to continue, Matthew turned toward the office where Paul busied himself with paperwork and shouted, "I'm leaving, Paul. Are you coming?"

Looking up, Paul glanced between the two men before calling back in a more moderate tone, "No, Father. I think I'll stay here with Lyle. He—"

"Do what you damned well please!"

Turning abruptly, Matthew strode through the doorway past the marching pickets and disappeared into the yard. Standing beside Lyle moments later, Paul gave a short laugh.

"Whatever you did to the old man sure lit a fire under his tail."

"The union is considering my proposal."

Paul appeared stunned, then gave a hoot of laughter. "Well, I'll be damned! The first sign of progress in a week, and you've managed it. No wonder Father's fit to be tied!"

But Lyle wasn't smiling. "They're going to accept the proposal, Paul. This mill will be back to full production by the end of the week, and I'll be in full charge, whether your father likes it or not."

"And I'll be on my way to Paris on the first ship." Paul gave another hoot of laughter before his jubilation slowly turned cautious. "But how can you be so sure they'll accept it?"

His gold eyes burning with a new heat, Lyle answered without hesitation, "Because my time here has finally come. I can feel it in my bones, and your father can, too. That's what's infuriating him. And I'm going to tell you something else, Cousin. Now that I have my chance, nothing is going to stand in my way. I'll make him eat his words. I'll run this mill more efficiently than he ever did, and I'll prove to him that I . . ."

Lyle halted abruptly, blinking. "I'm sorry, Paul. I'm afraid I'm obsessed with this whole thing."

Suddenly as serious as Lyle, Paul responded softly, "Don't let him do that to you."

"Do what?"

"Take the humanity out of you."

Staring into his cousin's pale eyes for long, silent moments, Lyle responded softly, "Don't worry about me. I'll survive. I always have. Now, if I were you, I'd hop on the nearest streetcar and go home to pack my bags."

"You're that sure . . ."

"I'm that sure."

Suddenly grinning, Paul slapped Lyle's broad shoulder. "Then I'm on my way!"

Grinning, too, as Paul disappeared through the doorway, Lyle suddenly felt his elation begin to drain. He looked around the silent mill. He knew what he wanted—what he had always wanted—but now that he was on the verge of getting it, he found his elation tempered by an entirely different concern.

Walking toward the door, Lyle looked out into the yard, searching the milling figures. He easily spotted Rosalie and Anna in a corner of the yard and made his way to their side. He nodded toward Anna and smiled as Rosalie looked at him expectantly.

"Truce, Rosalie. I don't want to talk about the strike, so don't look so apprehensive."

"What do you want to talk about, Mr. Kingston?"

Lyle sobered. "I want to talk about Sophia."

Rosalie was immediately on her guard. "Sophia's affairs are her own business."

"Sophia and I are friends."

Rosalie shrugged. "Sophia has many friends."

"Come on, Rosalie . . ."

264

Rosalie's rigidity wavered at the plea in Lyle's tone. "I don't know what you want me to tell you. Sophia's working for Madame Tourneau and she's very happy in her new position. We're all very proud of her."

"Even your mother?"

Rosalie's gaze flickered. "Sophia told you about Mama?" And then at his nod. "Mama will never change."

Lyle paused, his expression tightening. "I heard something that worried me, Rosalie . . . about Aaron Weiss and Sophia . . ."

Rosalie raised her chin in a manner so reminiscent of Sophia that Lyle felt his throat momentarily tighten. "Sophia can take care of herself."

"But—"

"Come on, Anna." Turning to Anna, who had remained silent through the exchange, Rosalie took her arm. "It's our turn to picket now."

In a minute the two girls were gone and Lyle's concern deepened. Rosalie's response to his inquiry had been more revealing than words. Back inside the mill a few moments later, he was frowning blackly. The union was going to vote tonight, and when they were done he was going to have the biggest job of his life ahead of him. He couldn't afford to allow thoughts of Sophia to cloud his mind. Rosalie was right. Sophia could take care of herself. She had taken the first step on her way toward the future she had always seen for herself, just as he had. Perhaps they'd meet on that path ahead of them.

And perhaps they wouldn't.

That thought suddenly too difficult to face, Lyle walked back into his office and slammed the door behind him.

Celeste Tourneau paused briefly at the drawn curtains to the rear room. She glanced at the clock on the wall nearby and gave a short sigh. The shop was closed, her employees had left, and she would soon be on her way home. It had been a difficult day and she was getting too old for the politics involved in her work. Ah for the luxury of merely designing and allowing others to handle the more difficult aspects of her profession.

Aaron Weiss's statement suddenly returned to mind, as it had several times that day. A recommendation to the Silk Association Council . . . Madame smiled, aware of the many benefits such a recommendation would entail. Inclusion in all the Silk Association Council activities—fashion shows, benefits, and exposure at the silk exposition in New York City. There she had the possibility of worldwide recognition of her talents. Ah . . . a beautiful dream.

But Madame Tourneau was not a dreamer. She was a worker and a schemer, both attributes that had taken her far in her chosen profession, and she had become aware that hiring the beautiful Sophia Marone was going to prove far more beneficial than she had ever dreamed. She fully intended using the young woman to the best advantage. Madame laughed aloud. As did the handsome, virile Aaron Weiss, no doubt.

Her mood becoming almost light-hearted, Celeste realized that she would profit in a most unexpected way from Aaron Weiss's lust. The exquisite Sophia Marone did not know what was in store.

His jaw rigid, Aaron sat beside Sophia as the carriage traveled the familiar route toward her home. He had been waiting for her as promised when she emerged from the salon at the conclusion of the day and they were again at an impasse. There was no doubting his distress was genuine as he turned to her abruptly and instructed, "Look out that window, Sophia. We've almost reached

Prospect Street. You'll be jumping out of the carriage in a minute and you'll be gone again. What then? Tomorrow, do we take up where we left off, never getting past foolish arguments which waste valuable time?"

Sophia turned her head from the sight of Aaron's anxiety, unwilling to admit to herself that her resistance to his entreaties was rapidly waning.

"Look at me, Sophia!" Aaron held her gaze, struggling visibly to restrain his emotions. "Is this *all* you want between us?"

"I don't know what you mean."

Aaron stared steadily into her eyes. His voice husky with emotion he whispered, "Yes, you do."

"I told you—"

"What *did* you tell me, Sophia? You told me that I couldn't buy you, and I've made no attempt to try. You told me that you can't let anything stand in the way of the goals you've set for yourself, and I've told you that I'll help you attain them. You've told me that you have no time for a casual affair, and I've told you that there would be nothing casual about an affair between us. Sophia . . ."

Aaron grasped her shoulders, drawing her close. His fervent persuasion echoed in Sophia's mind, even as her body warmed to his touch. She had heard similar words spoken many times, but this man wove a web around her senses, drawing her in, holding her captive with the passion in his voice and the ardor in his dark eyes.

"Sophia, listen to me . . ." Desperation entered Aaron's plea, even as Sophia fought to break free of his spell. "Meet me tonight. We can—"

The carriage drew to an unexpected halt, and Aaron looked up, muttering a soft curse as he glanced out onto the street. Angry, he tapped on the roof of the carriage.

"What's the matter, Harry? We haven't reached Prospect Street yet."

267

"I can't go any farther, sir." Harry's voice was rank with apology. "There's some sort of a fair being set up and the street is blocked off."

Sophia frowned at the intrusion of reality. "The Feast of the Madonna of Assunta starts tonight. It's a big holiday."

"I don't care about the holiday, Sophia. All I care about is us."

"I can't meet you."

"Why can't you?"

"Because I'm not like you." Summoning the strength to withdraw from his arms, Sophia whispered, "Please understand, Aaron, I believe what you say when you tell me that you care for me in a way you've never cared for another woman." Sophia paused, her voice dropping in timber when she continued. "And I believe you, too, when you say what we can mean to each other . . ."

"Then why—"

"I'm not the person you think I am—the person rumor has made me out to be!" Sophia shrugged. "I could never be that person. I'd disappoint you."

"You could never disappoint me, Sophia." Aaron's gaze dropped to her lips. "You're far more than I ever expected you to be." His voice dropped to a husky whisper. "And I promise, I won't disappoint you."

"Let me go, Aaron."

Freeing herself, Sophia reached for the door of the carriage only to be halted by the strain of Aaron's soft plea.

"Please, Sophia."

Wavering in that moment, coming closer to succumbing to the feelings rioting inside her than ever before, Sophia suddenly thrust the door open. Out on the street in a moment, she walked rapidly toward her home, refusing to look back.

"It's strange that a woman could be married to the

268

same man for twenty-eight years without realizing that he's truly a fool."

Unaware that Edith had entered to stand just inside the doorway of their room, Matthew looked up. Refusing to let her know the contempt in her tone had stung him, Matthew reached casually into the wardrobe for a fresh shirt.

"I'd say that statement speaks as poorly of you as it does of me, Edith."

"Oh, would you?" Advancing into the room, Edith closed the door behind her with obvious fury. "I wouldn't! Damn you, Matthew! What's happened to you?"

"Happened to me?" Matthew laughed, a sound without mirth. "What particular fiasco are you presently referring to? The strike at the mill, our son's imminent departure for France, or the expansion of Lyle's duties in supervision of the mill?"

"You know damned well what I mean?"

"You're wrong, Edith, because I don't! I should think you'd be happy with the progress of events here. Paul just returned from the mill and you were talking to him. Didn't he tell you that the union is looking favorably on our latest proposal and that they intend voting on it tonight? It appears they'll accept it and then everything will progress according to your plan."

"Bastard!"

"No, not I." Matthew raised a haughty brow. "Correct me if I'm wrong. It was your idea to encourage Paul to pursue his 'art,' wasn't it, and to have Lyle take a freer hand in supervision of the mill while he's gone so your dear son could have a clear mind while he's away?"

"Yes, but I didn't expect this to come about on *Lyle's* terms! Damn you, Matthew, you're playing Lyle's game, and I don't like it! Somehow he's managed to get the upper hand over you—something I thought I'd never witness. He's a bastard, Matthew! He has no place at the head of Kingston Mills!" Quaking visibly, Edith attempted to draw her outrage under control. "He has thwarted you at every step—throwing Hope back in our faces and now gaining control over the mill with guarantees for the future that you shouldn't have countenanced for a moment, much less agreed upon!"

Matthew's chin hardened under Edith's scathing gaze, and he laughed. "Your son made sure he told you everything, didn't he?"

"*Our* son, Matthew! Yes, and it's well that he did, since you seemed lacking in the courage to confess your stupidity!" Edith's gaze grew incredulous. "I can't believe you've allowed this to happen, but I should've seen it coming. Everything started getting out of hand after Julia visited you that night. What did she do . . . what did she say to make you—"

"Nothing! All this has nothing to do with Julia! It has to do with you and Paul, and Lyle and myself. And whether you care to admit to your part in this debacle, you played a major role in your overindulgence of *our* son, because Paul is what you've made him to be, Edith. He's an *artist*, interested solely in his *art*, and to hell with the rest of the world! And then there's Lyle . . ."

"This is your sister's fault, I say! If she hadn't brought that bastard into this family—"

"Leave my sister out of this!"

"No! The woman has lived on our patronage her entire life! She nursed that viper in our midst on the funds we provided! Well, that's all come to an end now. Tomorrow I'm going to tell her she's on her own. She can support herself and see how far she gets. Perhaps then she'll realize what loyalty means!"

His body rigid, Matthew took a sudden step forward that brought a moment of true fear into Edith's pale eyes. "You will do no such thing . . . do you hear me, Edith? My sister's health is poor."

"Or so she claims!"

"She has a weak heart, damn you! You'll keep your distance from Julia until your control is such that you'll be able to treat her in the same manner you've always treated her!"

"Like the indigent relation that she is?"

"Like the *lady* that she is and will always be! She is my sister, Edith, and I warn you now, if you go against my wishes, you'll see a side of me that you've never witnessed before . . . and that you'll hope never to witness again!"

Edith paused, finally managing a trace of her old hauteur. "Are you threatening me, Matthew?"

"Consider it a threat or a promise—whatever you like—but do as I say, Edith. For your own sake, and for the sake of us all."

Storming out of the room, Matthew was in the downstairs foyer when he suddenly realized that he was in his shirtsleeves. Glancing back toward the second floor, his rage such that he was unwilling to face his wife again in order to claim his coat, Matthew strode into the sitting room and the crystal decanter that rested on the corner table. With trembling hands, he pulled out the stopper and splashed the amber liquid into a glass. Downing it in one gulp, he refilled his glass and raised it again to his lips, grateful to feel the soothing effects of the spirits as he took another sip. He walked to the window, deliberately turning his back to the foyer as he closed his eyes.

A gasp escaped his lips as a dainty female image appeared before his mind's eye. Golden hair and golden eyes, small perfect features, and lips curved into a smile of complete adoration . . . an emotion he remembered returning with all his heart . . . Sweet Christine . . .

His anguish as strong as it had been those many years ago, Matthew swallowed, struggling to escape the loving smile that had turned to tears. How he had loved her.

Even now, after the passage of time, the sweet scent of her returned with vivid clarity, and the remembered gentleness of her touch tormented him. He had been so young, barely out of his teens when he had met Christine Clark, and he had been totally overwhelmed by the outpouring of love he had experienced for the shy, English-born immigrant. His ambitions for the future and the realization that the angelic-looking, uneducated girl was not of his class had had no effect on the power of his feelings. Hardly more than a child and totally alone in a new country after the unexpected death of her sponsor, Christine had responded to his attentions with all the fervor of her lonely existence. She gave all she had to give to him and he accepted it with a humility totally foreign to his nature, so great was his love.

It had not been difficult to convince Christine to become his mistress. She had been overjoyed to belong to someone at last and delighted with the Spartan quarters he arranged for her. He had wished desperately he could give her more and he remembered promising himself that he would never abandon his pledge to love her all of his life.

He had not taken into consideration, however, that Christine might someday abandon hers.

Matthew drank deeply from his glass, but the fiery liquid did little to quell the pain of memory. He had known Christine was not a virgin when he first took her to his bed, but he had read true innocence in her eyes and he was so certain she loved him. He became more certain as the days stretched into months and the months into a year, then two. His greatest difficulty had been in accepting the scope of emotions she raised within him. He had loved her more each day and was certain the same was true for her, until . . .

Damn it all!

Turning away from the window in hope of escaping the

image reflected in his mind's eye, Matthew threw his glass against the far wall, his fury as great as it had been that day. But he accomplished little with his violence, for fixed in his memory, was a vision of Christine and her lover in intimate embrace in the bedroom Christine and he had shared.

A familiar knife of pain cut deeply, drawing blood anew as Matthew turned back to the window in despair. He remembered Christine's shocked outcry at seeing him in the doorway, and her haste to escape her lover's arms. He remembered the sound of her voice following him as he ran to the door, and as he ran down the staircase refusing to look back, he remembered the sounds of her pitiful sobbing behind him.

Matthew breathed deeply once . . . twice. Swallowing the thick knot of emotion in his throat, he straightened his spine and raised his chin. All love inside him had died that day. And when Christine came to him later, appealing for forgiveness, telling him that she carried his child, he had laughed in her face.

Aware that he could survive the pain of Christine's infidelity no other way, he had allowed his heart to remain cold. He had pursued success and achieved it. He had found another woman who was everything that Christine was not, and married her. He had fathered a son and given him whatever love he was capable of giving. He had never looked back.

Matthew closed his eyes. Then when Christine died, alone and penniless, he had refused to shed a tear.

He had not, however, seen the last of her.

Lyle's sober face suddenly supplanted Christine's image in his mind, and Matthew snapped his eyes open with an angry grunt. Christine's bastard son had appeared to take his mother's revenge, and there was no escaping him.

Turning, Matthew furiously struck the crystal decanter to the floor with the back of his hand, hardly aware of the sound of shattering glass as he took another step and wiped the lamp from a nearby table and kicked it across the room. The wanton whore that she was, Christine still haunted him in the face of her son . . . *her* son, not his. *Never* his! The patrician air Lyle Clark assumed was feigned! He was common — as common as his treacherous mother! Matthew would never forgive Christine for her faithlessness. Neither would he forgive Lyle for being born.

Standing still in the debris of his fury, Matthew ignored the nervous servant who appeared in the doorway, as well as Edith, who stood midway on the staircase, staring at him in silence. Taunting him was the realization that everything Lyle had said that day was true. The union *would* accept Lyle's proposal tonight, and he *would* be forced to honor his foolish agreement to allow his "nephew" to take over complete supervision of the mill.

Still furious at his own stupidity and at a loss to understand why he had agreed to such a scheme, Matthew consoled himself that Lyle wouldn't win out in the end. He was sure of that, for he knew that despite the manner in which his nephew mimicked the airs of a gentleman, blood would tell. Like his mother before him, he would reveal his true self. Julia would see her precious Lyle for what he was then, and he would be free of Lyle Clark forever. It was just a matter of time.

The lively strains of "Finiculi, Finicula" filled the air, punctuated by bursts of laughter, the shouts of children, and the foreign rattle of rapid Italian as Aaron walked through the crowded street. Pushed and shoved on every side by the surging throng, he glanced scathingly around him at the carts that littered the street, offering every manner of purchase. Food, sweets, flavored ices, handmade articles, and gaudily painted religious statues abounded, and he frowned at the realization that he was

274

as out of place at the religious feast of these Italian peasants as his gleaming carriage had been beside the few wagons parked just beyond the string of lights marking its perimeter. Not for the first time he cursed the weakness that had forced him to come despite his reservations. He glanced around him, aware of the interest he attracted from many of the young women in passing. But he wasn't interested in that common lot. He had only one woman on his mind.

Straining for a glimpse of Sophia's brilliant tresses among the dark-haired throng, Aaron felt a growing desperation. He had been wandering aimlessly in the thickening crowd for more than half an hour and he was still unwilling to admit that he was wasting his time. He had been so sure Sophia's family would be in attendance, aware as he was of the importance these superstitious immigrants placed on their religious celebrations. He sensed that the strike at the Kingston Mill would make their homage to the Madonna even more significant.

Thrust roughly aside by an excited boy who raced past with a friend in hot pursuit, Aaron turned angrily, only to have comment wiped from his mind by the appearance of Sophia and her sisters at the far end of the street. His heart beginning a rapid pounding, he moved swiftly through the crowd, feigning astonishment as he halted abruptly beside her.

"Sophia, what a pleasant surprise!"

His smile broadened as Sophia swallowed and darted a nervous glance toward the middle-aged couple behind her. "Mr. Weiss . . . how nice to see you."

Nodding as Sophia made the necessary introductions, Aaron took an instant dislike to her sharp-eyed mother who appraised him critically. It was Sophia's father, however, who caused him the greatest shock. The man was homely and common beyond belief! Astounded that these two could have sired a daughter as magnificent as

Sophia, Aaron was unexpectedly saddened that despite her physical perfection, Sophia was so critically blemished by heredity.

"Mr. Weiss is a customer at Madame Tourneau's salon."

Sophia's explanation was directed to her mother, who replied in a caustic tone, "Ah, so? You have an interest in women's fashions, Mr. Weiss?"

Controlling the impulse to respond in kind, Aaron forced a smile. "My father's mill supplies most of the silk for Madame Tourneau. I'm also involved with the Silk Association Council. Madame Tourneau and Sophia will do some work for us at our next silk exposition in New York."

Maria Marone turned sharply toward her daughter. "That is so, Sophia?"

"I . . . I—"

Realizing Sophia was at a loss, Aaron interrupted. "I'm sorry. I don't think Madame has spoken to Sophia about the exposition yet."

Maria Marone's expression turned cold. "Sophia will not go to New York."

"Mama!"

"I said you will not go to New York!"

"Maria . . ." Sophia's father took his wife's arm. "We will talk about this later."

Realizing the situation was quickly slipping away from him, Aaron addressed Sophia's father directly.

"I wonder if you might spare Sophia for a short time, sir. I've heard the women of this church offer especially fine handmade articles for sale. My mother has expressed a desire for a crocheted tablecloth, but I'm at a loss in selecting one. I thought Sophia might be able to help me since she's more familiar—"

"No! Sophia will come with us."

Maria's abrupt interjection turned her husband toward

her with obvious vexation. His coarse features tightened as he ignored her discourteous response and addressed Sophia.

"Sophia, you will help Mr. Weiss."

"Sì, Papa."

With a brief farewell, Anthony gripped his wife's arm firmly and continued on. Aaron held his breath until he saw Sophia's sisters follow quietly behind them.

He turned back to Sophia, his smile fading at her obvious displeasure.

"Why are you here, Aaron?"

Grateful for the crush that suddenly thrust them closer, Aaron offered, "I wanted to see you. Is that so difficult to understand?"

Sophia darted a tense glance around her. "You see how it is with me, and you see the difficulty you cause me with your appearance here."

Aaron stiffened. "I don't understand your mother's attitude. What possible objection can she have to your participation in the silk exposition? You can only gain from working with well-educated people who can help you advance."

Sophia's smile was tight. "People like you, Aaron?"

"I didn't mean it the way it sounded."

"You didn't?"

Suddenly frustrated that their conversation had again taken a negative tone, Aaron abruptly took Sophia's arm and propelled her in the opposite direction from the one her family had taken.

"What are you doing? Let go of my arm!"

"No! I want to talk to you where there aren't dozens of people milling at our elbows. My carriage is parked nearby."

"No. People would think that you and I—"

"Do you think I'm concerned with what any of these people think?"

Sophia's response rang with sarcasm. "No, of course not. Why should you be?"

Halting abruptly, Aaron looked down at Sophia. Her expression was tinged with anger and she was more beautiful than any woman he had ever seen. His need for her echoed in his tormented tone as he whispered, "Sophia, don't you care for me at all?"

The band chose that moment to strike up another tune, and Aaron suffered another painful surge of frustration. "Come with me, Sophia . . . please," he rasped.

Silent for a long moment, Sophia shook her head. "Not to your carriage. Come. We can go into the church."

Sophia withdrew a scarf from her pocket and covered her head, conscious of Aaron's step behind her as she drew open the door of the church. The darkened interior was lit only by candles, and she released a relieved breath to find the pews were empty.

Sliding into a pew partially obscured by the shadow of a large pillar, Sophia slipped to her knees and closed her eyes, clasping her hands before her. But she did not pray. Instead, she sought to still the clamoring of her heart which escalated as Aaron drew her back to sit beside him. It gave her no satisfaction to see that Aaron was as distracted as she herself as he stretched his arm along the back of the seat and leaned toward her.

"We can't go on this way, Sophia." And when Sophia attempted a protest, he shook his head. "No, you've said all you can say and nothing has changed. We're still drawn to each other." He touched the throbbing pulse in her neck, his smile pained. "There's no use denying it. Your heart is pounding as wildly as mine."

Unable to bear the torment clearly visible in Aaron's face, Sophia attempted to look away, only to have him turn her face back to him as his mouth inched closer to hers. She was strangely unable to speak as he continued intensely. "Maybe everything you said about me is true, Sophia. Maybe I *am* selfish for not wanting to give you up, I don't know." He shook his head, appearing truly uncertain. "I only know that this time I want to *give* instead of receiving, and I have so much to offer you."

Sophia took a careful breath. "You said you didn't want to buy me . . ."

Aaron's dark eyes were suddenly bright with anger. "Is it buying you to tell you that there's something special between us that I can't let go? I've never wanted to share my feelings with a woman before. I've never wanted to know what's inside a woman, much less wanted any woman to know what's inside me, but with you it's different. Sophia, I don't know what I feel, but I know if I let you turn me away, we'll both regret it for the rest of our lives."

Barely resisting the appeal of the dark eyes that consumed her, of the warmth of his touch, Sophia whispered, "I can see that I was wrong about you, Aaron. You *are* a master at this game. You far surpass me with your skill."

Aaron drew back. "What are you talking about?"

"Your reputation is widespread. Somehow I can't help but wonder how many other women have made your heart pound the way it's pounding now. What can you possibly see in me that you haven't seen in a dozen women before me except, perhaps, that my hair is a brighter color, or my eyes a deeper blue? Or perhaps you still want to discover if all you've heard about me is true."

A muscle in Aaron's cheek ticked and he nodded. "You're partially right. When I first saw you I was stunned by your beauty, just like every other man who's ever seen you. And like every other man, I wondered if everything I had heard about you was true. I *wanted* it to

279

be true because I thought that would make it easier for me. But then I met you, and everything changed."

Sophia gave a scoffing laugh that turned Aaron's face hard. "Do you really think this is a joke, Sophia? Do you think I'd sit here, pleading with you, if I didn't think you were worth all the misery you've put me through? You're intelligent and quick. You have a true talent that excites me. You're ambitious and hungry for all the things that I've taken for granted my whole life, and you've made me view things differently since I've met you. You've awakened a part of me that I didn't know existed, and you've made me respect you for all you hope to achieve. I want to help you, and I want to share your success. I want to be a part of it all and I want to be a part of you."

The earnest sound of Aaron's voice was mesmerizing. He was wearing her down, confusing her, and touching her heart. Sophia felt a nudge of fear that added a sharpness to her reply.

"Beautiful words, Aaron. How many times have you said them before and then thrown them away after they've served your purpose?"

Anger, frustration, then determination clearly evident, Aaron suddenly grasped her arms. "Sophia, listen to me. From this moment on I want you to forget everything you've ever heard about me, because none of it is true any longer. I'm a different man from the one I was before I met you. I'm more different than I ever thought I could be, because I never believed I could feel this way about any woman. I believe in you, Sophia. I want you to believe in me. I respect you and all you hope to do. I want you to learn to respect me. Will you give me that chance?"

The sputtering flame of a nearby votive candle cast wavering shadows on Aaron's earnest expression, augmenting its intense appeal. The strength of his feelings was reflected in the trembling of his strong hands as they gripped her arms, and Sophia knew she was trembling as well. She was uncertain and pained by her uncertainty when Aaron rasped, "All I'm asking for is a chance, Sophia. Say yes . . . or I know we'll both regret this moment the rest of our lives."

The small break in Aaron's voice tearing at her control, Sophia swallowed against the lump in her throat with her brief word of consent.

"Yes."

Unable to speak as Aaron drew her close against him, Sophia surrendered to his hungry embrace. She was aware of the sacrifice of his restraint as he drew back from her.

"Let's get out of here before your father comes looking for you. We have a crocheted tablecloth to buy."

Rising to her feet on trembling legs, Sophia walked to the door. She attempted to push it open only to have Aaron halt her with a solemn pledge the moment before his lips touched hers.

"I promise you won't be sorry."

Chapter Thirteen

Rebecca Weiss sat at her dressing table engrossed in her coiffure as Samuel turned sharply toward her.

"Did you say Aaron has become involved with the Silk Association Council? Since when has your son been interested in the advancement of the industry? The only thing that's ever concerned him has been the advancement of his own interests."

Rebecca's back remained facing him and Samuel strained to see his wife's reflection in the mirror. His irritation increased as the shifting of his weight increased the pain in his throbbing foot. Damned gout . . .

Her small mouth tight with annoyance, Rebecca finally turned toward him. "There appears to be nothing Aaron can do to please you these days, Samuel. It's no wonder that he spends so much time away from home."

"The true crux of the problem is that Aaron is beginning to spend just as much time away from the office of late as he does away from home! That son of yours hasn't a spark of consideration! He knows damned well I'm in pain and need his help!"

"Samuel, you don't use your foot when you go over production figures or choose the next jacquard print or . . ."

Too late, Rebecca saw she had hit a nerve, and her full face flushed as Samuel nodded. "You're right, of course, but I had thought I surrendered jacquards to Aaron's expertise a few years ago. It seems I was wrong."

Rebecca turned back to the mirror abruptly and raised her chin. Samuel's small eyes narrowed. Oh, he knew that self-righteous expression, all right. His next words came out at a volume just below a bellow.

"All right, there's more to this than what you've said. What is it?"

His wife turned back sharply toward him, and Samuel took a moment's pause. Rebecca had never been a particularly pretty woman, but her small features and mild manner had been a comfortable fit for him since the first day he had met her. Her background and dowry had compensated for the lack of challenge in their marriage, and he had never regretted his choice. She was a good woman who had given him a surprisingly handsome son on whom she doted. But, it was time for the doting to stop.

"Rebecca?"

Rebecca stood abruptly, her well-fleshed shoulders as erect as a soldier as she announced, "Aaron has been helping *me*."

"Helping you?"

Rebecca smiled with pride. "You know what an excellent eye Aaron has for style. Well, I asked him to recommend someone to handle the silk fashions for the Silk Association Council and for the silk exposition next month."

"We've always used Elizabeth Morganfield for the exposition."

"The council is bored with Elizabeth Morganfield!"

"And Aaron had a replacement in mind?"

"Madame Céleste Tourneau."

"I don't like those French frogs."

"Samuel!" Rebecca shuddered. "It's not like you to be crass."

283

"I can be as crass as I like in my own bedroom, Rebecca." Samuel squinted as he hobbled to the bed and sat abruptly. "Tell me, when did the council decide it was bored with Elizabeth Morganfield? It didn't have any help from Aaron, did it?"

Avoiding his eye, Rebecca started toward the door. "I don't know when the council became bored, but I'm bored with this conversation, Samuel. And I'm ready for breakfast."

"Stop where you are!"

Rebecca turned indignantly. "Really, Samuel! Aaron mentioned that he thought Elizabeth Morganfield was slipping and that Madame Tourneau was rumored to have initiated a unique look in fashion that could set some new trends in silk. I invited Madame here with her sketches and found Aaron to be right. So I convinced the council to hire her. She's been marvelous to work with and I'm certain the council has taken a true step forward."

Pulling herself up in a huff as her husband continued his assessing stare, Rebecca said stiffly, "And *now* I'm going down to breakfast!"

The door closed emphatically behind her as Samuel drew himself cautiously to his feet and prepared to follow. Rebecca's departing words echoed in his mind, and he gave a low snort of disgust. The council might have taken a step forward or it might not have, but his son didn't fool him. Aaron didn't involve himself in anything if he didn't have a self-indulgent end in mind. Aaron was a dandy and an unscrupulous woman-chaser who was dedicated to his own amusement. Whatever his wife thought, Samuel knew his son and he—

The light suddenly dawning, Samuel stiffened. Hadn't he heard Allistair Marks going on and on about Madame Tourneau's newest mannequin at the last meeting of the Hamilton Club?

Samuel experienced a moment's true disgust. Damn it all! It appeared Aaron wasn't above using his own mother to advance the cause of his romantic affairs! Well, he was not about to let his son's personal weaknesses affect the performance of the mill or the industry's image.

The pain in Samuel's foot stabbed anew, and he groaned aloud as he reached the bedroom door. He'd look into this, damn it all! And then he'd see . . .

The din of the looms was reassuring as Lyle stepped out of his office and looked around the busy mill floor. It had been a long day and the end of a difficult week. His proposal to the union had been accepted on the first vote and the mill workers had returned to work the following day. Uncle Matthew had been silently furious to have been proven wrong, and Paul's abrupt departure for France three days later had not improved his disposition.

Lyle glanced back at the closed door to the inner office where Uncle Matthew had worked the entire day. True to their agreement, Uncle Matthew had turned over all management duties to him, allowing him full access to the details involved, but his distaste for the task had been clearly visible. Lyle withheld a laugh. It was the first, but he had determined it would not be the last, of the difficult lessons his uncle had in store for him.

Walking slowly across the floor, Lyle scrutinized the work in progress, noting the enthusiasm with which most of the employees had returned to work. He walked past the winders, briefly watching Rosalie Marone at work. She was such a bright, quick little girl. She had Sophia's spirit, if not her beauty and it was plain to see she was relieved to be working again. She returned his smile and Lyle's heart jumped at the shadow of Sophia he saw reflected in her face. He was suddenly more hungry for the sight of Sophia than he had thought he could ever be for another human being.

Uncle Matthew's snide remarks about Sophia and Aaron Weiss returned to haunt him anew and a familiar fury rose within him. Again his mind denied the rumor. Sophia could not be that much a fool . . .

Walking rapidly past the quilling machines, Lyle approached the looms and paused again. It hadn't taken long for the weavers to become attuned to the idea that a weaver who worked two looms earned almost twice as much as the weaver who worked one, and work was progressing smoothly. They were not aware, however, that the monetary relief would prove to be temporary. He knew the door had been opened for the acceptance of heavier loom assignments, and the result would be a reduction in piece rates until the situation reversed itself again and the weavers were running two looms for virtually the price of one. It was an inevitable step in industrialization that did not leave his conscience totally clear.

Lyle's scowl returned as he glanced toward the warping wheels and caught Moretti watching him with a snide smile. He was so tempted to . . .

Turning abruptly on his heel, Lyle walked back toward the office, his step slowing at the sight of Rosalie working beside Anna at Anna's machine. Anna lowered her head when she saw him, and his concern for the backward Marone sister deepened. Anna suffered sorely at Sophia's absence, easily panicking at her winder when things did not go well. It was obvious Rosalie strove to help her elder sister, and also obvious that she did not inspire the same confidence in Anna that Sophia had managed so well.

Realizing that Anna grew more frantic by the moment, he walked to the side of the machine and touched her arm. The girl's head snapped up and he saw fear darken her eyes in the moment before he offered smoothly,

"Don't get upset, Anna. We've had a lot of trouble with these skeins. You'll be getting better ones soon and the work will run smoother."

Anna nodded and went back to work without a word. Looking up, he saw Rosalie's appreciation. He warmed to the bond of friendship that firmed between them in that moment, only to hear an unexpected voice at his elbow.

"I'm leaving for the day, Nephew." And then in a softer tone as the girls moved to the other side of the machine, "I would've thought your experience with the older sister of these young tarts would've taught you something about Italian women, but it seems you're determined to walk down the same road again." He gave a short laugh. "I suppose you should give the red-haired baggage credit, though. From what I hear, Aaron Weiss has opened a lot of doors for her that would otherwise have been closed. I'm certain Weiss is being properly repaid for his efforts, of course . . ."

So his uncle sought to play the same old game. Lyle forced a smile.

"Sophia's too smart to become entangled with Weiss or his machinations."

Matthew laughed aloud. "So you think she's pining away for you, is that it? No . . ." He shook his head. "She's enjoying her new status as Weiss latest slu—"

"Don't go too far, Uncle!"

Aware that he had revealed himself and that his anger had provided his uncle with his only true satisfaction of the day, Lyle watched as Matthew strode toward the exit a few moments later. Grim with determination, Lyle turned back to the office.

Aaron Weiss stood silently beside her desk, and Celeste Tourneau's eyes narrowed as she considered his unexpected proposition cautiously. He had entered her office a short time earlier. Close association with him as they worked on plans for the silk exposition a month away allowed her the insight to recognize that he was annoyed that morning, short of patience, and a man with a purpose. That same close association had also served to increase her respect for him. She had come to realize that he was a supremely talented man, knowledgeable in silk and design, and that, youth and experience aside, his business acumen was second to none. He was also determined and relentless . . . and a very dangerous man when he wanted something badly. She knew he wanted Sophia and she also knew he would not hesitate to advance Sophia's cause at her expense if it served his purpose.

Celeste smiled, knowing she would not allow that to happen as she glanced down at the rough sketch on the desk in front of her her.

"You're telling me that you want this gown made up in time for the charity ball, and I'm telling you that it's impossible, monsieur. I've already hired three additional seamstresses to help with gowns being readied for the silk exposition."

"The silk exposition is a month away."

"And the charity ball is next week!"

"Madame, would it or would it not be a coup for you to be introduced to Paterson's elite at the charity ball as the new designer being sponsored by the Silk Association Council?"

Celeste carefully concealed the excitement Aaron's words evoked. "*Oui*, that would be beneficial."

"Is it worth the effort you will expend to have this gown made up on time?"

Celeste paused in response, cocking her head as she studied the black silk more closely. She could not deny the brilliance of the design.

"You would have Sophia show it?"

"I would have Sophia attend as your protégée."

Celeste's chin snapped up sharply. "You have already insisted that several of Sophia's sketches be incorporated into the showing at the exposition. Is that not enough?"

"No."

"I see. You intend to be the escort she has drawn so conveniently into the picture, and Sophia will be very impressed and grateful."

Aaron's smooth cheek ticked with anger he carefully suppressed as he kept his silence, and Celeste made a mental note that the arrogant fellow's feelings obviously went deeper than she had perceived. She proceeded cautiously.

"I think you're asking much more of me than I originally expected in this venture."

"And I think it's safe to say you'll be receiving more from this venture than you ever could have expected to achieve on your own, despite your modest success of the past."

"It is my 'modest success' and my reputation on which you will depend to advance Sophia's career, monsieur."

"You'll be amply reimbursed for the part you play, Madame. Your reputation will be greatly enhanced, and you'll be provided international exposure." Aaron paused for emphasis before continuing. "You *do* realize that several mills, including Weiss Silk, keep offices and showrooms in New York and Europe, and that we'll be represented at the next World's Fair" Celeste could feel Aaron's dark eyes burn into hers. "And you *do* realize what the right word dropped in the right circles could mean . . ."

Celeste attempted to conceal her growing excitement with a casual shrug. "I've worked for many years to achieve my status. I would not approve of Sophia's name being publicized along with mine . . ." Celeste watched Aaron's reaction carefully, noting the tightening of his lips before she continued. "But I suppose I could be persuaded to present Sophia as my protégée at the ball if I'm allowed to have some of my own silk gowns represented as well."

The tight line of Aaron's mouth loosened and Celeste proceeded, "And *if* Sophia will sign a contract agreeing to show her work solely in conjunction with mine for . . . let me say, the next three years?"

"Madame, what you ask is unreasonable!"

"Monsieur." Celeste raised her brows, "A woman alone must protect her future."

Aaron remained silent and Celeste was aware of his annoyance. She knew his short-tempered mood could work for or against her. She controlled a smile as Aaron finally nodded.

"Agreed. We can work out the details later."

"Very well, monsieur."

Celeste extended her hand toward Aaron and smiled as he shook it firmly. Her heart pounding, she waited until he turned out of sight in the salon before giving a short, incredulous laugh. Her career had advanced further in the few short weeks of Sophia Marone's employment than it had in the past five years of her life! Ah, but she knew she must approach this new turn in her fortunes with careful optimism, for all appeared to rest on Aaron Weiss's abounding passion for the beauteous Sophia. Unfortunately, Aaron Weiss could not be depended upon in his amorous pursuits. Rumor even hinted at a sadistic streak . . .

Recalling the heat with which the handsome Monsieur Weiss had stared her down a few moments earlier, Celeste felt an unexpected emotion rise inside her. He was dangerous, but so much a *man* . . .

Celeste paused to momentarily lament her lot. Too young to escape desire . . . too old to *be* desired . . .

Celeste consoled herself a moment later. She would indeed need to be young again to suffer the rigors of loving a man like Aaron Weiss, certain as she was that the pain in loving him would ultimately be considerable.

Running a hand against the upward sweep of her hair, Madame smiled. *Oui*, she would profit far more as a *voyeuse* in this game of love being enacted before her eyes, without risking the many pitfalls. She forced back the disconsolate sigh that rose in her throat. She supposed it was better that way after all.

Sophia's eyes were glorious pools of astonishment. Her lips were parted, and excitement had raised a flush to her cheeks. She was incredibly desirable, and Aaron wanted her so badly that he ached with the pain of it. But neither his frustrated desire nor his conversation with Madame were the cause of his present agitation as he drew Sophia into a corner of the salon out of sight. Sophia still had not responded to his announcement of the agreement he had struck with Madame a few minutes earlier. "Are you pleased, Sophia?" he prompted.

Sophia searched his face intently, and he wondered what she saw reflected there. Did she see the deep hunger he felt for her, around which his whole life now revolved? Did she know that he had surrendered to his debilitating feelings for her so completely that no other women interested him? Did she know that she was indeed the master here and that he would do anything to please her? Because he knew he would . . .

"What's the matter, Sophia?"

"I'm trying to see if there's any trace left of the Aaron Weiss I met that first day in Kingston Mill."

Aaron's smile was wry. "Oh, him . . . He's buried under a pile of regrets, never to show his face to you again."

Sophia remained sober. "I despised that Aaron Weiss."

Aaron's smile faded as he slipped his hand to her waist

to hold her fast under his scrutiny. "How do you feel about the fellow you're looking at right now?"

Obviously taking the question very seriously, Sophia replied hesitantly, "I . . . I think I like him very much."

Aaron's throat tightened with unexpected emotion.

"And I want to thank you, Aaron."

"I don't want your thanks." Aaron spoke in a husky rasp. "I want you to believe me when I say I care for you, that's all."

"I believe you."

"And I want you to trust me."

Sophia hesitated in reply. "You've done so much for me, but trust takes time, Aaron."

"Sophia, I—"

Suddenly conscious of the rising heat of his emotions and the lack of privacy that had been the bane of his existence in this torturous affair, Aaron consoled himself that he had finally forced the issue and he need wait only a little while longer. He took a necessary step back, fervently regretting relinquishing her.

"I have to go. Father's been in a damned nasty mood of late and he made sure he reminded me to get back to the office in time so we can leave for the Hamilton Club together this evening."

"Sophia . . ."

Sophia's head jerked toward the sound of Madame's voice. Aaron drew her out of the corner as the small Frenchwoman approached with a smile.

"Ah, there you are. I need your services, if you please, Sophia."

Bidding Aaron a hasty good-bye, Sophia accompanied Madame Tourneau to the back room and Aaron chafed under the Frenchwoman's smile. Madame had gone out of her way to demonstrate in her subtle way that she still maintained the upper hand, but Aaron was determined that it was only temporary.

"I forbid it!" Maria Marone turned from the washline stretched across the rear yard of her home. Sophia had found her there gathering laundry upon her return at the end of the day's work. She realized belatedly that she had made a mistake in confiding her good fortune at the salon as the older woman continued hotly, "You will tell the woman you work for that you will not go to the charity ball. You have no place there!"

Glancing around her, aware that her mother's shrill voice carried to the windows of the cold-water flats surrounding the small yard, Sophia pleaded softly, "Mama, why can't you be happy for me, or even try to understand how important this is? Madame is going to make up a gown that *I* designed for me to wear! It'll be the first time that I—"

"Why does this woman do this for you?"

Sophia shook her head. "I don't know. She thinks it'll impress the people there—all wealthy people, Mama!"

"She thinks you will impress the wealthy *men*."

Sophia stiffened, her enthusiasm turning cold. "She thinks I have talent that will be recognized."

"Stupida! This woman hopes to gain from you in some way. She wants to use you, and you are only too willing to be used."

The sudden appearance of Aaron's image before her mind's eye caused Sophia to flush at her mother's accusation. But she had done nothing wrong. Her throat closed as she saw her mother's familiar stiff stance, the suspicion in her eyes that had erupted into a blatant accusation, and the anger toward her that never seemed to abate. The question she had never dared ask slipped past Sophia's lips.

"Why do you hate me, Mama?"

Startled to see her mother's eyes fill, Sophia waited for a response that did not come as her mother turned back

293

to the clothes swaying gently on the line. Sophia spoke softly into the void.

"I've tried so many times to explain to you how I feel. There's something inside me, Mama, it's an image I see in my mind, and it tells me that I must keep trying to—"

Turning back to her with a snap, her temporary weakness turned to fury, Maria hissed, "You think to control me as you control your father, but I'm not the fool for you that he is. I hear what you're saying, but I see where your ambitions will take you, while he closes his eyes to what lies in store."

Her mother's words were knives that cut deeply, stirring defensive anger as Sophia raised her chin. "You undermine everything I do. Why don't you want me to improve myself? Are you jealous of me, Mama? Is that it?"

"Ingrata!" Maria took an aggressive step forward, her hand rising.

"Go ahead!" Sophia steeled herself for the expected blow, only to see her mother's hand freeze in midair, then drop back to her side. She gave a bitter laugh. "You call me an ingrate? Why should I be grateful when you've shown me little else but anger and tried to discourage me all my life? Papa's the only one who ever really listened to me or believed in me."

"Your papa, he doesn't know . . ." Maria halted, shuddering, then continuing. "He doesn't see what I see . . ."

"You see what you want to see, Mama, and you're afraid because you can't control me the way you control Anna and Rosalie."

"Anna and Rosalie are good girls. They will live good lives!"

"And I won't, just because I won't let you run mine?" Sophia shook her head. "I won't let your bitterness turn me into someone like you, and I won't let your fears hold me back. I'm going to the charity ball, and I'm going to the exposition, too."

"You will not!" Maria's enraged response reverberated in the yard. Her shrill voice followed Sophia as she turned and headed toward the alleyway.

"Come back here! Sophia!"

Coming face-to-face with her father as he emerged unexpectedly from the alleyway into the yard, Sophia opened her mouth to speak, only to have her voice fail her. Tears flooding her eyes, Sophia shook off her father's hand and broke into a run.

Outside on the street, Sophia controlled her step, walking rapidly, uncertain of her destination. Winding through the streets past the silent mills, she found herself climbing a familiar hill. She was breathing heavily as she reached the top and raced unconsciously toward the wrought-iron railing a distance away. Reaching it, she looked toward the falls, searching for the solace she had always gained from that special place.

A short laugh escaped her throat as a sob. The summer drought had taken its toll. The power of the mighty falls had been reduced to a trickling stream that trailed over the yawning precipice with little of its former grandeur. Her heart sank. Was it a sign? Was the vision in her mind that had driven her all of her life destined for the same inglorious end?

Doubts, regrets, sadness inundated her in successive waves, draining her until—

Lifting her head as a shaft of late-afternoon sun caught the modest spray at the base of the falls, Sophia saw it. A rainbow! It was pale and fleeting, unlike its more glorious predecessors, but it was there.

"Sophia . . .?"

Sophia turned abruptly at the sound of her name.

"Lyle . . ." Sober honey-colored eyes filled with compassion met hers, and she whispered, "How did you know I needed you?"

Lyle's arms were suddenly around her, and Sophia clutched him close. His strength renewed her and his touch warmed the cold core of her heart, restoring its life. Lyle was a sanctuary who would never fail her . . . a friend for all her life . . . a part of her.

Drawing back from her moments later, Lyle urged her to a nearby point of seclusion out of sight of passersby before he turned her toward him. He wiped the tears from her cheeks and searched her face with concern as she indulged herself in the comforting familiarity of him—heavy gold hair and brows, clear, fair skin and even features, glowing eyes stirred with sympathetic flecks of brown as they studied her intently, and full lips that brushed hers, soothing the ache inside her before he spoke.

"Tell me what's wrong, Sophia."

Resting her head against Lyle's chest, Sophia listened to the steady drumming of his heart and closed her eyes. She felt his response as she haltingly related the bitter words she and her mother had exchanged, and she felt his surprise as she confided Madame's plans for her. The words poured out of her, at first angry, then flat and empty, then touched with hope, and Sophia knew that in Lyle's arms the healing had begun.

Unwilling to part from him, Sophia pressed herself closer to Lyle, satisfied only when her head was tucked into the warm crevice at the side of his neck and her arms were locked around his waist. His hands made soothing circles on her back in the silence that came between them at last, and she waited, realizing suddenly that he hadn't spoken a word. When he did speak, his question was unexpected.

"Can you still read my thoughts, Sophia?" She sensed it was somehow important to him that she could as he whispered, "Tell me what I'm thinking now."

His question forcing her to draw back from him, Sophia studied Lyle's face as intently as he had studied hers moments earlier.

"You're thinking that we've both gotten the opportunity we've worked toward all our lives, and that we're finding the circumstances more difficult than we imagined they would be. And you're thinking that we both know that no matter how difficult it becomes, there's something inside us that forces us to continue."

A faint smile touched Sophia's mouth. "Am I right, *caro* Lyle."

"What else am I thinking?"

Reading a familiar torment in his eyes, Sophia continued. "You're thinking that our feelings are such for each other that although we've been separated, it now seems we've never been apart. And you're wondering . . ." Sophia paused, her smile slipping away. "You're worried . . ."

"Yes, I am."

"Why?"

Sophia could feel Lyle's sudden tension. "Did Aaron Weiss have anything to do with Madame Tourneau's decision to help you?"

Sophia stiffened and attempted to draw back, but Lyle held her fast.

"Did he?"

"So you've begun believing the rumors after all."

"I don't want to believe them."

"And if the rumors are true?"

"Sophia . . ." Lyle's face became pained. "I don't want you to get hurt."

Relenting, moved by the depth of Lyle's feelings for her, Sophia stroked the lines of concern on his face. This man touched her in ways she knew no other man ever would, and she knew he felt the same. She attempted to console him.

297

"Aaron cares for me, Lyle."

"Weiss cares only for himself."

"You're wrong."

"No, I'm not."

Sophia felt the depth of Lyle's anxiety. She didn't want him to suffer for her.

"He's not the same man you and I used to know, Lyle. He's changed. I can see his sincerity in his eyes. He's opened his heart to me in a way he hasn't with any other woman although I've given him little encouragement. I can't begin to explain the things he's done for me with no payment in return. If you could only hear him talk. He believes in me . . ."

"He'll use you, Sophia, just as he's used every other woman before you."

"I don't think so." Sophia held Lyle's gaze levelly. "The least I owe him is a chance."

Lyle's eyes were filled with regret. "This is all my fault, isn't it? You would never have considered accepting Weiss's help if I hadn't abandoned you when you needed me most."

Pausing at his question, unwilling to allow him to accept blame where there was none, Sophia whispered, "Think back, Lyle, and remember how it was. Things had become difficult between us. Our feelings were such that we had become a hindrance to each other. But I've learned from that, and you have, too. We're both on our way to proving we can do what we always knew we could."

"Weiss is a dishonest womanizer, Sophia. He can't be trusted."

"I know his reputation."

"Do you? I don't think so. He—"

"Lyle, please . . ." Pressing her fingertips against his lips, Sophia halted Lyle's words. "I don't want to hear any more of this and I don't want you to feel guilty or to worry about me. We're all responsible for our own actions. Any decisions I make are my own."

Glancing toward the western sky, Sophia sighed. "It's getting late. I have to go home."

"No, not yet. I want you to promise me something first—that you'll come to me if any of this goes bad."

"It won't. I won't let it."

Lyle attempted a smile. "Humor me, Sophia. I need to hear you say the words. It's important to me."

Lyle's words touched her heart and Sophia was torn by the torment she knew she caused him. Desperate to relieve his concern, Sophia slid her arms around his neck. Her voice was husky with the emotions she suppressed as she spoke.

"All right, I'll promise. But you must do something for me as well." Sophia raised her parted lips to his, the heat of tears filling her eyes. "Kiss me . . . because I want to feel you close to me for a little while longer, and because a kiss will heal our wounds."

"Sophia . . ."

A multitude of words that went unspoken was reflected in Lyle's voice in the moment before he slowly lowered his mouth to hers. Her soft sound of welcome as their lips touched was swallowed by his kiss and Sophia indulged the sweet consolation it evoked. Momentarily dismissing all that held them apart, she felt her softness meld to his strength, and she wished . . . she so fervently wished . . .

Straining her control to its limits, Sophia gradually drew back from the succor of Lyle's embrace. She was aware of the difficulty with which Lyle released her, for she shared it as well as she slipped her arm through his. Walking at his side moments later, the thought, *Separated, but never apart* came to mind and Sophia looked up. Reading acknowledgment in his eyes although the words had gone unspoken, Sophia forced a smile that tore at her heart.

Her chin high, her spirits restored after her meeting with Lyle, Sophia entered the kitchen. A glance around the room revealed her mother at the stove with her back to her and her father standing in the living-room doorway. Rosalie and Anna drifted anxiously into sight as she pulled the kitchen door closed behind her and held her breath.

Anthony's voice was gruff.

"Supper is ready."

It was not until later, when the dishes and pans had been cleaned and stored and Sophia stood alone on the porch, that she felt her father's touch on her arm. His dark eyes direct, he said simply, "Your mama was wrong. You will go."

Out of sight on the street below, Lyle looked up at the windows of Sophia's flat, watching shadowed figures pass the drawn shades. Fearing for Sophia's well-being in the face of her mother's unreasonable anger, he had been unable to leave, although Sophia had gone upstairs almost an hour earlier.

Consoling himself that all appeared quiet, he turned with one last glance and started back down the rapidly darkening street. Beautiful Sophia, so wise and yet so naive . . . What was it she had said? Weiss had changed. He was a different man. He cared for her.

Lyle controlled a bitter laugh. Weiss *wanted* Sophia, and he would remain the changed man she saw until he got her. Damn, why was she so blind to Weiss's tricks? Was it because she really cared for him?

That thought twisted a painful knife of jealousy inside Lyle, drawing blood. Thoughts of Sophia tormented him

. . . her head resting against his chest, her fingertips touching his face and lips, her arms wrapped around him as she held him close. His step faltered. The sweet taste of her mouth had called for more, but he had known only too well that to overstep the bounds of friendship now would be to lose her forever. It was a risk he had not been willing to take.

Turning onto Ellison Street at last, Lyle walked faster in an attempt to escape the burning knowledge that his misery was of his own making—and the realization that Sophia, who read his mind and heart so well, had misjudged one important factor. For she had not seen how deeply he loved her.

Chapter Fourteen

"Faster, Harry!"

Harry's response to Aaron's urging from inside the carriage was a crack of the whip that picked up the pace, but Aaron could not be satisfied. Plucking at the stiff collar of his formal evening wear, Aaron muttered an oath, then ran a nervous hand against his hair, scowling. If he didn't know better, he'd think that his father had deliberately delayed his leaving for the ball, but he knew that thought was farfetched. His father would have no way of knowing how involved he was in this particular charity ball and how much hinged on the success of his venture.

Releasing a tense breath as Madame Tourneau's salon came into view, Aaron sat forward. Damn, he was as tense as a spring!

Aware that anxiety had brought a full flush of perspiration to his brow despite the comfortable temperature of early September, Aaron drew his handkerchief across his brow. His mind wandered.

It had been a devilish torture working with Sophia through the long evening sessions of the past week, but while his frustration had deepened to the point of distress, his respect for her had grown. Working among the turmoil of seamstresses and fittings, finally doing much of the finishing of her gown herself, Sophia had shown a true genius for the execution of design, and he had continued to marvel that this young woman of such common parents could be so gifted.

Then, as the long days and extra hours had stretched on into a week and her exhaustion had increased, the person Sophia had so carefully hidden from him had begun to emerge.

An unanticipated tenderness swelling within him, Aaron remembered the previous evening as Sophia had sat beside him in his carriage. Fatigue and darkness became a catharsis that tore down the final barriers between Sophia and him as they had talked. The carriage had come to a halt at the usual spot, but for the first time Sophia had not hastened to leave. Her head had drooped against his shoulder and he had chafed at the restraint he had practiced as he slid his arm around her and drew her comfortingly close. Her earnest whisper as she spoke to him more intimately than ever before had touched him. She had claimed his heart completely as she had related her family's first difficult years after immigration and her determination to rise above those hard times. He had glimpsed her hidden anxieties then, and he had longed to make all the promises that would erase them from her mind. But he had not. He had known instinctively that Sophia was too proud to accept what she felt she had not earned and that she would regret her confidences if he did.

It had occurred to him then that the role he played in pursuit of this woman was no longer a guise. He still wanted her, but his feelings for her had somehow transcended the satisfaction of desire. His thoughts unsettled, he had spent part of the previous night exploring them without relief and the other part wanting Sophia more with each passing hour.

A smile tugged momentarily at Aaron's lips. He had worked just as diligently on another project during the past week—a surprise for Sophia that he hoped would give her pleasure.

303

Tensing, Aaron stepped down onto the sidewalk a moment after the carriage drew to a halt. He approached the front door of the salon, aware that his heart was pounding. The frenzied activity inside and the chatter of female voices stopped the moment he stepped through the door. Tempted to laugh, Aaron realized that if he had needed any assurances as to his appearance that night, it was well provided by the appreciative glances of the young women Madame had hired to show a brief sampling of gowns from her collection. They were lovely, two brunettes and a fragile blonde whose colorings complemented the vivid shades of the silk gowns they wore. Greatly reassured of the impression Madame Tourneau's work would make, Aaron smiled as Celeste stepped into sight from the back room. Garbed in an elaborate gray silk gown that emphasized her petite stature and narrow waist, Madame smiled broadly at the sight of him.

"Ah, Monsieur Weiss, how handsome you are! And how gallant of you to come to escort us to the ball."

"I wouldn't have missed it for the world, madame. You look lovely."

Madame's mock whisper raised his brows with surprise. "Careful, monsieur. You will turn my head."

About to reply, Aaron turned at the sound of a step to the rear of the salon, his breath catching in his throat as Sophia stepped into view.

Dazzling . . . magnificent . . . glorious . . . Superlatives raced across his mind as he sought the words that best described Sophia, but none would suffice. Black silk studded with the twinkle of a thousand stars . . . flame-red, upswept hair dusted with a sparkling halo . . . brilliant blue eyes that shone more brightly than the glittering precious stones at her ears and throat—and a mouth that drew him like a magnet as it rounded with a gasp.

Standing stock-still, Sophia surveyed him from head to toe. She swallowed with obvious difficulty, then whispered,

"You're far more handsome than the figure I drew, Aaron. You've brought my sketch to life."

At her side, Aaron took both of Sophia's hands into his, restraining the desire to take her into his arms as he whispered in return, "You know why I had these evening clothes made, don't you, Sophia?" He drew her hands against the black silk of his waistcoat, aware of the rapid acceleration of his heartbeat as he slid her hands up to touch the black silk revers of his coat jacket and then drew her palms to his lips. "I wanted this night to be exactly as you imagined it could be—"

"You will be the *pièce de résistance* of the ball, I have no doubt," Madame interrupted as she stepped to their side. Her small eyes darted between them, and Aaron suppressed the desire to shake off the firm hand she placed on his arm. "But it is time for us to leave if we're to make a suitable entrance."

Nodding, Aaron forced a smile. "I've arranged for a conveyance to transport your lovely models and you, madame. Sophia and I will follow in my carriage."

Celeste's smile stiffened. "I think it would be far better for the three of us to travel together since we are to be working so closely in the future." Celeste's small eyes pinned him. "That is the plan, is it not, monsieur?"

"Of course, madame."

Seated between the two women as the carriage moved briskly forward minutes later, Aaron silently cursed the astute Frenchwoman and deliberately took Sophia's hand.

The tense carriage ride behind her, Sophia stood inside the grand stone foyer of the city's most luxurious hotel. She breathed deeply, keenly aware of the rock of Aaron's presence behind her as he curled a possessive arm around her waist. The lilting strains of a waltz permeated the lobby and her excitement increased. Tonight she was the

305

woman she had always envisioned she would one day be. She was wearing a gown of her own creation that far surpassed even her own expectations. She had seen her reflection in Aaron's eyes, and in that moment she knew he had recognized himself in her drawing even before she had realized her unconscious intent.

Madame's low mumbling catching her ear, Sophia turned to find the Frenchwoman obviously concerned as she fussed with the mannequins' skirts in preparation for their entrance. Turning back to Aaron, Madame Tourneau offered tensely, "I can only hope that our late arrival will not be misconstrued."

Aaron dismissed Madame's anxiety. "We've arrived exactly on time. A full audience is preferable. I suggest you enter first with your ladies, madame, so everyone will be sure to recognize that the purpose of their presence is to introduce your work to them. Sophia and I will follow."

Madame nodded. "Your instinct for staging is excellent, monsieur. Of course we will comply."

Gathering her mannequins with a few sharp words, Madame stepped into full sight in the ballroom, pausing in the raised entrance of the room as they posed behind her. The required effect achieved, she moved slowly down the steps and into the crowd.

Her heart pounding as they prepared to step forward, Sophia looked up, making contact with Aaron's sober, intense gaze. Her heart did a little jump at the passion in his voice as he whispered, "You're standing on the brink of your future now. You'll remember this moment for the rest of your life, and when you do, I want you to remember what I'm telling you now. I love you, Sophia."

Knowing in her heart that Aaron meant every word, Sophia was unable to speak as he then took her arm.

"Let's go."

The music came to a temporary halt between dances as they took the final step forward into sight of the crowded floor. Gasps echoed in the room at their appearance, and Sophia responded to the pressure of Aaron's hand as he stayed her so the crowded room might view her unrestricted a few moments longer. Standing beside him, aware that she was the object of glowing comments and curious speculation as an excited murmur ran through the crowd, Sophia became suddenly numb. She had seen this all before—this room with its crystal chandeliers and satin brocaded walls. She had seen this orchestra and the maestro with his baton poised, and she had heard the whispers of ecstatic praise that had accompanied her appearance. It became suddenly clear that she had also seen the man at her side . . .

"Sophia . . ." Sophia looked up as the music began again. She saw pride, hunger, and love in Aaron's eyes as he whispered, "This night is ours."

Swept up into his arms, Sophia moved spontaneously to a dance she had never danced before, in the arms of a man she had not dared to trust but whom she now recognized as part of her destiny.

Lyle's face paled to a lifeless white as he stood beside his aunt on the crowded floor, and Julia felt a sudden stab of fear. Dear Lyle had selflessly agreed to escort her to this annual affair, rather than have her to go with Matthew and be subject to Edith's animosity, but he now appeared stricken . . .

Julia followed the line of Lyle's gaze to the ballroom floor where Aaron Weiss danced with the beautiful woman with whom he had entered moments earlier. Lyle seemed unable to tear his tortured gaze from her. Unwilling to view her nephew's distress in silence any longer, she whispered, "Who is she, Lyle?"

She saw the hopelessness and regret that Lyle was momentarily unable to conceal as he looked back at her.

307

"She's beautiful, isn't she? Her name is Sophia Marone. She used to work at the mill."

Julia was aghast. "She worked as a millhand? But—"

Lyle's face hardened. "Common beginnings don't necessarily mean a common end, Aunt Julia. I should've thought you'd be the first one to recognize that."

Lyle's defensive tone cut her. Jarred from her shock, Julia suddenly realized that she had fallen prey to judging from the same point of prejudice as the brother she condemned. She was ashamed.

Sliding her blue-veined hand onto Lyle's sleeve, Julia whispered, "I'm sorry." And then in a sudden flash of insight, "You . . . you love her, don't you, dear?"

Pausing as countless emotions went unspoken, Lyle answered simply, "Yes, I do."

"There she is, the common slut!" Watching from the sidelines as Aaron Weiss whirled his flame-haired partner out onto the floor, Matthew laughed aloud. "Let's see your nephew deny what she is now."

"Matthew!" Edith glanced around her, relieved when she saw no one had overheard her husband's crude comments. "What's wrong with you tonight? Who is that woman?"

"What's wrong with me? Nothing, Edith! I feel better than I've felt in days!" Matthew looked for Lyle, laughing again as he spotted him at the edge of the crowded floor. "Look at him! The fool is in misery!"

Edith's cold eyes became frigid. "I asked you who she is, Matthew."

Matthew turned to face his wife, smiling. "She's a cheap piece who used to work at the mill. Lyle couldn't keep his eyes off her." Edith's lips tightened with disapproval, and he whispered reassuringly, "Don't worry. Lyle won't stand a chance with her until Weiss is through with her. When he is, I don't think we'll have to worry—not if everything I hear about Weiss is true."

"I have no interest in anything your nephew does, Matthew." Edith's frigidity turned to pure ice. "I'd be pleased if I never had to hear his name or see his face again."

His spirits suddenly high, Matthew swept his wife out onto the floor, unable to resist a last jibe. "Really? You forget, *our* nephew is now the manager of *our* mill. And the idea was yours and yours alone, Edith! I'm afraid, temporarily at least, there's no escaping him."

Satisfied to feel his wife's slender frame stiffen further, Matthew whirled her faster, thoroughly enjoying himself.

"Damn that son of yours!"

"Samuel, please." The pleased flush her son's appearance in the entrance of the ballroom had evoked turned to an embarrassed heat as Rebecca whispered through a stiff smile, "People are staring! You should be proud of Aaron. He looks outstanding, and Madame's mannequin is a beautiful woman."

"Madame's mannequin . . . ?" Samuel turned toward his wife, eyes blazing. "You're telling me that woman is Madame Tourneau's mannequin and that she'll be working with Madame Tourneau on the Silk Association projects?"

"This ball and the silk exposition . . . yes. We've already signed the contract."

"Damn him!"

"Samuel . . ." Rebecca's brown eyes filled. "What's wrong?"

"I told him to stay away from that girl! She's trouble."

"You know her?"

"I know *of* her. Every young buck in town knows *of* her, and it appears your son has chosen to ignore my warnings so he might sample a bit of what she has to offer."

"You must be wrong, dear." Rebecca's anxiety intensified. "Aaron would never involve himself with such a woman."

Samuel blinked incredulously. "Rebecca, your son . . ."

"My son is a fine, honest young man of whom I'm very proud! You're wrong about him, Samuel, and I'm certain you're wrong about the young woman, too."

"Rebecca . . ."

"I won't listen to another word, Samuel!"

"But—"

"Stop, or I'll insist upon leaving now."

Samuel blinked again. It seemed to have slipped his wife's agitated mind that he had attended this ball under duress, that he would have liked nothing better than to have remained home, his foot elevated, and a headache powder dissolved in his glass. It seemed to have—

A tear slipped down Rebecca's full cheek, and Samuel inwardly groaned. Rebecca was a good wife and a mother who looked at her son through eyes of love. She didn't deserve this.

Samuel took a deep breath of forbearance. And he was going to make sure that neither he nor she would ever suffer another night of this humiliation again.

The balcony that surrounded the crowded dance floor was filled with tables where observers so inclined watched from the comfort of upholstered chairs, and Sophia felt their eyes upon her. Suddenly realizing she was trembling, Sophia felt Aaron's arm tighten around her waist, a reassuring gesture that went unnoticed in the midst of the crowd.

"Sophia . . ." Madame's voice turned Sophia's attention toward her as the Frenchwoman approached with a tall, stately woman close behind. "I should like you to meet Madame Tierny. She is a member of the Silk Association Council. I've explained to her that you will work along with me as my protégée and that, in fact, the gown you're wearing was designed by you under my tutelage."

With a smile Sophia assumed the role in which Madame had cast her. "How do you do, Madame Tierny."

The woman's gray brows rose with surprise. "That accent is Italian, isn't it?" Her tone became accusing as she turned back toward Madame Tourneau. "I thought she was French."

"Some of the finest silk in the world comes from Italy, Mrs. Tierny." Aaron's smooth interjection turned the woman with surprise. "Sophia's heredity has allowed her an instinctive feeling for silk, which Madame recognized immediately. Sophia will design exclusively in silk, you see, while Madame's designs, outside of her work for the Silk Association Council, will continue to employ many different fabrics. Madame has already approved a line of fashions which Sophia has conceived, called Seasons of Silk."

Madame's head snapped toward Aaron as he continued smoothly. "Madame will allow the first of these designs to be shown along with hers at the silk exposition."

"Really . . ." Mrs. Tierny appeared impressed. She scrutinized Sophia's gown more closely. "Marvelous detail . . . graceful flow . . . uniquely patterned beading. You've done an admirable job with this young woman, Madame."

"*Merci*, madame." Celeste's tone was gracious. "You have an excellent eye."

A burst of music overwhelmed their conversation, allowing Aaron to interject graciously, "If you'll excuse us."

Sophia was stunned to see Aaron's smile fall as he drew her out onto the floor.

"Damned bigoted bitch!" And as Sophia's eyes widened with surprise he continued, "She won't make any more comments about your accent. I've seen to that."

"My accent . . ." Sophia laughed, her mood undimmed by his anger. "I didn't realize I had an accent. I thought by now I spoke perfect English, but it appears I was wrong. But to be fluent in two languages when others speak

311

only one is an achievement to be proud of, no?"

"You don't have to worry what that woman says or thinks, Sophia." Aaron's tone was defensive. "You're the most beautiful and desirable woman in this room."

Aware that Aaron's anger lingered, Sophia fixed her eyes on his as the music swelled. "Tonight is too perfect for a frown. Smile, please, Aaron."

His eyes holding hers with glowing intensity, Aaron whispered, "You know that I'll do anything for you, don't you, Sophia?"

Aaron's burning zeal sent a quiver of emotion down Sophia's spine. It settled deep inside her as she gave herself up to the strains of the dance.

Breathless from the previous dance as the orchestra struck up anew, Sophia sipped from a delicate glass filled with champagne. A steady stream of introductions to many of the most prominent silk manufacturers in the city had left her dizzy with excitement, aware as she was that these same men would not have glanced her way a few weeks earlier.

Sophia's brilliant smile brightened. But she wasn't the same person she had been before! She had emerged from her cocoon, an exotic butterfly whose metamorphosis was complete as arranged by the passionately protective man at her side. Glancing at him, Sophia knew there could be no doubting Aaron's sincerity now. She was suddenly certain that whatever came to pass between them, she would have no regrets.

"What are you thinking, Sophia?"

Her thoughts too confusing to be conveyed, Sophia raised her glass again to her lips. "I'm thinking this wine is not at all like my papa's."

"It has bubbles . . ."

Sophia laughed, noting the sound seemed to rebound in

Aaron's smile as she whispered, "Bubbles, yes, and an intoxication I seem to feel with only two sips."

"It isn't the wine." Aaron drew her closer, dipping his head toward her as his smile broadened. "It's—"

His expression suddenly freezing as he stared at a point behind her, Aaron inquired sharply, "What do you want, Kingston?"

Turning, Sophia caught her breath. Lyle looked splendid, more handsome than she had ever seen him, in dark evening clothes that emphasized the heavy gold of his hair and eyes. His classic features softened with a warmth she knew was reserved for her alone as she reached toward him in greeting. Her throat choked closed as Lyle took her hand and raised it to his lips. She was unaware of Aaron's darkening demeanor as Lyle whispered, "I knew I would see you like this someday."

"Did you?" Aaron's tone was harsh. "But then hindsight is always clearer than foresight, isn't it?"

Lyle stiffened, and Sophia felt the coldness between the two men become frigid the moment before Madame appeared at her elbow with a gray-haired gentleman in tow.

"Sophia, Mr. Amsterdam has been wanting to meet you. He's an old acquaintance of mine who bears much influence in the field of silk in New York City. He has confided in me that he has been admiring you from afar. He would like to dance with you, if you will kindly oblige him."

Sophia darted a quick glance between the two antagonists beside her as Madame continued easily, "Don't concern yourself with these young gentlemen, *ma chère*. I will take good care of them for you."

Realizing she had no choice, Sophia turned to the distinguished older man. "It will be my pleasure to dance with you, Mr. Amsterdam."

Whirled out onto the floor in the fellow's capable arms, Sophia glanced warily over her shoulder, tense as Aaron and Lyle were blocked from her sight.

* * *

"Gentlemen, this type of conflict has no place here, *n'est-pas?*" Celeste's smile was firm as Sophia disappeared among the dancers on the floor, but her eyes were cold. "We would not like to spoil the evening for the mademoiselle and for the many others who have been watching her with such pleasure."

"You're right, of course, madame." Lyle forced a smile he did not feel, his loathing for Weiss never stronger. "I appreciate your concern for Sophia."

"Speak for yourself, Kingston. I don't need anyone to keep watch on my manner, especially someone who seeks to protect her own ends with the pretense of concern for Sophia."

"That's where you're wrong, monsieur!" Madame turned to Aaron, her gaze pure ice. "You need to be reminded that if you cause a scene you will defeat your own purpose here. I suggest that you take a deep breath and remember that you hope to establish Sophia's credibility — not discredit her! As for you, monsieur . . ." Madame turned to Lyle. "If you care for the lovely Mademoiselle Marone, I suggest you take another time to tell her so."

"If you'll excuse me for my outspokenness, madame, Sophia knows only too well that I care for her. But I do have something to say to Mr. Weiss." His gold eyes hot pinpoints of light, his voice dropping to a tone of unmistakable menace, Lyle spoke directly to his antagonist. "A simple warning, Weiss. Sophia isn't like the tramps you're used to dealing with, so take care. With Madame as my witness, if you hurt her, you'll answer to me."

"Bastard . . ."

Lyle's control visibly wavered. "Remember what I said." He paused, his voice lowering with unspoken promise. "To forget could cost your life . . ."

Madame Tourneau's low gasp did not affect Lyle's resolution, nor the realization as he slowly walked away that he had meant every word.

Sophia searched the crowd for sight of the two angry men she had left behind her, her anxiety concealed behind a polite mask as the dance came to an end. The planes of Mr. Amsterdam's jowled face lifted with admiration as he escorted her toward the sidelines.

"You're light as a feather on your feet, Miss Marone, and easily the most beautiful woman in the room. I'm looking forward to working with you and Madame during the silk exposition."

"And I look forward to working with you."

Back at Madame's side, Sophia waited only until the distinguished gentleman had turned away before inquiring tightly, "Where did they go, madame?" Her heartbeat rose to thunder in her ears. "They didn't—"

Obviously furious, Madame Tourneau interrupted in a restrained hiss, "I have saved our cause this evening, Sophia, but this game you play is a dangerous one that I will not allow!"

Sophia's anger flared. "I'm playing no games, madame. The conflict between Aaron and Lyle is of long standing."

"It is complicated by their feelings for you! I warn you, mademoiselle, if you wish to retain your position in my establishment, you will settle the matter once and for all."

Madame snapped her lips closed as Aaron appeared unexpectedly at their side. His emotions obviously under tight rein, Aaron grasped Sophia's arm without a word, refusing to yield his grip even as she strove covertly to shake it. Weaving his way back through the crowd, he drew her along behind him. His step did not slow until they slipped through the French doors and out into the semidarkness of the garden beyond.

"Aaron, what are you doing?" Struggling to free herself,

315

Sophia felt her anger soar as Aaron failed to respond. She protested as Aaron drew her out of sight under a huge oak tree nearby and closed his arms around her.

"No, don't pull away." Aaron's grating rasp gave Sophia a moment's pause as he continued. "I need to hold you, just for a few minutes."

Going still in his embrace, Sophia felt the restrained emotions that coursed through him as Aaron drew her closer, pressing his face against her hair. Her anger gradually dissipating, Sophia felt the reluctance with which he finally separated from her. She heard his self-directed anger as he whispered, "I'm sorry, Sophia. I almost ruined everything."

The depth of Aaron's concern caused her a moment's fear. She whispered harshly, "What happened? Where's Lyle?"

"Lyle?" Aaron stiffened. "I don't know where he is, and I don't care. But I suppose what really counts is how much *you* care."

"Lyle is my friend, Aaron."

"He's your *friend?* Is that why he threw you and your sketches out onto the street? Is that why he left you with nowhere to go to finish your work except that miserable library where an overweight lecher could threaten you?"

"That was as much my fault as Lyle's!"

His emotions rapidly rising out of control, Aaron gave Sophia a sharp shake. "I don't want to know what happened between Kingston and you. He gave up his claim to you that night when you raced out of his rooms and stumbled into my arms, and he's never going to get you back. You're going to belong to me more completely than you ever belonged to him."

"Aaron, you don't understand. I—"

"Sophia, listen to me . . ." Drawing her so close that his lips caressed hers as he spoke, Aaron whispered, "I don't want to understand. That was another time and another place. You were a different woman then, just as I was a different man. There are no yesterdays to regret and no tomorrows to concern us. There's only here and now."

His throbbing words draining her of her will, Aaron closed his mouth over hers. Cupping her chin with his hand, he guided her loving response, separating her lips with his, seeking out the hollows of her mouth and drinking from them fully. His loving assault relentless, he tore his lips from hers to follow a searing trail along her chin and the white column of her throat. His mouth moved warmly against her bare shoulders, against the soft rise of flesh above her neckline, and she gasped aloud.

Suddenly thrust against the hard trunk of the tree behind her, Sophia felt the full weight of Aaron's aroused body against hers as he showered kisses against her eyelids, the throbbing pulse in her temple, against the short bridge of her nose. Finding her mouth once more, Aaron settled deeply there, indulging his hunger for her, raising her with him to a new level of aching emotion.

He was breathing rapidly as he drew back from her, and Sophia saw her own feelings reflected on the shadowed planes of his face. Realizing the danger there, Sophia attempted to free herself, but her struggle succeeded only in stirring Aaron's passion anew as the thrill of Aaron's harsh whisper coursed down her spine.

"No, Sophia, don't try to get away from me. You know you don't want me to let you go."

The truth of Aaron's words rang deep inside her, spurring her to greater protest, and desperation touched Aaron's rasping plea.

"Listen to me, Sophia. I'll make it beautiful for you, I promise you that. I'll make you forget Kingston. I'll love you more than he ever was capable of loving you, and I'll make you love me."

Halting her struggle, Sophia looked up at Aaron, realizing as their hearts pounded in unison, that her mouth

317

craved the touch of his lips, that her body longed for the caress of his hands, that he had raised an aching need inside her that cried out for release.

Sanity raised a plaintive cry, forcing her throbbing whisper, "Aaron, I can't afford to let you love me. It will cost too much. I have no time for a casual affair."

"I've already made you a promise that there'll be nothing *casual* about a love affair between us, Sophia." Aaron's chest began a passionate heaving. "And I promise you more than that. I promise you ecstasy, Sophia, ecstasy that will far surpass anything you've ever known. It's there, waiting for us if we're bold enough to take it. You sense it. You know every word I say is true. I can see it in your eyes and I can feel it in the way your body responds to mine. Sophia, let me love you. I have so much to give."

Aaron's mouth was again on hers, and Sophia felt her resistance slowly slip away as Aaron ground his hard body against her softness, as he slid his fingers into her hair to hold her immobile under his kiss, as his hand cupped her chin, her neck, the full curve of her breast . . . She felt the cool evening air against her exposed flesh, and she gasped as he found the waiting crest of one breast, then the other. She felt his mouth against their full curves, nipping and biting, raising her passion to the point where she called his name, clutching him close. She was trembling, shuddering, aching, wanting more than she had ever wanted before when a burst of laughter close by shocked her from her impassioned thrall.

Clutching her close, protecting her partial nakedness with his broad back, Aaron moved her farther into the shadows. He brushed aside her trembling hands to restore her disheveled clothing with practiced ease, then raised her face to his as she sought to avoid his gaze.

"No, don't look away. Look at me, Sophia, so I can see your face when I tell you that I want to lie with you, that I want to hold you in my arms and feel your flesh against

318

me—that I want to worship your body with mine. Sophia, come with me now . . ."

"But . . ." Her breath short as Aaron caressed her lovingly, assaulting her senses anew, Sophia finally gained the strength to rasp, "We can't leave now. There'll be talk."

"No . . . no . . ." Aaron shook his head, halting his response for a shattering kiss that left her trembling. "I'll go back inside and tell Madame to make your apologies—that you're unwell and I'm going to take you home."

"But we've only been here an hour . . ."

"Long enough to accomplish our purpose. Now it's time for ourselves, Sophia. Sophia . . ."

Trailing his mouth against her cheek, Aaron teased the fragile shell of her ear with his tongue, whispering, "Tell me you want to go with me, Sophia. Tell me you *will* go."

Breathless, tortured beyond restraint by his loving ministrations, Sophia nodded. "Yes, I'll go."

Going stock-still for long seconds, Aaron drew back far enough to whisper against her lips, "You won't be sorry . . ."

Trembling, shaken, Sophia leaned back against the tree, watching as Aaron disappeared into the brightly lit ballroom. Reeling with the sensations he had evoked, she closed her eyes, unable to think past the remembered feeling of Aaron's mouth against her flesh and the driving desire he had aroused within her. Her eyes were still closed when she heard Aaron's step beside her, when she felt his mouth take hers again, when he tore his mouth from hers with a mumbled curse that snapped her eyes open to his unexpected anger.

"Damn you, Sophia. Another minute and you'll have me taking you here, under this tree, without a thought as to who could come up on us or . . ."

Taking a moment to rein his raging emotions under control, Aaron grasped her hand. A moment later their feet were flying.

The carriage wheels rattled against the cobbled street, echoing in the silence as Lyle turned beside him to Aunt Julia's small, pale face.

"Are you sure you don't want me to take you directly to Dr. Mason's office, Aunt Julia?"

"No, that won't be necessary. I'm all right, really. Rest will work the cure."

Julia attempted a smile. Guilty as she was for having exaggerated the brief bout of weakness that had unexpectedly assailed her, she found a smile extremely difficult, but she knew the untruth had been necessary. Lyle took her hand and squeezed it gently, raising her guilt anew.

Moments later he was staring back out the window, and Julia had no doubts where his thoughts had returned. Her heart resumed an erratic beating as she recalled the sharp confrontation she had witnessed between Aaron Weiss and her dear nephew. She had been stricken with fear at the tenuously controlled violence she had seen in Lyle's eyes. A single glimpse at Aaron Weiss had revealed the same depth of passion there. There was no need to guess what had inspired that fervor, for even after Lyle had returned to her side, his eyes had not left the beautiful Sophia Marone as she whirled around the floor in the arms of the elderly silk broker.

A few sharp words and Weiss left Madame Tourneau on the edge of the dance floor, with Lyle watching his every step. She had seen a potential disaster in the making, with Matthew grinning snidely in the other corner of the room, a ready witness to the impending scene, and the total body of the silk elite present to condemn her dear nephew for fighting over a woman whom they all considered many classes below them.

The erratic pounding of her heart and her resulting shortness of breath had provided the excuse she needed to remove Lyle from danger, and she had not hesitated.

But she still was not at ease with her deception.

Julia looked back at Lyle to find him frowning, and her thoughts came out in an unsteady question.

"W-will you return to the ball after you've left me at home, Lyle?"

Lyle's frown turned to a look of concern. "If you think you'll need me, I'll stay with you, Aunt Julia."

"No, Maggie can take care of me. I was just wondering . . . You didn't seem anxious to go to the ball at first."

"That was before . . ." Lyle halted abruptly, reconsidering before he continued. "I have some unfinished business to take care of there."

"You will be careful, won't you, Lyle?"

Lyle studied her concern. "You have a very discerning eye, Aunt Julia."

"And I love you dearly, Nephew."

Leaning toward her, Lyle kissed her pale cheek, and Julia realized the whole charade had been for naught.

Kiss after kiss, caress after caress, had left Sophia breathless and beyond conscious thought as Aaron's carriage traveled the darkened streets. Her lips, sensitized beyond bearing, separated under his. Her body filled with longing, sought his hard flesh. Her arms eager, wound around his neck, clutching, drawing him ever closer. She heard his soft groan and it echoed inside her as the carriage drew to a halt.

She glanced out at the street, uncertain as to their location as Aaron spoke a few short words to his driver and then helped her down onto the sidewalk before a modest residence. Suddenly conscious of her disheveled state, Sophia raised a hand to her hair.

"Don't worry. There's no one to see you here. These are my bachelor quarters."

A quick turn of the key and they were inside in a stillness that echoed with the sounds of their uneven breaths, in a darkness striped with gold shafts of light from the lamppost outside the window. Suddenly aware of the step she was about to take, Sophia stared at Aaron's shadowed face. In the dim light, he was again a stranger, a man she had kept at arm's length, a man who—

Aaron touched her, and everything changed. This man was part of her destiny, the shadowed figure always present but never quite discernible in her mind, and this was meant to be.

All conscious thought slipped away as Aaron's fingers moved in her hair, freeing the heavy tresses. She felt the erotic rain of kisses he showered against her face, her neck. She felt his warm mouth as it followed the rise of her breasts, and she breathed a sigh of relief as he stripped away her gown and released them. He kneeled before her, drawing down her petticoats, her underdrawers, rolling down her stockings and tossing them into the shadows.

Shielded only by the dim light of the room, Sophia stood before him, trembling. An ecstatic jolt of pleasure rocked through her as Aaron's hands moved against her bare flesh for the first time, as, still kneeling, he raised her to anticipation that left her knees weak and shaking.

Cupping her buttocks to hold her steady under his ministrations, Aaron trailed a moist, torrid path past the narrow rib cage that shielded her fluttering heart, stopping to lave her navel with his tongue in passionate assault. Pausing, shuddering violently, he spoke for the first time in a voice ragged with passion.

"I want to make you happy, Sophia. Speak to me. Tell me what you want."

When there was no response, Aaron dropped his head to nuzzle the tight curls between her thighs. His mouth slipped lower and a gasp escaped Sophia's lips.

He prompted softly, "Talk to me, darling."

Sophia's response was tortured. "Aaron, please . . ."

Aaron's tongue caressed the tender crease, increasing her shuddering as he pressed, "Tell me you want me to love you, Sophia."

Sophia swallowed tightly, her lips moving with words that had no sound.

"Say the words, darling. Tell me you want me."

"I . . . I want you, Aaron."

The brief silence that followed was heavy and prolonged as Aaron gazed up at her. His handsome features tight with passion, he whispered, "I'll give you what you want darling . . . what we both want."

Her heart racing, her mind a frenzy of longing and throbbing need, Sophia allowed him full access, giving herself up to him completely. She heard Aaron's soft sound of satisfaction as her knees buckled and he slowly lowered her to the floor. She felt his hands upon her as he spread her knees and settled himself between them. Cupping her buttocks, he raised her to him to find the aching bud of her passion, to fix his mouth fully against her, drawing deeply with his kiss.

Colors, brilliant and blinding, swirled wildly in Sophia's mind, finally exploding against Sophia's closed eyelids as a paralyzing spasm of ecstasy rocked her. Trembling, shuddering as spasm after wrenching spasm followed, Sophia was breathless and weak as Aaron continued drinking from her with unceasing ardor.

Still at last, too exhausted to speak, Sophia felt Aaron's breath against her lips. She opened her eyes to see him gazing down at her, myriad emotions reflected in his ebony gaze.

"No, I don't want you to sleep yet, darling. There's much more to come."

Drawing her to her feet, Aaron pulled her against his side as he led her toward a nearby doorway.

Stopping to light a lamp beside the bed, Aaron slipped

unexpectedly behind her, pulling her back tight against his chest as he turned her to face a nearby mirror. Sophia gasped. Her startling nakedness appeared more shocking with Aaron's fully clothed form behind her and Sophia felt a moment's shame. She searched Aaron's reflection for a sign of ridicule. Her throat tightened as she saw him cup her breasts in his hands, his gaze worshipful as he whispered, "You're perfect, Sophia, lovelier than I dared to dream." His hands slid down her naked flesh, eager fingers splayed as he continued, "No, don't close your eyes, Sophia. Watch me, darling. Watch me love you."

Satisfied only when Sophia was observing him intently in the mirror, Aaron caressed her breasts with one hand. With the other he followed a path he had previously followed with his lips until his fingers touched the sensitized font of her passion. He stroked her boldly.

"See how your body reacts to me, darling. It's shuddering. It's meeting my caress. It's warming to it." His ministrations grew more intense. "The ecstasy is returning, isn't it? It's building . . . growing stronger."

Succumbing to Aaron's intimate caresses, Sophia felt her will slip away. She was floating in a world of riotous sensation, attuned only to Aaron's touch, to the hypnotic sound of his voice. He was loving her totally, more deeply than she had ever dreamed she—

"Sophia, speak to me." Aaron's voice deepened. "I want to hear the words. Tell me you need me . . ."

Sophia groaned softly. "I need you, Aaron."

Aaron's touch grew bolder, robbing her of breath as he coached, "Tell me you love the way I make you feel . . . tell me you want me never to let you go."

Breathless, Sophia rasped, "Aaron . . ."

As breathless as she, Aaron caressed her with growing fervor, raising her high on translucent wings as he whispered, "Give to me Sophia. Give to me now . . . now . . ."

His throbbing words sending her over the edge of sustained ecstasy, Sophia plummeted from the precipice, her body pulsating to Aaron's unrelenting quest, giving as he asked, more than he asked, her body quaking as he quickly turned her in his arms and carried her to the bed.

Limp in the aftermath of her ecstatic convulsions, Sophia watched as Aaron slowly stripped away his clothes. His eyes never leaving her, he bared shoulders that were broader than she had dreamed. His chest heaving, he slipped his trousers down legs that were long and strong and covered with a fine mat of dark hair. As he flung away the last of his clothes, Sophia suppressed a gasp.

Poised above her, breathing heavily, Aaron whispered, "It's time to take me inside you, darling . . ."

Aaron paused briefly as his words registered in the brilliant blue of Sophia's eyes. He probed the moist delta awaiting him, then drove deep inside her as Sophia cried out against the pain of penetration.

Startled, incredulous at sudden realization, Aaron rasped, "Sophia, I didn't know . . ."

Suddenly past control, Aaron began moving inside her. His motions, at first controlled, became rapid and abandoned, and Sophia closed her eyes at his all-consuming possession. Acceptance became a groping heat that raised her to his thrusts, the sweet joy of the complete union growing stronger until she was meeting his strength with her own, clinging to him, rising with him, and crying out as they soared together in ultimate culmination.

Silent, his weight heavy upon her, Sophia felt Aaron stir. Her heart began pounding anew as he raised himself above her so he might clearly view her face. She saw a strange light in his eyes as he whispered, "Now you're mine."

Madame walked along the edge of the crowded dance floor. Her smile was pleased as she accepted congratulations and compliments along the way, then came to stand at a point of observance that allowed her a view of her lovely mannequins as their pleased partners whirled them around the floor. Her smile broadened.

Lucille, Denise, and Nicole . . . so very French with their flirtatious glances and winning ways. They were perfect for this occasion, despite the undependability which forced her to limit the use of their talents. But Celeste was also aware that their beauty had been completely overshadowed by Sophia's magnificent presence, and she gave a note of silent thanks for the opportunity Aaron Weiss had afforded her when he had spirited Sophia away.

Madame raised her chin, the heat inside her lending an unusual brightness to her pale eyes. Ah, to be that girl right now, the young and lovely Sophia who was doubtless lying in the arms of the handsome Monsieur Weiss. Celeste gave a short laugh. No, Aaron had not fooled her with his claim that Sophia was ill. She had seen the telltale flush of his passion, the tenseness about his lips. His hands had been shaking . . .

A thrill ran down Madame Tourneau's spine and she breathed deeply at the thought of what those smooth, knowledgeable hands were doing now . . .

Drawing herself sharply back to the present as the music again came to an end, Madame awaited the return of her mannequins. Her gowns had been a great success. The announcement of her proposed participation in the work of the Silk Association Council had been warmly received, and in the short time that Sophia had spent at the ball, Celeste knew that her beautiful protégée had made an indelible impression that added to the luster of her name.

Celeste smiled with satisfaction. She also knew that her smooth handling of inquiries after Sophia's departure would earn her Aaron Weiss's gratitude. She knew that such absences would undoubtedly increase in the future, and that she would be expected to cover them with the same aplomb.

Madame unconsciously shrugged. She would perform that service gladly, since the handsome Monsieur Weiss's gratitude would net her much in return. The situation was temporary in any case. Monsieur's interest was destined to fade—now that he had finally seduced the sultry Italian beauty.

Shaking off her heated thoughts, Celeste donned a professional smile as her three lovely employees reached her side.

Breathless, Denise whispered, "It is a lovely affair, *non*, madame?"

"Madame . . ." Lucille giggled, her blond head brushing Celeste's gray curls as she whispered, "I have found myself a wealthy admirer tonight. He wishes to take me home . . ."

"*Non*." Madame's smile became strained. "Tonight you work for me. Tomorrow is another day. You will tell the gentleman so."

"Ah, madame, you are cruel!"

Madame made a sudden decision in lieu of the problems she anticipated would come. "We leave in fifteen minutes, mademoiselles. Make haste to say your *adieus* so we may leave your admirers totally enraptured and wanting more."

Grateful that the resumption of the dance stole her pouting employees from her side, Celeste turned to see Lyle Kingston standing in the entrance. She gave a short laugh as he searched the crowd to no avail. Amused at the poor fellow's dismay, Celeste turned her back and looked away.

Lyle strove to hide his agitation as he stepped down onto the ballroom floor, carefully scanning the crowd.

Sophia was nowhere to be seen, and his uneasiness increased. He had a bad feeling . . .

Weiss's furious image returned to his mind, and he briefly closed his eyes.

Aaron has changed, Lyle. He cares for me . . .

Sophia, clever as she was, was incredibly naive, and he was certain Weiss would do his best to take advantage of that naivete after their confrontation an hour earlier.

The knot in Lyle's stomach tightened. Damn! He hadn't wanted to let Sophia out of his sight, but he had been unable to dismiss Aunt Julia's pallor and her shortness of breath. He had waited only until his aunt was in Maggie's capable hands before returning.

"Oh, there you are, Nephew! I thought you had left."

Turning sharply at the sound of Matthew's voice, Lyle forced a smile. He noted that his aunt, standing stiffly beside her husband, did not bother to return the courtesy as he nodded in greeting, but it was his uncle's jovial mood that sent the first tremors of apprehension down his spine.

"Edith and I were just about to leave." Matthew glanced back at his wife's stiff face. "As you can undoubtedly see, your aunt isn't in the mood to dance tonight. Unfortunate, in light of my own enjoyment of the festivities."

"Aunt Julia wasn't feeling well, so I took her home."

Matthew's bright expression momentarily dimmed. "It couldn't have been serious or you wouldn't have returned . . ."

"She'll be all right."

Matthew's bright demeanor returned with Lyle's reassurance. "It must be in the air—feeling unwell, I mean. It seems your 'friend,' the Marone girl, was similarly stricken."

Stiffening, Lyle stared at his uncle, aware that he was enjoying his little game too much to bring it to an early end. Lyle strengthened his forbearance, his heart beginning a heavy pounding as Matthew continued. "It was strange, though, the way Weiss dragged her out into the garden as soon as Amsterdam relinquished her, only to return to speak a few quiet words to the Frenchwoman before disappearing again. Weiss seemed in quite a hurry, as if he was incredibly anxious . . . almost as if he was in heat . . ."

"Matthew!" Edith spoke for the first time, her pale eyes icy. "Don't be uncouth!"

"Uncouth?" Matthew turned back to his wife. "You saw the fellow. I think it's a fair description."

Lyle bit back a reply as Matthew proceeded. "No one has seen either of them since, and I think it's safe to say Weiss and your Italian friend left together . . . in a terrible hurry."

Refusing to respond, Lyle held his uncle's gaze unflinchingly until all levity faded from the older man's expression and he said coldly, "Take my advice and forget the little slut. She isn't worth it."

Lyle took a hard step forward, his fists balled, only to hear his uncle grate, "That wouldn't be smart, Nephew — for such a clever fellow."

Lyle stared intently forward as his uncle and aunt walked out the entrance behind him. He had returned too late . . .

His throat so thick that he could hardly breathe past the lump lodged there, Lyle experienced a draining sense of loss.

He had given Sophia up, never truly believing he would lose her. But suddenly, incredibly painfully, he was certain he had.

Sophia lay warm against him in sleep, the smooth length of her stretched out against his hard flesh as Aaron raised himself on his elbow in intimate scrutiny. She was a breathtaking vision in her naked splendor. He knew he had never seen skin so clear and white, nor a physical perfection so complete. She was flawless, the most beautiful woman he had ever seen.

But she was more than that . . .

Strangely affected, Aaron clutched the gleaming, vibrant curls so close to his hand, weaving his fingers in their silky warmth as he brushed Sophia's lips with a kiss. She stirred and he remained still, not desiring to awaken her. He needed time . . . time to come to terms with the unexpected feelings rioting inside him.

He had been with many women, but he now knew he had never made love before. His abandonment to the emotion Sophia stirred inside him had been complete, but he had not been alone in his abandonment . . .

Aaron's heart began pounding anew as he recalled the total innocence of Sophia's response. Although startled at the intensity of his passion, she had held back nothing as he had brought her to culmination again and again. She was a passionate flower that had bloomed just for him, an aphrodisiac that left him with limitless desire. He had taken her once, and he knew he would not be satisfied until he had taken her again and again . . .

Slowly slipping his arms under and around her, Aaron drew Sophia closer, gasping as her head drooped and her lips grazed his chest. Breathing heavily, he realized they had only begun to explore the vast reaches of emotion they could touch together. She had been a virgin! Even now the thought was incredulous. A beauty of tarnished reputation . . . totally innocent, and totally loving.

A fierce jealousy suddenly overwhelmed Aaron. So many men wanted Sophia, but only he would have her. He would not share her in any way. He would help her with her work—keep her close to him, totally dependent on him, knowing and wanting solace or direction from no one else. He would be all and everything to her. He would give her everything and anything she wanted. And when the day came when this fire between them cooled . . .

Suddenly unable to face the thought of that inevitability, Aaron clutched Sophia tighter, his straining grip raising a sound of protest as he drank from the solace of her mouth.

Drunk on the taste of her, wanting more, he rolled himself atop her. Sophia came slowly awake as he kissed her again and again, searching the sweet recesses of her mouth, the hollows at the base of her throat, cupping her breasts to tease and suckle them until she cried out in an agony of desire. Moving the hard shaft of his passion against her, he urged, "Tell me you love me, Sophia."

Sophia did not respond, and a slow anxiety invaded Aaron's mind. He demanded more harshly, "Tell me you love me, Sophia . . ."

Her extraordinary eyes meeting his, Sophia hesitated, her lips moving though he heard no sound. Angry, he shook her lightly, and she rasped, "Is this love, this ache inside me that won't subside, this need to have you fill me? If it is, then I do love you."

His shuddering growing more intense, Aaron whispered, "You're not sure, are you, Sophia? I'll make you sure. In the same voice that I promised you ecstasy, I promise I'll make you sure that you love me."

Thrusting himself inside her, Aaron reveled in Sophia's sudden gasp, the flaring of her nostrils, and the sudden flush that signaled the rise of her passion. And he loved her, as he had never thought it was possible to love.

Chapter Fifteen

"Sophia, get up. It's late!"

Stirring from a heavy sleep, Sophia stared groggily at her sister as Rosalie leaned over the bed. She looked toward the window to see morning had already arrived and rasped, "What time is it?"

"Late! Anna's already sitting at the table and Mama will be in here to get you up in a minute." Rosalie's anxiety was apparent. "Mama was furious that you came home so late last night. She only held her temper because Papa stood up for you."

Feeling the heat of a slow flush, Sophia pulled herself to her feet beside the bed. Her body tender and aching, she straightened up slowly, the hours spent in Aaron's arms flooding back to her mind. Suddenly aware that Rosalie watched her in silence, she instructed sharply, "Tell Mama I'll be out in a minute."

The bedroom door closed behind Rosalie and Sophia slipped off her nightgown, only to freeze into stillness as she met her reflection in the dresser mirror. The hazy light of early morning did not conceal the small, dark marks of passion on her breasts and at the base of her neck. She looked down to see the same marks on her inner thighs and she closed her eyes. The sound of a soft gasp snapped her eyes open again to see that Rosalie stood just inside the door.

Her sister's voice was filled with despair as she whispered, "Oh, Sophia . . ."

A moment later Rosalie was gone. Attempting to dismiss the memory of her sister's dismay, Sophia dressed quickly and, with a quick brush of her hair, stepped out into the kitchen. Grateful to find her mother's back turned, she looked at Rosalie to see her sister glance away. She looked at Anna, only to have Mama demand her attention as she snapped, "Hurry, or you'll be late for work. You look tired, Sophia," she added pointedly as Sophia quickly seated herself. "But then we're all tired from waiting for you to come home last night."

Grateful that her mother chose to drop the subject there, Sophia decided on silence. Rosalie's hand took hers under the table and Sophia turned toward her. She was relieved almost to the point of tears as Rosalie smiled.

"So you've chosen to ignore my warning!" Samuel Weiss's sharp voice rang in the confines of his small office as he drew himself laboriously to his feet. The pain in his foot had worsened and he was still irate from the previous evening. His son's late arrival for work that morning had done nothing to ease his foul mood.

He leaned heavily on his desk, glaring. "I warned you about taking up with that young woman."

"I'm a grown man, Father. I make my own choices."

"You're my son! The Weiss family reputation is at stake here, and I won't have you demeaning the family name by your open association with that common young tart!"

"There's nothing at all common about Sophia." Aaron faced his father's anger, his eyes hard. "She beautiful, intelligent, and talented."

"Talented?" Samuel gave a scornful laugh. "Was it her talent that made you so impatient to whisk her away from the ball last night? Tongues were wagging the entire night."

To Samuel's surprise, Aaron flushed. "Sophia is working hard to escape her common beginnings. Madame Tourneau agrees with me that she can go far in fashion design."

"That French opportunist will tell you whatever you want to hear if it's to her advantage!"

"You're prejudiced against Sophia! You believe only what you choose to believe about her."

"This is a switch, isn't it, Aaron?" Samuel drew back, his small eyes narrowed. "Aren't you the one who told me a short time ago that Sophia Marone was a tart whose name was well known in bachelor circles? Can it be that my son is smitten?"

Pausing, Samuel suddenly laughed aloud. "Oh, no, not *my* son . . . the supreme whoremaster whose reputation with women is second to none! He couldn't be stupid enough to be taken over the hoops by his female counterpart . . ."

"Sophia's not like that!"

Samuel's laughter came to an abrupt halt. "What *is* she like, Aaron? Is she so good in bed that she's blinded you to what she is? She's using you! She's had many men before you, and she'll have many men after you. She'll make a fool of you, just as she did young Kingston!"

"You're wrong! Kingston never touched her. No man ever touched her!"

"Oh, no . . ." Samuel shook his head, incredulous. "You're trying to say that the girl was a virgin?"

Samuel waited for a response that did not come, and his incredulity grew. "Am I dreaming, Aaron . . . or are you attempting to be noble in holding your tongue about this woman?" He paused in contemplation of his son's rising color. "I didn't think you had a speck of nobility in you. Maybe this woman has wrought a change for the better in you after all." Suddenly slamming his palms down on the desk, Samuel shouted, "The next thing I know you'll be telling me that you want to marry her!"

"Don't be ridiculous, Father!"

His expression sober, Aaron drew himself erect. "I'm not the fool you seem to think I am. I know how far I can take this affair, and it isn't as far as the altar." Aaron's expression tightened. "I've seen where Sophia comes from. Her parents are common peasants—homely, ignorant people— and her sisters are dark-haired little wops. Her heredity is blemished beyond the point where it can be ignored, despite the fact that I'm obsessed with her."

"Obsessed with her!" Samuel's eyes widened. "Damn it, Aaron!"

"Don't worry." Resentment and a strange kind of sadness touched Aaron's expression. "I'm well aware of the limitations I must set on this affair, but I want it clear to you that it's not because of Sophia herself. I intend to do all I can to help her."

Pausing, Aaron continued more softly. "I want to make another thing clear, too. She's *mine*, Father. Make no mistake about it, I won't give her up one minute before I'm ready."

Samuel drew back, uncertain how to approach this new side of his son. Obsession? At least he hadn't been foolish enough to call his feelings for the woman love. Lust, possessiveness, jealousy . . . those were more apt descriptions of the symptoms he exhibited.

Samuel studied his son's adamant expression. "And if I'm not prepared to wait until you tire of her?"

"You don't have a choice, Father."

"Oh yes I do!" Snapping to attention, infuriated by his son's audacity, Samuel responded heatedly, "You're my son, but I can change your future with a flick of my pen! Remember that, Aaron! And while we're giving ultimatums here, I'll give you mine. You say you're obsessed with this tart. All right, I'll let you play that game for a while until you get her out of your system, but I won't stand for this affair to come out into the open! Only a business association on the surface, Aaron—that's all I'll tolerate! I won't have you flaunt her in front of your mother again, and I won't have the family name tainted!"

Aaron's jaw hardened. "I don't like being threatened."

"I don't care what you like! The matter is settled—finished! I don't want to hear about this woman or discuss her again. And I warn you, Aaron, get her out of your system quickly. I'm not getting any younger and I'm tiring rapidly. I don't intend to turn this business over to a fool who's obsessed with an ambitious slut who'll drag him down to her level! Is that understood?"

Waiting, truly uncertain what his son's response would be, Samuel held his breath.

Turning, Aaron walked out through the door and slammed it closed behind him. The echo of the sound drowned out Samuel's disgusted growl.

"The damned young fool . . ."

"This will not do, Sophia."

Madame Tourneau surveyed Sophia's appearance with a critical eye. It had been a busy day in the salon, a result, she was sure, of the acclaim she had received at the ball the previous night. And, perhaps, Madame admitted with reservation, due to curiosity about her lovely protégée who had stirred so much interest.

But Sophia had been less than fresh when she came to work that morning, and as the day wore on, it was apparent she was rapidly wilting. Madame's annoyance erupted in the sharpness of her tongue.

"You do little justice to my gowns in your present state, Sophia. Your skin is pale, your eyes are shadowed, and your vitality is at a low ebb. You must set some restrictions in your affair with Monsieur Weiss. He takes too much from you . . ."

Shocked at Madame's bluntness, Sophia drew back a

step and glanced around her. The shop was quiet. The two women going through the rack at the front of the store appeared oblivious to them, but Sophia was not content to allow Madame to get away with her unwanted opinions.

"My 'affair' with Aaron is none of your concern, madame!"

"Ma petite," Madame's sharpness warmed into a smile as she took a step closer and continued more softly. "I have no desire to direct the course of your private life. You have handled yourself admirably with Monsieur Weiss. I doubt that I would have had the strength of will hold him off as long as you did, no matter how beneficial it was to do so. But the resistance is now over, and it is clear for the experienced eye to see that the virile fellow did well by you."

"Madame—"

Sophia's fair skin flushed more darkly as Madame interrupted again. "You are fortunate. Two very handsome men vie for your attentions. In truth, I'm uncertain which of them I would've chosen. Monsieur Kingston is beautiful, too, *non?* Like a golden god. Poor fellow, he was bereft when he returned to find you gone."

"Lyle was looking for me after I left?" Madame's nod started a slow ache inside Sophia as tears rushed to her eyes.

"Careful, mademoiselle . . ." Celeste warned. "Monsieur Weiss is a jealous sort."

Sophia forced away the tears with supreme control, her anger flaring. "That's not your concern!"

"Ah, but it is! You are my protégée—as publicly established by your handsome lover. Everything you do reflects on me. But you mustn't worry. I will help you . . . and protect you. It's to my benefit, you see, to earn Monsieur Weiss's gratitude."

Not pausing for Sophia's response, Madame continued. "However, I advise you again to speak to your monsieur. Your condition today is . . ." Madame smiled, ". . . too re-

337

vealing, and while I envy you his ardent attentions, I tell you that people will talk."

Glancing at the clock on the wall, Madame frowned. "It is almost three. Perhaps you should go home early — get some rest."

Sophia glanced away from Madame's scrutiny. The woman's unwanted advice made her feel dirty and the loving interlude with Aaron sordid. She longed to escape, but she knew she could not go home to face a scrutiny even more intense than Madame's.

But Madame was right. She was tired . . .

The sound of the salon door opening behind her escaped conscious thought until Sophia saw a familiar light enter Madame's eyes. She turned abruptly, the moment before Aaron reached her side. Her heart began pounding as he slid his arm around her waist. Her lips parted as his gaze touched her mouth and she felt Aaron's response the moment before he turned to Madame.

"I've come to take Sophia home early today, madame. The excitement last night exhausted her and she's in need of some rest."

Madame's smile tightened the knot in Sophia's stomach. Aaron's hand at her waist moved caressingly, and she fought to control her reaction to his touch as the Frenchwoman smiled coyly.

"I was just telling Sophia the same thing. She needs only a moment to change into her own clothes and she may leave." Madame glanced momentarily at the gown Sophia wore. "Sophia was born to wear silk, *non, monsieur?* It is a shame for her to return to the simple garments she wears."

"Sophia was born to wear silk . . . and for much more, madame."

Aaron urged Sophia toward the back room, his eyes consuming her, and Sophia was too weak to do else but comply. Mary hastened to undo the fastenings on her dress as Sophia strove for control. The look in Aaron's eyes had started her trembling, leaving her without a voice to object to his proprietary manner, but she told herself she would settle everything between them when they had a chance to talk. Her trembling increased. Yes, they would go someplace where they could talk . . .

"What's wrong, Sophia? Aren't you well?"

Turning at the young seamstress's concern, Sophia merely shook her head. Out of her exquisite blue silk gown, Sophia escaped Mary's eye as quickly as possible. Fully clothed again at last, she drew back the curtain to find Aaron waiting.

His eyes speaking clearly the words he didn't dare speak, Aaron took her hand.

"I've been waiting for this moment all day."

Still unable to speak, Sophia followed his lead.

Moments later the carriage jerked into motion and Aaron took her into his arms. Her determinations fading, Sophia melted in his embrace, separating her lips to his kiss. She had no need to ask where they were going. She knew.

The balmy afternoon air slowed Maria's step as she passed the busy marketplace. Although her shopping sack was almost full, she surveyed the table heaped with tomatoes ripened to a bright red color by the sun. On the next table bright-yellow pears lent their sweet fragrance to the air, and she paused, breathing deeply. She had been shopping for an hour, carefully traveling from store to store in search of the best bargains to be found. Her legs were tired, but it was her sore and aching heart that lowered her spirits and caused her feet to drag.

Ah, Sophia . . . Sophia . . . Maria felt a tear rise to her eye.

Why do you hate me, Mama?

Maria had not dared reply to Sophia's whispered ques-

339

tion that day, but the words she had withheld now flooded across her mind in a unrelenting flow.

Hate you, Sophia? Never!

Fear for you? Yes.

But how could she make her understand, her beautiful daughter who had so clearly seen the path she wished to travel since childhood, that the path she saw as a glowing promise would only lead her to anguish? How could she make her daughter comprehend that the beauty others envied and adored would only hasten her down that path? How could she tell her daughter that she had cried with joy when Anna and Rosalie were born to see that they were plain, because she knew their way would be easier because of it.

The answer was simple. She could not. She had kept her tongue all these years and it was too late to explain now that she —

"Ah, Maria! *Come sta?*"

Maria turned sharply. The hackles on her spine rose as Marcella Negri smiled and squeezed her massive bulk between the produce tables to waddle toward her. The woman's gold tooth sparkled in the sun as her smile widened.

"You never come to visit me. What have you been doing with yourself?"

Maria forced a smile. "Things have been difficult at home lately, but now that the strike is over and my daughters are back to work, we're returning to normal."

"But you must be very proud of Sophia's rise in the world! To attend the charity ball . . ."

Maria suppressed a frown, galled at the notorious gossip's seemingly unlimited font of information. Determined to give her as little satisfaction as possible, Maria forced a smile.

"It was part of Sophia's duties in her new position. The Frenchwoman needed a mannequin to show her gown."

"The Frenchwoman . . . *sì.*" Marcella's prominent nose

340

twitched. "I hear she prefers to hire only young French-women in her shop because she thinks the society ladies who go there are more impressed with them. Sophia is fortunate that her sponsor spoke up for her or she would never have gotten the job."

Her sponsor? Maria turned toward the nearby table so Marcella might not see her surprise. "Ah, yes, Sophia's sponsor . . ."

"Mr. Weiss is a handsome man, no?" Marcella winked. "And he is so concerned about Sophia that he stops by the Frenchwoman's shop every day to check on her progress."

Maria looked up sharply. "You are well informed, Marcella. How do you know all of this?"

"My Angelo delivers bread to Montebello's, across the street from the Frenchwoman's shop. Mario Montebello told him."

Maria nodded, her pale eyes narrowing.

"My Angelo says Mr. Weiss was very proud of Sophia, but she must be careful with Mr. Weiss because he's not a nice man."

"Your Angelo is wrong. Mr. Weiss is a fine gentleman." Maria raised her chin with a superior air of confidence that she knew would impress the nosy gossip. "Anthony and I have met him . . . at the feast of the Madonna d'Assunta. He's been kind to Sophia because she helped him with some work for his mother."

Gratified to see Marcella taken aback with her response, Maria placed the tomato she had selected back on the table.

"It's getting late and I have a lot of work left to do today. *Arrivederci,* Marcella. I'll tell Sophia you were asking about her."

"*Sì . . .*"

Marcella was still staring as Maria turned away. Walking down the street moments later, Maria maintained rigid control over her expression, although she was badly

341

shaken. Her thoughts in a turmoil, she knew only that the thing she had feared most had begun.

His carriage had barely drawn to a halt in front of the mill before Matthew thrust open the door to stare furiously at his nephew where he stood near the entrance. Ignoring the workers milling nearby before the sounding of the whistle that would draw them back inside, he strode to Lyle's side. He turned to motion toward the short, seedy-looking fellow talking to a group of workers.

"Call the police and get that damned anarchist out of the yard!"

The whistle sounded, drowning out the angry rattle of Enrico Malatesta's words as he gestured dramatically to the few weavers gathered around him, but Matthew did not need to hear what the fellow said to know that the ardent rabblerouser spewed his own particular brand of socialist poison to whomever cared to listen.

"Lyle!"

"I heard you, Uncle." Lyle's face hardened. "However, I choose not to aggravate the situation at this particular moment."

"Damned coward! I'll take care of the fellow myself!"

Matthew turned, his step coming to an abrupt halt as his nephew commanded, "Stay where you are, Uncle! I don't want you to stir sympathy for Malatesta by throwing him off this property. Everyone will be inside in a minute. I'll take care of him then."

"But—"

"I'm the boss here, remember?"

Matthew paused, his lips tightening. The bastard was in command, all right, and he wasn't about to relinquish the authority he had usurped by so much as an inch.

His fury growing, Matthew stared into Lyle's cöld gold eyes, memories of earlier times and other gold eyes filled with love suddenly intervening. Breathing deeply against the unexpected assault of memory, Matthew grated harshly, "All right, handle it your way, but I'm warning you. I won't tolerate Malatesta's presence in the mill yard! He's a troublemaker and—"

"I know what he is! I also know we're just out of a difficult strike, and I'm not about to risk any more trouble. Use your head, Uncle! Malatesta's a countryman of many of your best weavers, and their loyalties run deep. They've avoided him here, for the most part, but if they see him attacked and thrown out, many of them will likely come to his aid."

"You overestimate these peasants, Nephew. They care only for the almighty dollar. Their scruples are easily bought."

Lyle's lips tightened and Matthew could feel the power of his nephew's contempt as Lyle grated, "That's your problem, Uncle . . . your lack of respect for any man's principles other than your own. You're more a fool than you've often accused me of being."

"Damned bastard!" Matthew took an aggressive step forward, and Lyle gave a short laugh. "That's right, Uncle, give your employees fodder for more gossip with a public display of the gist of things between us."

"I'll do as I damned well please in my own mill!"

"Even at the sacrifice of your profitability, I'm sure, because you could then blame your losses on my management, couldn't you?"

"Don't attempt to foist your problems on me, Nephew. You're in control here, and any difficulties that arise will be of your making."

"That suits me well enough. So, if you'll go into the office, I'll handle things my way."

Another blast of the mill whistle interrupting his reply, Matthew pulled himself erect, his glance scathing as the last of the workers trailed toward the door. A quick glance revealed Malatesta had been abandoned, and Matthew felt his fury rise. Turning on his heel without a word to his nephew, he walked into the mill and strode toward the office. He took up a silent stance beside the window that faced the yard as his office door slammed behind him.

His heart pounding, his fists clenched, Matthew watched as Lyle walked casually across the mill yard and paused beside the stiff-faced Malatesta. Realizing Lyle purposely kept his back toward him, he carefully watched Malatesta's expression, only to be startled when the shifty-eyed riffraff turned abruptly and walked back onto the street.

Drawing away from the window as Lyle turned back toward the mill, Matthew moved quickly to his desk and sat down. He had tossed his hat to a nearby chair and had picked up his pen in a pretended posture of absorption in the report in front of him when he suddenly exclaimed aloud, "Damn the bastard!"

He had been reduced to subterfuge in his own mill by a few short words in an authoritative tone that came as naturally to the arrogant pretender as his own!

At the sound of the outer office door opening, Matthew's lips tightened. Christine's son wasn't lacking in spunk, intelligence, or tenacity. He had always known that, hadn't he? But there was that basic flaw . . . It had fostered only resentment at first, but his feelings had rapidly deteriorated as the boy had matured, until now, when he looked at Lyle as a grown man, it was with an emotion akin to hatred. The breach between them was unbridgeable.

Matthew raised his chin, his determination renewed. Simply stated, the reason behind his antipathy was this. Lyle was another man's son.

Tearing herself from Aaron's arms, Sophia stepped back against the closed door of his bachelor quarters, her heart pounding. Aaron's expression darkened. He made a move to reclaim her but she shook off his touch with a harsh whisper.

"No, Aaron. I didn't come with you today for this. I . . . I think it's best that we talk."

"Talk, Sophia? About what?" Anger flashed in Aaron's dark eyes. "About how much I want you . . . about the way I woke up this morning thinking about you and about the way I haven't been able to get you out of my mind all day?"

"I didn't want this to happen." Sophia stiffened, seeking the control that had deserted her in Aaron's arms. "I can't afford this kind of distraction. It's taken me too long to come this far and I have too much to learn."

"I'll teach you everything you need to know, Sophia."

"Aaron, please . . ." Weakening, Sophia strove to maintain her resolve. "I've worked toward certain goals all my life."

"This is something neither of us planned." His expression pained, Aaron reached out to stroke a wisp of fiery hair back from Sophia's cheek. His fingers grazed her skin and a tremor ran down her spine as he continued. "I've wanted you from the first moment I saw you. I told myself that once I had made love to you I'd be able to walk away from you, just as I've walked away from so many other women, but it didn't work out that way. I want you more than ever, Sophia. I want you to want me."

"No, Aaron . . ."

"I won't let you push me away, Sophia." Aaron's voice begged her understanding. "You won't suffer for the passion between us, I promise you that. I've already opened doors for you that you would've found closed otherwise, and this is only the beginning. With my support—"

"I won't sell myself to you, Aaron."

"And I won't let you sacrifice me to your ambitions. That is what you're trying to do, isn't it?"

"No . . . yes . . ." Suddenly overwhelmed by conflicting desires, Sophia shook her head. What did she want? She wanted to feel Aaron's arms around her. She wanted to surrender to the emotions even now coursing through her, the aching need so new and so strong that Aaron raised with a touch, with a glance. She wanted to feel his mouth against hers, his hands stroking her. She wanted to lose herself in his arms. She wanted . . .

Suddenly she was in Aaron's arms. His mouth was on hers, separating her lips. His tongue sought hers, and Sophia felt her restraint slip away. His hard, aroused body moved against her and Sophia gasped with the ecstasy again coming clearly into view. Aaron's hands worked at the buttons of her shirtwaist, freeing her breasts, and she gasped at his touch. Raising her skirt, Aaron pushed aside her undergarments with rough, trembling hands. She heard the sound of her own indrawn breath as Aaron found her moist and waiting and caressed her boldly.

His voice was harsh as he whispered, *"This* is what you want, Sophia. You want me to make you feel good, and I will. You want me to make you a part of me again, and I'll do that, too." Fumbling at the closure of his trousers, Aaron slid himself under her skirts and Sophia gasped as his passion probed her moistness. Her eyes dropped closed, only to snap wide as Aaron ordered, "No, open your eyes and look at me." His expression almost savage, he rasped, "I want you to see how senseless it is to deny what we feel for each other, and I want there to be no mistaking my determination when I say I won't give you up."

Cupping her buttocks with his hands, Aaron slid himself inside her, his gaze victorious as Sophia's eyes glazed with passion. Moving slowly, tantalizingly, Aaron whispered, "Tell me you love me, Sophia."

"No, Aaron."

"Tell me!"

"I don't know . . ."

346

"You *do* know, but you're afraid. Don't be afraid. I won't hurt you. I only want to love you."

"Aaron, I—"

"No, don't talk anymore. Just *feel,* Sophia . . ."

Passion assuming control, Sophia gave vent to the tumultu·us emotions shaking her, knowing only the wonder of Aaron's touch, of being a part of him, of his hands supporting her as he raised her again and again with the force of his impetus. Rocking, clinging to Aaron's strength, Sophia was lost in the wonder of his arms as Aaron erupted inside her, his strong body carrying her with him as he shuddered to fulfillment.

Aaron held her close in the breathless silence that followed. She was uncertain of the exact moment when he withdrew from her and scooped her up into his arms. The bed was soft beneath her when she opened her eyes to find Aaron leaning over her, freeing her from her clothes. She heard the determination in his voice as he whispered, "I'll do anything you want, Sophia. The only thing I won't do is give you up."

His voice dropping a notch lower as he stripped away the last of her garments, Aaron stroked her erotically, starting her trembling anew as he whispered, "You're too inexperienced to realize how special this is between us, but I can tell you that we were made to be together. We're a perfect fit, like a hand in a glove. You'll see. I'll prove it to you."

"We're not, Aaron." Unaware of the tear that trailed from the corner of her eye into the bright hair at her temple, Sophia whispered, "In the eyes of the world we—"

"I don't care what anyone else says!"

Suddenly furious, Aaron stripped away his clothes and threw them to the floor. The bed sagged under his weight as he lay down beside her and drew her roughly into his arms. He drank deeply from her mouth before continuing in a hoarse whisper. "I've never felt this way about anyone

347

before, Sophia. The more I know you, the more I want you, and the more I have you, the more I need you. You've raised a thirst inside me that I can't quench."

Drowning in the emotions she saw in his eyes, Sophia whispered, "But lust is—"

"This isn't lust, Sophia . . . not for me. It's more. It's love."

Reading the doubt in Sophia's eyes, Aaron responded, his black eyes snapping. "All right, you can tell yourself you don't love me, but you can't tell me what *I* feel, and you can't tell yourself you don't want me."

Aaron stroked her boldly, a victorious smile touching his lips as her eyes fluttered closed with the rapid flaring of her passion. Suddenly rolling himself atop her, Aaron slid his hands into her hair, holding her fast as he traced her lips with his tongue, then bit her sharply.

"No . . . don't mark me. Madame said—"

"Don't mention that bitch's name now, or anyone else's. This time is ours."

Allowing her no response, Aaron kissed her deeply once more, and the words Sophia was about to say were lost in the swell of feelings that numbed her mind. Inside her again, he brought them both to rapid culmination before drawing himself free of her and slipping to the bed beside her. Turning her to face him, he fitted his body against the full length of her and held her close.

"Open your eyes, darling." When she did, Aaron continued heatedly. "It doesn't matter what the rest of the world thinks. You know as well as I do that it was meant to be this way between us. So we'll take what we want, and to hell with them all."

"Aaron, I don't—"

"No." Halting her protest with a searching kiss, Aaron drew back at last to rasp, "Ordinary rules weren't made for people like us. We'll do what *we* want and make them all like it."

Lost in the potency of Aaron's dark-eyed gaze, Sophia did not respond. Smiling, Aaron whispered, "Sleep. I'll wake you when it's time to leave."

Exhaustion assuming control, Sophia closed her eyes. As she drifted off to sleep, she felt Aaron draw her closer, as if he would never let her go.

Chapter Sixteen

Sophia looked out the window of Aaron's carriage as it moved briskly along the street. She shivered and drew her shawl tighter around her shoulders as the nip in the evening air penetrated the interior, and Aaron reached out automatically to draw her against his warmth. She glanced up, then settled against him, comfortable in his arms as her attention drifted back toward the passing street.

Satisfaction brought a brief smile to Aaron's lips. Several weeks had passed since the night of the charity ball when Sophia and he had first made love. They had made love several times since then, with each encounter more potent and soul-shattering than the last. He was only too keenly aware, however, that although he had spoken the words many times—from the heart—Sophia had never said she loved him.

Unconsciously drawing her closer, Aaron pressed a light kiss against Sophia's hair. He knew instinctively that her unconscious unwillingness to say those words was an after-effect of her former relationship with Lyle Kingston. A familiar jealousy flaring, Aaron comforted himself that although he had not been completely successful in driving the arrogant bastard from her heart, the lingering doubts Kingston had sowed in her mind about him were slowly eroding. Sophia no longer bad any hesitation in turning

350

to him for comfort when she was tired or uncertain, and she now accepted his touch unconditionally, even appearing to find succor in it. He knew, however, that his feelings for her were so strong that he would not be satisfied until he had displaced Kingston completely in her affections and he owned Sophia body and soul.

Sophia moved restlessly, and Aaron felt the nudge of concern. Sophia was exhausted. In the weeks since the ball, she had performed her regular duties in the salon during the day while working every evening to prepare for the silk association exposition. He knew much of Sophia's change of attitude toward him was not as much a result of their lovemaking as it was the effect of his unflagging devotion both to her and to her success at the exposition. His insistence upon selecting the designs to be used had disturbed her at first, and her resistance had annoyed him. Her respect for his judgment was obvious, however, and he knew that while she had not accepted all his suggestions in the execution of her designs, she had considered each one honestly. A trip to Weiss Mill one evening after closing so she might personally choose the silk for her gowns had been a brilliant strategy in winning her confidence. Sophia's selections had been brilliant and her appreciation sincere. The risk of incurring his father's further disfavor had been well worth taking.

Warming to the weight of Sophia's nearness, Aaron rested his cheek briefly against her hair. It was desperately important to him that Sophia's designs be accepted by the public. He wanted to see Sophia triumph. He wanted Madame Tourneau's meager offerings to pale in comparison with the splendor of Sophia's creative work. He wanted everyone to know that his "protégée" was more than a beautiful face and willing body. He wanted everyone to know she was *worthy* of the attention and time he had given her, and that his interest was not solely due to

351

the demands of the male part of his anatomy that was never truly dormant when she was near. But most of all, he wanted Sophia to achieve a success that would forever set her apart from her common background. Sophia deserved that much after suffering the cruel fate that had brought such an exquisite flower to life amidst weeds.

Aaron drew Sophia possessively closer, feeling again the demands of his constant desire for her and realizing the greatest drain on Sophia's energy did not come from the many hours spent at work. The intimate hours they had been able to steal from the day by unspoken agreement with Madame had drained his energy as well, but the effect on his passions had been negligible. The more he had of Sophia, the more he wanted. The more he wanted, the more he needed.

A momentary twinge of resentment darkened Aaron's brow. His feelings for Sophia were becoming more complicated and contradictory by the day. Without any effort at all, Sophia had succeeded in turning the tables on him in their loving affair, and he inwardly despised Sophia's control over him and lived for the moment when those roles would be reversed. He wanted the world to know she belonged to him alone while still unwilling to yield on the limitations his mind had set on their affair.

A familiar ache began inside Aaron as he adjusted Sophia against his side. Most of all, he wanted Sophia to say she loved him. He needed the victory in those words and the unequivocal commitment that would come with them. He knew he would not be satisfied with less.

Familiar streets came into view and Aaron cupped Sophia's chin with his hand, tilting her face up to his. With true regret he whispered, "We've almost reached Prospect Street and you'll be running off again. So kiss me now, darling—and make it good enough to last until tomorrow."

352

His heart beginning a heavy pounding, Aaron thought he saw regret in Sophia's eyes as well at their impending separation, but there was no regret as Sophia's arms closed around his neck and she surrendered fully to the fervor of his kiss. Pulling back as the carriage drew to a halt, Aaron cursed the twist of fate that held Sophia and him forever apart even while they were in each other's arms.

He was still lamenting his loss as Sophia turned the corner out of sight.

Night had fallen and the small bedroom Sophia shared with her sisters was in darkness. It was a darkness filled with the creak of worn bedsprings as Rosalie moved in her sleep and the rhythmic sound of Anna's breathing as she lay motionless in slumber, but Sophia felt little comfort in the familiarity of those sounds. Unable to sleep, she turned cautiously, aware that any undue movement might wake her sisters. She was unwilling to face their concern.

The sliver of moonlight that slanted through the gaping shade shone against the far wall and Sophia concentrated on the spot of light in an attempt to escape her whirling thoughts. Papa, Mama, Rosalie, Anna . . . the whole world was asleep while her mixed, tortured feelings tormented her.

Her throat thick, Sophia recalled Aaron's expression when she had parted from him earlier in the carriage. It had conveyed so many words that went unspoken and it had been difficult to leave him and return home where she knew her mother would strip away her joy. It was painful knowing that nothing she had accomplished or hoped to accomplish meant anything to Mama, and she suffered deeply knowing that for the first time her mother's suspicions about her were true. She knew she could never make her mother understand that Aaron was working as hard for her success as she herself was, and that he loved her. She knew he did.

She loved Aaron, too . . . didn't she?

The question rebounded in Sophia's mind, the answer eluding her, and Sophia experienced a familiar frustration. So much had happened in the past few weeks that she was uncertain what she truly felt. Her world had been turned upside down, with her dreams at the verge of becoming reality, and her reality becoming dreamlike. Never had she expected the haughty, arrogant Aaron Weiss to bring to fruition the image of herself she had cherished in her mind. Neither had she expected he would be the man who would bring her to other fulfillments as well.

Sophia ran an unsteady hand over her eyes, surprised to find them moist. It was difficult to explain the emotions she felt when she was in Aaron's arms, but she somehow knew that it was right that Aaron and she should be together now. It was as if another part of her, a woman she barely knew, had been waiting for Aaron all her life. That other part of her had emerged to accept his loving and to love him in return. And the loving was beautiful . . . Her body flushed with heat each time she recalled the wonder Aaron evoked in her, his passion, and the supreme tenderness of which he was capable. She felt cherished and protected. She knew his love wasn't feigned, no matter what her mother would claim.

A tear slipped out of the corner of Sophia's eye. She felt so much for Aaron, not the least of which was gratitude for his faith in her. He had given her so much.

So why couldn't she say the words *I love you* . . . They were simple enough. She had said them before.

Lyle's image returned unexpectedly to her mind and Sophia gasped at the strength of the vision. She recalled the instant bonding she had felt with the handsome, angry nephew of the boss, despite his original antagonism toward her. She remembered the day they had stood on the bridge over the falls and she had looked into the glowing gold of his eyes and become certain for the first time that their hearts and minds were completely open to each other. She experienced again the feeling that Lyle was as close to her now as he had ever been, that his thoughts were with her, and that despite the distance between them, with the slightest effort, she would be able to speak directly into his heart. They had not shared more than a kiss, but she knew Lyle loved her, and that she loved him in a way she could never love Aaron.

Sophia paused in her thoughts. Could it be that her feelings for Lyle were holding her back from saying the words to Aaron even though she had given herself to Aaron so completely in other ways? Or was it something else?

Sophia closed her eyes in an effort to shut away her confusion, but it remained. It pinched. It teased. It hurt . . .

The smell of cigar smoke . . .

Sophia snapped her eyes open to see a blue curl of smoke enter the room through the slight opening between window and sill, and her heart leaped to a heavy pounding. Not everyone was asleep. Not Papa . . .

Moving carefully to the edge of the bed, Sophia grasped her dressing gown and slipped it on, turning for a last look at her sisters' sleeping faces as she drew the door open and slipped out of the room. Moments later she was on the porch looking at her father's familiar stocky frame outlined against the moonlight. At his side in a moment, she slid her arm around his waist and smiled at his low grunt of surprise. Anthony's dark eyes reflected the silver light as he turned toward her with concern.

"Something is wrong, Sophia? You don't feel well?"

"No, I'm fine, Papa." Sophia barely maintained a smile. "I couldn't sleep."

Tears filled Sophia's eyes at the familiar touch of her father's calloused hand against her cheek and the worry in his voice as he whispered, "You're working too hard and you're tired. You should be sleeping, *figlia mia.*"

"You should be sleeping, too, Papa. You work harder than I do."

Anthony shrugged. "With me it's different. I'm an old man. During the night my selfish mistakes haunt me."

"You? Selfish?" Sophia shook her head. "No, not you."

"*Sí, figlia mia . . .*"

"No. You're a saint, Papa."

"Your papa a saint?" Anthony smiled sadly. "No. You think that of me because I've always protected you against your mother's anger. But you don't realize that I made your mother the woman she is by failing her in ways she never failed me."

Suddenly angry at her father's self-deprecatory words, Sophia shook her head angrily. "No, Papa. You never failed anyone. You always did your best for all of us."

"You're wrong. There are things you don't know . . ." Anthony paused, appearing to weigh the adamancy of her words before he smiled sadly. "I didn't do what was best for your mama, Sophia. I should not have married her, because I knew she didn't love me. Her mother wanted her to marry me because she thought I could provide for her with the bad times coming. I knew she was deserving of more than I would ever be able to give her, but I was selfish. I wanted her too much to give her up." Anthony sighed. "Your mama has spent her life regretting the day she took my name, and her regrets have made her the bitter woman that she is today."

"No, Papa. Mama is Mama. She is what she is."

"Your mama is what *I* have made of her." His eyes filling unexpectedly, Anthony again stroked Sophia's cheek. "I know that to be the truth, and I don't hide from it. But your papa isn't so much a fool that he would see that same mistake repeated again with someone he loved. For that reason, I've stood strongly between your mama and you and I wouldn't let her force you to marry Joey, even though she believed she was doing what was best for you. And it's for that reason that I tell her that she must ignore the jealous tongues that wag about you even now. I've told her that you're a good girl and that you would never do anything that would reflect poorly on your family. I've told her that she should be proud that you're out of the mill and that she should trust you to do the right thing, as I do."

"Papa . . ." Sophia's heart ached with the words she could not make herself speak.

His voice dropping a note softer, Anthony spoke into the silence as Sophia's voice trailed away.

"I love all my daughters, Sophia, but you were always special to me . . ."

"No, Papa."

"*Sì*. My pride is greater in you, and you are a part of me in a way Rosalie and Anna are not."

"Oh, Papa . . ." Sophia swallowed against the hard knot in her throat. "What if something were to happen that made things change? What if it all went bad?"

"Shh. No more of this talk." Reprimand sounding in his voice for the first time, Anthony continued firmly. "You will do well, Sophia. I know it in my heart. Your work will be special in the way *you* are special, and everyone at the silk exposition will know your name."

"But what if . . . if you're disappointed?"

"Sophia, *figlia mia*, you're my daughter and my blood

runs in your veins. No one can take that pride from me. As for the rest . . ."

Shrugging, appearing suddenly unable to go on, Anthony forced a smile. "Go to bed now."

Words suddenly beyond her, as well, Sophia hugged her father, a sob catching in her throat as his strong arms closed tightly around her. Drawing back a moment later, Sophia kissed his cheek before turning and walking quickly to her room.

Lying abed a short time later, Sophia watched a fresh curl of smoke filter through the window. She breathed deeply of the pungent odor, guilts and regrets swelling to a deadening ache.

"Sophia . . ." Rosalie's unexpected whisper pierced the darkness, turning Sophia toward the sound of her younger sister's voice as she asked softly, "Do you love Aaron Weiss?"

Caught unprepared by Rosalie's unexpected question, Sophia hesitated. Unwilling to practice another deceit, Sophia spoke in hushed response.

"I don't know."

"I don't understand."

Her own confusion causing her to pause in response, Sophia whispered, "A part of me loves him . . . very much. But another part of me holds back."

"Does he love you?"

"Yes."

Rosalie hesitated, then spoke with uncertainty. "You aren't sure of your own feelings . . . so how can you be sure he loves you?"

Myriad responses rose to Sophia's lips before she answered simply, "I'm sure."

Rosalie's small, calloused hand slipped into hers. Appearing to regret the doubt she had expressed moments earlier, she whispered, "But how could he

358

help but love you, Sophia? Everybody loves you."

Sophia closed her eyes in the darkness. Smiling at last, she held her sister's hand tightly, knowing Rosalie's whispered words of reassurance were far from the truth. But she allowed them to console her, for a little while.

Raising his head from the production report in front of him, Lyle looked out onto the mill floor, his mind unconsciously monitoring the sound. There was a time when he would have been elated at the roar of full production, knowing that he was responsible for restoring it and keeping labors problems subdued, but somehow the satisfaction he had expected to experience escaped him.

Lyle ran a heavy hand through his hair, sighing deeply before drawing himself to his feet. He was tired . . . more than tired, and he knew the long hours he had spent at the mill during the past few weeks had little to do with his exhaustion. He was sleeping poorly and seemed to have little appetite of late, a result of the images of Sophia that haunted him and the lump in his throat that appeared every time he thought of her.

Still staring through the glass onto the mill floor, Lyle took a few steps and paused, his hand on the doorknob. It was strange. Everything was going extremely well at the mill, much to his uncle's discomfort. He was well aware that his uncle would gladly have sacrificed production for the pleasure of having been proved right about his bastard nephew, but he hadn't been afforded the opportunity. In the time since Paul had left and he had assumed control of the mill, Lyle had gotten the weavers to accept their new situation with grace . . . almost with eagerness. He had soothed the feelings of the other workers who had begun looking on the weavers' new situation and increased income with a jealous eye by manipulating the flow of the work so they might also see increased income. Production had soared, and it appeared everyone was happy, with one exception. No, two . . .

Lyle gave a short laugh. He knew the reason for his uncle's discontent. As for himself . . .

Refusing to continue with that last thought, Lyle drew the office door open and stepped out onto the floor. His gaze moved automatically toward the winder where a heavy, dark-haired girl worked feverishly among the ends, her full face flushed. Josephine was a poor replacement for Sophia. But then, there were few who could measure up to Sophia in any way.

The knot inside him tightening, Lyle strode onto the floor. He paused as he came abreast of Rosalie's winder. He watched as Sophia's younger sister moved quickly along her machine, her head turned from him. He had taken to stopping to talk to her when he passed, and had even gotten Anna to speak a few friendly words. Talking to the two Marone girls made him feel closer to Sophia somehow, and he had come to enjoy their exchanges.

Rosalie turned unexpectedly toward him and Lyle started with surprise. The girl's eyes were brimming with tears and her face was flushed. She looked away upon seeing him, and Lyle felt an unexpectedly protective instinct rise.

At her side, Lyle whispered, "What happened, Rosalie?"

"Nothing." Rosalie shook her head. "It's nothing."

Moving quickly to the other side of her machine, Rosalie slipped from sight, but Lyle was not satisfied. He was short-tempered, tired, and irritable, and if anyone—

Suddenly noticing a few workers grouped a short distance away, he strode forward in time to see Joey Moretti among them. A glimpse of Joey the moment before the group became aware of his presence revealed a peculiarly stricken expression on his face. Lyle made a move to follow them when they disbursed, only to be halted by a light touch on his arm.

Rosalie's face was blotchy, her eyes red-rimmed as Lyle looked down at her with sudden insight.

"They were talking about Sophia, weren't they?"

Rosalie raised her chin. "Sophia would have laughed in their faces if she had heard them, and we should do the same."

The heat of Lyle's anger intensified. "But you're not laughing, are you, Rosalie. Well, neither am I."

"I'm not as strong as Sophia, but I won't give them the satisfaction of seeing they've upset me." Seeing his agitation, Rosalie pleaded softly, "Please . . . Sophia wouldn't want trouble here because of her. It would only make more talk, and Mama would hear of it."

Rosalie halted abruptly, glancing toward the far machine where Anna watched them soberly. Lyle saw her quiet sister's eyes were similarly filled and the knot of frustration inside him tightened.

Damn it all, it was no good! The position he had striven for all of his life was now almost secured, but it had all become flat and meaningless to him. It had taken only the brimming eyes of these two girls to bring his feelings out into the open and to make him realize he would give it all up for another chance to—

Lyle's racing thoughts came to a sudden stop. It was too late for regrets. Sophia has slipped away from him and into someone else's arms.

Realizing Rosalie awaited his next move, Lyle forced a smile. "All right, Rosalie. Don't worry. As far as I'm concerned, this never happened."

Back inside his office minutes later, Lyle watched as Rosalie and Anna resumed work, realizing that with his brief words of reassurance he had lied.

* * *

Waiting until Madame Tourneau and her seamstress walked to the back of the salon and out of earshot, Aaron inquired softly, "What's wrong, Sophia?"

Sophia's looked up, and Aaron's anxiety increased. Something had changed between them. He had noticed it when he had arrived at closing time, prepared to lend his help in the final stages of preparation for the exposition. In the time since, he had searched his mind for a reason for the distance Sophia had subtly put between them. Remembering the spontaneity with which she had turned into his arms before leaving him the previous evening, he was at a loss to explain it.

Sophia did not respond to his question and he urged, "I know something's wrong. I want you to tell me what it is."

"Nothing's wrong." Sophia's smile was cool. "I'm tired and a little nervous. The exposition is only a few days away."

"Of course you're tired." Aaron forced a smile. "You've worked every night this week and you need some time to yourself. We need some time together." Aaron made a sudden decision. "Come on, let's get out of here. Phoebe can finish the trim on that gown."

"No! I mean . . ." Sophia's hand tightened revealingly on the ribbon in her hand. "Phoebe's busy with Madame's work."

"Mary, then. She won't mind coming in here tonight. She'll be glad for the opportunity to earn a little more money."

Sophia shook her head. "No, I'll do it myself."

Suddenly angry, Aaron jerked the ribbon from Sophia's hand. "It's not the work that's bothering you, is it? Sophia, look at me! Did I do something to make you angry? Is that it?"

"No." Sophia shook her head. "It's just—"

Sophia turned abruptly, but not before Aaron saw the

tears that filled her eyes. Incredulous, Aaron was momentarily unable to react. He had never seen Sophia display so much as a moment's weakness.

Suddenly unwilling to expose Sophia to Madame's scrutiny, Aaron curved his arm around Sophia's shoulders and drew her toward him as the Frenchwoman returned from the back room.

"Sophia isn't feeling well, madame. We'll be leaving early this evening. I suggest you call Mary in to finish for her. Sophia's exhausted."

The Frenchwoman's small eyes narrowed with unexpected resentment. "We are all tired, monsieur, even I! And I do not expect to add to my expenses by having Mary finish Sophia's work! The responsibility is hers, and if she's not up to it—"

"I ask you to remember that you've borne none of the expense for Sophia's gowns, madame, and that she's worked on them on her own time. I'll pay Mary's wage just as I've paid for everything else associated with Sophia's contribution to the exposition. I think you'll agree that Sophia's talent is an excellent risk."

Madame's pointed chin hardened stubbornly. Resentment flashed anew in her eyes as she returned haughtily, "I cannot spare Phoebe from her duties and there is no one else to send for Mary. Sophia's work will have to wait."

Annoyance quickly escalating to anger, Aaron returned in a voice heavy with threat, "Sophia and I are leaving, and I tell you now, if Sophia's work isn't ready to be shown at the exposition, I will see that yours isn't shown, either!"

Turning without another word, Aaron ignored the indignation that colored Madame's face. His attention devoted to Sophia, who had remained uncharacteristically silent through the exchange, he shrugged his coat onto his shoulders, draped Sophia's shawl around her, and urged her toward the door.

The carriage drew to a halt on the darkened street and Sophia looked up for the first time since Aaron had assumed a place at her side. She flushed hotly as she stared at the door of his bachelor quarters.

"You've made a mistake in bringing me here, Aaron."

"I don't want to take you home yet, and there's no other place we can go." Aaron's anxiety grew at the frigidity of Sophia's tone. "You've hardly spoken at all tonight. You can't tell me nothing's wrong. I don't believe you."

"I don't care what you believe."

"Yes, you do, Sophia. Sophia, look at me!"

Grasping her shoulders, Aaron turned Sophia toward him. Her body was rigid and her eyes were cold. Panic touched his mind. Reacting instinctively, he attempted to take her into his arms, but Sophia pushed him away.

"No, don't!"

A nagging suspicion becoming full blown at Sophia's rejection, Aaron whispered tightly, "What kind of a game are you playing, Sophia? Last night you came willingly into my arms, and today you want nothing to do with me. Could your sudden aversion have anything to do with the fact that your gowns for the exposition are almost finished and you don't think you need me anymore? Or has Madame Tourneau been talking to you? Has she told you that you'd be better off turning your talents toward impressing silk brokers like Wilfred Amsterdam who might be able to advance your work further once you get to New York? Is that it?"

Sophia's glorious eyes widened. She stared at him in silence for long moments before whispering, "So you think me to be a whore after all."

Sophia turned away from him and reached toward the door, but Aaron would not allow her escape. His heart pounding, his stomach tied in painful knots, he turned her forcefully back to face him.

"No, I know you're not a whore. God . . . no . . ." Aaron closed his eyes briefly, unwilling to admit even to himself that even if she were, he couldn't stop wanting her. "But I know something's wrong, and I've had too many women attempt to use me not to realize—"

"If there's been anyone who's been used in this affair, Aaron, it's been I."

"You're saying I used you?" Aaron gave a short, self-deprecating laugh. "I've used many women, Sophia, but that's never been with case with you." Suddenly more earnest than he had ever been before, Aaron whispered intensely, "I've believed in you and worked alongside you from the beginning. I've helped you take giant steps toward realizing your goals because they became my goals as well. I've fought for you, defended you, and lain awake at night thinking about you. And I've loved you, Sophia . . . with more love than I thought I had inside me."

"You've believed in me . . ." Tears rose again in Sophia's eyes. "Yet you accuse me of selling myself to you in exchange for your favors."

"I didn't mean that, Sophia."

"You did!"

"Sophia, listen to me!" His hands tightening on her shoulders, Aaron rasped, "I love you, and you were pushing me away. I thought you had had enough of me and you wanted to put an end to everything between us. I thought—" His voice breaking, Aaron suddenly crushed Sophia close. "I couldn't stand it if I lost you . . ."

Aaron's desperate grip tightened as the silence in the carriage stretched painfully. Close to despair, he felt

Sophia's shudder before she slowly slipped her arms around him in return.

Her warm breath brushed his neck as she whispered, "I'm sorry. I'm so sorry, Aaron."

Allowing Sophia to draw back from him, Aaron stared down into her magnificent face. He saw confusion, contrition, and sorrow clearly reflected there. Her lips trembling, she continued softly. "Everything has been happening so fast. I couldn't sleep last night. I went out on the porch and I—" Pausing, Sophia searched his face, then started again, "I became unsure of myself and began doubting everything—my dreams, myself. I suddenly wanted to get away from it all, but now I know it was foolish of me to think I could escape myself, and it was unfair of me to take my insecurities out on you. Because the truth is, through all my uncertainties, Aaron, I never doubted that you loved me."

"I'm sorry, too. I said some things I didn't mean."

Sophia took his hand and smiled. "Let's go inside, Aaron."

Holding back, Aaron whispered, "I never believed you sold yourself to me in exchange for my help."

"I know."

"I love you, Sophia."

Sophia's smile wobbled. "I know."

Sophia stood beside him moments later as Aaron fumbled for his key. His hands trembled with the anxiety that Sophia might again change her mind before he could close them away from the rest of the world and take her into his arms. He had glimpsed the desolation he would face one day when he would be forced to give Sophia up. He still quaked with the pain of it, but he was determined to put it out of his mind for now. He would drown himself in loving her and forget everything else, despite the shadows of despair that still lingered.

The lock clicked open and Aaron turned to Sophia. His gaze intense, his love for her a burning ache inside him, he took her hand.

Trembling, Joey stared at the drawn blinds of Aaron Weiss's bachelor quarters, where Weiss and Sophia had entered only moments earlier. Watching from a point of seclusion across the street, his mind a frenzy of jealousy, he barely restrained the desire to burst through the door and tear Sophia from the rich man's arms. Instead, he cursed aloud and brushed the tears from his eyes, the knot of pain inside him excruciating.

Sophia had used him and pushed him aside, and he had suffered. However, his humiliation had reached a new peak that afternoon in the mill when Gino Scalzone had laughingly related to the group of men around him how Angelo Negri had seen Weiss and Sophia coming out of this place after their lovers' tryst.

Pain, shame, and frustrated desire had overwhelmed Joey in successive, devastating waves. Sophia's shame was a secret no longer, and in the back of his mind, he knew he had come here and waited, hoping desperately to discover Angelo had lied.

A sob rose in Joey's throat and he closed his eyes against his distress. He had loved Sophia. He had offered her his life and his name, but she had thrown it back in his face. She had dishonored him in front of his family, his friends, and in front of the same fellow who now held her in his arms, until he, who was the pride of his family, had barely been able to hold up his head.

Joey attempted to draw his emotions under control, the need for vengeance rapidly replacing his misery. He knew Weiss's reputation, and he had no doubt the infamous womanizer would toss Sophia aside when he had had his fill of her, but Joey knew that would not be enough. His mortification was such that he would not be satisfied until Sophia's humiliation equaled his own.

She was a bitch . . . a whore! Joey trembled with his increasing rage. She was a fallen woman, and he would see to it that everyone knew her for what she was!

Swallowing against the painful lump in his throat, Joey squared his shoulders, still unable to tear his eyes from the drawn blinds that shielded Sophia's sin from the world. Sophia had laughed at him in the past, caring little for her reputation or his threats against it. There was one place, however, where he knew she could not dismiss her shame.

Forcing himself to turn away, Joey started down the street, his pace rapidly accelerating.

"It's true, I tell you! Everything Joey Moretti told me is true! Sophia has lain with Aaron Weiss in order to gain his favors. She has disgraced us!"

Anthony stared at Maria, numbed by her outburst. The unnatural silence of their bedroom, where Maria had dragged him immediately upon his return from work, grew prolonged. Not a sound came from the kitchen where they had left Anna and Rosalie white-faced behind them.

Still silent, Anthony assessed the wildness of Maria's eyes and her blotchy color. Looking as she did now, strands of graying hair loosened from her normally tidy bun, her lined face twitching with suppressed emotion, she was almost unrecognizable as the beautiful woman he had loved and married those many years ago. Tears welled again inside him for the wretched creature his selfish love for her had wrought. Sadly, he shook his head.

"No, Maria. Joey wants Sophia. He can't have her, so

he lies. You're too eager to believe the worst of Sophia because you don't understand her. You never have. I know now you never will."

You're a fool, Anthony!" Spittle sprayed from Maria's lips with her scathing hiss. "You think *you* understand Sophia better than I do because she twists you around her finger and makes you believe everything she says. You laughed at me when I said you encouraged her behavior with your permissiveness. Then you became angry, and now you pity me because you believe me to be a frustrated old woman who is jealous of her daughter. But it isn't so! Don't you understand? *I'm* the only one who truly understands Sophia's hungers! She is my daughter—my flesh and blood! I know how she thinks and what will happen if we don't—"

"Enough, Maria!" His pity disappearing with a sudden swell of anger, Anthony snapped, "Sophia is my flesh and blood, too!"

"No! She is not!"

Halting abruptly as the words left her lips, Maria whitened. She took a small, defensive step backward as her declaration rang in the silence of the room. She swallowed visibly, her body quaking as Anthony glowered threateningly.

"What are you saying? Take back that lie, Maria, or I will—"

"What will you do, Anthony?" Tears suddenly heavy in Maria's faded eyes, she whispered thickly, "It's the truth. There's nothing you can do to make Sophia your daughter when she is not."

Grasping her thin arms, Anthony shook his wife roughly. "What are you talking about? Tell me!"

"I'm sorry, Anthony . . ." Tears streamed down Maria's face as her agitation increased. "I hoped you would never have to know, but I had to tell you! You believed Sophia was good because you believed your goodness flowed through Sophia's veins, but it doesn't! Sophia cares for nothing but her own selfish desires. She is her father's daughter!"

"Sophia is *my* daughter!"

"No."

Reading the truth in Maria's eyes, Anthony took a staggering step backward. The urge to flee almost overwhelming, he forced himself to remain as he mumbled a single word in reply.

"Who . . . ?"

Maria swallowed, her voice hoarse as she whispered, "The countess who took me into her home and educated me when I was a young girl . . . everyone knew of her kindnesses to me, but no one realized how the life I led each summer at her villa changed me inside. I was beautiful, Anthony, you remember . . . The countess didn't have a daughter, so she clothed me, fussed and petted over me, and I started to believe my childish dreams could come true. The countess's son, Edoardo . . . do you remember him? He was tall and handsome, and that last year when I was sixteen, he told me he loved me. I believed him."

Her face suddenly hardening, Maria drew herself up stiffly. When she spoke again, her tone was scathing.

"Edoardo soon tired of me, and when I told him I carried his child, he laughed! He said the child would be his parting gift to me! He left the villa and went back to the city. I never saw him again . . ."

Maria took a deep, shuddering breath. "The countess would listen to nothing I said about her son. She told me I was an ungrateful young woman who sought to better herself at his expense. She banished me from the beautiful villa on the hill, and I returned to my mother in disgrace."

Closing her eyes as the parade of painful memories again marched across her mind, Maria continued in a hushed tone. "Mama said little when I told her what had happened, but I saw her eyes. I had killed the part of her where her love for me resided. She said I had paid for my vanity and pride, but she would not allow my sins to disgrace the family by allowing me to bear a bastard child. She said everyone knew you loved me and wanted me . . ."

A low sound, almost a sob, escaped Anthony's lips, but Maria seemed not to hear. Involved as she was in the torment of the past, she continued without reaction to his pain.

"It was so easy for Mama. As filled with guilt as I was for my disgrace, I obeyed her without question. I tricked you into believing I was a virgin on our wedding night." Maria gave an incongruous laugh. "A simple midwife's trick, that was all that was needed, because you were a simple man, and you loved and trusted me. It took only another of the midwife's powders to have the child born prematurely and you never suspected my treachery."

Maria slowly closed her eyes. "You believed Sophia was yours, and you loved her . . . but *I* knew whose blood mixed with mine in Sophia's veins. She was only a child when she first told me of the vision of herself she saw in her dreams . . . of the fine lady she would be one day, wearing beautiful dresses, with everyone bowing to her as she passed . . . and I suddenly knew the whole nightmare that I had lived through would happen again if I didn't stop it. I became afraid. I became afraid for Sophia and for you . . . and for myself, because . . ." The tears again flowing, Maria reached tentatively toward Anthony, a plea in her reddened eyes, "Because by this time I loved you in a way I had never loved Edoardo. I didn't want to lose you . . ."

Stiff, finally able to think past the deadening shock of loss Maria's words had evoked, Anthony whispered, "All these years you made me think I was at fault for the anguish that had embittered you. You robbed the joy from those years, Maria. You stole from me. But you were frightened and confused . . . I could understand that." His heavy features suddenly darkening, all trace of compassion deserting his expression, Anthony continued with growing heat, "But I could not . . . I *will* not . . . ever . . . forgive you for stealing my daughter from me!" Unaware that tears streamed from his dark eyes, Anthony continued in a hoarse whisper. "Sophia is *your* daughter, but in her heart *I* am her papa. She would never betray my trust in her. Sophia is a good girl. She is innocent of all you say!"

The flush returning to Maria's face, she suddenly raged, "Must I prove to you that I know my daughter better than you? Must I prove to you that she has used you to get her way, the way her father used me? Must I prove to you that she is her father's daughter in a way she was never yours?" Seeing her husband's adamancy, Maria rasped, her lips tight. "All right, we will go to the place Joey spoke of and we'll see."

Knowing Maria could be proved wrong no other way, Anthony followed her into the kitchen. Ignoring his daughters' pale faces, he donned his coat and walked down the steps behind her into the yard. His heart breaking as they stepped out onto the street, Anthony silently prayed. For himself and for Sophia, and for all he stood to lose that night, he prayed.

Arriving across the street from the address to which Joey had directed them, Anthony paused, Maria standing stiffly at his side. He knew Sophia would not be there. He knew she was at the salon working, as she had claimed to be every evening for the past few weeks. He knew this was all a waste of time that would only serve to prove to Maria once and for all that Sophia—

The front door at which Anthony stared suddenly opened. His heart began a heavy pounding as Aaron Weiss stepped into sight and paused briefly there before turning to a figure coming into sight behind him. As Anthony watched with dismay, the handsome mill owner's son reached back inside with a smile and drew Sophia out beside him.

The moment of revelation was deadening as Anthony watched Weiss slip a possessive arm around Sophia, as Sophia smiled up into his face, and as Weiss brushed her lips lightly with his before drawing her down the steps to usher her into the carriage awaiting them.

Numb, Anthony stared after Weiss's carriage as it pulled away. Unaware of Maria's agonized expression, he was conscious only of a paralyzing sense of loss. The Sophia who was his flesh and blood, the Sophia he had loved more deeply than he had ever loved anyone else, had never existed. This true Sophia was her mother's child, her father's daughter, who had betrayed his trust and proved to him that he had never known her at all. This Sophia was a stranger.

The darkness of evening closed around her as Sophia slipped into the alleyway beside her home and emerged into the backyard with an soft sigh of exhaustion. She smiled wearily at the small black cat that brushed against her legs, its tail high in welcome, and leaned down to stroke him briefly. She was aware that she had been unfair with Aaron earlier. He had not deserved her hostility and had been inordinately patient with her. Sensitive to her feelings, he had taken her into his arms as soon as the

373

door of his rooms had closed behind them, but he had not pressed her to make love. Instead they had talked, and she was grateful for that, for her emotions had been too troubled and her mind too confused. She was uncertain how long they had remained there before returning to the salon to make a tentative peace with Madame Tourneau. But Sophia knew the Frenchwoman was still angry. She also knew it was only Aaron's influence that had saved her from suffering from Madame's wounded pride. But, in truth, Sophia realized that her confusion was still such that she presently cared very little about what Madame Tourneau said or thought.

What was wrong with her, anyway?

Reaching the staircase, Sophia glanced up at the porch where she and Papa had spoken so intimately the night before. Her throat tightened and her sense of guilt deepened. Papa was so proud of her. She had always had his understanding and approval, and it hadn't been until they had spoken the previous night that she had fully realized this time it might be different.

Taking a deep breath as she reached the third floor, Sophia approached the kitchen door. The sound of her step drew her mother into sight and Sophia hesitated.

"You do well to be wary, Sophia." Maria's voice held a shrill quality that Sophia immediately recognized as her mother directed abruptly, "Come inside. We have been waiting for you."

In the kitchen, Sophia glanced around her. Rosalie and Anna watched silently from the open doorway into the living room, and Papa stood a short distance away from Mama. But his eyes were strangely cold.

"I won't ask where you were, Sophia, because I know." Mama's fury was building. "I know everything!"

Feeling the blood drain from her face, Sophia glanced at her father again. Anthony was motionless and stiff, as

374

if carved from stone, and Sophia's stomach clenched at the absence of love in his eyes. Reacting more sharply to her father's alienation than to her mother's anger, she questioned hoarsely, "What do you know?"

"We saw you come out of Aaron Weiss's rooms! We saw the way he touched you . . . smiled at you. We saw it all and we were put to shame because of it!"

"Mama, you don't understand . . ."

"I understand! I understand too well! You have turned your back on decency. You have sacrificed our good name for the sake of your ambition. You have betrayed our trust in you!"

"Trust, Mama?" Suddenly coming alive under her mother's attack, Sophia raised her chin. "*You* never trusted me. You've accused me many times of these same things you accuse me of now, never caring that they were without cause."

"I knew what was inside you! I knew where your vanity and pride would lead you."

"You knew nothing but your suspicions, Mama! And even now you don't care about learning the whole truth. Aaron loves me!"

"He loves you?" Maria nodded knowingly. "He will marry you then, and give you his name."

Sophia remained silent.

"This rich man who 'loves' you has never spoken of marriage, has he?" And when Sophia did not respond. "Has he?"

"No, but—"

"But what? What would he do if I went to him now and demanded that he marry you?"

"Mama . . ."

"Answer me!"

"I don't know."

"I'll tell you what he'd do. He'd laugh at me!"

"No, he—"

"He would laugh, and he would be right to laugh, for only a fool would think that you mean any more to him than the many women he has had before you!"

Realizing argument was futile, Sophia appealed softly to her father.

"Papa, please. Tell Mama everything will be all right."

"You waste your time speaking to your papa, Sophia." Maria's voice was strangely flat. "Your papa doesn't hear you. You will listen to *me* now, and you will do what I say. You will tell Mr. Weiss that you'll never see him again. Then you will leave the Frenchwoman's employ and go back to your job at the mill."

"I can't, Mama!"

"You will! You will go back to the mill and beg for your old position if you must."

"Aaron would never let me go. He loves me."

"*Stupida!* He uses you as he has used many women before you, but you're too vain to see!"

"You're wrong, Mama! But even if it were true, I couldn't walk away from everything now. I've worked hard, and the exposition will soon—"

"I will discuss this with you no further!" Her tight face gray and twitching, Maria drew herself up stiffly. "You will do as I say if you wish to remain in this house. I will not be party to your shame."

"I can't, Mama."

"You will do what I say or you will leave this house . . . now!"

"Mama . . ." Sophia shot a pleading glance toward her father, but his expression remained unchanged. "Papa . . ."

"You will speak only to me!" Maria took a threatening step forward. "Will you do what I say?"

"Mama, I—"

"Will you?"

"No!" Tears brimming, Sophia responded emphatically, "No, I won't let you do this to me! I won't let you make me give up everything I've worked for to grow old and worn and bitter like you and to blame everyone else for my misery when the truth is that cowardliness held me back from being what I wanted to be! I won't do it because I don't want to be like you!"

The silence that followed was a palpable force that held all within the room motionless as Maria stared at her daughter's beautiful, tormented face. Her own face so gray as to appear drained of life, Maria whispered, "Leave this house, Sophia. You are no longer welcome here."

"Mama—"

"Get out."

"But Mama—"

"Get out!"

Reacting instinctively, Sophia pushed open the door and ran down the steps. Moments later she emerged onto the darkened street, her feet flying.

Edith turned to stare at her husband with astonishment as he attempted to fix his tie before their bedroom mirror. Hostility was rife in her voice.

"Say that again, Matthew. I can't believe what I'm hearing."

"You heard me correctly, Edith." Matthew used the silvered glass to return his wife's gaze. "I said Lyle is managing the mill better than I ever expected he could."

Edith's narrow jaw hardened. "You're saying that to aggravate me. You're always trying to aggravate me these days."

"I've invited him here tonight."

Edith went suddenly still. "How dare you!"

"I dare because I choose to dare, Edith!"

"I told you I don't want that bastard in my home again! My sister will never forget the humiliation of having him turn up his nose at Hope. Despite that insult, you've given him a free hand at Kingston Mill and now you've invited him back here as if he's an honored guest. What's next, Matthew? Will you let him take over this house and throw us out onto the street?"

Matthew flicked his gaze over his wife's slender figure, her proud carriage, and softly upswept hair. "You seem to forget that allowing Lyle to manage the mill was your idea, Edith—a part of your very sly machinations."

"My machinations? I don't know what you're talking about!"

"Don't you?" Matthew turned to face his wife directly, his gaze cold. "It was all for Paul's sake, wasn't it? You wanted your son to pursue his art without suffering pangs of conscience for having abandoned his family responsibility. Well, now you have what you wanted, and it chafes." Matthew's eyes hardened. "Well it chafes me, too, Edith, and I don't propose to suffer alone. You thought to handle me so well . . . and you did. You convinced me to go along with your plans, but you failed to realize that Lyle, clever fellow that he is, might take your plan a step farther, and that I, for whatever reasons prevailed at the time, might actually go along with him. Well, it's all come to pass, and we're all one big happy family now."

"We are not! That bastard will never be a part of my family!"

"Are you so sure, Edith?"

"Matthew, what's happened to you?" Edith swayed visibly and Matthew felt his first moment of regret as his wife obviously strove to withhold tears. "I don't know you anymore! Since that night Julia came here for that secretive talk with you, you've changed! You've hardened to my councils. You—"

"If you mean by that, that you've found it more difficult to wrap me around your finger since then, you're probably right, Edith, but I'm tired of your blaming my sister for everything that's changed. It's more than that and you know it."

"I know nothing of the sort!"

"Don't you?" Matthew gave a hard laugh. "You don't like taking a backseat to anyone, much less a bastard, and now that Lyle's taken over the mill, that's exactly what's happened. You're on the outside looking in, Edith, and it infuriates you. But I don't intend to allow you to escape your portion of the blame in this affair, so I'll add that none of this would have happened in the first place if you hadn't indulged Paul past redemption."

Slowly straightening, his gaze unwavering, Matthew added, "If I must pay the price of your son's abdication, then so must you. Our dinner party tonight is a business affair. I don't intend omitting my mill manager from the guest list or any list on which I choose to include him." Matthew laughed again. "Strangely, you've proven to be Lyle's strongest ally by assuring him entrance where he might never have been welcome before." Pausing, Matthew added, "And all for the sake of a few splashes of paint on canvas . . ."

"All for the sake of my son's happiness!" Suddenly livid, Edith responded, "Yes, I did maneuver and connive for Paul, and I'd do it again to save him from your insensitive oppression!"

His face flaming, Matthew went stock-still. Forcing a smile a moment later, he took his wife's arm and replied in a tightly controlled voice, "Then I suggest you suffer the result of your handiwork in silence and consider your outrage a noble sacrifice for your darling son. And . . ."

Matthew paused to direct a look of steel into his wife's pale eyes, "Since I have no intention of reneging on my given word, you had better hope I'm able to find an honorable way out of this mess you've instigated, or we'll be stuck with the bastard for the rest of our lives!"

Silently drawing his wife's arm through his, Matthew turned to walk beside her as he urged her toward the hall.

"As for now, Edith, I hear our guests in the foyer downstairs, and I also hear your 'nephew's' voice among the arrivals. Strange, isn't it, that Lyle's voice carries so well in this house that it can be discerned clearly above the rest, despite the fact that he speaks quite softly? Do you suppose we should look upon that phenomenon as a sign?"

Edith's choked response evoked a soft snort from Matthew as he ordered, "Smile, dear. And remember that this uncomfortable bed is one in which you chose to lie . . . and that I'm lying in it beside you, sharing your discomfort. You may find small relief in that fact, but I find it all the solace available to me, and I'm discovering that I'm enjoying that consolation immensely."

Drawing his wife along beside him with a sudden jerk, Matthew took further consolation in his wife's biting glance as she assumed a dignified step.

Breathless, ignoring the curious glances she evoked, Sophia ran down the familiar street. Still incredulous at what had come to pass, she heard the shrill echo of her mother's voice.

"Get out! Get out!"

Catching her breath on a sob, Sophia halted momentarily and brushed the tears from her cheeks. She remembered the shock on Rosalie's small face as she turned toward the door, and the fear in Anna's, but most vivid of all before her mind's eye was Papa's frozen expression.

Papa had turned against her.

Covering her mouth with a trembling hand, Sophia began walking again, her gaze trained on a doorway near the end of the street where a streetlight blazed in welcome. The pain of that last thought more than she could stand, Sophia hastened to a run, finally halting before the familiar door. Brushing her hair back from her face and taking care to wipe the tears from her cheeks, she attempted to push it open, only to find it locked.

Knocking, waiting with growing agitation for a response, Sophia felt hope leap inside her as the door finally opened a crack.

"What do you want?"

The face revealed through the narrow opening between door and jamb was old and wrinkled, and Sophia attempted a smile as Lyle's landlady observed her without a smile.

"I . . . I didn't expect the street door to be locked. Is Mr. Kingston in? I have to see him."

"No, he isn't. He left about an hour ago."

"Are you sure?"

The old woman drew back, her eyes narrowing. "Of course, I'm sure. I'm not too old to know what I saw."

"Please, I have to talk to him. Would you mind if I went up to check?"

Pinning Sophia with her gaze, the woman inquired bluntly, "Are you in trouble? I don't want trouble around here."

"N-no." Sophia forced a smile. "I just want to make sure he's not home."

Scrutinizing her face for a moment, the woman finally nodded. "All right. But I'll watch you from here, and if Mr. Kingston isn't in, you come right back down."

Slipping through the doorway, Sophia took the steps quickly and paused in the hallway in front of Lyle's door.

Taking a deep breath, she knocked softly. Her heart pounding, she listened for the sound of footsteps beyond, but there were none. She knocked again.

"I told you he isn't home! You come right back down here, now."

Waiting only a moment longer, Sophia retraced her steps, her feet dragging. Pausing in the downstairs hallway, she attempted a smile. "Would it be all right if I waited for Lyle here? I could—"

"No." The old woman's face was suddenly suspicious. "And I'm telling you now that I'm going to lock this door again as soon as you leave. Don't you go waiting on my doorstep, either, or I'll have the police after you for loitering!"

The door slammed closed behind Sophia the moment she stepped down onto the sidewalk, and she paused, realizing she had been thrown out onto the street for the second time that night.

Walking again, aware that the night air was becoming more chilled, Sophia fought back her tears. She had wanted so desperately to talk to Lyle. She knew if she saw him, everything would be all right. His gold eyes would warm the ache inside her, and his arms would still her quaking.

But he wasn't there.

Uncertain how long she had been walking, Sophia looked up to find herself standing in front of a familiar brick-faced house, but there was no light in Aaron's bachelor quarters, and her heart fell. Despairing, knowing the effort was useless, she rang the bell.

Unexpectedly, the door opened. Fully dressed as if ready to leave, Aaron looked at her with surprise for a long, silent moment before pulling her up the step and into his arms. Sobbing so loudly that she could hardly speak, Sophia surrendered to Aaron's comforting embrace, allowing him to draw her into the living room and to seat her on the settee. Seated beside her, he wiped the tears from her face, his voice tight with concern.

"What happened, Sophia?"

Suddenly ashamed of her weakness, Sophia forced up her chin. "I can't go back home. My mother knows . . ."

A slow fury dawned in Aaron's eyes as he whispered, "They threw you out of the house because of me, didn't they—just as you are, without clothes, without—"

"I'll be all right." Sophia drew back, determined to regain control. "I'll ask Madame for my wages tomorrow, and I'll rent a room."

"You'll stay here." Stilling the last remaining tremor or her lips with a gentle kiss, Aaron halted her again as she attempted to speak. "No, don't say anything else, Sophia. You don't have to tell me what happened or how it happened until you're ready, but I don't want you to worry, darling. This place is yours for as long as you want it."

Aaron's kindness stirred tears anew, but Sophia forced them away with an attempt at a smile. "Just for tonight, Aaron. Maybe tomorrow Mama will . . ." She paused, knowing in her heart that the new day would have no effect on her mother's rage.

"Sophia, look at me." Obeying his soft command, Sophia felt the full impact of Aaron's love for her as he whispered gently, "You can stay here as long as you want, with no strings. By that I mean . . ." Aaron hesitated, holding her gaze. "I'll go, or I'll stay, whatever you like. It's up to you."

Not waiting for her reply, Aaron took her into his arms. He rocked her gently, and Sophia closed her eyes to the solace of his embrace. His soft words of endearment comforted her, his gentle caresses relieved her stress, his strength renewed hers, until slowly, with meticulous accuracy, she poured out the details of the shattering confrontation with her mother.

Silent as she concluded, Aaron drew back to look into Sophia's stricken face. She saw myriad emotions reflected in his eyes the moment before he scooped her up into his arms, carried her into the bedroom, and laid her on the bed. Lying down beside her, he drew her comfortingly into his arms.

"Sleep, darling. I'll stay with you as long as you like . . . as long as you need me."

Closing her eyes in the semidarkness, realizing she had neither the strength nor the will to do more, Sophia felt Aaron's kiss against her hair, her cheek, her lips, and she relaxed to its gentle reassurance.

Chapter Seventeen

The windows of the dye shop dripped with condensed steam, the effect of the chilled late-afternoon air and the boiling chemicals in the tubs at which Anthony worked. But Anthony was oblivious to the growing discomfort of his surroundings and the mumbling complaints of his fellow workers. His mind far from the dye swirling before him, Anthony returned again to the startling revelations of the previous night.

Sophia, his favored child, his pride and joy, was not his child at all. Struck with a pain so fierce that it stole his breath, Anthony staggered, drawing curious stares, but he knew his ailment wasn't physical. It was simply that his heart was breaking.

Unconsciously watching the master dyer as he dipped his finger into the tub to taste the dye thoughtfully, Anthony waited for the result of the test. To add more chemicals or less chemicals, to make the color darker or lighter, it all meant very little to him now.

Sophia had not come home the previous night, and he knew now she would not return, for Maria would not relent on her demands. His wife was a woman obsessed with the shame that had befallen her again, this time in the form of her daughter's transgression. She was determined to distance herself from it so her other daughters would not suffer, but Anthony knew it was already too late.

Angry tears hiding behind his eyes, Anthony cursed himself for the vanity that had allowed him to believe that a homely, ignorant man such as he could have been responsible for bringing to life as extraordinary a young woman as Sophia. When he had been unable to credit himself for her physical beauty, he had credited himself for the spirit he saw inside her, for the honesty he had read in her eyes, and for the ambition he had encouraged despite Maria's warnings. Maria had seen the truth from the beginning, but he had only just come to realize that behind Sophia's smile and loving ways was a young woman who was a stranger to him, who had made a mockery of his trust in her, and who had turned his pride to dust.

Anthony stirred the chemicals in the vat in front of him, adding a measure more at a signal from the master dyer, his gaze moving to the clock on the wall as he did. The day had been endless but he had no desire to go home. Home was an empty place now, just as empty as his heart.

He had not spoken a word in defense of Sophia the previous evening because it was no longer his place. As for his wife who had deceived him for so many years, Anthony felt little at all. In stealing Sophia from him, Maria had stolen his love for her as well. All that remained were two daughters who served only to remind him of the one he had lost.

The blast of a whistle interrupting his thoughts, Anthony sighed. He would finish with this vat and leave the rest of his work for tomorrow. It would be a tomorrow that was as empty as today, and all the other tomorrows that would follow.

Her hands tightly clasped in front of her, Sophia strained to see past the large wagon that partially blocked the entrance of Stein's Dye House. She took a quick, nervous breath and raised a hand to smooth her unbound hair. She had not slept well the previous night, and she knew she did not look well. She had awakened fully dressed to find a note from Aaron on the bed beside her, and she had been peculiarly embarrassed at the situation in which she found herself.

It had not been any easier for her at the salon with Madame in a foul mood from the previous day's altercation with Aaron, but Sophia had spent little time concerned with the situation there. Her mind had been filled with the image of Papa, his coldness and his silence. The day had not passed quickly enough for her to make her way to see him at the conclusion of his shift.

The first workers began filing through the dye-house doors and Sophia scrutinized the group for the man she sought. Many familiar faces, many interested glances, but the one she sought was not among them. Panic had begun making inroads into her mind when the short, stocky figure of her father emerged. Her heart beginning a heavy pounding, she swallowed thickly, following his approach with her gaze, only to realize that he was about to walk past her. She grasped his arm.

"Papa . . . stop, please!"

Anthony turned toward her, his eyes darkly shadowed, his expression grave. "I'm not your papa and you're not my daughter. The Sophia I knew does not exist."

"I didn't mean to hurt you, Papa." Sophia took a shuddering breath, not believing her father's coldness. "I wanted to tell you about Aaron, but I didn't know how."

His black eyes intent, Anthony responded, "It's no longer my business what you do. You're your mother's daughter."

The pain of her father's rejection was almost more than she could bear, Sophia clutched his arm. "You know why I left the house last night . . . why I can't do what Mama wants me to do, don't you? You understand . . . ?"

"Your mother understands."

Sophia took a step closer to her father, her eyes brimming. "Mama doesn't understand. She never could, but I want *you* to understand."

Carefully removing her hand from his arm, Anthony responded in a whisper, "I understand. For the first time, I truly understand. Good-bye, Sophia."

Her pain growing with each step her father took away from her, Sophia suddenly turned and fled. She was still running as she approached the house that had become her new home. Her breath coming in deep, labored gasps, her face covered with perspiration although the day was chilly, she withdrew the key Aaron had left her from her pocket with shaking hands. Unlocking the door, she pushed it open to halt suddenly as Aaron appeared in the foyer. One look at her face and Aaron enclosed her in his arms. She was sobbing breathlessly as Aaron asked, "What happened, Sophia?"

"I went to talk to him, but he wouldn't listen to me."

Jealousy cutting deeply, Aaron demanded harshly, "You went to talk to whom? Who, Sophia?"

Sophia swallowed, then rasped, "Papa . . ."

Aaron clutched her close, his relief profound as he whispered earnestly, "Don't worry about him. Don't worry about anyone. You don't need anyone but me. I'll take care of you. I'll see that you get everything you've ever wanted or dreamed of having. We're going to have a wonderful time together, darling . . . a new life for both of us. You'll see."

Suffering her pain while another part of him softly rejoiced, Aaron drew her closer. Fate had wrested Sophia away from the common parentage that had so demeaned her, and that same fate had delivered her to him. Sophia was his alone, at last . . .

His desire soaring, Aaron raised Sophia's face to his. He kissed the dampness of tears from her face and the sob from her lips. Curling his hands tightly in her hair, he held her fast as he kissed her persistently, persuasively, satisfied only when her sorrow became passion and she returned his kiss fully, without restraint.

Later, lying beside her, loving her as he had never loved

388

before, Aaron brought Sophia to satisfaction again and again. In his mind he vowed to erase her pain with his loving, to make her forget everything and everyone but himself, now and forever . . . for as long as forever might last . . .

Anna shot a covert glance at Rosalie as the silence at the dinner table grew heavy. Her eyes on her plate, Rosalie ate without speaking, contrary to her usual manner of enthusiastic conversation, but Anna was not surprised. Sophia's absence from the house, their uncertainty where she had gone and how she had fared, had left a pall over the remaining members of the family. Papa had returned from work an hour earlier and had not spoken a word. Mama was rigid with anxiety. The terrible confrontation with Sophia, which had been the result of Mama and Papa's secret conversation a short time earlier, had split the family in a way she had not believed possible.

Unable to eat a bite, Anna pushed her rapidly cooling food around on her plate. The bed she had shared with her sisters all of her life had seemed peculiarly empty without Sophia beside her, and the day had been long and anxious, but she knew Mama was not fully to blame for the terrible crisis that had beset the family. Sophia had gone a step too far in taking up so scandalously with Aaron Weiss, and Mama had been forced to confront her. Anna had never expected, however, that the confrontation would come to this and that Papa would turn his back on Sophia, his eldest daughter and the one he loved the most.

Mama sought to conceal her tears as she turned away, and Anna's heart bled for her mother's pain. Anthony rose unexpectedly, pushing back his chair with a careless hand that sent it slapping back against the floor, and his face flushed as he reached for his coat without a word and walked silently toward the door. She heard the panic in Mama's voice as she questioned shrilly, "Where are you going, Anthony?"

Anthony turned sharply toward his wife, the animosity in his gaze stealing Anna's breath as he responded sharply, "Don't worry, Maria. I go nowhere in particular, and I will return. This is my home and my responsibilities are here. You will always have bread on the table and a roof over your head while I'm well enough to keep them there." His homely face hardening into an almost unrecognizable mask, he then added, "And *our* daughters will always have a place here. That is all you ever wanted, and you should be happy with that. You *must* be happy with that, Maria, for that's all your husband now offers you."

Waiting until the sound of her husband's footsteps on the stairs could be heard no more, Maria drew herself to her feet. Her skin gray, her dull eyes surprisingly without tears, she whispered softly, "Your father doesn't understand. From the beginning, I did what I knew I must. I sought to correct a terrible mistake and to see that mistake was not repeated, but somehow it all went wrong." Maria's eyes abruptly brimming, she shook her head. "He doesn't understand . . ."

Suddenly on her feet, Anna ran to her mother's side. Throwing her arms around her, Anna spoke softly through her own tears.

"I understand, Mama. I know you've always done what you thought was best for us. You're not responsible for Sophia's mistakes."

"Anna!" Rosalie was standing as well, her small face flushed. "How can you talk like that? Whatever Sophia did, she did honestly, with good intent!"

Turning back to Rosalie, Anna whispered, "Yes, and when she did, she broke Mama's heart."

Comforting Mama gently, Anna felt an unaccustomed strength come to life inside her. Mama needed her now. In all of her life, only Paul Kingston had needed her, but he had quickly forgotten her when his need for her was gone. She suddenly knew that it would not be the same with Mama.

An unexpected confidence growing inside her, Anna realized that Sophia had made her feel needed in a way she never was before. As usual, Sophia had shown her the way. She only wished it had not been at such a terrible price.

Lyle approached his rooming house wearily. The end of the day had not come soon enough, as tired as he was from the extended hours he had been spending at the mill and the late dinner party at his uncle's house the previous evening.

He recalled his first glimpse of Uncle Matthew and Aunt Edith as they had walked down the staircase to greet their guests. Were it not for the presence of several of the city's most influential men, he was certain Aunt Edith would have ignored him completely. The feigned warmth with which she had greeted him had been a moment of silent triumph, which, strangely enough, had left him cold.

Even the social acceptance of mill owners who had carefully overlooked him a month earlier had not raised his spirits. He had returned home to be tormented during the night with dreams of a beautiful, red-haired woman who slipped through his fingers to stand just beyond his reach. He had awakened to the knowledge that his dream was reality and his torment real.

Unbuttoning his coat and loosening his tie as he neared the front door, Lyle dug into his pocket for the key. He paused in disgust, remembering that he had left it in the pocket of his other coat, then knocked heavily, certain he would not escape his landlady's complaints.

Forcing his grimace into a smile as the door opened, Lyle did not have to wait long.

"Forget your key again, Mr. Kingston?"

Lyle strove to retain his patience. "I'm sorry, Mrs. Monroe. It won't happen again."

Stepping aside, the old woman allowed him past her. He was making a hasty retreat up the staircase when she stopped him with her unexpected comment.

"Seems like you forgot an appointment last night, too. That young woman who showed up on your doorstep was real upset. Not that I approve of you havin' women in your rooms, but it didn't seem right to leave her waiting like that."

Lyle turned, suddenly tense. "What young woman?"

"A red-haired girl." The woman shrugged a rounded shoulder. "I suppose she might've been real pretty if her face hadn't been all blotched from crying."

"Crying?" Lyle felt his agitation rise. "Why didn't you tell me this sooner?"

"She didn't ask to leave a message, that's why. She just walked away."

Withdrawing his pocketwatch, his fatigue forgotten, Lyle frowned. Rosalie had told him that Sophia was working late every night at the salon. If he was lucky, he'd would be able to catch her before she left.

Turning quickly, he started back down the stairs, ignoring the old woman's muttering as she closed the door behind him.

Grateful to see a light still lit in the rear of Madame Tourneau's salon, Lyle peered inside, knocking briskly as he did. Within moments the small Frenchwoman made her way toward the door, her small eyes taking on a gleam of interest as she recognized him. Drawing the door open, she purred, "Ah, Monsieur Kingston, how nice to see you again. But you have come too late, as you can see. My poor establishment is closed for the evening."

Impatient with the game the woman played, Lyle forced a smile. "I came to see Sophia, madame. I understand she's been working late on some special work for you."

"Special work for me? No, monsieur." The Frenchwoman's face tightened. "Sophia does not work late for me, but she isn't here tonight, in any case. She left early."

"She's gone home, then." Lyle's frustration increased.

"No, monsieur, not home." The Frenchwoman smiled more broadly. "The young mademoiselle has made other plans." Seeing she had piqued his interest, Madame opened the door wider. "Come in, *s'il vous plaît*, I will be happy to explain."

Knowing he had no choice, but certain he would regret it, Lyle stepped inside.

Aaron had left for an appointment a short time earlier, and Sophia walked through the quiet rooms, silently grateful for time alone after the tumultuous interlude they had shared. She needed to come to terms with her new situation, without Aaron's distracting presence.

A brief talk with Madame that morning had made it abundantly clear that she could expect no help from that quarter. She would be forced to take advantage of Aaron's generosity for an indeterminate period, for the truth was that she was destitute — without money, without clothes, without family . . .

Sophia forced back the tears to which she had surrendered too often of late, telling herself she was done with crying. Determined to consign that pain to the past, she looked around her as she continued through the parlor and dining room, past the surprisingly well-equipped kitchen, to pause at the doorway of the bedroom that was now her own. She looked at the packages on the bed, the change of clothing and essentials Aaron had arranged to have delivered. Knowing she would refuse to take money from him outright, he had arranged for unlimited credit for her with Madame Tourneau, and for Harry to make the same arrangements in the Weiss name at the local establishments where she would find it necessary to shop.

Her discomfort growing, Sophia told herself that she should be grateful for Aaron's help and for the fact that he loved her. She told herself that she was not truly a kept woman because the situation was temporary and as soon as she was able, she would pay Aaron back. She told herself that she was on the way to fulfilling her dreams and she had no choice now but to go forward and never look back.

The empty rooms around her rang with silence as a voice inside her reminded that it was not supposed to be this way. She was not supposed to be alone.

Taking a firm hold on her emotions, Sophia told herself that she was not truly alone. Aaron loved her. In his arms a short time earlier, she had thought of nothing but the beauty of his touch, the wonder of his kiss, and the power they achieved in their joining. It was only afterward, when their passions had cooled, that unwanted thoughts had returned to loom larger than before.

And she wondered, as she had many times through the long, previous night, how different things might be right now if Lyle had been home when she had gone to him . . .

But it was too late now for wondering. And if she knew that a part of her was bound to Lyle with ties too strong to break, she also knew that another part of her loved Aaron as much as he loved her. She only wished . . .

An unexpected knock raised Sophia's head sharply toward the sound. Her knees suddenly unsteady, she started toward the door. The knock sounded again as Sophia drew it open. Her throat tightening at the sight of Rosalie's small, sober face, Sophia took a quick step forward and threw her arms around her. Separating herself from Rosalie at last, Sophia looked down the steps behind her sister.

"Where's Anna?"

Rosalie's small eyes misted. "I came alone, Sophia."

"Oh."

Biting her lips against the pain of the words that had

gone unspoken, Sophia drew Rosalie inside and closed the door. She paused awkwardly as Rosalie looked around the impressive room.

"So, you see my new home." Sophia's eyes were revealingly bright. "Aaron said I could use it until I can find a place for myself."

Rosalie attempted a smile. "It's beautiful."

Sophia nodded, without attempting a smile in return.

"I . . . I couldn't bring your clothes, Sophia. Mama is still too upset."

"It's all right. Aaron has arranged . . ."

Sophia's words slowed to a halt, and her face flushed. "I'm sorry for the trouble I've caused everyone, Rosalie."

Taking Sophia's hand, her grip surprisingly strong, Rosalie whispered in a rush, "I know the way things were with Mama, Sophia, and I know what you felt inside you. You did what you had to do, just as Mama feels she did. I'm proud of you, Sophia. I'll always be proud of you."

"No matter what others say?"

"I hear nothing they say. I hear only the voice inside me that tells me you're good and beautiful . . . and that you're my sister."

Tears so heavy in her throat that Sophia could hardly speak, she whispered, *Mia sorella fedela . . .*

"I'm your faithful sister, *sì*, but not so brave as you are, Sophia." Rosalie grimaced. "Because I must rush home now before Mama finds out I came here."

"You will come back?"

Rosalie's hand tightened around hers, the promise in her eyes bright. "I'll come back."

Clutching her arms against the chill evening air, Sophia remained staring down the street after Rosalie's petite figure had turned out of sight. She drew herself erect as she saw the approach of a familiar black carriage.

The carriage door opened as soon as it drew to a halt and

Aaron bounded up the stairs to her side. Obviously alarmed, he grasped her arms.

"Why are you waiting out here? Is something wrong?"

Gratitude swelling inside her for the loving concern she saw in Aaron's eyes, Sophia whispered, "No, nothing's wrong now that you're back."

His expression sober, his eyes revealing more than words could convey, Aaron curved his arm around her shoulders. Turning her with him, he closed the door behind them and took her into his arms.

Watching from a point of seclusion as the door closed behind Sophia and Weiss, Lyle felt his heart sink. He had recognized the address Madame Tourneau had supplied immediately, and he knew he had not disappointed her with his reaction to the tale she told. But he was not concerned with Madame.

The tightness in Lyle's throat was painful, the ache in his heart almost more than he could bear. Beautiful Sophia, with red hair streaming over the shoulders of the simple white blouse she wore, clutching her arms against the chill of the evening air, the brilliance of her great blue eyes visible even at a distance . . . He had once held her beauty in his arms. He had once felt her sweet breath against his lips as she told him she loved him. He had once known he was closer to Sophia than anyone else in the world. But all that was finished now.

Madame had told him with great relish the basic facts of Sophia's separation from her family. With even greater relish, she had related that Sophia was now under Aaron Weiss's protection. It was little comfort to know that Sophia had come to him first, for the result was the same. He had not been there for her when she had needed him before, and he had not been there again. He was too late. Sophia's choice had been made. Her future was temporarily secure in the hands of a man who could advance her dreams further than Lyle ever could.

Lyle took a deep, shuddering breath. He wished he could be happy for Sophia, but he could not. He wished he could strike her from his mind. He wished he could cancel the day from his life that he had first encountered the beautiful redhaired temptress who had brought his heart to life and then torn it in two. He wished . . .

Halting in his thoughts, Lyle knew that what he truly wished most of all was that he had never let Sophia go.

Chapter Eighteen

Rebecca looked up at her son, assessing his reaction as he politely took her arm and escorted her down the front steps of the Weiss mansion. She had spoken to Samuel earlier, telling him that she needed Aaron for some important Silk Association matters, and after considerable argument she had succeeded in winning her son for the morning. That step achieved, however, she was at a loss to begin. Aaron had been so distant of late, and she saw so little of him. He was a grown man with quarters of his own that he maintained in town, and she knew she had no right to question him on the occasions when he failed to return to the family residence at night. But he had been returning home less and less frequently of late, until he was seldom home at all.

She had done her best to deny her son's involvement with the Marone woman. The girl was an incredible beauty and had a talent for design, but she was common. Her background was inferior, as was her education, unlike Aaron who had gone to the best schools and had known nothing but the best all his life. She had expected that when Aaron became seriously involved with a woman, it would be with a woman of his own caliber and that he would marry and settle down. His scandalous relationship with the Marone girl was a far cry from that. The young woman's reputation alone revealed that she was not worthy of him, but the difficulty, she feared, would be in convincing Aaron of that truth.

Aaron's stiff expression was more revealing than words as they reached their carriage, and Rebecca's dread for the task ahead of her deepened. He had not wanted to accompany her to the lawyer's office that morning so they might discuss the lease on the floor space in one of Paterson's newest buildings that she intended to recommend to the association. He had arrived home that morning in time to change his clothes, obviously with other plans in mind, but he had not dared refuse her in the face of his father's agitation.

Waiting only until Aaron was sitting beside her and the carriage snapped into motion, Rebecca spoke softly.

"I appreciate your taking the time to help me, Aaron. I'm afraid I'm at a loss in legal matters."

"I offered my help before the exposition, Mother, so you mustn't feel it's an imposition."

Aware that Aaron's smile was forced, Rebecca responded hesitantly. "I do respect your judgment and business acumen, dear. It's only in your private affairs that I feel you're acting unwisely."

Aaron's attention was immediately acute, his words clipped. "Oh, you disapprove of the way I conduct my personal affairs?"

"Aaron, dear, don't be angry." Feeling a moment's despair, Rebecca continued earnestly. "I wouldn't have arranged this opportunity to speak to you if I didn't feel it was absolutely necessary. It's just that I know how strained relations have been between you and your father since he spoke to you about that woman."

"That woman, Mother? I think you're aware that her name is Sophia Marone."

"You're right. I know her name quite well . . . as do most of the young men of your set, I understand."

399

"You understand incorrectly, but I don't intend to argue with you in defense of Sophia's reputation. Her reputation is poor, and her association with me has worsened it, but most of the gossip is inspired by jealousy."

"Aaron, please." Rebecca sought to calm her son's rising agitation. "I don't want to argue with you about Miss Marone's reputation, either. I've instigated this conversation with another thought entirely in mind. Dear, I hope you'll take me seriously when I tell you that you're on shaky ground with your father."

"I told Father—"

"Allow me to finish speaking, please, because it's urgent that you become aware of some facts. Your father isn't well, Aaron."

Aaron gave a scoffing snort. "Gout isn't a fatal disease, Mother."

"Don't dismiss your father's illness too easily, Aaron." Reprimand entering her voice for the first time, Rebecca drew herself up rigidly. "Your interest in your love affair has blinded you to the obvious. Your father's gout has gotten progressively worse. He's now in constant pain, which is a greater drain on his energies than you seem capable of understanding. For the first time in his life, he has been seriously considering conceding primary responsibility for the mill to you, and he is outraged by his belief that your involvement with this woman and her affairs has allowed your interest in the mill to lag to the point where you're incapable of handling it."

"That's nonsense, Mother, and Father knows it!"

"He's frightened that you're becoming serious with that woman."

"Serious? In what respect? I've already told him that I have no intention of marrying her. It isn't necessary, in any case. I'm perfectly satisfied with the status of affairs, and so is Sophia."

Rebecca paused. "Your father doesn't trust the situation. He says you're infatuated with the woman."

Aaron's face flamed. "I am. That should be fairly obvious."

"He says you're infatuated to the point where your judgment is impaired. He says your affair with her is a public scandal, and he won't trust passing the mill into your hands while you're still involved with her."

Acutely aware that her son's chest was beginning to heave with anger suppressed for her sake, Rebecca persisted determinedly, "Your father has told me — and I know he was sincere in every word he said — that he would rather *sell* the mill than turn it over to you under those conditions. He also said," Rebecca hesitated, tears filling her eyes as she repeated the words that cut her heart to shreds, "that if he's forced to do that because of your adamant attachment to that woman, he'll cut you out of his will and leave you a pauper!"

Aaron's flush abruptly drained, leaving his shocked face colorless as he responded simply, "He wouldn't do that."

"My dear . . ." Rebecca's words emerged from her choked throat with a sob. "I'm afraid he would."

Suffering for the words she had been forced to speak, Rebecca dabbed at her tears with a lace-trimmed handkerchief. Aaron's jaw was rigid, but she was resolved that her son would comprehend the true peril in continuing his flagrant affair.

"There's no threat to the mill in my relationship with Sophia, Mother. I've told Father that."

"There's only one way you can truly convince him, dear. Your father wants you to marry."

"Marry! Is he insane?"

Rebecca continued relentlessly. "He has a young woman already picked out. Kathryn Vandermere, of the New York Vandermere family. You must remember her. She remembers *you* very well. You met her at a party in New York last year. She's lovely and intelligent. She has so much to offer. She was educated abroad, I believe."

Aaron gave a scoffing laugh. "So was Sophia."

"Be serious, Aaron! This isn't a laughing matter!"

"I am serious, Mother. I won't give Sophia up."

Rebecca raised her chin. "Your father's concerns are directly related to your deep feelings for that woman, Aaron. He thinks that she'll secure some kind of hold over you—that she'll threaten you in some way and you'll lose your judgment completely. He says he won't have a harlot for a daughter-in-law."

More rigid than before, Aaron hissed, "I'm in control in this affair, Mother, not Sophia! She's completely dependent on me for everything, even her present success. She knows I can take it all away from her with a snap of my fingers, and she won't take a chance of incurring my disfavor."

"Aaron, dear, listen to me. I understand your position. You're young and you want this woman. Your father's had little objection to your amorous affairs in the past, and he'd have no objection now if he didn't feel this woman poses a threat. He isn't demanding that you give her up. He wants you to marry so that your position will be secure. He has no objection if you continue to see that woman in secret. He confided to me that passions of this sort rarely last for the bong term, and he expects that you'll eventually cast her aside. Kathryn need never know about her."

Unexpectedly shocked at the scenario his mother proposed, Aaron gave a short laugh. "You're more a woman of the world than I realized, Mother."

"No, Aaron." Rebecca corrected her son sharply. "I'm the woman I always have been, one who loves her son and seeks to protect him from his own weaknesses."

Contrite, Aaron took her trembling hand. "I'm sorry,

Mother. But I hope you'll understand when I say I won't prostitute myself for the sake of my father's insecurities."

"Don't refuse before you've had time to give all of this some thought, please, Aaron. Your father suspects I intended speaking to you this morning, and this is the perfect opportunity to gain some time so things might work out on their own. Let me tell him that you're considering visiting the Vandermeres on their Long Island estate. The invitation has already been extended, you know—through your father. There's no time limit on it. Perhaps around the holidays . . . when it would seem more natural to visit. That's over a month away. Who knows what will happen by that time? You may feel differently."

"I won't."

"Let me tell your father you're considering it—please, dear."

Silent for long moments, Aaron nodded. "If it'll make you feel better, Mother."

Tears of relief welling in her eyes, Rebecca rasped, "Thank you, dear. I'll tell your father as soon as I return home." Pausing, Rebecca continued softly, "You know we're doing this because we love you."

Aaron nodded, although Rebecca saw that his mind had slipped away from her as he turned toward the window to stare out at the passing street. But she was relieved, and temporarily content.

Sophia walked briskly along the busy thorougjfare, oblivious to the nip in the morning air. She had been sleeping poorly, had overslept, and was extremely annoyed with herself. She would be late for work, and she was keenly aware of Madame Tourneau's views on tardiness. She knew that she would suffer no more than a few sharp words from Madame, for the Frenchwoman was not of a mind to risk Aaron's displeasure of late by reprimanding her harshly. However, that realization only annoyed her more.

Sophia glanced into a storefront in passing, only to be brought to a temporary halt at her reflection in the glass. Could that young woman dressed so smartly in a fashionable, tailored costume, her brilliant hair confined under a close-fitting bonnet, really be her? Sophia continued walking, amused at her own reaction. So much had happened in the past few months. Her appearance reflected the changes in her life so closely that she was often startled, as she had been a moment before, at her own reflection.

The exposition had come and gone, and her designs had been a great success—so much so that in recent weeks her gowns had become almost as avidly sought after in the salon as Madame's. The full extent of Madame's cleverness had become clear to her then, but she felt little resentment in knowing that the agreement she had signed kept her bound to Madame Tourneau as her protégée for three years, for her experience was still limited and her financial situation dire.

Her position in the salon had not changed, except that she was in more constant demand as a mannequin from curious matrons than ever before. She knew, however, that their interest was not totally due to the success of her designs. Word traveled quickly, and it was commonly accepted that she was Aaron Weiss's mistress. As such, she was a curiosity, for it seemed Aaron's amorous escapades were legend in some circles, as was his reputation for being fickle. She had even overheard that wagers were being taken as to when she would be replaced in his affections.

But she spent little time worrying about that eventuality, because she knew Aaron loved her. If there had been any change at all in the relationship between them recently, it was that he had only come to love her more. He had fulfilled his promises to her in every way possible, although she had never sought to hold him to them. Despite her protests, she now had a closet filled with gowns, many of them silk, more than she needed or had ever hoped to own. Since the exposition, she had traveled with Aaron to New York many times where she had been dined and entertained along with him by silk brokers and individuals important in international trade. She had gone for carriage rides in Central Park with Aaron, shopped on Fifth Avenue, and attended the opera, and her education in the trade and otherwise had grown. She knew that Aaron was proud of her—unfortunately, jealously so.

It was Aaron's jealousy and growing possessiveness that caused her the greatest concern, for the simplest compliment from an admiring male was enough to send him into a quiet rage. Her own guilts plagued her then, for she knew she could not love as Aaron loved—with a passion that excluded everyone else from mind, and she sensed he knew that. The part of her committed elsewhere remained committed, despite her love for him.

She was also uncomfortable with the realization that Aaron resented Rosalie's visits and that he was jealous of her affection for her younger sister. She sensed he would prefer that last link of communication between her family and her be severed. Struggling to understand him, Sophia had concluded that as a spoiled, indulged, only child of wealthy parents, Aaron had never learned to share love. But she consoled herself that if Aaron erred in loving too much, she must forgive him.

The increasing traffic on the street was an indication of the lateness of the hour, and Sophia pushed herself to walk faster. She could not afford to allow the malaise with which she had awakened to set the pace for the day, because she did not want to slip into remembering. Remembering brought pain, and she—

Coming to an abrupt halt, her heart pounding, Sophia stared at the man who had stepped out of a doorway in front of her. Her shock was reflected in the familiar gold of his eyes as Sophia and the man stood stock-still, looking at each other for a long, silent moment.

Moving spontaneously into each other's arms, they clasped each other close. Her eyes closed, Sophia indulged the sheer joy of Lyle's embrace, wanting never to let him go, only to become gradually aware of the curious glances of passersby. Drawing back, she saw Lyle was as reluctant as she to break away.

"Sophia . . ."

"I've missed you, too, Lyle."

"No." Lyle shook his head soberly. "No more of that. I don't want you reading my mind and speaking the words for me. I want to say them myself . . . because I need to say them. I've missed you, Sophia. Are you all right? Are you happy?"

"I'm all right." The joy in Sophia's eyes dimmed as the reality of Lyle's presence intensified feelings she had thought subdued. "But I miss . . ."

Her eyes suddenly filling, Sophia was unable to speak. Noting her distress, Lyle took her hand and tucked it under his arm. Drawing her firmly against his side, he urged her along beside him. "There's a little cafe around the corner where we can sit for a few minutes and talk."

"But . . ."

"Just for a little while, Sophia."

Seated across from Lyle in the cafe minutes later, a cup of demitasse in front of her, Sophia indulged herself with the sight of him. She had not remembered how blond his hair was, or how clear his skin, but she had not forgotten the burning intensity of his gaze when he looked at her, the firm line of his jaw, and the pride unconsciously displayed there. Fit, so good-looking that it somehow hurt, dressed modestly but with instinctive taste, he was the true "golden god" that Madame Tourneau had named him. Without conscious effort he still exuded the same strength and virility that had always drawn her to him. It drew her to him still.

But something new had been added—a sense of quiet confidence and authority that had been absent before. She knew those two last qualities had been sorely won from the uncle who had sought to denigrate him all his life, and she was intensely proud.

Lyle smiled his rare smile and she treasured it. She reached across the table toward him and he took her hand, curling it in his as he said softly, "You look beautiful, Sophia."

"Yes, I do." The Sophia of old momentarily emerging, she laughed. "I surprise myself at times to see how grand I have become." Her smile dimmed. "But the old Sophia lies inside, behind the beautiful fabric and fashionable clothes."

"Sophia . . ." Lyle squeezed her hand. "You've become a great success and the talk of silk fashion circles."

Sophia forced a smile. "I've become the talk of other, less favorable circles as well, so much so that I don't know where my 'fame' is greater."

"I've heard Madame Tourneau is going to allow you to do a full line of designs for the spring."

"Ah, so those plans have become public knowledge. But what most don't know is that Madame takes the risk only because Aaron has guaranteed her against loss."

Lyle's smile faded and all effort at casual conversation ceased. "Are you happy with Weiss, Sophia? Does he treat you well?"

"Very well." Sophia's voice dropped a notch softer. "He's very generous, and he loves me."

"He loves you . . ." The words emerged harshly from Lyle's lips. "Do you love him?"

407

Sophia blinked. Lyle's hand had tightened on hers to the point of pain. She knew she must be completely honest for both their sakes, but the words were surprisingly difficult to say as she whispered, "Yes, I do." And then in a rush, "But I love you, too, Lyle."

Regretting the words the moment they had left her lips, Sophia attempted to withdraw her hand, only to have Lyle hold it more firmly than before.

"Don't regret being open with me, Sophia. I'll never take advantage of anything you say to me."

Her heart warming in a way it did with no other, Sophia whispered, "I wish . . ."

Sophia's voice trailed away, and Lyle commented with a touch of unexpected bitterness, "Wishing is a useless habit. I learned that truth the hard way, even though I've fallen prey to it again myself in recent months."

"I'm so proud of you, Lyle." Sophia held his gaze intently. "Rosalie says you've earned everyone's respect at the mill, even your uncle's, and that you've even managed to discourage the agitators from coming to the mill yard because there are so few disgruntled workers. She says—"

"Rosalie is a dear girl." And then after a pause, "I'm sorry about the way things are between you and your family. I know how you feel about them—about your father."

Sophia stiffened. "My father says he's no longer my father."

"He was angry. He didn't mean that."

"He did. I saw it in his eyes. I never thought he would turn against me." Sophia's eyes filled as she continued. "We're both on our way to getting what we always wanted, aren't we, Lyle?" Lyle nodded and she paused to continue a moment later with a sudden, desperate earnestness. "But I never meant it to be this way. I never meant to give up those I love."

"We both have our regrets, Sophia. I—" Lyle's gaze

dropped to her lips and Sophia felt his longing in the moment before he whispered, "I think we should go."

Reading the agreement in her eyes, Lyle ignored the cups that lay untouched in front of them. He helped her to her feet and took her hand again as they started toward the door, gripping it with a desperation Sophia keenly shared. Pausing with his hand on the knob, he looked soberly down at her, but Sophia did not hesitate. Standing on her toes, she kissed his lips, unmindful of the gasp of the countergirl. The sweet taste of Lyle's mouth lingered as they stepped out onto the sidewalk and he pulled the door closed behind them.

Aching with the words she suppressed, Sophia forced herself to say the only words she dared.

"Good-bye, Lyle."

"Good-bye, Sophia. If you need me—"

"I know."

The pain of parting was more than she could bear, and Sophia turned abruptly and walked away. She did not turn back as she rounded the corner and started to run. Truly uncertain of what and from whom she was running, she did not stop until she could run no more.

His fury unabating, Aaron paced the small jewelry store. The proprietor's extended absence as he retired to the safe in the rear of the store to retrieve another tray of diamond earrings was trying his patience. He had made fast work of the Silk Association lease with his mother and put her back in the carriage for home. He had breathed a silent sigh of relief as he had watched the carriage disappear from sight, relieved to be free of the need to keep his anger under control.

Damn his father! The old man must be getting senile to believe he would allow his situation with Sophia to get out of hand. In the time Sophia and he had been together, things had progressed exactly as he had planned them. As he had told his mother, he was in complete control, with Sophia totally dependent upon him.

Aaron felt a momentary surge of satisfaction. He had been aware of Sophia's intentions from the first. Living in his house was to be a temporary arrangement. She had intended to find a place for herself and to pay him back for everything he had advanced her, but he was too clever for her. He had gradually filled her closets with clothes and her life with luxuries to which she was unaccustomed, inwardly grateful for Madame Tourneau's farsightedness in having forced the restrictive contract with Sophia as a prerequisite of accepting her as a protégée. Living in unaccustomed style with the best of everything at her fingertips, Sophia was still earning the meager wages of a mannequin, and her "debt" to him grew larger each day.

He recalled her protest of his "generosity." She had failed to realize that those presents were the bonds with which he bound her to him. There had been little truth in his statement that Sophia feared to chance his disfavor because of his control of her financial situation, however. Sophia did not fear him in the least. She never failed to challenge him when she disagreed with a point in question, and he knew she worried more about his growing preoccupation with her than she did about losing him.

Touched by a familiar spark of disquiet at that last thought, Aaron consoled himself with his greatest victory. Sophia had finally said she loved him. The thrill of those words on her lips was still fresh in his mind. He never tired of hearing them.

He had been totally honest with his mother, however, when he had maintained that he would never marry Sophia. His convictions in that regard had not changed, no matter how dearly he wished they could.

Darting a glance toward the rear of the store, Aaron drummed his fingers impatiently on the glass case in front of him, realizing that he should be grateful for his mother's intervention this morning, despite the aggravation it had caused him. She would tell his father that he had agreed to the plan to visit Kathryn Vandermere. The old man would be appeased. Aaron had decided he would make an effort to show a greater interest in mill business than he had of late, and his father would be pleased with that, too. In the end, he would have it all. He would take over the mill as he was meant to do, and he would keep Sophia as long as it suited him to keep her. If his interest in her didn't wane, he would then give his mother's suggestion greater thought.

But that was in the future. He was concerned with the present and the diamond earrings with which he intended to surprise Sophia that evening. For the truth of it all was that Sophia was born to wear diamonds and silk and it gave him great pleasure to see them lying against her perfect skin.

His impatient pacing taking him toward the window, Aaron stared out onto the street, only to go rigid with shock as the door of Baldanzo's Cafe across the street opened and a striking couple stepped out onto the sidewalk. There was no mistaking that fiery hair, that perfect profile, and the flash of brilliant blue eyes as Sophia turned to the man at her side—just as there was no mistaking Lyle Kingston as he spoke softly to Sophia, his gaze on her lips.

In a moment they separated and Sophia turned the corner out of sight. Staring after her for long moments, Kingston then proceeded down the street and out of sight as well.

"Well, here they are, Mr. Weiss."

Aaron turned at the sound of the jeweler's voice. His

411

jealous fury concealed behind a tight facade, he approached the balding fellow and looked down into the tray.

"Which are the largest? These?" He pointed at a particularly extravagant pair of earrings.

"Genuine blue-white diamonds, sir. Perfectly matched at almost a karat each."

"I'll take them. Put it on my account." Ignoring the fellow's gleeful smile, Aaron snapped, "Hurry up. I'm tired of waiting."

Out on the street a few minutes later, Aaron slipped the box into his pocket, jealousy devouring him. Sophia and Kingston . . . Kingston and Sophia . . . the words drummed through his mind. How long had they been meeting, and how far had it gone?

He would find out . . . tonight. The right time and the right opportunity, and he would make Sophia tell him all.

Rosalie raised her head from her machine as Lyle entered the mill, her gaze stopping cold at the sight of him. He had left the mill on an errand shortly after the whistle had sounded, unexpectedly leaving Jacques Montepelier to oversee the floor in the elder Kingston's absence. It had been a gesture of faith which had been well received by the workers, and she knew the trust he had evidenced had earned him trust in return.

Lyle glanced briefly toward her, and Rosalie knew . . . She walked quickly to his side, her concern evident as she questioned abruptly, "You saw Sophia. Is something wrong?"

Lyle's eyes narrowed. "No, nothing is wrong. How did you know I saw her?"

"It . . . it was the look of you." Faltering in her response, Rosalie finally concluded in a hush, "Only Sophia brings that expression into your eyes."

412

Lyle's gaze did not waver. "I didn't realize it was so obvious that I love her."

"Only to me—because I love her as well."

Pausing, Lyle whispered with a note of despair, "Are we blessed or cursed with that love, Rosalie?"

Aching for the consolation she could not supply, Rosalie turned back to her work, and Lyle moved on.

The creak of the oversize bed sounded loudly in the room, but Aaron paid it little mind, engrossed as he was in his lovemaking. Sophia's smooth flesh was warm beneath him as he trailed his mouth along the slender column of her throat. He nipped the delicate skin sharply, her small whimper of discomfort driving him to more active play as he tightened his fingers in her hair to hold her fast. Smothering the sounds of her protest with his kiss, he ground his mouth deeply into hers until all dissent ceased and her arms wound tightly around his neck.

Tearing his mouth from hers, Aaron pressed hot, moist kisses along Sophia's chin and shoulder, seeking and finding the rise of her full breasts. Shuddering, he fastened his mouth on an erect crest, drawing deeply, her soft moans of passion lifting him to a level of aching hunger almost beyond endurance.

Raising himself above her, Aaron looked down into Sophia's magnificent, love-flushed face, realizing that her nakedness was not solely physical. Revealed in her brilliant azure eyes was a desire that matched his own, and reflected on her trembling lips was an eagerness that would go unanswered no longer.

The warm, moist delta between Sophia's thighs awaited him, and Aaron nudged it briefly before plunging deeply with a sudden violent thrust. At rest inside her, he felt elation rise as Sophia's passion-filled gaze met his. He re-

413

mained deliberately motionless, waiting, enjoying the light of uncertainty that slowly dawned in Sophia's eyes. He heard her first tentative whisper. She reached out to draw him down upon her, but he drew back from her, aloof. He saw her confused anxiety and his expression hardened.

He would make this beauteous witch suffer for the agony he had endured after seeing Lyle and her together. He would make her beg for his loving as he had so many women before her, and when she did, he would laugh. He would make her —

With a quick, agile movement, Sophia slipped out from underneath him and was on her feet beside the bed before he had time to react. The unbound length of her hair was a glorious curtain that partially shielded her nakedness as she stood motionless for a long second before reaching for her dressing gown.

On his feet beside her, Aaron took it roughly from her hand.

"Where do you think you're going?"

Sophia did not respond as she snatched the dressing gown back from him.

"You like to play games, don't you, Sophia . . . but you don't like it when I set the rules."

Sophia paused. "I don't know what you're talking about."

Unwilling to conceal his mounting fury any longer, Aaron responded, "I saw you with Kingston today."

Momentarily silent, Sophia whispered, "So, that's it. You're angry because you saw me with a friend."

"A friend?" Aaron laughed harshly. "Do you expect me to believe that? I saw the way Kingston was looking at you."

"You saw what you wanted to see. There's nothing but friendship between Lyle and me. That's all there ever has been."

"I don't want Kingston to be your 'friend.' "

"You have no control over that, Aaron."

"I don't want you to see him again."

Silence her only response, Sophia turned away, and panic touched Aaron's mind. He grasped her arm.

"I asked you where you're going." And when there was still no response, "Sophia!"

"Let me go, Aaron."

"No, damn you! I spent most of the day waiting to settle this between us, and when I came here you greeted me as if nothing at all happened this morning."

"Nothing did happen, other than a short conversation between two people who respect each other and wish each other well."

"Kingston wants you. He always has."

Jerking her arm from his grip, Sophia turned on him, her eyes bright with anger. "I won't listen to any more of this! I've told you what happened—a chance meeting! If you choose to torment yourself, you may, but I won't let you torment me as well."

"Sophia, wait!" Aaron grasped her arm again, anger turning to fear at the resolution he read in her eyes. Reading innocence there as well, he held her fast. His voice dropped to a whisper.

"Please wait. I'm sorry."

Sophia sought to free herself, but Aaron would not allow it. "I was jealous. I don't want any man looking at you the way Kingston was looking at you. I love you."

"You say you love me." Sophia's voice was suddenly weary, "But I don't think you know the meaning of the word."

"I do!" Earnest, Aaron whispered, "You're never far from my mind, day or night. I ache with wanting you, and when you look at another man the way you looked at Kingston today . . ." Aaron paused, a shudder shaking him. His voice was ragged when

415

he spoke again. "How can you do this to me, Sophia?"

"You do it to yourself, Aaron."

Sophia's voice was cold, but Aaron knew he had never wanted her more.

"Do you know how beautiful you are, Sophia? You're perfect, like a priceless statue."

Sophia's expression saddened. "Is that all you see in me—my beauty?"

"You know I see more—much more. But I want you all to myself. I don't want to share you with anyone."

"You already have all I can give you."

"I want you to tell me you love me."

"I've already said—"

"Tell me again."

"Aaron . . ." Reconsidering what she had intended saying, Sophia whispered, "I do love you, Aaron."

Aaron drew her closer, his voice a low plea. "Tell me you love me more than you've ever loved anyone else."

Sophia's glorious eyes filled. "I love you in a way I've never loved another man, and I've done my best to make you believe that. Something inside you won't allow you to trust me, and I'm not certain if that's my fault or yours, but I'm at a loss to fight it." Her eyes brimming, Sophia whispered, "Oh, Aaron, I wish . . ."

Feeling the hopelessness that had taken hold inside her, Aaron suddenly realized his jealousy was a greater threat than any other man could be, and his heart began a ragged pounding. Drawing Sophia against him, he clutched her close.

"You wish . . . Tell me what you wish, Sophia. Tell me and I'll make it come true."

"You can't."

"I will. I promise."

Motionless in his arms, her breath warm against his chest, Sophia whispered, "I wish you believed me. I wish you trusted me. I wish you realized that I haven't given myself to you lightly and that I wouldn't stay with you solely for the comforts you've given me. I wish you would accept the truth when I tell you that the words 'I love you' mean as much to me as a vow, and that I would never dishonor them. I wish—"

Unable to bear more, Aaron stopped Sophia's words with his kiss. His hands in her hair, his mouth gently caressing hers, Aaron felt a new depth to the incredible emotion Sophia raised inside him as his mind drummed an endless litany . . .

I love you, Sophia . . . I need you, Sophia . . . I want you, Sophia . . .

Sophia's arms wound around his neck, and Aaron's hunger for her swelled. Scooping her slenderness up into his arms, Aaron took the few steps back to the bed they had abandoned minutes before, his ardor true and consuming.

Warm lips . . . sweet flesh . . . soaring ecstasy, and Sophia and he were again one. Pausing on the brink of culmination, Aaron looked down at Sophia where she lay beneath him. The words he spoke reverberated deep inside him as he whispered, "I'm sorry, Sophia. I love you. I cherish you. I—"

Unable to withhold the force of his passion any longer, Aaron shuddered his love into the intimate warmth of Sophia, exhilaration brightening the scope of his emotions as Sophia clutched him close in receiving him.

Sated but unwilling to release her, Aaron slid to the bed beside her. Wrapping his arms around Sophia, he held her close until her breathing became slow and even and her limbs became relaxed. Allowing her head to fall back against the pillow at last, he declared against her lips, "You're mine."

* * *

Awaking from a heavy sleep, Sophia struggled to move, suddenly aware as she did that she was confined in Aaron's arms. Moonlight streamed into the room through the slitted blind, and she knew a moment's disquiet. She shook Aaron lightly. His grunt of acknowledgment was accompanied by the tightening of his embrace.

"Are you staying tonight?" she whispered.

Aaron drew her closer. "Yes."

"You're staying too often, Aaron."

Aaron's dark eyes opened into narrow slits, but Sophia knew he was more alert than he appeared to be as he responded, "This is where I want to be."

"But—"

"I don't care what people think or what conclusions they draw." Aaron silenced her further response with a kiss. "Go to sleep."

His breathing deep and even a few moments later, Aaron did not speak again, but as Sophia lay in his arms, sleep was somehow beyond her.

Chapter Nineteen

The frigid December air whistled noisily in the street outside, rattling the windowpanes, the only sound within her otherwise quiet rooms as Sophia sat back and viewed the sketch in front of her with a critical eye. Frequent trips to the showrooms of New York designers in recent weeks had broadened her education considerably, but the experience had been illuminating in a way she had not expected. It had confirmed what she had known instinctively from the first, that her own ability when working with silk was unique — a gift that was somehow inborn. She knew what others had only recently discovered in Madame Tourneau's salon, that her gowns flowed more gracefully than the others, that her designs were inherently suited to the particular colors and feel of the silk she chose, and that the final result of her work, in every case, was *the* gown for which that silk had been created.

A wave of disturbing physical discomfort unexpectedly overwhelming her, Sophia lowered her pencil to the table and sat back. She had suffered bouts of malaise more frequently of late. She did not sleep well and she knew her appearance had suffered as a result, but she was unable to escape the images that haunted her when her mind was unoccupied. It was then that she saw Papa, his homely, warm face gone cold; Mama, with a light akin to hatred in her eyes; Anna, who had turned her back on her. And

419

then there was Lyle and the memory of the myriad feelings he stirred within her, and the realization that even the consolation of his friendship was now denied her.

Forcing her mind from the painful memories where it lingered, Sophia glanced up at the clock on the dining-room wall. Eight o'clock and Aaron had not yet arrived. Sophia sighed, her feelings torn. She had grown closer to Aaron in so many ways since the break with her family and she knew she valued his guidance and concern for her welfare almost as much as she valued his love. But he was overwhelming. The battle to maintain her personal independence, however much she relied on him financially, was difficult and constant. She had finished only a few of the designs needed for the spring designs of Seasons of Silk, and Madame was getting impatient. Frustrated, needing time, she had reminded Aaron a week earlier that he had promised the rooms were hers when he first offered them to her, and that he would stay over on invitation only. That reminder had been a mistake.

She knew in her heart that Aaron still had not forgiven her, and it pained her to know she had hurt him so badly. Raising her hand, Sophia touched the earrings she wore. Diamonds. She looked down at her dressing gown. Velvet and silk. And when she stepped out into the cold the following morning, she would be wearing a fur coat and boots made of the finest leather. All of it was a result of Aaron's generosity to her — a generosity inspired by love. Sophia's eyes filled unexpectedly. She loved Aaron, and as the pain of her ostracism from her family grew, she became increasingly aware of the value of that love.

Sophia paused in her thoughts as a wave of weakness assailed her. She raised an unsteady hand to her forehead, aware that it had become beaded with sweat. Over in a minute, with only a faint nausea remaining, it was a malaise she had suffered with increasing frequency in the past month. Had she not had her monthly flow regularly, she would have suspected . . .

Breathing deeply, Sophia shrugged off the thought. She had not had much appetite lately and had lost considerable weight. Madame had passed the remark that she was not showing her gowns to greatest advantage because of her weight loss, and Sophia knew it was a point well taken. She also knew the reason for her physical decline was her mental distress. She only wished . . .

Lyle returned unexpectedly to mind, and Sophia recalled his words: *"Wishing is a useless habit. I learned that a long time ago . . ."*

Sophia unconsciously nodded. She had learned that same difficult lesson long ago, but still she wished . . .

"Going out again, Aaron?"

Turning abruptly toward his father where the sharp-eyed older man stood in the sitting-room doorway, Aaron paused in an attempt to retain his patience. He had spent each day since his talk with his mother almost a month earlier evincing open interest in assuming greater responsibility in the mill. He had been in attendance at all business meetings, attentive to details, quick with suggestions, and he had accompanied his father on all business trips. His campaign had been a concerted effort to show his father that he cared. He had owed his father that, but he had not stopped there.

He had made certain to remain at home for dinner most evenings, even though he had much preferred to have a quiet dinner with Sophia. He had made little compromise in another area, however, finding himself unable to leave Sophia on most occasions when they lay in each other's arms. Sophia had become a part of him as no other woman ever had, and as his father stared at him with his particularly piercing gaze, Aaron had the feeling that the old man had realized that fact long before he himself had been aware of it.

Steeling himself against the conversation that he knew was to come, Aaron responded, "Yes, I'm going out again, Father." I didn't think it was necessary for me to give you an accounting of my nightly rounds."

"No, it *isn't* necessary. I know where you're going."

Fast losing his patience, Aaron nodded. "Then I'll be on my way."

"Not before I say what I have to say to you, if you don't mind."

"But I *do* mind." Buttoning his overcoat, Aaron turned toward the door.

"Don't take another step, Aaron! I want to make some things clear to you, and I don't intend to wait another day . . . or night." Aaron turned slowly toward him, and Samuel continued. "You continue to see that woman, despite your mother's and my disapproval of her."

"That's my business."

"No it isn't. It's mine! Your mother explained to you how I feel, and I don't intend going over that same ground again, but I want you to know that you haven't fooled me with this elaborate act you've been performing for the past month. You haven't called on the Vandermeres, and you have no intention of calling on them, do you?"

Aaron stiffened. "I haven't decided . . . but that has no relation to my work at the mill."

"If you don't get your private life back on track, you won't *have* any work at the mill!"

Samuel paled, obviously in pain, but Aaron felt no compassion for his father's physical distress, so deep was his fury as he whispered, "You can't threaten me into giving Sophia up. I *won't* give her up."

"Then accept that invitation from the Vandermeres,

damn you!" His complexion taking on a ghastly gray pallor, Samuel gripped the back of a nearby chair to steady himself. "I don't intend to punish myself for your idiocy! I'm not well, Aaron, and my patience is growing thin. Keep the woman if you're so obsessed with her, but protect your family name and business with marriage to a woman who won't trample them both into the dirt! Kathryn Vandermere knows your reputation and she's still interested in you, more the fool she. You'll not get another opportunity to save yourself, I tell you. Own up to your responsibility and act like a man!"

"I've been more a man since I met Sophia than I've ever been in my life, Father. She awakened me to some things that I never—"

"I don't want to hear it!" Livid, Samuel hissed, "Make your decision, Aaron! You have until the first of the year, and after that time—with God as my witness—if you haven't taken an appropriate step, I'll put the mill up for sale!"

Speaking into the silence that followed his announcement, Samuel added, "So, go to your woman and indulge yourself, and ask yourself while you're sleeping by her side if she's worth the future you would sacrifice for her."

Furious, knowing there was no response that he dared to make, Aaron turned silently toward the door.

Lyle glanced around Uncle Matthew's lavishly decorated great room. The holidays officially began with the first of Aunt Edith's parties, but he recognized the farce involved in his presence there that evening. Aunt Edith had given both Aunt Julia and him a wide berth since they had entered, while concealing her animosity with the skill of a master. He supposed he should feel some satisfaction in the realization that he had been present at social affairs at his uncle's house more often in the past few months than he had in the previous few years of his life, but he did not.

Instead, Lyle looked at his diminutive aunt, concern for her taking precedence over his personal discomfort. Smiling a rare smile, he patted the hand she rested on his arm.

"Are you having a good time, Aunt Julia?"

"Are *you* having a good time, Lyle?"

"Aunt Julia . . ." Guiltily aware that the present rift between Aunt Edith and Aunt Julia was somehow related to him, Lyle responded honestly, "I've never enjoyed Uncle Matthew's parties. I never will."

"My dear, you view these affairs improperly."

Lyle's light brows rose with surprise. "Really . . ."

"Yes, really, Lyle." Aunt Julia moved closer to his side as she whispered with elaborate confidentiality, "Edith is a snob and a bore. Matthew is almost as big a snob as she, and he's condescending as well. Their parties are pretentious, and their guests, for the most part, are either vain social-climbers, business acquaintances in whom I have no interest, or arrogant fools. Their repast, however, can usually be counted upon to be extravagant, unique, and beyond compare. As a result, I usually leave Edith's parties feeling very impressed with my own intelligence, with a greater appreciation of my own home and friends, and with a very satisfied palate. Lyle, dear, I wouldn't miss one of these parties for the world!"

Amused, Lyle leaned toward his smiling aunt. "I would."

Aunt Julia laughed aloud, then covered her lips with her fingers, her laughter more contained. She turned as a heavy, gaudily dressed woman approached her and was actively involved in conversation with her a few moments later.

Turning to catch his eye as he strolled toward the corner, Aunt Julia winked unexpectedly, and Lyle smiled. His dear aunt *was* enjoying herself, and he had the suspicion

Aunt Edith's annoyance in seeing her so amused was one of the major reasons for his dear aunt's enjoyment.

Lyle paused in his thoughts, acknowledging silently that another reason for Aunt Julia's high spirits of late was his new position at the mill and the success he had met in handling it. He only wished he could enjoy his success as much as she.

"Hello, Lyle."

Lyle turned, surprised at the appearance of Hope Moray at his side. Looking much the same as she had at the awkward dinner party a few months earlier, she was still plain and distressingly thin, but the smile with which she greeted him was new.

"Hello, Hope. I would've spoken to you earlier, but I didn't think you'd want to speak to me."

"I suppose you were wrong then."

Unconsciously noting that Hope wasn't as homely as he had originally believed with a smile picking up the planes of her narrow face and brightening her eyes, he remained silent, allowing her to continue.

"I hear you're doing extremely well at Uncle Matthew's mill. Your superb handling of the strike is the talk of the city. Aunt Edith is furious. She would so much have preferred to see you fail miserably so she might complain bitterly about you."

Surprised at her candor, Lyle responded, "I didn't realize that you kept abreast of Kingston Mill affairs."

"I do in your case. You can't really fault me for my interest, can you?" Hope's thin face sobered. "I want to thank you for raising my opinion of men, Lyle. There aren't many in your position who would've turned down the opportunity that was offered to you, even if the woman attached to it wasn't appealing. Money usually makes men blind to women's deficiencies."

"I don't consider myself in a position to judge anyone

else's defects, Hope. I never have. I did recognize, however, that the proposition that brought us to this house that evening was insulting to both of us."

Hope held his gaze. "I respect you for that." Her gaze deepened. "And there are few men whom I respect. I also want to thank you for your honesty and generosity in speaking to me so civilly tonight when I was rude and obnoxious to you at our last meeting. But you see, I had always considered you an outsider and an opportunist."

"I'm still an outsider."

"No, you aren't—except to Aunt Edith and Uncle Matthew. You've earned everyone else's respect in these few short months. And you proved to me that night and in the time since that you aren't an opportunist."

"Yes, I am."

Hope considered his response. "I suppose . . . to a degree, but not in the way I believed."

"Thank you, Hope. Then we can be friends after all?"

Accepting the hand he extended toward her, Hope again smiled. "It'll be my pleasure to be your friend."

"As such, you'll be the only 'friend' I have here. So, would you care to join me at the sumptuous repast that Aunt Julia has been raving about? There has to be something good about these parties."

Laughing, Hope fell in beside him. An unlikely couple, they strolled toward the buffet table awaiting them.

Marvelously gowned, the smile of the perfect hostess on her lips, Edith watched Hope and Lyle as they strolled toward the buffet in apparent enjoyment of each other's company. Fuming but still smiling, she poked Matthew sharply and grated through clenched teeth, "Do you see that? Damn him!"

Turning with annoyance, Matthew stared blankly at the

426

unexpected sight of his nephew and Hope in pleasant conversation. He shot his wife an acid glance.

"Well, *you* must be pleased to see them together," he said dryly.

"I'm not, and you know it! I wanted this to happen under *my* terms, Matthew! Not under his! But I'm telling you now, he'll never get away with it! I'll speak to Muriel and tell her what Lyle is!"

"What will you tell her, Edith?"

"That he's a bastard . . . the son of a whore . . . that he isn't good enough—"

"Lyle was a bastard and the son of a whore when you came up with the idea of this alliance in the first place, and I told you that you were a fool then!"

"He's a bastard literally and figuratively!"

Matthew's smile was hard. "But Hope seems to like him." Matthew twisted the knife. "You're an excellent matchmaker."

"Damn you, Matthew!"

"Thank you, dear."

"I won't let him get away with it, I tell you!"

Matthew took his wife's arm. Pressing a firm kiss against her lips unexpectedly, he whispered, "Keep smiling, dear, or you'll have tongues wagging."

Obliging him with a smile for the benefit of observers, Edith looked up into her husband's face and whispered, "Kiss me again and I'll bite your lip off."

Sliding his arm under hers, Matthew drew her forward with what appeared to be a loving whisper as he murmured, "You're a bitch, Edith." To his own surprise he added in afterthought, "The problem is, I'm beginning to believe we deserve each other."

"That nice, Sophia, but I think you've limited the sweep

of that skirt to the point where it's a detriment to the style."

Sitting behind her, Aaron leaned over Sophia's shoulder, his mind wandering from the sketches on which Sophia worked as a bright curl of hair brushed his cheek. Firming his intentions, he considered the sketch again. "Perhaps you should—"

"I've narrowed the skirt purposely, Aaron." Brown brows drawn in a light frown as she turned to look at him over her shoulder, Sophia continued. "I'm going to add a silk overcoat with a collar that's lightly beaded to match the beading on the neck and hemline of the gown."

The brilliant blue of Sophia's eyes bathed his face as she awaited his reply, and Aaron was momentarily in her thrall. Up close . . . so very close. . . . Sophia never failed to stun him with her beauty. Again forcing his mind back to the task at hand, he replied honestly, "I should've realized you had something special in mind. You continue to amaze me, darling."

Sophia scrutinized him in silence, and he knew she was assessing his sincerity. Apparently satisfied, she turned back to her work, and Aaron felt a nudge of irrational annoyance. He had been waiting for Sophia to finish working for almost an hour, and he was tired of seeing the back of her head. The argument he had had with his father earlier in defense of his feelings for her had not improved his disposition. He wanted to reassure himself that he had done the right thing. He wanted to make the positive outweigh the negative this night, and he knew there was only one way he could do that.

"Sophia . . .

Sophia's shoulders stiffened at the sound of his voice, and Aaron felt a rush of anger.

"What's the matter, Sophia? Am I disturbing you?"

Sophia turned toward him, unsmiling. "Yes, you are,

Aaron. I need some time to work tonight. Madame wants—"

"I don't care what Madame wants! I care what *I* want. And right now I want you."

Sophia sighed. "I'm not feeling well this evening, Aaron."

Aaron searched Sophia's face, surprised to see that she *was* flushed. He touched her forehead, his brows knitting into a frown. "You're warm. You have a fever."

"No, I don't."

His frown tightened. "You've been restless at night and now you're losing weight. Of course, you don't feel well. You're working too hard. Madame has no right to ask so much of you. I'm going to tell her—"

"No, Aaron! Madame resents your interference. It only makes things more difficult for me."

Aaron stiffened. "If that witch has been abusing you . . ."

"She hasn't. Aaron, please . . . try to understand. I'm just not feeling well. Madame Tourneau has nothing to do with it."

"Then come to bed."

Sophia gave a short laugh. Relenting from her stiff posture, she stroked his cheek. "I need *rest*, Aaron."

Aaron didn't smile. "I'm not the monster you think I am, Sophia. I don't intend forcing myself on you. I just need to hold you in my arms for a little while, until you fall asleep. And if you're determined to finish that sketch, I'll wake you up when I leave in the morning. That should give you an hour or so to work on it before you have to leave." Noting the shadows under Sophia's eyes that he hadn't seen before, he whispered, "Please, darling."

Pausing only a moment, Sophia lay down her pencil, and Aaron released an unconscious breath. A short time later the house was in darkness and Sophia was lying in his arms. She was quiet, but he knew she wasn't sleeping.

He drew her closer, his father's words unconsciously running through his mind.

". . . *ask yourself while you're sleeping by her side if she's worth the future you would sacrifice for her.*"

Tangling his hand in her hair, Aaron kissed the throbbing pulse in Sophia's temple, knowing his father was a fool. If he were to have any doubts about this affair with Sophia, it would not be when she was lying in his arms. She was everything to him then, just as she was everything to him now. It was only in the cold light of morning when he was far removed from her that he sometimes saw himself as a fool as well.

But a compromise need be made, for he had recognized that look in his father's eyes, and he knew what it meant. The old man would not relent. Aaron also knew himself. He wanted Weiss Silk Mill for his own.

Aaron drew Sophia closer. He'd talk to his father tomorrow . . . and then he'd pay that call.

His breath making frosty puffs on the night air, Anthony stood in the dimly lit yard. He was tired and wanted to sleep, but Maria was still in the kitchen talking to Anna, and he had made it a policy since Sophia had left not to go to bed until his wife was already asleep. He then lay down beside her and, never touching her, went to sleep as well.

Glancing up at the third-floor porch, Anthony took a deep breath, coughing as the frigid air reached his lungs. He hardly recognized Maria since Sophia had left, so silent and withdrawn had she become. But then, he hardly recognized himself, for there was little of the old Anthony Marone left inside him. How could there be? After eighteen years of marriage he had discovered that the woman he had believed he married had never existed. He had lived all those years with a woman who had carried another man's child into their marriage bed. That woman had allowed him to suffer guilt when there was none on his part. She had allowed him to believe Sophia was his daughter and had then cruelly stolen her from him by telling him that the blood of a stranger flowed in Sophia's veins. She had then proved to him by revealing Sophia's treachery that he had never truly known her at all.

With that, Maria had destroyed his pride, his love . . .

"Papa . . ."

Anthony turned at the sound of Rosalie's voice. His voice emerged sharply.

"What is it? Your mother sends you after me?"

"No, Papa." Rosalie took a step closer. A shaft of light touched her sober face as she whispered, "You miss Sophia."

"No, I do not!"

"You do, Papa, and she misses you. I know she does."

"You know nothing. You're a little girl."

"Sophia's my sister and she's your daughter."

"No."

"She loves you, Papa!"

Anthony took a painful breath, knowing even as he spoke the words, Rosalie did not comprehend their full meaning. "She's not my daughter. She deceived me. She lives in sin. She disgraces us all."

"Papa . . ."

"Go upstairs, Rosalie, and leave your papa alone." The anger suddenly gone, Anthony's voice was reduced to a whisper. "Go to bed."

"What about you, Papa? You're tired."

"When your mama goes to bed, I will follow."

"Papa . . ." A single tear trailed from Rosalie's heavily laden eyes. "Won't you ever come back to us?"

Wiping it away with his calloused palm, Anthony then

431

kissed the damp skin of her cheek. "Go to sleep, Rosalie."

Waiting only a moment more, Rosalie then turned toward the stairs. Drawing the stump of a stogie from his pocket, Anthony placed it between his lips. Out of habit, he lit it, although the enjoyment of smoking had somehow left him. Just as with his life, the pleasure was gone.

Chapter Twenty

Afternoon had turned into evening as Sophia walked across the salon floor toward Madame Tourneau, aware of the impatience the Frenchwoman strove to hide. The extended hours at the salon had seemed to stretch on endlessly, increasing the exhaustion she concealed as she smoothed down the waistline of the blue velvet gown she wore and adjusted the neckline. The gown fit poorly, even more poorly than it had the previous week, but Sophia knew the fit was no reflection on Madame Tourneau's talents as a dressmaker.

Suddenly warm in the heavy garment as she turned at Madame's direction, Sophia took a deep breath. She had been grateful that she was alone upon awakening that morning because she had felt too ill to speak, much less to answer Aaron's worried inquiries. She had not expected her condition to improve, however, since her sleeplessness had worsened and her appetite had fallen off even more sharply in the past few days. Aaron's concern had not eased the situation and she had begun pretending a wellness that she did not feel in order to alleviate his anxiety.

"Sophia, turn again, please."

Sophia obliged Madame, only to have the room continue spinning around her when she was still. Reaching out to grasp a nearby rack, Sophia steadied herself, the sound of Madame's voice ringing in her ears as she looked up. Her momentary dizziness past, Sophia forced a smile.

"You are well, Sophia?" Madame's small eyes narrowed assessingly. "Madame Harrington and I will be happy to excuse you if you are not."

"No, madame, I'm fine."

Forcing a steadiness to her step that she did not feel as she returned to the back room, Sophia sat abruptly. She was still sitting, resting her head on her hand when Madame appeared unexpectedly at the door.

"What's wrong, Sophia?"

"A temporary malaise, madame. I'll be all right in a moment."

Madame walked closer to speak in a confidential tone. "You do not look well, Sophia. I've told you that several times over the last few weeks." She gave a short laugh. "At first I thought your paleness a few minutes ago was a result of having overheard my conversation with Madame Harrington, but now I can see I was wrong."

Sophia became immediately alert at Madame's tone. The Frenchwoman had some news to impart. Begrudging the satisfaction she provided with her inquiry, Sophia questioned politely, "How did your conversation with Madame Harrington concern me, madame?"

"It didn't concern you, exactly, *ma chère*. It concerned a friend of yours."

"A friend?"

"Your very handsome friend, Monsieur Lyle Kingston. Madame Harrington told me that he has been seen in the company of Mademoiselle Hope Moray of late. The rather plain and rather wealthy mademoiselle seemed very taken with him, and he with her. Tongues are wagging of an announcement that will soon be made—perhaps in time for the Noel."

Swallowing, determined not to allow Madame to see the distress her words had evoked, Sophia forced a smile. "Lyle is a wonderful man. Mademoiselle Moray is fortunate."

"Ah, yes, so handsome a man . . . so virile . . . so proud.

434

Like a golden god. You will doubtless be aggrieved to lose him."

"You're mistaken, madame. I won't lose Lyle because of this liaison. He'll always be my friend."

"But the young Mademoiselle Moray may not approve of such a 'friendship.' "

Drawing herself to her feet, Sophia stood unsteadily, determined not to allow the conversation to go any further. "Perhaps you're right." And at the Frenchwoman's raised brow, "I'm not feeling very well after all, madame. I think it would be best if I leave for the evening."

Madame stiffened at Sophia's tone of dismissal. "Monsieur Weiss usually picks you up on Friday evenings. He will be annoyed to find you're not here when he arrives."

"Perhaps." Sophia's gaze was direct. "If you will excuse me, madame."

Abruptly turning her back on Madame Tourneau, Sophia walked to the rear of the room where Mary watched the Frenchwoman's annoyance with barely concealed amusement.

"Will you undo my back, Mary?"

The sound of the curtain whipping shut behind Sophia turned her in time to hear Madame's footsteps move back to the front of the salon. Sophia looked up as the young seamstress giggled softly.

"I guess you told her, Sophia! If I had an admirer like Mr. Weiss, I wouldn't let her talk to me that way, either."

Nodding, Sophia slipped out of the gown and back into her own clothes. Struck with another bout of weakness, Sophia stood momentarily still. Again steady, she fought the sadness that had welled inside her at Madame's gleefully imparted words. So, Lyle had found himself someone to love who was free to love him in return. Sophia's heart squeezed with pain. She wondered if the young woman knew how lucky she was.

Slipping into her coat and hat, Sophia took another deep

breath and started resolutely toward the door. Out on the street moments later, she fought to steady herself, exasperated at the persistent weakness assailing her. She was halfway down the street, walking resolutely toward the street-car stand when she paused abruptly in front of a house bearing a familiar sign.

Howard Matteson, M.D.

She had heard many of Madame's patrons speak well of Dr. Matteson . . .

Submitting to impulse, Sophia turned up the stairs. A moment later, she rang the bell.

Pacing impatiently, Aaron looked out the window onto the darkened street. Where in hell was Sophia?

She was nowhere in sight and Aaron gave a low growl. He had arrived at the salon only to find Sophia had left early, and he could not really blame Madame Tourneau for her annoyance. Sophia was getting too independent of late — in all quarters. He was not about to put up with it.

Aaron's cheek twitched with suppressed anger. Sophia had become too sure of him, and he supposed it was his fault that she had. He spoiled her, and the depth of his feelings for her was too transparent. Worse, he could not seem to keep his hands off her, and the words "I love you" were always at the tip of his tongue to the point where he sometimes had to force himself to hold them back. But she had gone too far this time — leaving the salon with an inadequate excuse when she was expecting him, and then disappearing for over two hours while he waited for her to return. Where could she be? She had nowhere to go. Or did she . . . ?

Aaron's pacing faltered as jealousy flared anew. He would make Sophia account for every minute of her time when she returned, and then he would make sure that she never tried this trick again. He was not a man who appreciated being kept waiting — especially tonight . . .

A sound at the outer door alerting him, Aaron strode forward and pulled it open, startling Sophia as she stood with the key in her hand. Grasping her arm, he pulled her inside and slammed the door shut behind her. He stood silently for long moments, looking down at her, realizing few people would have recognized this startlingly lovely young woman wrapped in a hooded cape lavishly trimmed with Persian lamb fur as the Sophia Marone who had arrived on his doorstep months earlier with only the clothes she wore on her back. This was the Sophia Marone *he* had created — *his* mistress . . . the woman for whom he had defied his father . . . the woman for whom he risked his entire future. The little fool did not seem to realize what he had jeopardized for her!

His anger swelling, Aaron demanded, "Where have you been?"

His voice was ringing in the silence of the room when Aaron first noticed Sophia's pallor and the strangely distracted manner with which she returned his gaze.

"I've been walking."

"Walking! You *were* expecting me to call for you at the salon, weren't you?"

Sophia nodded, her stiff fingers moving absentmindedly at the closure of her cape.

"It's freezing outside and it's been dark for an hour. Do you realize you've kept me waiting all this time?" When she did not respond, Aaron stiffened. "Were you with someone — is that it? Who was it? Tell me!"

Sophia dropped her cape onto the nearby chair. Her expression was devoid of emotion. "I wasn't feeling well. I went to see a doctor." She paused, her gaze tight on his face. "Aaron . . . I'm going to have your child . . ."

Momentarily motionless, Aaron then took a sharp step backwards. "That's impossible."

"It's true."

Staring at Sophia in silence for a long moment as his heart

437

plummeted with the pain of her treachery, Aaron suddenly gave a sharp laugh. "So, my father was right after all. He said I couldn't trust you. He said you'd eventually try to pressure me into a situation I'd regret, but I said you were too honest. I said . . ." He laughed more harshly than before. "It doesn't matter what I said, does it? Somehow word got back to you about the problems I'm having with my father and you came up with this story to try to force my hand."

"I don't know what you're talking about . . . but what I've told you is true."

"No, it isn't!" Aaron shook his head. "Do you really take me for that much of a fool? You forget, I'm not ignorant of the functions of a woman's body, and I'm intimately acquainted with yours, Sophia. Your menses has been regular each and every month since I first took you."

"Yes, it has . . . That's why I didn't suspect—"

"Stop this, Sophia! It will do you no good to continue with this lie!"

"It's not a lie, Aaron. It's the truth."

Her face whitening, Sophia swayed and Aaron reached spontaneously for her only to have her avoid contact with his hands as she gripped the back of a nearby chair to steady herself. "No, I'll be all right. Dr. Matteson said this dizziness is common in—"

"Dr. Matteson!" Aaron could feel his face drain of color. "You went to Dr. Matteson? Why did you go to see him?"

Sophia scrutinized his face, uncertain. "Because his office is near the salon."

"No, that wasn't the reason, was it? You went to him because he's my mother's physician . . ." Aaron paused in that thought. "But knowing that, how did you expect to get away with this trick? Didn't you realize I could check with him to verify everything you're telling me now?" Taking a sharp step forward, Aaron rasped, "Didn't you, Sophia? Damn you, tell me!"

438

Tears suddenly brimming in Sophia's glorious eyes, she whispered, "I didn't know he was your mother's doctor. But everything I've told you is true. I didn't believe it at first, either, but Dr. Matteson said in some rare cases women maintain a steady menses throughout their confinement. It's the way of things with them . . . and it appears it will be the way of things with me."

"I can check every word that you're telling me, Sophia! Dr. Matteson will tell me the truth!"

Sophia's lips trembled revealingly. "I've already told you the truth, Aaron."

Incredulity wiping his mind free of thought, Aaron watched as Sophia strove to retain control. The effort was almost beyond her, and he suddenly knew there was no need to verify the truth of Sophia's announcement. She had never lied to him before. She was not lying to him now. Acknowledgment was a lead weight inside him as he whispered, "It's true, then . . ."

Anger coming to his immediate rescue, Aaron then snapped, "How did this happen? The powders the midwife gave you. She said they'd protect you."

Sophia averted her gaze. "Dr. Matteson laughed at me of my stupidity. He said the powders are useless . . . that only a fool would be taken in by the nonsense the midwife told me." Pausing, Sophia continued in a difficult whisper, "He said the child will be born in July."

"No it won't!"

Sophia took a deep, shuddering breath. "It happened, Aaron. I can't take it back."

"Yes, you can—and you will!" Rage flushing hotly through him, Aaron grasped Sophia's arms roughly. "I tell you this now—I will not have a bastard child haunt me the rest of my days! You'll get rid of it now—tomorrow!"

"Get rid of it?" Sophia gasped, her eyes widening. "You don't mean—"

"I mean you'll go to that midwife who gave you those powders, and you'll throw them back in her face! I mean you'll tell her that she'll take care of the mistake *she* made or you'll have the police on her!"

Sophia shook her head incredulously, her eyes widening. "No, I couldn't do that!"

"Yes, you can!" Aaron felt Sophia's shock even as he shook her roughly, his own desperation growing. She could not have the child! It would be the final straw in the strained relations with his father. His father would turn his back on him for good and put the mill up for sale as he had threatened.

Staring into Sophia's white face, Aaron continued hotly. "You have no choice! You'll do what I tell you now, or it's the end of everything between us. What will you do then? You'll be unable to work for Madame Tourneau or anyone else as a mannequin before long, and at a word from me, Madame will enforce the terms of the contract she holds with you. The fashion field will be closed to you for three years and you'll be out on the street again with only the clothes on your back."

Aaron's lips tightened. "You could go back to working in a mill, of course, if you could find a mill that would accept a woman in disgrace. And I wouldn't count on your 'friend,' Kingston. He's found someone to take your place, you see . . . a young woman with money and social position that will help him rise above his 'bastard' status. You can be sure that he won't involve himself with another bastard at this point in time, especially when it isn't his own."

Steeling himself against Sophia's silence and the look in her eyes, Aaron hissed, "You'll go to the midwife tomorrow! You'll get it done immediately."

"I can't!"

"You can and you will!"

Shuddering with rage, Aaron stared down at Sophia.

Bitch! Whore! She had carefully trapped him, but she would see that she had not won out. She would see that he—

"You said you cherished me . . ."

Aaron's rage halted abruptly at Sophia's whispered words. A low, keening wail come alive in his mind at the pain in her voice. He didn't want it to be this way between Sophia and him. He only wanted—

"You said you loved me . . ."

The wail grew louder, drowning out Aaron's fury, leaving him only the barely restrained desire to crush Sophia in his arms, to kiss the tears from her eyes and to assuage her pain as he rasped, "Love isn't enough, Sophia." He paused, his voice breaking roughly, "Yes, I love you, but I swear to you, I will *not* let that love interfere with what I know I must do! I will never acknowledge a bastard child as my own! I will never look at it or hold it in my arms! I will never admit to its existence! And if you bear it contrary to my wishes, I will refuse to acknowledge your existence as well."

Realizing Sophia was shuddering, Aaron pressed with a callousness born of desperation, "Tomorrow, Sophia. I want it done tomorrow, with no excuses!"

"I can't . . ."

Aaron took a deep breath, forcing a steadiness to his voice that he did not feel as he continued. "I'm leaving for Long Island in the morning on family business. I'll be away a week. I want it over and done when I return."

Unmoving in his tight grip, Sophia closed her eyes. A single tear slid from beneath her lids in the moment before she opened them again to whisper, "You say you love me. How could that be true?"

Aaron steeled himself against the softening he felt growing inside him. Releasing Sophia abruptly, he snatched up his coat and hat. Turning toward her once more when he reached the door, he repeated, "I want it done tomorrow."

Walking down the street moments later, Sophia's tear-filled

eyes haunting him, Aaron faced a harsh reality. He had betrayed Sophia not only once but twice. He had betrayed her in what he had already done, and in what he intended to do.

But the Vandermeres were waiting—and so was his father. He wouldn't get a second chance.

Still staring at the door which Aaron had closed firmly behind him, Sophia breathed deeply once, twice, in an effort to retain control. Taking a few short steps, she sat on the nearby settee, her hands clenched in her lap as she tried to come to terms with the events of the last few hours.

Dr. Matteson had been kind, but it was only now that she realized the true reason behind his surprise when she had walked through the doorway of his office. She did not care to remember her humiliation in learning that she was to have a child, or the evasive answers she had given to Dr. Matteson's questions. She had known Aaron would be upset, but she had never expected that he would turn on her so cruelly.

Sophia closed her eyes against the torment of Aaron's defection, a single sob escaping her lips. He had said he still loved her, and strangely enough, she believed him. But he didn't love her enough to comfort her or to share her distress. He didn't love her enough to love the child she could give him. And, in the end, he didn't love her enough to choose her over all.

A vision of clear gold eyes came to mind, but Sophia forced them away. She had made a choice those months ago. Lyle was her friend, but she couldn't burden him with problems that she had brought upon herself—especially now, when things were going so well for him.

Sliding the flat of her hand against her stomach, Sophia took a deep breath. Was Aaron's seed really growing inside her, or was this all a frightening, overwhelming dream? Was everything she had worked for finished now—the future which had seemed so bright only a few hours earlier, the "Seasons of Silk" on which she had worked so diligently? Were her hopes for eventual reconciliation with her family dashed forever with this last humiliation she would deal them? Had Mama been right in her prediction that the shadows of her disgrace would fall on them all?

Suddenly getting to her feet, Sophia walked into the bedroom. She halted abruptly as she passed her reflection in the mirror, stunned at what she saw. Gone was the smiling, self-confident Sophia Marone she had once been, the young woman who had been so certain of the great future that lay ahead of her. In her place was a pathetic young woman she did not recognize, a woman who had given up everything she held dear for the sake of a dream that had crumbled into dust.

Another bout of weakness gave vent to queasiness and Sophia felt control slipping away. Leaning over the washstand moments later, she retched and retched again, then collapsed weakly on the bed. She closed her eyes to see Aaron's dark eyes again accusing. Why hadn't she realized the limitations of Aaron's love? Why had she made herself believe that he loved her enough to stand by her?

The answer was simple. She had made herself believe what she wanted to believe, and she was now caught in her own self-deception.

But others, innocents, were caught as well, and the thought of the shame that would fall on them because of her was more than she could bear. In an attempt to escape it all, Sophia closed her eyes and tried to sleep.

A new day had dawned after a night of sleepless anxiety. Sitting rigidly in his carriage as it moved through the frozen, early-morning streets, Aaron found his mind moving in the same frenzied circles in which it had whirled all through the night. Impatient as the carriage slowed at an intersection,

443

Aaron glanced outside, aware that Sophia was only a few streets away.

It had been one of the most trying mornings of his life, maintaining a casual facade in the face of his mother's excited chattering at the breakfast table, and his father's cautious scrutiny. The railroad station his destination, it had been more difficult than he had imagined it could be not to direct Harry there by way of the Park Avenue address where he was certain Sophia had also spent a wakeful night.

Aaron paused in his thoughts, determined. He would not relent, no matter the depth of Sophia's distress. Sophia would come to her senses and see that she had no choice but to do as he told her. She faced the prospect of being without money, without a place to live or a means to support herself. She could not return to her family in her condition and he knew she was too proud to go to the bastard Kingston with another man's bastard growing inside her. Sophia was at his mercy.

Aaron took a fortifying breath. Strangely, he felt little satisfaction in the realization that Sophia was totally dependent upon him at last. Just as strangely, through the shock, anger, and panic he had experienced in the last few hours, he knew he had never loved Sophia more. It had pained him to see her reduced to tears and to know she was suffering. The week he would spend at the Vandermeres would be long and tedious with this affair hanging over his head, and he was already anxious to return to Sophia and to take her into his arms. He would be more cautious after this, however, dispensing with powders and the like and relying solely upon his self-control to avoid repetition of this potentially disastrous situation. But he would love Sophia—with all his heart, he would love her.

As for Kathryn Vandermere, he would do his best to win her over as quickly as possible. He needed to pacify his father's fears . . . and his own as well. Once Kathryn and he were married, he would be free to do as he chose, and he would choose to continue loving Sophia . . . he feared for as

444

long as he would live.

The gray winter morning had dawned heavily overcast, but Sophia paid little attention to the cheerless sky. She had been sick upon awakening and it had been only with the sheerest strength of will that she had been able to drag herself from her bed and dress. The desire to run and hide was overwhelming, but she knew that it was senseless to run and that there was nowhere to hide.

The pain of Sophia's distress deepened as Aaron's words returned again to her mind, as they had countless times during the sleepless night.

"Tomorrow, Sophia! I want it done tomorrow!"

Aaron had said he loved and cherished her, but he would not love or cherish the child she could give him. He would turn his back on her and walk away.

The emptiness inside her expanding, Sophia reached for her cape and slipped it onto her shoulders. As she approached the door, she realized the temporary nature of the life she had lived for the past few months. There would be no brilliant future for her. The image she had seen of herself in her mind since childhood would never truly come to be. She was without a home, without friends, without a way to support herself . . . or the child that grew within her.

Sophia stepped out onto the street, the first blast of freezing morning air causing her to catch her breath. She looked around her. A few other people emerged from nearby alleyways and started on their way, and uncertain of her own destination, Sophia followed. She ran for the streetcar when they ran, and she climbed aboard and sat when they sat. Rising instinctively from her seat a short time later, she alighted at a familiar stop and began walking briskly. It was only when she reached the corner of Prospect and Ellison Streets that she halted. A gasp escaped her lips at her unconscious intent.

No . . . she could not go home!

Suddenly unsteady, the frigid gusts of winter wind numbing her mind, Sophia stepped into a nearby doorway, waiting. Uncertain how much time had passed as she shivered expectantly, Sophia felt her heart leap in her chest as a short, muscular figure appeared in her line of vision. The stretch of his shoulders was comfortingly familiar as he pulled his worn cap down further on his forehead in protection against the cold. The man looked up toward a spot in the distance, and Sophia glimpsed his dark eyes, his full mustache, and lean, homely face.

Papa . . .

Drawing back into the shadows of the doorway as her father turned unexpectedly in her direction, glimpsing a sorrow he could not conceal, Sophia muffled an anguished cry. *She* had done this to Papa! She had taken the smile from his eyes and left sadness in its stead. She knew her mother suffered as well, and she knew this disgrace she would bring upon them both would be the final blow.

Hiding, determined not to let her father see her, Sophia waited until he turned out of sight. The wind whipped the folds of her cape and she drew it closer around her, her shivering increasing, but she was not yet willing to leave. Her patience rewarded a short time later, Sophia indulged herself in the sight of her sisters as they walked toward the mills, heads bent into the wind. Rosalie was talking, and at a brisk gust of wind, she grasped the shawl that covered her head and burst out laughing. Looking up, Anna joined in, laughing along with her, and Sophia was struck with the new maturity she glimpsed briefly on Anna's face. Instinctive love and pride in her sisters rising inside her, Sophia followed their progress down the street. They turned out of sight, and her sense of loss was so acute that she was physically stricken.

Leaning back against the protection of the doorway, Sophia fought to keep herself on her feet, her head spinning.

She touched her forehead in an effort to still the dizzying motion, only to find it covered with perspiration despite the frigid temperature.

Stable again at last, Sophia burst from the doorway. She had run a few feet in an unconscious direction when she halted abruptly, suddenly aware of her intent.

No! That was the one place she could not go! She would not be able to watch Lyle from afar as she had watched her father and her sisters without going to him—without throwing herself into his arms—without abandoning herself to the warmth of his honeyed gaze and the consolation she knew he would never refuse her. She could not do that to him!

Turning, Sophia began walking swiftly in the opposite direction. She had chosen the path she would take those months ago, and she had chosen Aaron as well. Her choice made, she knew she must now have the courage to live with it. She must have the courage to do what she must do—for her sake, for Aaron's sake, and for the sake of those innocents threatened by what she had done . . .

Her mind frozen, her body shuddering uncontrollably, Sophia paused before a shabby frame residence a short time later. She looked up at the front door, an anguished cry starting inside her mind as she climbed the steps. The door opened slowly after the third ring, and Sophia looked at the heavy woman who eyed her assessingly. The midwife's breath was heavy with alcohol as she questioned tightly, "What are you doing here so early in the morning?"

Her lips frozen, Sophia faltered, "I need . . . I want you to . . ."

The midwife stared at her for silent moments, then nodded. "Sí. I know what you need. Come inside."

Sophia hesitated. Her heart and mind rebelling, she was unable to move until the woman pulled her inside and closed the door behind her. Patting Sophia's arm, she said gruffly, "A few minutes and it will all be over. Come."

The cry inside her mind growing louder, the ache in her heart overwhelming all conscious thought, Sophia took one step, and then another . . . and then another . . .

The train whistle was shrill and piercing as Aaron glanced around the crowded car. Finding a double seat that was unoccupied, Aaron put his bag into the overhead carrier and sat abruptly. The car jerked into motion as Aaron settled himself at the window and unfastened his coat. He was determined to get some sleep on the way. He had no desire to arrive at the Vandermeres in a state of complete exhaustion. Too much depended upon the impression he would make and his ability to charm the waiting Kathryn.

Suddenly disgusted, Aaron removed his hat and slapped it down on the seat beside him. He hated this business — all of it! He hated the thought of the week to come, during which he would be forced to degrade himself for the sake of his father's fears and his own ambitions. He hated the thought of spending that time in the company of one woman when his thoughts would be with another. He hated everything and anything that kept him from where he wished to be . . . at Sophia's side . . . but he knew he would do what he must.

His mind set, Aaron willed himself to sleep, knowing that in the end, he would have it all.

Swaying weakly, Sophia followed the midwife back to the front door. Reaching into the inner pocket of her cape, she withdrew some bills and held them out to her.

"Is this enough?"

The woman shrugged and took the money from her hand, eyeing her warily. "You will feel better soon. Go home and rest."

Wracked by another wave of pain, Sophia leaned against

the wall, breathing deeply until it passed, only to hear the midwife's grunt of disgust. "You must expect some pain for a while. It's the price you pay for your folly, but it's nothing like the pain you have saved yourself . . . and the shame. Go home now."

Sophia stood uncertainly on the steps as the midwife's door closed firmly behind her. She felt the frigid wind buffet her face and she remained motionless, hoping that it would sweep the horror of the last hour from her mind. It did not.

Walking unsteadily down the steps, Sophia turned toward Market Street, uncertain of her destination. Seized by another wave of pain, Sophia held her breath. The midwife had said she must expect some pain, but the midwife had not realized that the pain in her body was mild compared with the pain in her heart.

The cry inside her grew louder, and Sophia fought to restrain a sob. It was over and done. She no longer need fear the final disgrace she would bring upon her family. They were saved. It was only she who was now damned with a far deeper shame than she had ever known before.

Searing knives of pain slashed again, cutting deeply, stealing her breath as Sophia emerged onto the corner of the street. She saw a streetcar approaching in the distance, but it was too far away. Turning in growing panic as a hack turned the corner in front of her, she raised her hand in summons, striving to hold herself upright as it drew to a stop.

Suddenly at her side, the driver inquired anxiously, "Are you sick, ma'am? Where do you want to go?"

The words, "Park Avenue," slipped through her lips as the concerned man helped her into the carriage and closed the door behind her. Unconscious of the passage of time, Sophia raised her pain-drugged lids in time to direct the driver to her front door. She attempted a smile as he helped her down onto the sidewalk.

"Do you need a doctor?" The old fellow's wiry brows were

449

knit with concern. "I'll get one for you."

"I'll be all right." Withdrawing the last of the bills from her pocket, she pressed them into his hand and forced a steady step toward her door. She did not turn to see him staring after her as she unlocked the door and slipped inside.

A sudden piercing pain, and Sophia felt a hot, sticky wetness on her legs, but she paid it little mind as she staggered toward the bedroom door. She had somehow known it would be this way—a fitting end to a shameful deed.

The room reeling around her, she approached the bed, dropping her cape to the floor as she lay down. The heated wetness continued to flow from her, and Sophia closed her eyes. In doing so she blotted out the pain, she blotted out the shame, knowing in her heart she would never open her eyes again.

The gusts of wind had grown more chill since morning, but Rosalie was impervious to the icy blasts as she stepped down from the streetcar and started toward the brick-faced house near the end of the block. A power outage at the mill and the resulting complications had sent most of the workers home early, but she had told Anna to make up an excuse for her and had gone to visit Sophia at the salon. She had been startled to find that Sophia had not reported for work and that Madame Tourneau was in a quiet fury.

Rosalie recalled the Frenchwoman's hissed comments with annoyance.

"Your sister thinks me to be a fool, but I am not! Monsieur Weiss has gone away for a week, and she thinks she will pass that time working here at her leisure because she believes I won't risk his displeasure by reprimanding her. But she is wrong! You will be wise to advise your sister that I will expect her here on time tomorrow or she will arrive to find someone else hired in her place!"

A hot flush touched Rosalie's rosy cheeks despite the bite of the cold. Madame Tourneau was a jealous old woman who envied Sophia the devotion of Mr. Weiss. She knew that if Sophia had not appeared for work, it was because she was not well, but she would tell Sophia what the Frenchwoman had said. Sophia would take care of her!

Anger accelerating her pace, Rosalie was breathing heavily as she ran up the steps to Sophia's front door. She knocked, then knocked again. Surprised at the lack of response, Rosalie turned the knob, a sudden sense of uneasiness touching her mind as the door opened easily.

Walking into the living room, she called out, "Sophia, are you here?"

An eerie silence her response, Rosalie felt a shudder run down her spine as she took another step. She called out again, her heart beginning a slow pounding as she started slowly toward the bedroom door. Pausing a moment, she stepped into the room, only to be shocked into silence at the sight of Sophia's motionless form lying on the bed. Suddenly conscious of the blood that stained the coverlet underneath her, trailing the side of the bed onto the floor, Rosalie gasped. Crying, praying, calling Sophia's name, she rushed to her side.

Her breath escaping in a sob at the gray color of her sister's skin, Rosalie touched the pulse in Sophia's temple, then in her throat, crying aloud when she found it beating weakly there.

Frantic, more frightened than she had ever been in her life, Rosalie cried, "Sophia! Sophia, can you hear me?"

Still lids fluttered and Rosalie felt a moment's hope. Clutching Sophia's hand she rasped, "Sophia, talk to me. Tell me what to do!"

Sophia's heavy lids rose to allow a peek of dulled blue eyes as she whispered, "Don't tell Papa . . . Mama . . ."

A sob escaped Rosalie's throat. "But Sophia . . ."

"Promise . . . promise . . ."

Nodding a whispered promise, Rosalie saw Sophia's eyes fall closed again, and panic assumed control. Sophia's skin was growing colder . . .

Remembering the telephone she had seen in the corner of the living room, Rosalie ran toward it with uncertainty. She had never used such an instrument before, but she knew she must try.

Removing the receiver from the hook, Rosalie put it to her ear. In reply to the nasal inquiry of the operator, she whispered in a shaking voice, "I want to talk to Kingston Mill. Quickly, please . . ."

Holding her breath at the sound of ringing on the wire, Rosalie sobbed aloud when she heard Lyle's voice. Her fervent plea shattered the silence of the room as she rasped, "Mr. Kingston — Lyle — please come!" She sobbed again. "Sophia is dying!"

Chapter Twenty-one

The darkness around her was not without sound. Floating in a netherworld without light, Sophia became attuned to the hissing whispers, the sounds of movement, the drone of voices growing louder in volume, only to become hissing whispers once more. She felt a touch on her cheek, heard a voice in her ear pleading softly, but she had no desire to respond. It was safe in the darkness. There was no threat—no guilt—no shame.

"Sophia . . ."

Someone spoke her name. The deep voice was familiar, raising a warmth inside her that had gone cold, but she could not—she *would* not respond.

"Sophia, please."

The voice held a new note. Desperation . . . pain, and Sophia wondered how it could be that she caused pain even when she had ceased to exist.

"Open your eyes. Damn it, open your eyes!"

Orders . . . she would take no more orders—but the darkness around her lightened, drawing her to the anxiety in the husky voice as it continued softly. "You're not going to do this to me, Sophia. You're not going to give up. I won't let you!"

"Please open your eyes, Sophia . . ."

Rosalie's voice.

Sophia stirred at the desperation of her sister's plea as she continued. "Please. I don't know what to do."

Rosalie was frightened. Seeking to alleviate her sister's fear, Sophia fought the shadows in which she had hidden only moments before, but they oppressed her, holding her back. She heard sobbing and whispered words of comfort, but the sobbing continued.

Struggling, forcing herself free of the darkness, Sophia strained to open her eyes. The first sliver of light sent physical pain surging anew and Sophia gasped aloud, aware of the rumble of voices around her as she strained to identify them more clearly. She forced her eyes wider to find only blurred images meet her view.

"Oh, Sophia . . ." Rosalie's voice was closer. Sophia felt the words brush her face. She tried to turn toward her sister, but it was difficult to move, difficult to fight the shadows again swelling to claim her.

Her vision gradually clearing, Sophia saw Rosalie's small face was blotched from crying. She suffered anew, whispering, "Don't cry . . ."

A strange face intruded into her line of vision. The stranger touched her, examined her, then spoke.

"She's very weak. She should be in a hospital."

"No!" The force of Sophia's rasped objection set her to shaking.

"She doesn't want to go to the hospital. Just tell me what to do and I'll take care of her."

That strong male voice again. Sophia knew who it was. She tried to smile as the shadows hovered around her, as her sister clasped her hand and whispered, "Tell me what to do, Sophia. I want to stay with you, but Mama and Papa will come looking for me if I don't go home soon."

"No . . . don't want them to know . . ." Sophia rasped. "You promised . . ."

"Go home, Rosalie." The deep voice was firm. "If you

454

stay, your parents will know something's wrong. Sophia will be all right. I'll take care of her and you can come back in the morning."

"But—"

"Please go home, Rosalie. Sophia will only become more upset if you don't."

Rosalie moved away and the voices dimmed, but Sophia felt a strong hand take hers. Sight and sound faded as the hand continued to clutch hers tightly, and she relaxed, knowing Lyle held her safe and secure at last.

Sophia's hand went limp, and Lyle glanced up, panicking as Dr. Levine brushed him roughly aside to assume his place at her bedside. His heart pounding, Lyle watched as the small, wiry doctor's ministrations abruptly stopped and the man drew himself slowly erect.

Lyle's voice escaped in a choked whisper. "Doctor, is she—?"

"She's sleeping."

Running his hand roughly through his hair, Lyle gave a short laugh, then laughed again, his relief overwhelming. "I thought . . ."

His throat suddenly too tight to speak, Lyle turned away from the bed, only to feel Dr. Levine's reassuring hand on his shoulder.

"She's not out of the woods yet, but we have more to be optimistic about than we did when I arrived here a few hours ago. The bleeding has stopped and her heartbeat is weak but steady. She seems to be a healthy young woman. Barring any unforeseen incident, she should survive."

"*Should* survive?" Lyle took a deep breath and blinked his eyes clear of tears.

"Your young lady did a very foolish thing. Whoever did this to her was a . . ." His brows knitting, the old physician took an angry breath, choosing not to finish the thought. "I

455

can't be certain at this time if there's permanent damage, and the risk of infection is very strong." Dr. Levine paused again, pinning him with his gaze. "Very honestly, I find this situation difficult to understand." The old physician stared harder. "It"s obvious that you love this young woman and that neither of you are committed elsewhere, if I'm to judge from the absence of rings. There was no reason for such a desperate step. You're two healthy young people. A baby is a gift from God. It wasn't meant to be thrown back in His face."

Bearing the weight of the doctor's scrutiny, Lyle responded softly, "I didn't know she . . ." He paused and started again. "If I had known what she intended doing, I would have stopped her."

Studying his face a moment longer, Dr. Levine shrugged wearily. "I suppose it's too late now for regrets. I can only tell you that she'll need close care for the next few days. She's lost too much blood to run the risk of losing any more. Complete bed rest, the powders I've left for her, good nourishing meals so her body may rebuild itself . . ." He looked back at Sophia again. "She's a beautiful woman . . ."

Lyle nodded as Dr. Levine reached for his coat.

"I've done all I can for her now. The rest is up to her. I'll stop back first thing in the morning." He raised bloodshot eyes to Lyle's, repeating, "She needs close care. Isn't there anyone you can call to help you?"

"I'll take care of her."

Pausing in the doorway, the old man smiled. "Yes, I can see that you will. Send someone if you need me."

Turning back to the bed, Lyle stared at Sophia for a long, silent moment. The sound of the front door closing registered in the back of his mind as he took the few steps to her bedside and crouched beside her. He took her hand, wincing at its coldness. Adjusting the blankets around her, he crouched back down beside her.

The agony of his love for her rife in his voice, unable to keep the tears from flowing, Lyle whispered, "Don't try to slip away from me again, because I won't let you go, Sophia."

Her hand tight in his, Lyle raised it to his lips. He knew he had never loved her more than at this moment.

Julia walked slowly down the staircase of her home, pausing midway as she reached the small circular window to stare out at the somber morning sky. The naked branches of maple trees that had stood there for the greater portion of her life waved wildly in the wind, and she unconsciously shivered. She had never liked winter. As she grew older, she liked it even less. The only bright spot in the entire season was the Christmas holidays, and they had been too brief.

Shrugging, she continued down into the foyer, determined to make the best of a day that appeared destined to be gray and endlessly cheerless. Julia paused at the foyer mirror to adjust the collar of her dark gown, a smile picking up the corners of her lips. She would force her concentration past the daylight hours and think of the evening to come, when Lyle would come to dinner and they would talk.

Julia's smile warmed. Everything was going so well for Lyle. He had surpassed even her highest hopes in his management of the mill—first settling a strike that under other conditions might have had a frightening impact on profitability. He had then made improvements in processing that had increased production, and, surprising all who had said it could not be done, he had established a rapport with the workers that was totally inconsistent with the mood of the industry. He had established Kingston Mill as one of the most stable mills in the city in the period of a few months. She knew his success was the result of his intelligence, talent, honesty, and strength of character, which had won him the respect of his peers and the mill employees.

Julia paused in her thoughts. She only wished she could say that he had earned Matthew's respect as well, but she feared her brother's prejudices and obstinacy would keep them forever apart. Lyle's unexpected friendship with Hope Moray was even looked upon with suspicion by her brother.

Acclimated, however, to the tenor of things between her dear nephew and her stubborn brother, Julia was confident that Lyle would eventually win a permanent place in the mill. Matthew was many things, but he was not a man who would renege on his given word. Lyle had a true future ahead of him for the first time in his life — a future to which he was born, although that inherent right had not been acknowledged. She —

An unexpected knock on the door turned Julia's head as Maggie's heavy step sounded in the hallway. The dour Scotswoman opened the door to a hack driver who questioned briefly, "Is Miss Kingston at home? I have a note for her from a gentleman who asked me to wait for her reply."

Taking a few quick steps, Julia took the letter from the driver's hand, her heart beginning a rapid pounding the moment she recognized Lyle's writing. The note was brief and to the point. Looking up, Julia instructed tersely, "Get your coat, Maggie. We're going out." And at Maggie's questioning gaze, she replied, "Lyle needs us."

Her purpose firm, oddly immune to the frigid cold, Julia stepped out onto the street minutes later, Maggie behind her.

Strangely disoriented, Sophia opened her eyes. It had been a long, black night, filled with pain. Her memory dim, she recalled only Lyle's gentle touch and comforting whisper when she felt she could stand no more. She had

458

silently questioned then how Lyle had come to be beside her in the room she had shared so intimately with Aaron. The answer had escaped her, but her need for him had not.

Wanting to speak to him but strangely unable to form the words, Sophia reached unsteadily for his hand. He gripped it tightly, concern deepening his frown as he leaned closer, his breath brushing her lips.

"How are you feeling, Sophia?" His gold eyes studied her, bathing her with unspoken love as he whispered, "Talk to me, darling. Tell me you're going to be all right. I want you to tell me you believe that as surely as I do."

Sophia attempted to speak, but the words would not move past her dry lips. Noting her distress, Lyle dipped a cloth into a nearby bowl and bathed her face. He waited as she rasped, "It wasn't supposed to be this way . . ."

His expression pained, Lyle whispered in return, "How was it supposed to be, Sophia? Tell me. I'll make it be whatever way you want it to be."

"I thought it was over . . . closed my eyes . . . didn't want to open them again." And then at the pain her words brought to Lyle's face, "Better that way."

Angry, Lyle responded sharply, "Better for whom, Sophia? Better for Weiss? Better for you? Certainly not better for me, or for Rosalie. Don't you know how I felt, thinking you were slipping away from me?"

"I know." A tear slid from Sophia's weary eyes. "Sorry."

A muttered curse escaped Lyle's lips, and he gripped her hand more tightly. "No, don't cry. You've cried enough."

"You don't know what I've done."

Drawing closer still, Lyle rested his cheek lightly against hers. His morning stubble scratched her skin, but she felt only the consolation of his nearness as he whispered, "I know." He paused, swallowing hard. "Why didn't you come to me, Sophia? I thought you knew I'd always be there if you needed me."

459

"Couldn't . . . you shouldn't be here."

Drawing back as her agitation grew, Lyle pressed a finger against her trembling lips.

"Shh. What's done can't be undone, darling."

"It would've been better if I had—"

"Don't say that!" Anger lighting the blazing gold of his eyes, Lyle cupped her face with his palms. "You're good and honest and loving. The world hasn't been good and honest and loving with you in return, and you've suffered, but you're not going to suffer anymore. I'll see to that."

Sophia fought the warmth rising inside her as Lyle whispered, "I'm going to tell you now what I should've told you long ago—before the opportunity again passes me by. I love you, Sophia. I've always loved you. As a friend loves—as a lover loves—in every way a man can love a woman. I've regretted letting you go with all my heart. Nothing I've achieved means anything to me knowing that I gave you up in order to get it. If I had it to do over, I'd take you in my arms and never let you go. Everything that's happened to you is my fault."

"No."

Lyle paused at her denial, then whispered, "Answer me this. If I hadn't pulled back from you that day I held you in my arms . . . if I hadn't decided that my ongoing war with Uncle Matthew placed first with me, that I had to win it at any expense, would you have gone to Aaron Weiss?"

Silent, Sophia returned his stare. The memory of Aaron's dark eyes filled with love, however limited the emotion, the echo of his voice heavy with passion, the wonder of the emotions he evoked within her, the pain of his betrayal—all returned. Incredibly, love still remained.

Her response was a ragged whisper. "I . . . I don't know."

Supreme sadness filling his eyes, Lyle whispered in return, *"I do."*

Weary, strangely numb, Sophia closed her eyes. She felt

Lyle's lips brush hers and she heard the fervor in his voice as he whispered, "I love you, Sophia. Remember that. Take it to sleep with you and hold it in your heart. Try to forgive me . . . and if it's not too late, try to love me the way I love you." She didn't answer and he whispered unevenly as she drifted off to sleep, "Try, darling . . . please try."

Sophia slept, but Lyle did not relinquish her hand. He held it close to his chest, then pressed it to his lips. He hoped. He prayed. He needed another chance. He needed to love her. He needed to make her understand that he would love and protect her all of his life. He needed . . .

Lyle sighed. He needed Sophia, any way she would come to him — as a friend, as a lover, as the one woman for him, forever. He knew that now. Nothing, neither his personal war nor ambition, would come —

A sound at the outer door snapped Lyle to attention. Releasing Sophia's hand to place it gently on the bed beside her, he walked quickly toward the sound, a smile moving across his tired face as he opened the door to see Aunt Julia on the step. She walked into the room, Maggie behind her. Waiting only until they had removed their outerwear and stood hesitantly before him, he took Aunt Julia's hand and drew her to the settee beside him. He motioned Maggie toward the other chair.

Holding his aunt's gaze firmly, he whispered, "Sophia's in the other room. She's very ill, but she's sleeping. I have some things to explain to you, Aunt Julia, so you'll understand everything that's happened completely and so you'll know how important all this is to me. I'm going to tell you how I came to love Sophia, and why I love her, and when I'm done, I hope you'll understand why I'm going to do what I must do."

Aunt Julia's gaze did not waver as Lyle started to speak.

461

* * *

Matthew stood in the doorway of his mill office, staring intently through the glass onto the mill floor. Furiously angry, he attempted to ignore the nagging concern that threatened to negate his ire as the day's production began at the mill, unsupervised.

Damn it, where was Lyle? He was already an hour late without sending any word. It was unlike him, but he knew he should have expected it. Lyle was getting too sure of himself. His success of the past few months—his recent "friendship" with Hope—it was all going to his head. His bastard nephew was beginning to show his true colors, just as he had always known he would.

Straightening his shoulders, Matthew attempted to dismiss the sorrow that thought evoked. He should be happy to see his predictions come to pass so quickly. He should be grateful that the adopted Kingston was finally revealing his true nature. He should be pleased to know that the mill would soon revert back to his sole supervision without the terms of his oral agreement with Lyle being breached.

He knew he should . . . but he somehow wasn't.

Another glance at the wall clock and Matthew gave a low snort of disgust. Stripping off his jacket, he rolled up his sleeves and prepared to step out onto the mill floor. It had been years since he had been forced to work directly with his mill laborers. He had thought that period to be over in his life, that his son would assume the responsibility as it was meant to be.

Matthew frowned, an unexpected sense of loss deepening. Paul had never been "his" son. Paul had been Edith's son from the first day of his birth, but he had refused to recognize that fact until it was almost too late. It had only been in recent months, as Lyle had assumed the position he had always believed Paul would take, that he had begun coming to terms with that truth for the first time in his life.

Forcibly halting his train of thought, shocked at the direction in which it was leading, Matthew took a deep, strengthening breath. He didn't need Paul and he didn't need his bastard nephew! He didn't need anyone! He had worked alone and built up his business by himself, and he could manage the mill alone again!

Lyle unexpectedly stepped into sight on the mill floor and Matthew's mind froze. Something was very wrong. Lyle was carelessly dressed, his face unshaven. Weariness was evident in the deep circles beneath his eyes and in the tight lines of his face, but there was something else there as well — a determination, a resolve that he had never seen before.

Catching and holding his eye, Lyle strode toward him, his gaze as hard as steel, and Matthew suddenly knew . . .

Closing the office door firmly behind him, Lyle approached his uncle directly. He halted within a few feet of him, his eyes meeting his uncle's guarded gaze levelly, and Lyle was momentarily amused at the moment's irony.

"Don't look so apprehensive, Uncle. You're about to have your fondest wish come true."

Matthew stiffened. "And what is that wish, may I ask?"

"You're about to be rid of me."

Matthew's silence revealed his shock and Lyle gave a harsh laugh. "You surprise me, Uncle. I thought this would be the happiest moment of your life."

His expression unexpectedly tense, Matthew offered tightly, "Enough of this ambiguity, Lyle! Tell me what you're saying."

Lyle was suddenly weary. "I'm telling you what you want to hear. I'm saying that I've finally realized what's really important to me — what I may have lost for the sake of a grievance that would not die. I'm telling you that you've won, that our bargain isn't the driving force in my life anymore."

"You're not making any sense. What are you talking about?"

Lyle paused in response, scrutinizing the handsome, tense face of the man who had been his nemesis most of his life.

"Do you really care, *Father?*"

Matthew's face whitened. He took a spontaneous step backwards, his reply emerging in a hiss.

"You're *not* my son!"

"I am." The truth of those words freeing him, Lyle finally smiled. "You know it and I know it, Father."

"I'm not your father, I say! Who put that thought into your mind? Julia?"

"No. I learned the truth when I was seven years old, from a source beyond refuting. I heard it from my dying mother's lips."

Matthew whitened, visibly shaken, and Lyle was struck with a moment's sadness at how deeply he had rocked his father's world by simply claiming true right to his name. He watched the workings of Matthew's lips with unexpected pity as his father sought to form the words of his response.

"You . . . you want me to accept that you believed this ridiculous claim all your life and you never mentioned it before this moment? Do you really expect me to believe that with the rancor of our past exchanges, you never brought it up because you chose not to? You must believe me to be a fool!"

"No, Father, neither you nor I is a fool. I was merely faithful to a promise I made my mother. She told me that she made a grave error that turned you against her. She said she had loved someone before she met you and believed him dead, and that when he suddenly appeared again in her life, she was overwhelmed by her feelings. She said you

464

never forgave her that one terrible mistake and refused to believe that the child she carried was yours, although it *was* yours beyond a doubt. She swore to me that she had never been untrue to you before that day, and was never untrue to you from that day on, although you never spoke to her again. She said she sent the other man away, although she knew you would never acknowledge me and that your pride would always be between us. She said she never intended to tell me the sad truth, but she couldn't carry the secret to her grave."

"You're not my son . . ." Matthew face suddenly old and weary, he whispered, "Christine was a whore. You could be any man's son."

Lyle took a hard step forward, his hands balling into fists as the blood surged to his head—only to be stopped by the unexpected pain in Matthew's eyes as he continued in an anguished whisper. "I loved her. I trusted her, and she betrayed me."

His fury draining in the face of his father's unexpected distress, Lyle whispered in return, "You loved my mother, but not enough to marry her. You sacrificed her to your ambitions and whatever self-interests drove you to do the things you did then." Lyle gave a short, self-deprecating laugh. "I despised you for that. I swore that I would one day make you acknowledge me. I dreamed of the day when I would stand at your side, vindicating my mother by forcing you to concede the truth of my birthright. But I was wrong in thinking that I could ever make you believe other than what you wanted to believe or that I could ever make you concede that the bastard you despised was your son."

Pausing, Lyle continued more softly. "But I'm my father's son more than I realized, so much so that I nearly sacrificed the woman I love to my driving need for retribution. So I'm here to tell you now, Father, that I don't intend to perpetuate that mistake. I intend to correct it, whatever price I may pay, and if it means giving up my newly won position here, then it's done."

Lyle continued softly. "I'm going to take some time off away from this place to try to correct my mistakes. I don't know how long it will take me . . . a week, a month, or maybe two. When everything is well again, I'll come back."

Obviously shaken, Matthew gave a short laugh. "Just like that? No further explanations?" He laughed more harshly. "If you're entertaining any thought that your position will be here waiting for you when you decide to return, you're fooling yourself even more grievously than you've fooled yourself in the past! You're not my son. You have no inherent right here. You're an employee, the same as any other man on that floor out there, and if you walk out of here now, you'll get the same treatment they would get under the same circumstances. You'll be fired."

Lyle's gaze did not waver. "So be it, then. I'll do what I must, and so will you. Good-bye, Father."

"Don't call me that! You're not my son!"

Turning without response, Lyle walked to the door as Matthew declared more vehemently than before, "You're not my son!"

The hypocrisy of those words ringing in his ears, Lyle closed the door behind him.

Rosalie remained silent, watching the confrontation between Lyle and the elder Kingston through the glass partition that separated the office from the mill floor. Her heart pounding, she glanced toward Anna to see she was working along her machine, unaware of the drama being enacted a few yards away.

Rosalie closed her eyes, shaken. Sophia's secret was a difficult burden to carry. Through the long night she had suffered for the promise she had made, certain neither the anger of her mother or her father would keep them from Sophia's side if they knew the severity of her illness. Rosalie withheld a sob, knowing that even now, Sophia could be . . .

"Rosalie . . ."

Startled to find Lyle beside her, Rosalie looked up expectantly to meet his smile. He took her hand with his brief whisper.

"Don't worry about Sophia. She'll be all right."

Turning toward the door, Lyle was gone as quickly as he had appeared.

Suddenly at Rosalie's side, Anna searched her face, anxiety in her eyes as she whispered, "What happened, Rosalie? What did he say to you? Was it something about Sophia?"

Her promise weighing heavily upon her, Rosalie forced a smile. "He said he had seen Sophia this morning, and she was fine."

Unable to say more, Rosalie turned back to her machine, her heart breaking.

The darkness that surrounded her was familiar, but Sophia had not expected the flames. The fiery tongues leaped at her, singeing her, threatening to devour her, even as the pain swelled once more. She could not escape them and she groaned aloud.

She heard concerned voices in response, and sought to open her eyes, but she could not. She felt cool water on her brow, but the fire continued to rage. She swallowed the liquid that met her lips, but the heat consumed it. She cried out in despair, but there was no response.

Then she heard it, a whisper that grew more demanding, and she opened her eyes. She saw Lyle, and she reached out to him, but he faded from sight and the flames soared higher.

* * *

Sophia reached out to him, her eyes wide, searching, and Lyle's panic soared. Helpless against her agony, he watched as she twitched and turned in her bed, mumbling incoherently as he sought to reassure her, but she didn't hear him.

Turning to Dr. Levine as he stood ineffectually nearby, Lyle questioned harshly, "What happened to her? She was fine when I left her an hour ago."

Dr. Levine's expression was grave. "Infection is common in these cases, Mr. Kingston. I had hoped the powders would prevent that complication, but . . ." He shook his head, choosing not to continue.

"What're you saying?" Lyle turned an anxious glance toward the bed. "Surely you can do something . . ."

"I'm doing all that can be done, Mr. Kingston."

Lyle looked back at Sophia. Her glorious eyes were bright with fever, unseeing, her brilliant hair soaked with perspiration, and fear soared inside him.

"We must do something!"

"Cool towels to reduce the fever, force liquids, continue the medicine, and pray that the infection can be checked—that's all we can do."

"Lyle, dear . . ." Turning toward Aunt Julia, Lyle read anguish in the worried lines of her face as she laid a trembling hand on his arm. "We'll stay as long as you need us. Just tell us what you want us to do."

"All right." His heart pounding, Lyle turned to Maggie, "Fill another basin, Maggie, and get more towels. Sophia's going to get better. We'll *make* her get better."

His throat choking at the defeat he read in Dr. Levine's eyes, Lyle crouched beside the bed once more and took Sophia's hand. "Do you hear me, Sophia?" His pledge more sacred than a holy vow, he whispered softly, "I won't leave you again. You're going to get better, and when this is all

468

done, we'll put all this behind us. I love you, Sophia." Lyle paused, his voice breaking as he whispered again, "Do you hear me, darling? I love you . . ."

There was no response.

The luxurious dining room of the Vandermere mansion buzzed with conversation as the dinner party continued. Glancing around a table bright with sterling and crystal, laden with delicacies that were the effort of the Vandermeres' new French chef, Aaron smiled. Bankers, captains of industry, pillars of society surrounded him, and at his side the lovely Kathryn raised a delicate glass of vintage wine to her lips.

At ease in the affluent setting, Aaron rested momentarily on his laurels. He had made an excellent impression on the Vandermere family and their guests in general, and on Kathryn in particular. He knew that as far as the younger women present were concerned, he was the most handsome man in the room. He suppressed a laugh. In a little over twenty-four hours, he already had the fair Kathryn wrapped around his little finger.

Taking a moment to flash the surprisingly shy young woman his most endearing smile, Aaron then turned his attention back to his plate. His facade inwardly cracking, Aaron was strangely weary. Damn! What was wrong with him?

Aaron paused a moment on that thought. The answer was simple. He didn't want to be here. Despite the splendor of his surrounding and the prize that lay at his fingertips waiting for him to snatch it, his enthusiasm was forced. Kathryn, with her warm glances, intelligent conversation, and appealing presence, was not Sophia. She had none of Sophia's flamboyance, either physically or mentally. Her gray eyes held none of Sophia's passion for life, her cultured tones were void of the titillating appeal of Sophia's heavily accented conversation, and he saw in her none of the consistent challenge of the devastating, total woman that Sophia was. In analysis, he liked Kathryn, but he loved Sophia.

However, he silently conceded that his father was right. Kathryn suited this atmosphere in ways that Sophia never would. Kathryn would make him an ideal, socially acceptable wife, and Kathryn's children would suit in a way that Sophia's children never could.

Aaron looked up from his plate to find Kathryn studying him covertly, and the glance he returned colored her delicate complexion. No, his life and his family fortune would never be at risk with Kathryn. Neither would his heart.

His decision abruptly made, anxious to get on with things so he might return to relieve his mind and console Sophia for the difficult step he was certain she had already taken, Aaron smiled more warmly and took Kathryn's hand.

A single lamp burned in the silent bedroom. Outside, the city was dark as Lyle studied Sophia's sleeping form. Seated in the upholstered chair he had pulled up to her bedside, he leaned forward to touch her forehead again, relieved to find the heat there still subdued.

Releasing a relieved breath, Lyle stroked damp tendrils back from Sophia's temple, noting the toll her dire state of health had already taken. The classic lines of her face had grown sharper and deeply shadowed, and the incredible length of her dark lashes lay against cheeks that were frighteningly pale. But he consoled himself that her temperature had been normal for several hours.

Slipping back into his chair, Lyle closed his eyes. Dr. Levine, his age revealing its limitations, had left shortly

470

after Sophia's temperature fell below the danger point, but Aunt Julia and Maggie had been unwilling to leave. He had only succeeded in convincing his aunt to get some rest by accepting their promise to return the next morning. In truth, he was grateful for their help, knowing Sophia's secret was secure in their hands—a situation he could not guarantee under any other circumstances. He had needed that guarantee, since he knew Sophia wouldn't be able to bear for the truth to become general knowledge—not for *her* sake, but for the sake of the shame it would bring down on her parents. That theme had been repeated over and again in Sophia's fevered ramblings, and he sensed it ran through her mind even now, in sleep.

Lyle rubbed his hand against his chin, wincing at the stubble there. He hadn't bathed or shaved since he was summoned by Rosalie. How many days had it been? One? Two? He had lost count. He only knew that each minute had stretched into an hour, and the hours had been endless while Sophia had lain in bed suffering. During those endless hours, he had made a solemn vow. He would make Weiss pay.

Sophia's unexpected whimper brought him to attention, and Lyle slid forward, leaning toward the bed. Her eyes opened unexpectedly and Sophia looked at him, obviously disoriented. A sudden, violent shudder wracked her, startling him in the moment before she began shivering furiously. His heart pounding, Lyle caressed her cheek, finding it surprisingly cool. She didn't speak, and he urged softly, "What's wrong, Sophia? Are you in pain?"

"N—no." Her teeth chattering so profusely that she could barely form the words, Sophia rasped, "C-cold . . . so cold . . ."

Immediately on his feet, Lyle looked around the room, frustration soaring. Striding to the closet, he was relieved to see an extra blanket there, and within moments he had

471

stretched it across the bed—to no avail. Her cape stretched out upon her, and then his own coat, had no effect, and Lyle's panic swelled. Sophia was shivering with increasing violence. The hand he clutched tightly was cold as ice and her lips had taken on a sickly shade of blue when Lyle made a sudden decision.

Kicking off his shoes, Lyle lifted the covers and slid into the bed beside Sophia, his heart drumming louder at the icy feel of her as he drew her into his arms. Dire mental pictures moving across his mind, he clutched her close, willing his warmth into her, whispering soft reassurances that were incoherent even to his own ears.

Uncertain how long he had been clutching her close, Lyle held his breath as the tremors of Sophia's slender frame appeared to ease. Peering down into her face, he thought he saw a lessening of the frightening pallor there as well, and his throat was suddenly tight as she returned his gaze with true clarity for the first time. His voice ragged, he whispered, "Are you feeling better, darling?"

Sophia's short nod sending his spirits soaring, he pressed his lips lightly against hers, then adjusted her more comfortably in his arms. Tucking her head into the curve of his shoulder, he whispered against her hair, "This is where you belong, Sophia—in my arms. You've always belonged here, but we were both too blind to see it." He paused momentarily in silent self-condemnation, continuing. "But that's all in the past now. Don't try to slip away from me again, because I won't let you."

Still, except for an occasional shudder moments later, Sophia lay quietly nestled in his arms, and Lyle closed his eyes, determined never to let her go.

Awakening from a troubled dream, Sophia was suddenly alert to the male presence lying beside her in bed, the strong arms that clutched her close, and the warm breath fanning her cheek. She strained to see the shadowed face so close to hers, suddenly uncertain. But the head that lay beside hers on the pillow was covered with light hair, not dark, and the eyes that slowly opened to meet hers were not an unfathomable black, but a warm, glowing gold.

Pain still with her, uncertain of many things, Sophia closed her eyes, finally at rest.

Chapter Twenty-two

In his shirtsleeves, Matthew walked between the machines. He ignored the curious glances he received from his employees—the same glances he had been receiving in the time since Lyle had made his bold declaration and walked out of the mill. He gritted his teeth, his distaste for the position he had been forced to assume growing greater by the day.

Noting a sneer from a nearby worker, Matthew cautioned sharply, "Keep your eyes on your work, Marco. You're not irreplaceable, you know!"

Satisfied when the man turned back to the loom without response, he looked around him. The few glances that met his were not friendly, and he was aware that direct supervision had never been his forte. He knew it never would be.

Back in the office a few minutes later, Matthew slammed the door behind him, grateful when the din of the mill was again muted by glass. He had forgotten how much he despised working on the floor and how endless a job it was to keep the workers on their toes and the work flowing smoothly. Under any other circumstances he would have—

All thought abruptly leaving his mind, Matthew stared with disbelief toward the entrance of the mill as the door opened to reveal Edith, her conservatively stylish elegance never more obvious as she stood imperiously there. She walked directly toward the office without a glance at either side of her, and he prepared himself as she opened the door, entered, and closed it sharply behind her. She raked him with her gaze, disapproval of his appearance in every quiver of her dilated nostrils as she demanded, "Where's Lyle?"

Silently cursing, Matthew responded, "He's not here right now."

Edith's smile was pure acid. "So it's true, then!"

"What's true, Edith? What are you talking about?"

"The story that's being bantered all over town, that Lyle walked out of here last week! That's he's through at Kingston Mill!"

"The story is false."

"If the story is false, where is he? Why isn't he here?"

"He's taking care of an emergency—some personal matters. He'll be back when they're settled."

"Damn you, Matthew! What's the matter with you? He walked in here and declared himself a holiday, that's what he did! He's taken off for parts unknown, and like the fool that you are, you've taken to the floor to fill in for him! Are you insane? Don't you realize you've been afforded the opportunity you've been waiting for? Why haven't you attempted to replace him? Why don't you have a temporary supervisor sitting in here so that the word will get around that he need not even attempt to return? Why are you standing there in ineffectual silence when you should be—"

"That's enough, Edith!"

"What did you say?"

"I said, that's enough, and I meant it." Unyielding in the face of Edith's tight-lipped fury, Matthew continued. "The mill is *my* business, not yours, and I'll handle it in whatever way I see fit."

Momentarily silent, Edith responded with careful control. "You seem to forget, Matthew, that a part of this mill

475

is in *my* name—a legality my father insisted upon when we—"

"I'm tired of hearing about your father, too!" Suddenly unwilling to discuss the matter any further, he directed with quiet authority, "Go home, Edith. You have no place here. If I had wanted to tell you about my dealings with Lyle, I would have. I'll replace Lyle if and when I'm ready, and not before, and I'm not going to let you maneuver or push me into anything I'm not ready to do, so don't try."

Suddenly weary, Matthew scrutinized his wife's open shock at his dismissal of her. Unexpectedly, he was struck with sympathy for the plight of this forceful, intelligent woman who abruptly realized all manner of coercion and persuasion was useless. Speaking softly, he said with more understanding than he had exhibited in many years, "I'm sorry, Edith. You're stunned, unhappy, frustrated. You're wondering if I'm really the man you married. The truth is, I'm not certain I am anymore. I only know that whatever I do in this mill now is *my* decision, and you have no part in it." He paused again and added, "Please, dear, go home."

Her eyes filling at the unexpected softening of her husband's tone, Edith whispered, "Matthew, can't you tell me what's wrong?"

Taking a step toward her, realizing he couldn't explain his reaction to this unexpected situation with Lyle simply because he couldn't explain it to himself, Matthew kissed his wife firmly on the lips, smiling sadly as a tear trailed down her cheek. He wiped it away with his palm, then kissed her again.

"Go home, Edith."

Holding his gaze a moment longer, Edith turned and left. Her eyes still glazed, she did not look back.

* * *

Gasping, breathless in her attempt to draw herself to a seated position in bed, Sophia surrendered to her weakness and lay back against the pillow, closing her eyes. Opening them again a moment later, she looked around the bedroom where the past helpless few days had stretched into a lifetime.

Sophia closed her eyes as pain stabbed anew. Cramping, nausea, intermittent pain, and a debilitating weakness were still her constant companions, but she knew she could not complain. Lyle had saved her life with his care. She didn't have to question the reason. He had made it very clear. He loved her in a way that she had never fully realized he loved her.

An uncontrollable sadness bringing a new depth to her pain, Sophia recalled the passion with which those same words had been spoken to her by another man—in this same room . . . in this same bed. She could not seem to drive them from her mind.

Sophia looked up to see Julia Kingston bustle into the room, and she felt a familiar pang of disquiet. Lyle's aunt and her housekeeper had been so good to her. They had fussed over her, bathed her, brushed her hair, and changed her clothes, and she wondered at the generosity of spirit they showed her—for she was certain they knew what she had done.

Pausing in her step, Julia Kingston questioned, "Are you all right, Sophia? Would you like me to call Lyle or Dr. Levine?"

"I'm fine." Sophia attempted a smile. "But I'd appreciate it if you'd call Lyle."

At her bedside in a moment, Lyle appeared alarmed. "What's the matter, Sophia?" He laid his hand on her brow, frowning. "You don't have a fever."

"I want to get up."

"Get up?"

"I want to walk, Lyle. I have to start taking care of myself sooner or later."

Lyle's short laugh was incredulous. "You can hardly hold up your head. Do you realize how much blood you lost?"

Sophia did not blink. "Yes, I do."

Lyle leaned closer, his expression intense. "No, you don't. You almost died, Sophia. Your body was almost drained before Dr. Levine managed to stop your bleeding. Your infection hasn't been completely cured, either. You still run fevers occasionally and you'll be a long while in healing, so I'm telling you now that I don't intend to get you on your feet one minute before Dr. Levine says you're ready. Understand?"

Sophia's eyes sparked with momentary anger.

"You're not my boss or my keeper, Lyle!"

Lyle moved within a hairbreadth of her lips. "Yes, I am. So get used to it."

"I *want* to get up!" Sophia pressed insistently.

"And I want to fly, but I can't."

"Oh, Lyle!" Sophia couldn't suppress a weary smile. "You take advantage of me."

"Yes." Lyle brushed her lips with his. "I do. But you'll have plenty of chance to get even with me when you're better."

Aware that Aunt Julia had slipped out of the room the moment Lyle had taken charge, Sophia questioned softly, "How long will that be, Lyle? I want to know."

"Dr. Levine says a few weeks. Maybe a month."

"That's too long. I have to be out of here soon. Aaron—"

"Forget Aaron."

"This is his house."

"It's yours as long as you need it. I'll make sure of that."

"Lyle, please . . ."

478

"I said, I'll take care of it." Dismissing her worried glance, Lyle continued smoothly. "And now you're in for a treat. Maggie's made some of her special Scottish broth. You're going to love it."

"I'm not hungry."

Lyle's eyes narrowed. "I said, you're going to love it."

A fleeting smile touched Sophia's lips as she wagged a finger weakly. "You wait, *mi bello ragazzo*. When I'm better, you'll be sorry."

"Oh no I won't. Because then you'll take care of me." Pausing, Lyle raised an affected hand to his brow. "I've been having these headaches, you see."

Sophia laughed aloud. "And I can cure mumps and sties . . ."

A sudden loud crack sounded in the room and Sophia jumped, then whitened. She stared at the picture that had fallen off the wall to land, its protective glass cracked, on the floor. She looked back up at Lyle, apprehensive.

"It's nothing." Noting her obvious alarm, Lyle smiled. "I can get the glass fixed."

Sophia shook her head. "It's not the glass . . . A picture falling off the wall means a visitor is on the way."

Lyle held her gaze firmly, aware of the direction her thoughts were taking. "Nobody comes in here unless I let him, Sophia."

Sophia felt the reassuring warmth of Lyle's mouth as it touched hers briefly, and then repeated, "Nobody."

Aunt Julia heaved an exhausted sigh, then turned toward Maggie, where the silent Scotswoman sat beside her in the carriage. Her smile wobbled.

"Lyle loves Sophia very much, doesn't he, Maggie."

"Aye."

"Do you think she loves him, too?"

479

Pausing Maggie slowly nodded. "The lass loves him, I've no doubt. But it's not as simple as that."

Julia whispered, "He wants to marry her."

"Aye, I know, but I've me doubts about what the lass will do." Maggie shook her head. "She's a deep one. I'm thinkin' she loved the other laddie and willna' turn from one to the other easily, despite the calloused way the other laddie treated her."

Julia nodded, her eyes following the curve of the street as their carriage turned onto Broadway. "I feel the same, and I've been wondering if Lyle realizes what a difficult fight he has ahead of him."

Maggie's strong brows furrowed as she returned the gaze of the small, anxious woman beside her with concern. "It's in me mind that Master Lyle is primed for a fight. Ye've but to hear the mention of young Master Weiss's name to see his color rise."

"I'm frightened, Maggie."

"Ye've no cause to worry." The old housekeeper's chin rose with obvious pride. "The young master's up to the task."

"I don't mean that." The depth of her inner torment reflected in her voice, Julia whispered, "If the girl should decide against Lyle, it'll break his heart."

In an uncharacteristic display of emotion, Maggie paused to blink back tears. "Aye, it will."

The silence that followed was broken by Julia's sudden intake of breath as her home came into view. The black carriage parked in front of it was familiar. She exchanged an anxious glance with Maggie, her worst fears confirmed as Matthew stepped down onto the sidewalk as soon as her own carriage drew to a halt.

Drawing the door open, Matthew extended his hand courteously toward her. Facing her brother in the sitting room minutes later, Julia immediately dispensed with formality. "What do you want, Matthew?"

His anger apparent, Matthew was direct in return. "I want to know why Lyle came into the mill almost a week ago and for all intents and purposes threw everything he had worked for away with a few short words! I want to know what happened to him, what he's doing—where he is. He hasn't been back to his rooms in days." He paused, his lips tightening. "I'd be a fool if I didn't realize it has something to do with a woman—and I know it isn't Hope who's gotten him in this state. It's that redheaded tart, Sophia Marone, isn't it?"

Julia raised her chin, her emotions carefully controlled. "What makes you think I know what you're talking about? And if I did, why would I possibly tell you? Whatever Lyle is doing is *his* business, and no one else's."

Studying her face intently for long moments, Matthew whispered, "You know what's going on, and I want to know, too. I've considered Lyle many things in the past, but I've never considered him a fool—yet he's behaving like one. There's no explanation other than a woman that fits his behavior, and the only woman he's ever been really interested in is that Italian slut."

"You'll watch your language if you have any hopes of continuing this conversation, Matthew! You're blackening the name of a young woman you don't truly know."

"And you *do* know her, is that it?" Matthew grasped her arms with unexpected fervor. "What's going on, Julia? Tell me!"

"Let go of me, Matthew."

Appearing momentarily shocked at his own behavior, Matthew released her and took an involuntary step back. "I'm sorry." Pausing, he continued more softly. "But I'm trying to understand what's happened, Julia, can't you see that? I want to know why Lyle walked into the mill and sacrificed everything he worked for without a blink of an eye. I know he didn't do it lightly. I want to understand . . ."

"I doubt that you *could* understand, Matthew."

Matthew stiffened. "What do you mean by that?"

"I mean that your *son* is more of a man than you've ever been, or could ever hope to be." That statement delivered without malice, Julia continued softly. "Lyle's awakened to the reality that there's more of you in him than he cared to see. He doesn't want to make the same mistakes you made, because he doesn't want to turn into a man like you. He doesn't want to sacrifice the woman he loves to his pride. It's as simple as that . . . and that's why I said I doubted that you could understand."

Matthew's jaw tightened, and Julia felt a familiar futility rise as he stated flatly, "Lyle is *not* my son. He has earned my concern, however, and you're right in other things you've said. I *don't* understand. That young woman is a trollop. She'll drag him down to her level and then she'll—"

"That's enough, Matthew!" Her eyes welling, Julia whispered, "You're incapable of understanding, so don't even try. But I'll tell you now, my dear brother, that I respect Lyle for what he's doing. I respect him for his compassion, his sensitivity, for his willingness to accept his portion of the blame for any misdeeds, and for the scope of love of which he is capable. I respect him and any decisions he will make in a way that I never respected you, Matthew, because he has *earned* my respect as you never did."

Matthew held his sister's gaze in silence for long moments before turning abruptly and walking out of the room. Julia raised her chin, unaware of the tear that trailed down her cheek at the sound of the front door closing behind him.

* * *

482

Aaron fidgeted in his seat as the train rocked and swayed along the tracks. Each progressive stop had increased his anticipation until he was uncertain he would be able to bear the wait until the lights of the city of Paterson came into view.

Attempting to occupy his mind, Aaron sat back and cautiously reviewed again the week he had spent with the Vandermeres. First into his thoughts was the particularly affectionate farewell Kathryn had given him that afternoon. He remembered still the warmth of her slenderness in his arms as she had fervently returned his kiss. He remembered that she had pressed herself against him, her body pulsing with subdued passion. He smiled. He had gone to the Vandermeres hoping to commence a careful campaign, but victory was now a foregone conclusion. Kathryn was his anytime he wanted her.

Aaron's smile paled. The problem was, he didn't want her.

Aaron took a moment to correct the fall of his jacket against his shoulders, annoyed with himself that he had worn this new, particularly expensive garment for the long journey home. He knew the reason he had, of course. He wanted to look his best for Sophia. He wanted to show her what she had missed, that he looked better than she remembered. And then he wanted, more than he had ever wanted anything in his life, to *prove* to her what she had missed—kiss by loving kiss, caress by heated caress.

Realizing his body was reacting predictably to the stimulus of his thoughts, Aaron gave a short laugh. Even the thought of Sophia aroused him, but he knew his reaction to her was not purely physical. Sophia's fire—her enthusiasm and zest for life, the challenge in her eyes, and the pure, unadulterated joy which she stirred in him with the briefest glance—was a total assault on his emotions. It annoyed him to admit to himself that she had stolen his heart, that this affair which he had begun with devious motives and intentions in mind had backfired on him until he was the one who had become a moth to Sophia's flame, fascinated by her, addicted to her, willing to do anything to keep her.

His mind moving momentarily to the demand he had made so angrily of her before he left, Aaron unconsciously firmed the set of his jaw. But he was not so much a fool for Sophia that he would allow her to hold a pregnancy over his head, and he had told her that in no uncertain terms. He consoled himself that whatever discomfort she had experienced in doing what needed to be done was in the past now. He had already determined his strategy in dealing with it. He would refuse to discuss the details of the matter with her, treating it as if it never happened. He would wait patiently until Sophia was again physically healed and would prove to her with his loving attentions that the sacrifice she had made for him was worthwhile. He would spoil her, indulge her, cater to her. He would dress her in silks far more beautiful than her most extravagant dreams, and he would provide Madame Tourneau the proper incentives to bring Sophia's work along as quickly as possible. With the pleasure of the present, he would force that past unpleasantness from her mind.

As for Kathryn Vandermere—that would be his secret until it could be kept a secret no longer. He would impress his parents with the need for caution, lest the Vandermeres become suspicious of undue haste. He would satisfy their anxiety with the promise he had made to return to visit Kathryn the following weekend.

His heart beginning a heavy pounding as the train began its approach to the Paterson terminal, Aaron drew himself erect and withdrew his watch from his pocket. Seven o'clock. It was late. He had wanted to leave the Vandermeres earlier, but Kathryn had pleaded . . .

Irritated as the vision of Kathryn's cloying smile returned, he jammed his watch back in his pocket and reached up to the overhead rack for his coat. He would send his bag home and go directly to the Park Avenue address to see Sophia. If he became too involved to tear himself away, he would see his father tomorrow. Sophia's face replaced Kathryn's in his mind's eye, and Aaron felt his heart begin a new pounding.

The old man could wait—whether he liked it or not.

Lyle listened intently as Sophia's halting whisper drained weakly away. He raised a hand to her forehead and smiled as she protested his caution.

"I'm not sick. I'm just tired."

But Lyle knew Sophia did not see what he saw. She didn't see the total lack of color that lent her appearance an almost ethereal air. Nor did she see the new gauntness to the graceful planes of her face, or the dark circles that emphasized the alarming brilliance of her eyes. She wasn't aware of the overwhelming frailty of the picture she presented, as if she were a fragile porcelain doll that must be handled delicately or it would break.

Neither did Sophia truly realize how close she had come to death. Lyle tensed at the thought, the possibility of having lost her still overwhelming. It haunted him, awake and sleeping, and had become one of the main reasons he had refused to leave her side, even at night. He had not slept in her bed since that first night when, sick and shivering, she had clung to him so desperately.

Pressing a light kiss against her lips, he whispered, "I know you're tired, darling, but there are some things I want to discuss with you now that Aunt Julia and Maggie have gone." And then at the revealing twitch of her cheek, "Are you uncomfortable with them, Sophia? Is that it?"

485

"No. They've been very kind. It's just that I feel so helpless."

"It's only for a little while. You'll be better soon, and then we'll get you out of here."

"Lyle, I—"

The sound of a key in the front-door lock jerked Lyle's head up abruptly. He heard Sophia's sharp intake of breath as he turned toward the living room with a step just short of a run. He was nearly at the door when it opened to reveal Aaron Weiss standing there.

Moving aggressively forward, Lyle growled, "Get out of here, Weiss."

Weiss took a step into the room and slammed the door shut behind him, demanding, "What are you doing here, Kingston? Where's Sophia?"

"I said, get out . . ."

"You seem to be a little confused!" Aaron bristled, "This is *my* house, not yours, and I want to know where Sophia is!"

The heat of Lyle's fury lent a red-hot haze to his vision as his hands balled into fists and he rasped, "You may have paid the rent on this place, but you don't belong here anymore. You sacrificed that right when you left a week ago. I'm warning you now, Weiss, the only way you're going to take another step into this house is over my dead body."

Weiss's reply was a snarl. "Where is she?"

A weak call from the bedroom snapped both their heads in its direction. Weiss started toward the sound and Lyle swung, his fist connecting sharply with Aaron's chin, sending him staggering backward against the door.

Taking a moment to regain his senses, Aaron lunged toward him, halting abruptly as Sophia called again, "Please, Lyle . . . Aaron . . . I don't want you to fight! Lyle, please let Aaron come in."

·The agitation in Sophia's voice more than he could bear, Lyle hesitated, then stepped abruptly to the side, allowing Aaron past him. Entering the bedroom behind Weiss, he walked directly to Sophia's bedside as Aaron froze in the doorway in apparent shock at his first sight of her.

The strain of Aaron's appearance was apparent as Sophia strove to speak. Lyle crouched beside her, taking her hand as his gaze fused with hers and he whispered, "You don't have to talk to him, Sophia."

Her eyes suddenly brimming, Sophia rasped in return, "I have to see him sooner or later, Lyle. He's not solely to blame for my condition. I'm as guilty as he."

"No, Sophia. You—"

"Please, Lyle. I just want this to be over."

Hesitant, uncertain as he scrutinized Sophia's quiet adamancy, Lyle nodded abruptly. "All right. But I'm not going to leave you alone with him."

Sophia smiled weakly. *"Caro* Lyle. Please trust me."

Her plea cutting deeply, Lyle looked up at Weiss as he stood unmoving a few steps away. The desire to bring the vicious, selfish bastard to his knees never stronger, Lyle whispered rigidly, "Just for a few minutes, and then I'm going to throw him out, whether he's finished talking or not."

Turning abruptly, Lyle strode past Weiss into the living room. Standing stiffly just out of sight of the bedroom door, he ran a shaking hand through his hair and attempted to control the anxiety suddenly besetting him.

On his knees beside the bed in a moment, Aaron grasped Sophia's hand. It was as cold as death, and Aaron shivered. Sophia's face was gaunt and white. Her eyes were haunted. Panic overwhelmed him as Sophia sought to

487

extricate her hand from his grasp and he rasped, "Tell me what happened, Sophia."

Sophia's struggle suddenly ceased. "What happened? It didn't go well, Aaron, but it's done. You're safe from the humiliation of my bastard child."

Aaron touched Sophia's pale cheek, vicious knots twisting in his stomach at the shadows of pain there as she spoke again. "I hadn't given a thought to how I must look, but I can see in your eyes that I look poorly."

"No." Aaron shook his head. "You're still beautiful."

Sophia didn't smile. "If I am, I'm beautiful only on the outside. Inside I'm as ugly as the deed I committed."

Aaron's throat was suddenly tight as he rasped, "I . . . I don't want to talk about it, Sophia. It's over—done. It's in the past." He swallowed and continued. "Neither am I going to ask you what Kingston's doing here, and why he thinks he has the right to order me out of this house. I'm back now, and I'll take care of you."

"As you took care of me before, Aaron?" Sophia's eyes did not waver. "Will you love and cherish me as you did before?" Answering her own question, Sophia shook her head. "No, I think not."

Aaron clutched her hand more tightly. "You knew I was coming back to you. I told you I would."

"Yes, I remember—only too well." Sophia's eyes fluttered weakly closed and Aaron's panic swelled in the moment before she opened them again to continue with obvious resolution. "I wanted to talk to you so I could tell you the reasons why I did as you demanded. I wanted you to know I didn't do it out of fear of your threats or the disgrace I would suffer, but . . . but I realize now that there aren't any reasons that are good enough. I can't forgive myself, Aaron . . . and I can't forgive you."

"No, Sophia . . . no." He sought to draw her into his arms, to kiss the lips that had spoken the words he

488

dreaded to hear, but Sophia avoided him. Her eyes were cold as he whispered, "You're ill, and you aren't thinking clearly. You'll feel differently in a few days. I'll stay with you. I'll take care of you."

"It's too late, Aaron."

"Sophia . . ." Aaron's voice broke on a low plea. "I love you . . . and you love me."

Tears streamed freely from Sophia's eyes as she responded, "I'm going to leave here as soon as I'm able."

"No!"

"You heard her, Weiss. Get away from her."

Suddenly beside the bed, Lyle tore Sophia's hand from his, his expression rabid as he hissed, "Go home, Weiss. Don't come back."

His hatred for the bastard Kingston never stronger, Aaron slowly drew himself to his feet. His hands knotted into fists as he took a quick step forward, only to be halted by Sophia's rasp, "If you love me as you say you do, Aaron, you'll go now."

Aaron's head snapped back to Sophia with disbelief. She was asking him to leave! He swallowed, and attempted a smile. "You don't mean that, Sophia. You don't really want me to go."

Sophia was breathing rapidly, her face paling to a frightening gray as she responded breathlessly, "I do. Please . . ."

Shaken as much by Sophia's obvious physical distress as he was by the words she spoke, Aaron was unable to oppose her. "I'll come back tomorrow, Sophia," he whispered. "You'll feel differently then."

"No, she won't!"

Turning toward Kingston, Aaron did not deign to reply. He looked back at Sophia once more. "I'll see you tomorrow, darling."

Turning abruptly, Aaron walked unsteadily toward the

door, aware of Kingston's footsteps close behind him. Out of sight of the bedroom, Aaron turned to stand his ground as Lyle grasped his arm, warning menacingly, "Don't try to come back here, Weiss."

Aaron ripped his arm free of Lyle's furious grip, seething. "This is *my* house and Sophia belongs to me! You're the outsider here, Kingston! Sophia doesn't need you anymore. I'll take care of her."

"I've seen how you take care of Sophia." Lyle's gaze burning shafts of light, he hissed, "Bastard! You almost killed her!"

Aaron blinked, then shook his head. "You're lying. She's weak, but—"

"You're the one who's lying—to yourself now, just as you lied to Sophia when you said you loved her."

"I do love her."

"You don't know the meaning of the word!"

"And *you* do . . ."

Lyle drew back, slashing viciously with the hot, burning blade of his fury. "I know that I love Sophia enough to accept any child she could give me. I know I love her enough not to force her into a despicable act that would tear her heart in two. I know that I love her enough not to abandon her to bleed to death in her lonely bed. Bastard! You betrayed Sophia once and she almost died! I'm not going to give you a chance to do it again."

"Aren't you?" Regaining control of his emotions, Aaron laughed harshly. "You think you're in command here, don't you, Kingston? Well, you aren't. Sophia's hurt, and she's listening to you now, but this situation is temporary. The fright she suffered will all begin to fade a few days from now . . . a week at the most . . . and then she'll start remembering what it was like between us—"

"You swine . . ."

"She'll want me back, Kingston." Aaron laughed again,

his self-confidence growing with each word he spoke. "Because I had her first. She won't forget the commitment made in loving me totally, without holding back."

Suddenly rocked from his feet as Lyle shoved him roughly, Aaron staggered a few steps backward, righting himself as Lyle ordered, "Get out, now!"

Aaron stared at Kingston's enraged expression, suddenly determined not to allow him the satisfaction of a fight. He whispered a quiet threat in return.

"Take good care of Sophia, Kingston, because if anything happens to her, I'll hold you personally responsible."

Aware that Kingston was shuddering with suppressed fury, Aaron adjusted his coat with slow deliberation, then picked up his hat.

Pausing with his hand on the knob, his eyes as hard as onyx, Aaron whispered, "I'm going now, but I'll be back. You can try to keep me away, but in the end, Sophia won't let you. You see, she loves me."

Smiling as Lyle pushed his hand off the doorknob and jerked open the door, Aaron stepped out onto the doorstep. He laughed aloud as Lyle slammed the door in his face, but his laughter, forced for effect, rapidly faded.

Starting down the steps, he turned into the frigid wind, immune to its bite as he raised his hand to signal a passing hack. Moments later, his face as hard as stone, Aaron climbed inside.

Sophia closed her eyes as the muffled conversation in the next room grew more heated. It halted abruptly, and her heart jumped at the sounds of struggle. She heard the front door open and slam closed. In the silence that followed, she thought of the words of love with which this whole affair had begun — and the bitterness that remained.

The low, mourning wail inside her mind resumed.

491

Stricken to the heart, she clamped her hands over her ears, willing away the sorrowful sound that would not cease.

Lyle paused to regain his composure as the sound of Weiss's laughter faded away. His hatred of the man an intense ache inside him, he turned and marched resolutely back into Sophia's room.

He halted as he stepped through the doorway. Eyes squeezed tightly closed, Sophia lay with her hands covering her ears, her face a mask of grief.

Sophia's distress more than he could bear, Lyle moved immediately to her side. Removing her hands from her ears, he took her into his arms, whispering, "It's over, Sophia. You never have to see him again."

Sophia and Kingston . . . Kingston and Sophia . . . The words drummed through Aaron's brain as the carriage rattled through the dark streets, tormenting him. Sophia had sent him away, and even now she was probably calling Kingston to her bedside.

Sophia's pale, wasted image returned, and a sudden thickness in Aaron's throat turned to pain. What had he done to her? He hadn't realized the danger in what he had asked her to do. If he had he wouldn't have—

Aaron halted in that thought. If he had known the risk, would he have insisted anyway? Aaron closed his eyes, refusing to face the answer. The knot in his throat tightened, squeezing unexpected tears from his eyes. Sophia had suffered . . . nearly died, while he had spent the time seeking Kathryn Vandermere's favor.

Consoling himself a moment later, Aaron told himself that Sophia loved him. Kingston had been there for her, and she was grateful, but gratitude could not replace love. He forced a smile. He'd get her back.

All sign of his emotional upheaval carefully erased, Aaron approached the front entrance of the Weiss mansion. He smiled as the door opened abruptly to reveal his father standing in the foyer. As he entered, he noted that his suitcase was on the floor just inside the door, obviously where it had been placed after being delivered from the railroad terminal.

Noticeably irritated, his father did not bother to smile in return.

"Hello, Aaron. I admit to surprise that you bothered to come home tonight at all. It was nice of you to send your dirty clothes home to your mother and me so we might know you were back in the city, however." Pausing to allow his sarcasm to be totally absorbed, he continued more tightly. "How did it go at the Vandermeres?"

"Very well." Aaron arched a brow. "Did you have any doubts?"

"And Kathryn?"

"It's all taken care of, Father. I'm going back next weekend. She's mine whenever I want her," Aaron stated flatly.

"You're so sure."

"Yes."

Samuel's cheek twitched with suppressed anger. "Vain, arrogant young pup!"

"It's what you wanted, isn't it?"

Samuel stared hard at his son. "You don't intend to make it any easier for me, do you?"

"Why should I?" His resentment openly displayed, Aaron responded tightly, "Have you made it easy on me? You know how I feel about all this."

"Yes, I do. You'd prefer me to ignore the fact that you're in love with a beguiling young whore."

"Sophia's not a whore!" Furious, Aaron took off his hat and slapped it down on the foyer table. "She doesn't meet the standards you've set for my wife, but she isn't—"

His lined face suddenly livid, Samuel rasped, "I don't intend to stand here listening to you defend your mistress in one breath while you talk about the woman you intend to marry in the next!"

"This duplicity was your idea, remember, Father?"

"And you went along with it so easily. I'm ashamed to say that you took to the idea as if you were born to it."

"So you say!"

Samuel shook his head. "The damndest thing is, I feel sorry for Kathryn Vandermere. She doesn't really know what she's getting into, does she?"

"Do any of us ever know for sure?" Aaron responded without a trace of a smile.

"Perhaps not. But my own personal feelings aside, I'll expect you to follow through with your trip to Long Island this weekend, and every weekend for as long as it takes to accomplish your purpose. And I caution you, Aaron," Samuel's small eyes hardened, "you will not seduce Kathryn Vandermere as you have every other young woman you've ever shown an interest in. You will treat her with respect until you place your ring on her finger."

Aaron laughed harshly. "Do you have any instructions for afterward, Father?"

Samuel's gaze did not flicker. "No, I can only assume by your past success that you need no guidance there." Pausing, Samuel continued. "Your mother is waiting for you in the sitting room. You'll go in to see her now and you'll relieve the many anxieties she's suffered, even if you have to lie through your teeth to do it. Do you understand me, Aaron?"

Aaron was no longer smiling. "I understand you."

Turning, Samuel continued in abrupt conclusion. "As for myself, I've had enough for tonight. Good night."

Watching his father walk laboriously up the staircase,

494

Aaron felt a familiar resentment swell. Because of an old man's fears, he had almost lost the woman he loved to another man. The thought rankled. But the situation was temporary. He would marry Kathryn Vandermere, but before he did, he would get Sophia back. And when Sophia was in his arms where she belonged, no one . . . *no one* . . . would ever force him to let her go again.

That thought allowing him the consolation he needed to get him through the night, Aaron turned toward the sitting room as his father closed his bedroom door behind him.

Chapter Twenty-three

Aaron slapped the jacquard pattern he had been attempting to study down on the desk in front of him, his frustration soaring. The angry sound raised the head of the clerk seated outside his office door, but Aaron paid the fellow's curious glance little mind as he drew himself abruptly to his feet and gave the wastepaper basket beside his feet a savage kick. The basket bounced off the far wall, scattering paper in all directions as Aaron resumed the tense pacing he had abandoned a few minutes earlier.

Three weeks had passed since he had returned from Long Island that first time to find Sophia ill and in the care of Lyle Kingston, and Aaron had finally conceded that wresting her away from the bastard Kingston wasn't going to be as easy as he had thought. Three weeks, during which he had managed to talk to Sophia three times . . .

Damn that Kingston! Jerking at his collar with complete disregard for the damage he did his meticulous appearance, Aaron stripped off his tie and threw it on a nearby chair, realizing even as he did that it would not relieve the anger choking him. Were he not so furious, he would have admired the strategy with which Kingston had met the situation. It had been brilliant. Dispensing with the need for a personal confrontation, Kingston had arranged to have the doctor waiting for him when he came to visit Sophia the morning after he returned from his trip to Long Island.

Aaron frowned as he recalled Dr. Levine's scrutiny and the

contempt he had read in the old man's eyes as the doctor had spoken in a hard, flat voice.

"I must say that your appearance on this scene clarifies a situation that I previously found very confusing, Mr. Weiss. And since you weren't on hand during my patient's most critical period, I think there are some things I should make perfectly clear to you. Sophia is very weak and her condition is unstable. In fact, she's lucky to be alive at all. She was extremely upset when I arrived this morning, and I can tell you now that her emotional condition has impacted negatively on the slow progress she has been achieving. Stress is too draining on Sophia's limited strength."

Aaron recalled his instinctive protest, to which the doctor replied, "Do you profess to love this woman — or at least care about her in some degree, Mr. Weiss?" Shaking his head, the old man had then muttered, "No, don't answer that. I don't think I want to hear your response. Suffice it for me to say that my patient nearly succumbed to her condition a few days ago, and that a setback at this point may be irreversible."

Pausing for effect, the doctor had continued. "I understand this is your house and you feel you have a right to free access here. That point is obviously well taken, but it doesn't change the fact that in exercising that right, you'll be putting Sophia in danger. Neither can Sophia be moved from here with complete safety now. Maybe in two or three weeks . . . I can't say exactly how long . . . she'll be strong enough. Of course, you have the right to throw her out on the street . . ."

At the tense twitch of Aaron's cheek, the old man had continued. "But if you *really* care for her you'll allow her to recuperate slowly with only those around her who afford her positive reinforcement."

Aaron's pacing grew more intense as he recalled his departure immediately after that session. He had been allowed two visits with Sophia since that time, each fully supervised and limited. Those visits had been enough, however, to confirm that he wanted Sophia more than he ever had, that his enforced separation from her only made him more determined to get her back, and that she *was* steadily progressing toward good health. She had, in fact, looked so beautiful to him on his last visit, with a faint tracing of color returning to her cheeks and some of the spark returning to her wary eyes, that he had almost been tempted to put an end to the whole charade then and there by taking her into his arms and by refusing to let her go.

He had not done that, however, and he knew instinctively that time was running short. He knew that he need speak to Sophia alone soon or he might lose her. And he also knew that his feelings were such that he would take any risk that was needed before he would allow that to happen.

Totally disgusted with his own ineffectiveness, Aaron drew his frantic pacing to a halt. The irony of his present situation was galling. His life was falling to pieces around him on one front, the most important front, while he was having tremendous success on another. Throughout the grueling ordeal with Sophia and Kingston, he had returned to Long Island each weekend to pay determined court to Kathryn, and he was well aware that he had won Kathryn's parents over totally. So well had they accepted him that he had decided to stay away for a week in order to slow the rush of events. Above all, he knew he must win Sophia back before any word of a possible betrothal got out or he would lose her for good.

Walking unconsciously toward the window, Aaron stared out at the bleak February sky. Clouds rushed overhead, blocking out the sun as the wind whipped through the streets with an almost galelike force. It was bitter cold as it had been most of the month of January, the only point in his favor, for Dr. Levine seemed reluctant to chance allowing Sophia out while weather conditions were so poor. Aaron was grateful for that, for he sensed Sophia's first outing would take her away from him, and he knew that there was only one place where she could go.

Cursing himself for his thoughtless panic that had forced this whole chain of events, Aaron made a silent, threefold oath. First, he would get Sophia back. Second, he would see that Lyle Kingston paid dearly for taking Sophia away from him, even for so short a time. Third, he would never let Sophia go again.

Evening had again come as Sophia walked slowly into the living room, her step deliberate and paced. Day and night had passed without distinction during the weeks she had lain gravely ill. It had only been during the past week that time had begun to drag as she had become impatient with the slow progress of her recuperation.

Unconsciously smoothing the waistline of the gown she wore, Sophia was uncomfortably aware that her clothes hung loosely against her, but she knew that was not the only change in her that the past three weeks had wrought. Her complexion continued to be pale, her smile was rare, and eyes that had formerly been mirrors of her enthusiasm for life now mirrored only dark uncertainties.

Raising her chin, Sophia continued walking. She was determined to regain her strength so she might function again on her own. Obviously sensing her desire for independence, Lyle's aunt and her housekeeper had spent less and less time with them of late, and she had been grateful for their sensitivity.

Dr. Levine was satisfied with the progress she was making, Julia Kingston and Maggie had seemed awed by her recuperative powers, and she was grateful that her progress had not seen any setbacks, such as the one that had threatened after the first time Aaron had visited.

Forcibly putting Aaron from her mind, unwilling to face

the turmoil that thoughts of him evoked, Sophia realized that the only person who seemed dissatisfied with her was Lyle.

Glancing up as Lyle approached, Sophia felt again the heat of his penetrating stare as he held a sketching pad and colored pencils out toward her. Refusing to accept them, Sophia spoke with unaccustomed sharpness.

"I don't want them."

"Why not?"

"You know why." Sophia swallowed past the lump that had formed in her throat as Lyle dropped them on a nearby table. "It's because of ambitions that I couldn't let go—my fine dreams of one day wearing the silk I wound on my machines—that all this happened. I'm separated from my family and I've done something that I never thought . . ." Momentarily unable to go on, Sophia then continued more softly. "I've become a person I hardly recognize—a woman I never believed I could be."

"I don't want to hear you talk like that, Sophia."

"I know what I've done, Lyle, and so do you."

"The past is over and done. It's time to put it behind you and go on with your life."

"My life?" Sophia shook her head. "I've made a mess of it, and I've damaged yours, too." Recalling the secret Lyle had revealed to her during a long, wakeful night recently past, Sophia continued. "You've worked all your life toward making your father recognize you for the man you are, and now you've jeopardized the progress you've made by staying here to take care of me."

"You haven't damaged my life, Sophia. All you did was force me to face some things I should've faced earlier. I despised my father for deserting my mother when she needed him, and you made me see that I was no better than he was. I don't want to be like him, Sophia. I don't want to spend my life knowing I sacrificed the woman I love for ambition or for anything else. And I don't want to wake up one day to find myself a hard, cynical old man whose life is empty of all the things that are really important."

Unable to face the emotions she read in Lyle's eyes, Sophia again averted her face.

"Look at me, Sophia."

Sophia turned obediently toward him, allowing the glow of Lyle's love to warm her, at the same time despising herself for the swell of feelings it raised in return. She was confused and uncertain as he touched her cheek tentatively, then wrapped his arms around her to hold her comfortingly close. She could feel the heavy pounding of his heart as he rasped huskily against her hair, "What I did for you I did with entirely selfish motives. I love you. I'll always love you. I chose you over my position at the mill because I wanted to—because you were more important to me. Staying here with you and caring for you isn't a duty. It's a privilege. If I have my choice, I'll be with you for the rest of my life."

The ache inside her almost more than she could bear, Sophia slid her arms around Lyle's waist, comfortable in his embrace as she was in no other's. She attempted a reply that would not come.

Did she love Lyle?

She knew she had never loved him more.

Did she love him in the way he loved her?

She knew she could, so easily.

Did she still love Aaron?

Sophia closed her eyes as intimate, loving memories assaulted her. With each she had made an unspoken commitment that would allow her little peace. Aaron had left her in her moment of crisis with an ultimatum that made a mockery of the words of love he had spoken. He had returned with those same words of love on his lips. But somehow she knew he truly loved her. And if Aaron was less than he should be . . . was he any different than she?

"Sophia . . ."

Sophia opened her eyes. The piercing gold of Lyle's gaze drew her in. She felt his empathy and knew he shared her pain and turmoil as vividly as if it was his own. She felt the love that flowed between them, binding them even as it kept them apart. She felt the full depth of his desire for her, knowing it was not merely physical, but a total, complex emotion that in so many ways would demand more of her than Aaron ever had demanded, while giving more than Aaron could ever have conceived of returning. Her aching heart cried out for the fulfillment of that total emotion, to return it full measure, but it was battered and sore. Looking at Lyle with more love than she had thought she could raise inside her, she realized that his presence was a consolation and a torment—a contradiction as potent as her confused feelings could endure.

She shuddered, and Lyle drew her closer, rocking her gently as he laid his cheek against her hair and whispered, "Now it's my turn to read *your* mind, darling. I know what you're thinking, and it's all right. You don't know how you feel right now. You're confused and physically weak. If you could, you'd run away from everything and everyone until your mind cleared, but we both know that isn't possible right now." Separating himself from her so he might look directly into her eyes, Lyle continued. "I won't press you, Sophia, and I won't let anyone else press you, either. Dr. Levine said you'll soon be well enough to go out. As soon as he does, we're going to leave here. I'm going to take you back home with me and—"

"No . . ." Sophia shook her head. "I can't." Her eyes filled. "I'll spoil everything for you."

"You'll spoil everything for me if you don't."

"No."

"Yes."

"Oh, Lyle . . ."

"Once you're settled, you're going to start working on your

502

designs again. If Madame Tourneau doesn't want them because of Weiss, we'll find someone who does."

"No . . . I can't. I have a contract with Madame."

"We'll break it."

"Your father will turn against you completely if he knows you've taken me in."

"I'll find another job. The city has plenty of silk mills, and I've suddenly become a valuable entity."

Sophia shook her head. "Kingston Mill is the place you want to be. I can't let you do that."

"You can't stop me." Lyle paused, wary. His voice slipped a notch lower. "Unless you're thinking that you want to go back to your parents . . ."

Sophia closed her eyes.

"Then you're coming home with me."

"But —"

"It's settled."

"Is it?" His domineering tone raising a trace of her flagging spirit, Sophia replied slowly, "I will allow no man to dictate to me, *caro* Lyle."

Lowering his face closer to hers with a smile, Lyle whispered, "This man will." He kissed her lightly. "For a little while, at least."

His smile unexpectedly drawing one in return, Sophia whispered, "Did no one ever warn you that Italian women are headstrong — that they don't take orders easily?"

"No."

Sophia's smile slowly warmed. "Then you have much to learn."

"As long as you're the one to teach me . . ."

Holding his gaze long and hard, Sophia found her response turning to a hard lump in her throat. Lyle's gaze dropped to her lips, caressing them with almost physical warmth as he whispered, "You're tired, Sophia. Come on, it's time for bed."

Feeling the difficulty with which Lyle released her, Sophia knew in her heart that it was the hardest thing he had ever done. Lyle slipped his arm casually around her waist as he turned her toward her room. "We'll talk about the sketches tomorrow."

Walking beside him, Sophia leaned her head against his shoulder and closed her eyes. Maybe they would . . .

The car barn of the Paterson Street Railway Company was dark and deserted as the watchman made his rounds. His step slowed as the smell of smoke caught his notice and he turned, catching his breath as a tongue of flame burst from the rear wall of the building. Momentarily frozen as another burst, then another, sent more flames to join those licking at the ceiling of the cavernous building, the watchman backed out into the freezing night. The force of the wind almost knocking him from his feet, he ran to sound the alarm, fighting his way back to the building as sparks broke through the roof and were swept high into the sky.

His eyes widened as the rear of the building became engulfed in flames, the frigid gusts fanning the blaze into a roaring fury. With horror, he turned to flee.

Bells ringing, horses laboring, the fire engines turned the corner, halting him in his flight. A frenzy of activity commenced as the flames roared and cracked, whipped into an inferno by the galelike winds. Shivering in the cold, choking as the spiraling smoke grew thicker, the watchman drew back farther, knowing in his heart it was too late.

Lyle twisted and turned in a restless sleep while tormenting visions assumed control of his mind. Sophia lying unconscious in a pool of her own blood—Dr. Levine laboring over her—the sounds of Rosalie's sobs, and then his own . . . The visions changed—Aaron Weiss kneeling beside Sophia's bed—Weiss holding her hand—Weiss whispering into her ear, and then Sophia's loving smile . . .

Lyle snapped suddenly awake, his heart pounding. It was the same dream, the same nightmare that haunted him. He was determined that it would not come true, but he was afraid. He had seen the look in Sophia's eyes at the mention of Weiss's name. There was no bitterness there — no hatred for the act which Weiss had forced upon her. Instead, he had seen a strange commiseration in her eyes, and he had known then that whatever had come to pass, Sophia still believed Weiss when he said he loved her.

Lyle breathed deeply in an effort to rein his emotions under control, the question that burned inside him returning again. Did Sophia still love Weiss?

The possibility of that thought plaguing him, Lyle drew himself to his feet and began the tense pacing with which he had spent many nights. Whether Sophia loved Weiss or not was immaterial. He would not let her throw herself away on the selfish bastard again. He would protect her from Weiss at any cost. He would —

His attention caught by sounds rising over the battering of the wind, Lyle turned toward the window. He listened more intently. Fire bells ringing . . . the sounds growing closer . . .

Lyle glanced at the clock on the dresser. One o'clock.

Drawing on his pants and shirt, Lyle walked quickly toward his bedroom door. He stepped into the hallway to meet Sophia standing uncertainly there. Glorious red hair tumbling against the shoulders of her full white nightgown, her brilliant eyes still groggy from sleep, she reached out hesitantly to him.

"What's happening, Lyle? All that noise . . ."

"I don't know." Taking her hand in his, Lyle halted her a safe distance from the front door as he opened it to the frigid night air and looked outside. He was startled to see considerable traffic on the street, all of it moving in the direction of the unnaturally bright sky to the west. A heavily dressed man

505

hurried by, hunched against the wind as Lyle called out, "Do you know what's burning over there?"

The man turned back, shouting over the roar of the wind, "The mills are on fire!"

His heart going cold, Lyle drew back and closed the front door. He turned to Sophia where she stood rigidly a few feet away.

"Did you hear?"

"Yes."

Swallowing, knowing what he must do, Lyle walked to Sophia's side. His gaze held hers intently as he grasped her shoulders. "If the engines are being called out from all over the city, it must be a bad fire." He paused, his voice dropping a notch lower. "I have to go there, Sophia."

"I know."

"Go to bed. I'll return as soon as I can."

Dressed and at the door a few minutes later, Lyle turned back to Sophia to see fear in her eyes. Suddenly at his side, she slid her arms around him and hugged him close. He heard the quiver in her voice as she whispered, "Be careful."

Attempting a smile, Lyle whispered, "Don't worry. I will. I'll be back as soon as I can." He brushed her lips lightly with his. "Go back to bed, darling."

Sophia nodded and Lyle slipped out the door. On the street a few moments later, he flagged down a passing wagon and climbed aboard.

His clothes hastily donned, Aaron stood at the front door of his home, waiting impatiently as his father made his way laboriously down the stairs. Another fire engine galloped past, and Aaron's patience strained at the breaking point.

"Hurry up, Father!"

Samuel shot his son a sharp glance. "Don't worry, Aaron. The fire can wait a few minutes more."

"You shouldn't be going, dear!" Walking behind her husband, Rebecca spoke worriedly, "It's not safe for you to be there. You can't move as fast as you should. What if—"

"That's enough, Rebecca!" Panting as he stepped down on the foyer, Samuel continued. "Neither Aaron nor I will do anything foolish. If the mill is ablaze . . ." Samuel shuddered, then raised his chin. "But I know it isn't. It's all some kind of mistake."

Wrapping his muffler more tightly around his neck, Samuel reached for his hat.

"Are you ready, Aaron?"

Too annoyed to respond, Aaron took his father's arm and opened the door. His mother was right, but he knew his father was too stubborn to listen to reason.

The smell of smoke was heavy on the air as they stepped out onto the porch. Nearly rocked from his feet by the thrust of the wind, Aaron glanced toward the curb to see their carriage waiting. Waiting only until his father was safely seated inside, Aaron shouted over the roaring wind, "Get us to the mill as fast as you can, Harry."

Aaron had barely closed the door behind him when the carriage snapped into motion.

The wind buffeted Anthony relentlessly as he stood on his back porch, looking toward the fire-reddened sky. The smell of smoke caught in his throat and he coughed, then shivered in another icy blast. The sky had grown increasingly brighter in the past hour as fire bells had continued to ring. He knew the blaze was spreading, and he had carefully tracked the reflections of its progress against the night sky as it moved through the main business district of the city.

Turning at the sound of a step behind him, Anthony saw Rosalie, heavily wrapped, step out onto the porch. Behind her, Maria and Anna remained inside, peering at the brilliant display through the window. Sliding his arm around Rosalie, Anthony felt the tremors that shook her. He knew instinctively they were not due solely to the cold as he said, "Don't be afraid, Rosalie. The wind is blowing the fire away from us. We're safe here." He paused, looking intently into Rosalie's frightened face as he then addressed the unexpressed fear he saw there. "Sophia is safe, too. The fire is far from the house where she lives."

Rosalie's dark eyes searched his face. "Is that why you stayed out here watching the fire, Papa? Because you were worried about Sophia?"

Anthony's throat choked closed as the endless torment of the past few months again rose strongly inside him. He whispered the truth he could no longer deny. "Sophia is gone from my house, but she is not gone from my heart."

Her dark eyes holding his as another frigid blast rocked them, Rosalie responded above the wind's roar, "I wish she knew that, Papa. She would be so happy . . ."

Pausing, the words costing him dearly, Anthony returned, "Then you must tell her, Rosalie. When you see her again, you must tell her . . ."

The wind whistled through the streets, swirling sparks and bits of fiery debris in the air as the wagon in which Lyle rode drew to a halt. The burly driver turned, shouting over the roar of the wind, "You'll have to get off here. I'm not going any closer to the fire."

His face stiff from the cold even as the flying sparks singed him, Lyle jumped to the ground with a quick salute. The smoke thickened as he slipped past the hastily erected barricades, looking past City Hall to see Ellison Street ablaze. Market Street was a chaos of sound as he ran past the melee of excited firemen, anxious spectators, and fire engine horses rendered unmanageable by the falling embers. He halted

508

abruptly at his first sight of the spectacle of Main Street totally engulfed in flames.

Cinders falling like snowflakes were whipped by wind into a blinding screen as Lyle made his way laboriously through streets clogged with evacuees, where the wind whistled its eerie threat, and blazing boards, carried east and south by the wind, ignited new fires wherever they fell. Carefully skirting the perimeter of the fire, Lyle arrived on the lower end of Van Houten Street and halted abruptly, startled by the sight that met his eyes. Standing in a long, noble row, the silk mills were untouched—free and clear of any trace of damage—while a few streets away the city was being consumed!

Aware that the direction of the gale-force winds had spared the mills and that the winds might reverse direction at any time subjecting the mills to the same barrage of flying embers that was setting the city aflame, two fire companies worked diligently, wetting down the roofs of the mills and nearby structures and keeping watch against airborne flames. Driven past the scene of their determined efforts by an instinctive need, Lyle halted abruptly once more as Kingston Mill came into view. His heart pounding as the freezing winds whipped him, he stared at the brick structure, the focus of his angry, frustrated dreams. He had been an outsider there for the greater part of his life, an inherent right denied him, yet the building and all it represented had become a part of him. He knew his own personal loss would have been severe had it succumbed.

A single light glowed in the mill-office window. Battered by the howling wind, Lyle realized the moment toward which he had moved all his life was finally upon him. He walked spontaneously toward it.

The rattle of the carriage was overwhelmed by the frightening power of nature's elements gone wild as the Weiss carriage moved carefully along Van Houten Street. Glancing at his father where the old man sat beside him, Aaron saw the physical deterioration to which his own self-absorption had blinded him for so long. His father's complexion was a frightening shade of purple, his breathing erratic as he shivered from cold or the stress of excitement, he was uncertain which. They had arrived at Weiss Mill to find it, along with other nearby mills, untouched by the blaze that continued to raze the main business district of the city. Their fears had been immediately placated by the fire companies working at protecting the mills, but it had been obvious that the stress of the ongoing threat was exhorting a heavy price on his father.

A familiar irritation nudged as Aaron recalled the part his father had inadvertently played in the turmoil between Sophia and him. His father had been coldly ruthless in his demands, a fact that had diluted the concern he felt for the old man's physical condition. His annoyance was not such, however, that he would allow his father to return home alone right now, when he was feeling poorly.

Staring out the window as Harry followed a circuitous route in an attempt to avoid the overflow from the fire, Aaron surveyed the mills in passing. Untouched by the disaster that lit the night sky as it raged out of control, they stood dark and strong. Industry Mill, Phoenix Silk, Kingston Mill, Neuburger Silk, Waverly Mill, all were—

His introspection coming to an abrupt halt, Aaron squinted assessingly at the man he saw bent against the wind as he made his way determinedly down the street. Was that really Lyle Kingston turning onto the raceway bridge toward Kingston Mill?

The man stopped walking abruptly, the wind battering him as he stood resolutely, staring at a lit office window. A slow elation assuming control of his mind, Aaron saw the bright-blond hair almost hidden by the hat pulled well down over the man's forehead. He recognized the square set of the

510

man's shoulders, his stance arrogant, assured, even as he was abraded by the wailing elements. The man turned unexpectedly, allowing a brief glimpse of his profile, and Aaron almost laughed aloud. It was Kingston without a doubt!

Watching as Kingston strode suddenly forward, his track straight for the solitary light that glimmered in the darkness of the mill, Aaron's joy knew no bounds. The fool had made a fatal mistake! He had left Sophia alone!

Glancing cautiously at his father, Aaron saw that the old man was shivering and disinterested in what was happening on the street as he strove to adjust his lap robe for more comfort. Suddenly realizing that he had little time to spare, Aaron hammered the roof of the carriage with his fist.

"Hurry up, Harry! Get us home!"

Removing his robe from his lap, Aaron adjusted it across his father's knees, smiling as his father looked up at him. "We'll be home soon, Father. Don't worry. I'll go back and stay at the mill to make sure everything is all right."

Looking out onto the street as the carriage began an accelerated pace, Aaron felt excitement rise at the thought of the sweet meeting to come.

Lyle stepped through the unlocked entrance of Kingston Mill, struggling to close the door as the wind threatened to drag it from his frozen grip. He breathed deeply, relieved to be sheltered from the raging elements as he unwrapped his muffler, pulled his hat from his head, and ran a hand through his hair.

Beginning the long walk across the unlit mill floor, past silent machines converted into impotent shadows in the semi-darkness, he continued toward the dim light that beckoned him. Pausing briefly, he pushed open the office door as Matthew raised his head. Matthew's tone chilled him in a way the winter wind had not as he questioned abruptly, "What are you doing here?"

Deliberately delaying his response, Lyle scrutinized his father in silence. The haste with which Matthew had dressed was apparent in his uncharacteristic disarray—his carelessly donned clothing, his uncombed hair, and in the dark stubble that shadowed his chin. More disturbing still was the look about his eyes—a disorientation or a lapse of composure Lyle had never witnessed there before. Although he knew he looked similarly unkempt, Lyle was strangely affected by the sight of his father suddenly unprotected by the aura of cold authority and polished superiority he had always sought to project. The man standing before Lyle was a human being with vulnerabilities and frailties. The lines in his face, not normally so pronounced, cut deeply into skin that seemed pallid and aging, and gray strands formerly only obvious at his temples seemed to have recently made rapid inroads into the dark. Most startling of all was the innate weariness in Matthew's eyes which he strove to negate with the sharpness of his tone.

"I asked you what you're doing here!"

However, the arrogance remained . . .

"I suddenly find myself wondering the same thing."

Matthew straightened up. His emotions carefully controlled he stated flatly, "I find it incongruous that you should bother to come here now, Lyle."

"Do you?"

"Yes, I do. Through all the years that we were at odds, I thought you to be many things, but I never thought you to be a fool—yet a fool is what you've proved to be." Not waiting for a response, Matthew continued. "I gave you the opportunity of a lifetime! I gave you a chance to prove yourself, but what did you do with that chance? You threw it back in my face, that's what! You walked into my office a month ago, casually shrugging off all the responsibility that you had so eagerly assumed a few months earlier. You boldly declared yourself a

512

holiday—"

"Not a holiday!"

"No? What then? You never bothered to explain."

His slow smile reflecting sadness rather than joy, Lyle responded softly, "The truth is that I believed then, as I do now, that you were incapable of understanding the situation that led to my actions, that no explanation would satisfy you, and that you'd jump at the opportunity to escape the bargain we had made."

"Oh, did you?" Matthew took a sharp step forward. "You were doing well here, better than I had believed you were capable of doing. I was beginning to trust you. I was actually beginning to think . . ." Matthew halted abruptly, obviously regretting his brief words of praise. "But that's all in the past now. Why *did* you come back?"

The sadness inside Lyle deepened. "If you don't know why, I suppose there's no use in my trying to explain." He gave a short, self-deprecating laugh. "I really thought I'd been able to put the past behind me, but it seems it'll be a long time before I can train myself not to care what happens here."

Matthew took another step forward, his eyes holding Lyle's levelly as he questioned, *"Do* you care, Lyle?"

The question was unexpected. It caught Lyle unawares, without one of the patented responses with which he normally would have protected himself when questioned so closely by this man. Holding his father's gaze, feeling its full weight, Lyle knew this was no ordinary night—that time and circumstance had built up to the point in time where only an honest response would do. Keenly aware of the vulnerability he willingly exposed for the first time in his life, Lyle responded softly, "Yes, I care."

"Then why did you throw it all away?"

"I didn't." Lyle's jaw firmed unconsciously. "I told you I'd be back."

"And you expected me to hold your position for you—without any explanations?"

Lyle shook his head. "No, I didn't expect you to . . . and now I realize I was a fool to hope you would."

"Why should I have held it for you when you chose your loyalty to a woman over your loyalty to me? Can you tell me that?"

His hostility returning, Lyle responded sharply, "The answer to that is simple. Because I had already proved to you all that needed to be proven—because you should have known that I wouldn't have jeopardized everything I'd worked for if the situation wasn't dire—because if you weren't able to take my word on trust by then, I knew you never would. And . . ." Lyle paused. "Because I'm your son."

Beginning to tremble noticeably, Matthew muttered, "You're not my son."

"You know as well as I do that that's a lie!" Hostility turning to fury, Lyle demanded, "Look at me, Father! Damn it, look at me! Not only am I the image of you physically, but I'm like you in so many ways that it began frightening me! A near tragedy a month ago brought me to the rude awakening that I had sacrificed the woman I loved for something that might never be. And I determined then that if you wouldn't acknowledge me as your son on the merits of truth and long-overdue reason, I didn't want your acknowledgment at all!"

His fury fading as quickly as it had come, Lyle continued, a trace of a smile returning. "You see, Father, I've lived most of my life as a bastard, while the man who I knew was my father looked right through me. That cut me deeply as a child, but I'm not a child anymore. I've come to the point in my life where other priorities forced me to put that hurt aside—priorities you would never understand."

"I understand *priorities*. I've set them for myself all of my life."

"At a terrible expense to those who loved you . . ."

"So, you've judged me and the way I've conducted my life and found me wanting! I should've expected that you'd lay the blame for your deficiencies on me. It's much easier that way."

"Actually, Father, it isn't." Unblinking in the face of Matthew's mounting anger, Lyle continued softly, the aching truth that had lain unspoken inside him all his life emerging in a whisper. "The truth is that I wanted to respect you. I wanted to think that you had loved my mother and that under other circumstances, you would have loved me. I've only recently come to see, however, that I was deluding myself. My mother wasn't good enough for the new life you were building. Given enough time, you would have cast her aside and forgotten her. I suppose my mother never realized that in making that one solitary mistake, she burned a place for herself in your memory that she wouldn't have been granted otherwise. As for myself, I've come to see that I bear the same stigma as my mother in your eyes—that I wasn't good enough for you from the day I was born, and no matter how hard I work or how much I achieve, I'll *never* be good enough."

Matthew raised his chin. His trembling increased and Lyle was struck with a devastating sadness. Pausing, he continued softly, "Strangely enough, Father, after all the years of resentment and animosity that have passed between us, I find that all I feel for you now is pity for all you've thrown away. It's because of that pity, and an inexplicable sense of obligation that I seem unable to disregard, that I came here tonight. You see, Father, it suddenly occurred to me that if you lost the mill, you'd lose the only thing that was really important to you. Somehow, I wanted to spare you that."

Matthew stood rigidly, without response. With a rueful shake of his head, Lyle continued. "But, as usual, I came to offer you something that you neither needed nor wanted."

The deadening ache inside Lyle deepened. "You needn't worry that you'll be bothered with my unwanted solicitude again, though. You've finally gotten through to me. You want no part of me and never will. My only regret is that I wasn't able to accept that realization sooner. It would've saved so much—"

Halting as Matthew turned away abruptly and began stuffing papers into a leather bag, Lyle gave a short laugh. "Well, I guess everything's been said that's worth saying. There's only one thing left." Lyle paused. "Good-bye, Father."

With a sense of finality that was both relief and pain, Lyle turned toward the door. Stepping out into the frigid wind moments later, he steadied himself against the unrelenting blasts, realizing that his father had remained true to himself to the end. He hadn't even bothered to say good-bye.

The streets through which Aaron's carriage traveled on the outskirts of the fire were as light as noon, and Aaron was suddenly aware of the true scope of the holocaust that had struck the city. He needed no official notification to realize that the primary business district of the city had already been consumed, and he had the feeling as he continued to peruse a night sky brilliant with red arcs of flame, and as he suffered the sting of fiery ash even in the confines of his carriage, that it would be a long and wearying night.

Rapping loudly on the roof of the carriage, Aaron urged again, "Hurry up, Harry!"

A responsive jump in the pace of the carriage was his driver's only reply as Aaron sat back, silently congratulating himself on his foresight. He had directed Harry to take protective canvas from the carriage house to cover both himself and his stalwart gelding from the fiery sparks that had caused so much concern on the way back to the Weiss mansion. He had then installed his father at home in the care of his anxious mother.

Finally acceding to his father's rapid debilitation, Aaron knew there was an even greater need to settle the situation with Sophia. His father would not wait much longer, and he was determined not to progress a step further in his courtship of Kathryn Vandermere until Sophia was safely his again.

Keenly aware of the whirling sparks that danced on the wind, Aaron assessed the streets around him as the carriage turned onto Market Street and narrowly avoided a racing fire engine heading in the opposite direction. He squinted at the name emblazoned on the side of the vehicle — Jersey City Fire Company No. 3 — then gave a relieved laugh. Apparatus was obviously being brought in by railroad flat cars from all sections of the state. With that kind of help on line, it would be no time at all until the fire was contained.

The wind gusted again, rocking the carriage, and Aaron was momentarily uncertain. The wind was the only complication. He could only hope that —

All thought was swept from his mind as Park Avenue came into view and Aaron was grateful that Sophia was far removed from the flames. That fact had afforded him the opportunity he had been awaiting, and he was suddenly certain that destiny had intervened to grant him a second chance with the woman he loved. He would not waste it.

The familiar brick front of his bachelor residence came within sight, and Aaron's heart began a rapid pounding.

The lamp beside her bed cast elongated shadows on the flowered wall as Sophia attempted to shut out the sounds of the fire, but her efforts were of little use. She closed her eyes again, disgusted with the weakness that had forced her to remain behind, her anxieties growing greater by the moment. There was little doubt that the fire had worsened, and she feared that the whole block of mills where the fire had started

517

might be endangered. She consoled herself that her family faced little peril several blocks away from the fiery scene.

Anxiety forming a lump in her throat, Sophia knew that Lyle was the one who might be endangered. She had known the moment he had heard the news of the fire that the strange bond between Lyle and his father, forged by youthful hatred, contempt, and a reluctant admiration, had not been severed. She had sensed that bond from the first, but had only come to comprehend it completely after Lyle had confided his secret to her during that long night a few weeks earlier.

Sophia's anxiety increased as another powerful blast of wind rattled the windowpanes. Lyle had gone to help the father who had never acknowledged him, serving a bond of blood that his father had regarded with shame all of his life — and she had once told Lyle that he could never understand . . .

A sound at the door and Sophia sat upright in bed. Was it the wind or . . . ? Her heart taking wing at the sound of a key in the lock, Sophia threw back the covers. On her feet in a moment, she ran unsteadily toward the bedroom door, her joyful smile dying on her lips at first sight of the person standing just inside the entrance.

"Aaron!"

Swaying weakly, Sophia grasped the door for support. She took an uncertain step backward as Aaron walked directly toward her, stripping off his hat and coat as he walked, running a hand through his hair as he searched her face for a sign of welcome. She saw true despair register in the darkness of his eyes as he whispered, "Aren't you glad to see me, Sophia?"

Breathless from the rapid pounding of her heart, Sophia rasped, "How did you know—"

"How did I know you were alone?" Aaron gave a short laugh and walked closer. "I saw Kingston go into the mill. His uncle was evidently inside and he—"

Halting abruptly as Sophia paled and swayed again, Aaron grasped her arms in support as she gasped, "The mill—is it on fire?"

"You're worried about the bastard, is that it, Sophia?" A familiar jealousy curled Aaron's lips. "Well, you needn't be. The mills are safe. They're out of the path of the fire. The business district is burning—a portion of Van Houten Street and Ellison Street, both sides of Main Street . . ."

Stunned at the unexpected news, Sophia whispered, "What about Prospect Street?"

"Safe."

Sophia released a tense breath, adding in afterthought, "Madame's salon . . . ?"

Aaron laughed. "Gone, along with your contract with her! The French bitch will be looking for financing to start again when this is over. I may agree to help if she consents to a full partnership." Aaron laughed again, suddenly amused. "Or I may hire her to work for us . . ."

Aaron's hands burned her arms through the light fabric of her gown as Sophia whispered, "There is no 'us,' Aaron."

The laughter drained from Aaron's face. "You don't mean that, Sophia."

"Yes . . . yes, I do."

"No." His agitation growing, Aaron drew her closer despite her protest, wrapping his arms around her, forcing the full length of her body against his as he whispered, "No, you don't. You're angry with me, and I don't blame you. I panicked when you told me you were going to have a child. I couldn't see past the complications your condition would cause. I left you with an ultimatum that I didn't really mean."

"Didn't you, Aaron?"

Aaron blinked in the face of her unexpected doubt. "Yes, I suppose I meant it, but I knew you loved me and that you wouldn't let anything come between us. I was certain you'd follow through with what I had told you to do."

"You knew me so well . . ."

Her sarcasm escaping him, Aaron whispered, "I knew you loved me."

"I did love you."

"You *do* love me!"

"No."

The force of the wind shook the room, rocking them, lending an eerie urgency to the passion enfolding between them as true panic dawned in Aaron's eyes. "Yes! Sophia, listen to me, please. I made a mistake — a terrible mistake. I regret it more than I've regretted anything in my life. I want to make all this up to you. I want to take care of you, to love you, to make all your dreams come true."

"My dreams . . ." The words were a hard lump in her throat, and Sophia rasped, "I no longer dream, Aaron."

Aaron was momentarily silent as his dark eyes searched hers, as he read the truth of her words. "I'll restore your dreams, Sophia. I promise you I will. I'll make you forget the suffering you've endured. I'll make you forget the day it all went bad between us. I'll make you forget everything and everyone except the love that we shared — how beautiful it was between us . . . how beautiful it can be between us again."

Aaron's earnest plea tearing at her, the knowledge that this proud man was begging, tortured a heart already battered and weary as she whispered harshly in return, "Can you drive away the echoes of a baby's cry I'll never hear? Can you take away the blurred images of the child I'll never see? Can you make me forget what I did?"

Silent in the face of her anguish, Aaron briefly closed his eyes. She felt the heavy pounding of his heart against her breast and the tremors that shook him. Startled, she saw tears slip from beneath his closed lids and she gasped at his soft cry as he crushed her closer still, muttering low, tormented words against her hair. Suffering his grief as she had suffered her own, Sophia held herself rigid in his arms, refusing to console him.

"Forgive me, Sophia. Please forgive me." Pressing light kisses against her hair, Aaron rasped, "I didn't really know what it meant to love. I realized what it meant only when I nearly lost you and found how bleak the days would be if I could never hold you in my arms again. I need you, Sophia. Don't turn your back on me."

Taking no pleasure in the words she knew she must say, Sophia responded, "It's too late, Aaron."

"No, it isn't!"

"Too many things have happened that can't be undone."

"I love you, Sophia." Aaron drew back to look down into her face, and Sophia shuddered at the pain she saw openly displayed. "I'll prove to you that you can love me again. I'll make you see . . ."

Cupping her chin in his hand, Aaron kissed her once, twice, his face distorted with anxiety as she sought to escape him. Holding her fast, he covered her mouth with his, forcing her lips apart, kissing her over and over again until she was weak from the struggle to escape him.

His mouth trailing from her bruised lips, Aaron pressed heated kisses against her throat, her shoulders, his trembling hands tearing at her gown as she protested, again struggling to escape him. Suddenly swept up into his arms, Sophia felt the room sweep past her, then the softness of the bed beneath her back. She cried out in protest as Aaron's mouth met the warm flesh of her breasts as he caressed them, tortured them with his kisses. Weak, unable to fight him any longer, Sophia felt consciousness drift away under his heady ministrations, only to hear the renewed panic in Aaron's voice as he shook her, demanding, "Sophia . . . Sophia open your eyes, darling. I didn't want to hurt you. I only wanted to love you . . . to make you love me. Sophia, please . . ."

Struggling her way out of the blackness that threatened to

engulf her, Sophia read the true torment on Aaron's face, and her sorrow was profound. Where there was once love, only compassion remained.

"I love you, Sophia. I've never loved anyone the way I love you. I never will. Tell me you forgive me."

"I forgive you."

"Tell me you can love me again."

Filled with sadness, Sophia whispered, "You ask too much."

The kiss that met her lips then was angry. It was touched with desperation, remorse, pain. Raising her hand to Aaron's cheek, she returned it, seeking to assuage his distress while knowing that a part of her had gone cold, never to be touched by his kiss again.

His cheek was warm as it rested against hers. She felt the moistness of his tears and she shuddered, her mind repeating, "Too late . . . too late . . ."

"I'll make you love me again, Sophia. You know I will."

Silent, Sophia closed her eyes. Tears streaked from their corners into the fiery hair at her temples. Yes, she knew . . . many things . . .

His weight suddenly lifted from her, Aaron leaned over her, restoring her gown, fastening the buttons he had ripped open so viciously only minutes earlier. Drawing the blanket up over her, Aaron turned to the night table. Recognizing the packets he saw there, he emptied one into a glass and filled it with water. Supporting her with his arm, he held the glass to her lips.

"Here, drink this, Sophia. It'll make you sleep, but before you do, I want you to think about what I'm telling you now." His dark eyes bright with fervor, his handsome face filled with pain, Aaron continued. "I've done many things in my life that I should've been ashamed of . . . things I should've regretted, but I never felt a moment's regret or shame—until now. If I could change what happened—" His voice breaking,

Aaron sought for control, then rasped, "But you loved me once, darling, and I promise you, you'll love me again. I'll *make* you love me, and I'll make you put all the heartache behind you. Then I'll love you and cherish you for the rest of my life."

"No. It's too late, Aaron."

Pressing a gentle kiss against her lips, Aaron whispered, "I have to go now. I have to go back to the mill, but I'll return tomorrow. I'll take you away from here, to somewhere we can begin to put the past behind us."

"No . . ."

"Don't talk, darling. Just drink."

Settling her back against the pillow when the glass was drained, Aaron kissed Sophia deeply, with a gentleness that started tears anew. Tenderly wiping them from her face, he whispered, "Good night, darling."

Sophia heard the front door open, then close, and she knew he was gone. She turned to stare at the window, at the unnatural light slanting through the blinds.

Yes, she knew many things, and as sleep slowly overwhelmed her, she remembered . . .

The catastrophe raged on, spilling into the streets at the perimeter of the fire where refugees clustered, children cried, and the frantic activity to protect the mills continued. The roadway was choked with people, vehicles, animals hoping to escape the devouring flames, all coming together in a knot of fear behind the main lines of the effort.

Gravely affected by the plight of the desperate people gathered there as he sought to make his way home, Lyle found himself drawn into the tumult once more as he spotted a child wandering in the street behind him. In a few rapid steps, he snatched the boy up, holding him protectively against the relentless gusts until a woman rushed to claim him. Turning into the wind, the mother took the child to a nearby doorway where the rest of her family clustered. Lyle followed the woman's unsteady progress with his gaze, watching as the children bundled for protection against the cold.

Another great arc of flame shot against the night sky, raising a wail from those behind him, and Lyle unconsciously shuddered. He was unable to measure the passage of time since he had left the mill. He frowned as the sky assumed the light of day in reflection of the blaze that raged unrestricted a few blocks away. The smell of smoke had seemed to grow greater. It choked him, even as the battering wind rocked him more viciously than before. Drawing himself erect, Lyle stared to the southeast, studying the sky.

The sound of hoofbeats turned Lyle to the street behind him in time to see the arrival of an excited horseman. Leaning down to the fire captain, the fellow shouted a message that was lost to Lyle over the roar of the wind. The captain's acknowledgment his cue, the rider then kicked the horse into motion again and quickly disappeared from sight around the curve in the street.

Apprehension soared to a driving fear inside Lyle as the captain snapped into motion, shouting to his men. The firemen had mounted the fire apparatus, ready to roll, when Lyle reached their side. Grasping the captain's arm, he shouted, "Where're you going, Captain? What happened?"

"The fire's jumped the railroad tracks! All the engines on the perimeters have been called in to fight the fire there!"

Lyle's heart leaped with fear. It wasn't possible! The fire couldn't have traveled that far or that fast! He had thought Sophia was safe!

The fire engine jerked into motion and Lyle leaped, catching the rear of the wagon as it began rolling. His throat thick with fear, Lyle clutched the wagon rails, cursing himself, and desperately hoping . . .

Following the fire wagon with his gaze as it raced out of

sight, Matthew felt fear rise inside him. Standing in the shadows, he had heard the grave pronouncement of the progress of the fire and he had seen Lyle's agitation as he had leaped aboard the wagon.

Matthew briefly closed his eyes against the portent of the scene. The world he knew was burning down around him, but as Lyle's face appeared again before his mind's eye, he was suddenly keenly aware that much more than his mill was threatened.

Apprehension and anxiety teamed with a deep, heartfelt regret to lend a new motivation to his step as Matthew started forward. He clutched the leather bag he had filled so carefully, realizing the papers he had frantically stuffed inside meant little in the face what he had almost thrown away.

Pride had forced him to turn Lyle away all of his life. He had tried to discourage him, demean him, to make him believe he was less than he was, but none of it had worked. Lyle had only grown stronger under his attack and more determined, until, in the end, Lyle had demonstrated more clearly than Matthew had been able to acknowledge as they had stood face-to-face in the mill a short time earlier, that he was the better man.

Matthew raised his chin against the thrust of the wind. He knew now what he must do. He would go directly home to his wife, and he would speak gently and honestly, but with a firmness that bespoke the truth he could no longer deny. He would say:

"Edith, there's something I have to tell you . . . something I should've told you a long time ago. It's about Lyle. You see, dear, he's my son . . ."

Anthony shuddered in the wind, his eyes on the night sky as he stood on the sidewalk in front of his house. The streets around him were filled with the overflow from the fire — wagons, equipment, people clustered in every available niche that provided shelter from the elements. An occasional shout or wail was heard over the roar of the ceaseless wind, but all present were otherwise silent as they watched the destructive path of the fire glowing against the sky.

Another tremor shook Anthony. At the same moment he felt a touch on his arm. He turned to see Maria, wrapped in a heavy blanket, standing by his side. Her pale eyes avoided his face as she held out a steaming cup of coffee.

"Here. Drink. It will warm you."

Accepting it, Anthony took a sip, than another, closing his eyes as the hot liquid warmed a path to his stomach. Snapping them open again, he turned to Maria as she spoke.

"Come inside now, Anthony. You'll get sick."

Anthony shook his head. "No, I'll be all right."

"But why must you stand here? It will do no good."

Ignoring his wife, Anthony drank deeply from the cup, then draining it, he gave it back to her. "Go inside. Your daughters are alone."

"But—"

No longer listening, Anthony snapped toward the sound of fire bells as a racing fire engine turned up the street. A steamer, then a hook and ladder . . . Anthony's heart began a heavy pounding. Something was happening . . .

Bells again, and Anthony saw a fire wagon racing behind. He shouted out to it, struck to the heart with fear as the fireman on the rear shouted back, "The fire's jumped the tracks!"

Looking back at Maria, Anthony saw the same thought had struck them simultaneously as she grasped his arm, rasping, "You must go to her, Anthony!" Tears overflowed her eyes to streak her lined, remorse-filled face as she continued. "You must bring Sophia home where it's safe before it's too late!" Maria's trembling hand tightened. "Please, Anthony, tell her I was wrong. Tell her I'm sorry . . . for everything."

Not waiting to respond, propelled into a run by fear that was a hard knot inside him, Anthony started down the street. The vision of Sophia's beautiful face vied with Maria's tear-streaked visage in his mind, the two women he still loved more than life.

Sophia was dreaming. It was so warm and the air was thick and heavy. It pressed on her chest, making it difficult to breathe and she struggled to get a clear breath. Aaron's face . . . then Lyle's . . . swam in front of her. She heard their voices calling her, but she could not seem to awaken.

A fierce wind battered her, bathing her in its warm heat. She heard it rattle at the windows. She heard it whistle through the streets. She heard bells . . .

Fire bells . . .

Sophia forced open her heavy eyelids. She was surrounded in a gray fog. No, it was smoke. It caught in her throat and she choked, than coughed, struggling to escape the heavy weight of her limbs. It was so hot.

Forcing herself to a seated position, Sophia attempted to clear her head, but it swam dizzyingly. She drew herself to her feet, suddenly realizing, as breathing became more diffi-cult, that the room was filling with smoke. She strained for breath.

Glancing around her, she grasped her dressing gown from the chair, holding it over her face in an attempt to block out the smoke, but it was to no avail. She dropped weakly to her knees to crawl toward the door, but the opening eluded her. She was lost . . . the thickening smoke disorienting her, the battle for breath too much for her limited strength. She felt the blackness close in to steal her life and she mused as the harsh reality faded that she had not thought it would end this way . . .

Lyle's heart pumped with a fear that blocked out the cold and negated the effect of the ruthless wind, leaving only the horrendous scenes of destruction that met his eyes as the fire wagon charged through the burning streets. Suddenly whipped by a storm of colored fire as flying cinders stung his face and hands, he clung desperately to the rails, hearing the ring of screaming voices muted by the screeching wind as great walls of flames raged uncontested, felling everything in their path. Momentarily blinded by the vicious sparks, Lyle felt the wagon turn, skirting the fire as it arrived at the railroad tracks and plunged onward toward the line of buildings burning beyond.

With horror, Lyle watched one block pass, then two where the fire raged on. He hoped . . . he prayed . . .

Aaron steadied himself against the bump and sway of the carriage as Harry negotiated another quick turn to avoid flames pouring from side streets they had traveled only a short time earlier. His fears soared!

He had been so certain the fire would be contained! Turned back time and time again by impassable streets, he had instructed Harry to take a circuitous route back to Weiss Mill when he had noticed the wild rush of engines toward the southeast. The surge of fear he had experienced in learning that the fire had jumped the tracks had momentarily paralyzed him and that hesitation had been his undoing. His order to turn and follow the path of the engines had come moments too late as a thunderous roar precipitated a building collapse that blocked the roadway. Explosions of fire were everywhere, impeding their progress until he was beside himself with desperation.

The heat intense, the great dazzling light of the fire growing brighter, Aaron felt his apprehension mount as the carriage turned onto a clear strip where they began traveling freely once more.

Trembling, Aaron closed his eyes. What had he done? He had thought the fire would soon be controlled, and he had left Sophia. He had given her a sleeping draught, making her more vulnerable to the fire. She was alone . . . in danger. He should not have left her!

Opening his eyes again, Aaron stared out at the passing street as they crossed the tracks a distance from the fire. He swore a heartfelt oath. He would get Sophia out of that house and to a point of safety, and he would nurse her back to health. When she was well again, he would take her away . . . away from all the things that threatened to come between them. He would love her and keep her with him forever. He would make no further sacrifices to his father's demands or to his own senseless prejudices. He would love her, and he would make her love him. They would be together forever . . . Sophia and him.

Sophia . . . his love . . . if he could get to her in time . . .

The fire wagon drew to a sudden halt, the powerful horses blowing hard from the strain of their effort as Lyle hit the ground at a run. He was nearing the end of the street when he saw the familiar brick-faced house he sought was wrapped in a cloud of smoke as burning embers driven by the ferocious wind beat against it, covering the roof and windowsills with a glittering rain of fire.

Pushing his way through the assembled throng, he grasped the nearest fireman roughly as he shouted over the roar of the wind, gesticulating wildly in the direction of the house.

A hard shake of the head confirmed his greatest fears. Sophia had not emerged.

Almost knocked from his feet by a sudden, vicious blast of wind, Lyle stared in horror as a great body of flame was hurtled from a burning building beyond onto the roof of the house. Bolting forward, escaping the clutching hands that sought to restrain him as the roof exploded into flame, Lyle thrust open the front door.

Momentarily blinded by the choking smoke inside, unable to catch his breath, Lyle hesitated briefly, then ran forward, shouting Sophia's name. His only response the crackle of flames that grew increasing louder, Lyle stumbled onward, finally reaching the bedroom doorway, where he gasped at the sight of a broken window and the bed fully aflame. He shouted over the growing din of whistling wind and crackling blaze, stumbling forward as his foot struck an object on the floor.

Startled at the sight of Sophia lying there, Lyle fell to his knees. Coughing, straining for breath, he gathered Sophia into his arms, desperation giving him the strength he needed to lift her from the floor and run, with all his might, toward the front door.

Gasping, hardly aware of the hands that grasped him in support, Lyle labored for breath, relinquishing Sophia to the fireman who carried her a safe distance from the fire and wrapped her in a blanket. Tears streaming from his eyes, Lyle followed and fell to the ground beside her. Coughing, his chest heaving, he watched Sophia's still, smoke-blackened face, a sob rising in his throat as the agony inside him expanded to excruciating pain.

"Sophia . . ." His trembling hands touched her face. She was so still. "Sophia . . ."

Her delicate lids fluttered. Lyle held his breath.

Suddenly wracked by a deep spasm, Sophia began coughing, her slender body rocked by the violent exertions. Relief exploding inside him, Lyle started to laugh. He was laughing still, shuddering with the effort, tears streaming from his eyes as he took Sophia into his arms.

Bracing himself as the carriage drew to a screeching halt, Aaron snapped forward on his seat as Harry called out from atop, "I can't get any closer, sir! The street's blocked!"

Out of the door in a moment, Aaron jumped to the ground and started running, his panic-stricken gaze on the row of buildings a short distance away where fire burned brightly. Wheezing and breathless from his frantic pace, he turned the corner, coming to an abrupt halt at the sight that met his eyes. The upper portion of his house was engulfed in flames!

Horror assuming control of his mind, Aaron broke into a run. He charged through the crowd, suffering a premonition of loss so acute that it caused physical pain as he shouted Sophia's name. A parade of horror flashed across his mind when she was nowhere to be found within the crowd, and he inched closer to the blaze, fear slashing viciously at his control as he paused.

He heard it then, a voice coming from within! It was Sophia! She was calling him!

His breath emerging in a sob, Aaron rushed forward. Thrusting open the front door, he burst into the dense, choking smoke.

"Stop that man!"

A shout from the fireman standing beside them raised Lyle's head as the fellow gasped incredulously, "Someone's running into that house you just came out of! He's crazy! It's ready to go!"

Relinquishing Sophia to the fireman's ministrations, Lyle jumped to his feet, swaying, staring with disbelief as Aaron disappeared through the doorway. He turned at Sophia's frightened rasp.

"What happened, Lyle? Who was it?"

Lyle swallowed tightly. "It was Weiss. He ran into the house."

"He's looking for me!" Pushing the blanket off her, Sophia attempted to draw herself to her feet. She resisted Lyle's aid, fighting his attempt to restrain her as she lunged forward, protesting hoarsely, "I have to stop him!"

Debility thwarting her, Sophia managed a few steps before swaying weakly. She was unconscious of the arms supporting her, of the blanket draped around her shoulders as her eyes widened with horror. The house shook in the ravages of fire and relentless wind, and she screamed into the unrelenting din, "Aaron, come out! I'm here! I'm here!"

Intent on the doorway through which Aaron had disappeared, Sophia felt terror consume her mind at the building's first warning shudder. Flames licking upward toward the sky became stronger, brighter, sending out a spectacular brilliance in the moment before a huge, explosive boom momentarily blocked out all other sound.

A sudden silence overwhelming her mind, Sophia watched as the house appeared to flutter in the wind. It shuddered once more with a grace that belied the savage destruction incurred as it tumbled slowly, with infinite, deadly brilliance to the ground.

Tears streaming from her eyes as her mind recorded a horror which she refused to fully absorb, Sophia shook her head. She looked up unsteadily at Lyle as he wrapped his arms around her.

"No . . ."

The trailing whisper fraught with anguish escaped her lips in the moment before merciful darkness assumed control.

Chapter Twenty-four

Huge rolling columns of smoke barreled in upon Sophia, choking her. She screamed aloud, her voice echoing in the empty, smoke-filled void surrounding her.

Terror . . . pain . . . fear . . .

She saw his face then . . . Aaron. His dark eyes were earnest and filled with regret. The love in his deep voice was etched with pain as he whispered, "I didn't mean to hurt you. I didn't know what it meant to love. I've never loved anyone the way I love you. I'll make you love me again."

No . . . no. Too late . . .

She saw it again . . . the house shuddering in the throes of its consumption by the fire, swaying hypnotically in the few seconds before it burst into a brilliant light and fell, gracefully, lethally, to the ground.

Her eyes snapping open in escape from the horrifying images, Sophia gasped aloud. The world rocked and jolted beneath her as her blurred vision slowly cleared to meet gold eyes instead of dark, filled with concern. She looked around her to see the inside of an ambulance, and glancing outside through the window opposite her, she glimpsed the fire-ravaged streets of the city.

It was true.

Unaware of the tears that streamed down her smoke-stained cheeks, Sophia rasped, "It wasn't a dream. Aaron's dead . . ."

Lyle took her hands in his. "Yes, it's true. There was nothing you could do. Nothing anyone could do. It was a tragic mistake."

"He was trying to save me, Lyle! He did it because he loved me."

Lyle hesitated, the price he paid for his words heavy in his voice as he whispered, "Yes, he did."

Lyle's simple response an unexpected catharsis, Sophia was suddenly sobbing violently, her body shuddering with grief for all that had once been and was no more . . . for all that could have been and would never be . . . for the waste of love and life . . . for Aaron.

Allowing her grief full measure, Lyle held her close, comforting her. As her sobs drew to a halt, he wiped her tears from her cheeks and drew back from her unexpectedly. Sophia's protest died on her lips as the shift of his broad shoulders revealed the smaller man behind him. Her breath caught in her throat at the sight of the warm, homely face, the dark, tear-filled eyes and great quivering mustache.

"Papa . . ."

Sophia reached out to him with a sob, the harsh words and distance between them bridged by the torment she read on his face and the love that soared between them as his shaking arms closed around her. Trembling as he trembled, crying as he cried, she clutched him desperately close and closed her eyes. She was a child again in her father's arms. She was safe, protected, understood as only he understood her, loved as only he loved her. She was filled with the warmth and goodness of him, home at last.

But her happiness was fleeting as reality returned and she drew back, heartfelt words quavering on her lips.

"I'm so sorry I hurt you, Papa. Please forgive me. I've missed you so much."

Her father drew her close once more. His mustache

534

brushed her face and she felt the dampness of his cheek, heard the tremor in his voice as he whispered, "Papa's sorry, too, *figlia mia*. There's been no joy without you, but that's all over now. Don't cry. Everything will be all right."

The unexpressed anguish of separation shuddered in her father's strong arms, and it shuddered inside Sophia as well. She heard his soft, almost incoherent words of regret mumbled against her hair, and she seconded them in her mind. She was touched by the unique consolation she received only from the sound of his softly accented voice speaking so earnestly from the heart.

But the pain remained. And Sophia knew . . .

She was not a child anymore. Her love for her father, no matter how deep, did not have the power to erase the sorrow of the woman she had become. Her heart rent in two, she rasped, "Oh, Papa, somehow everything went wrong . . ."

Anthony's heavy features twitched with suppressed emotion as he strained for control. "*Sì*. It went wrong when your papa turned his back on you. It went wrong when he put his foolish pride before his love for you. It went wrong when he spilled his own life's blood by denying you, daughter of my heart." Pausing to still the trembling of his full lips, Anthony continued fervently. "But that's all over now. We will turn our back on the past and put the bad things behind us. We will forget."

"I can't forget, Papa." Sophia's voice cracked on a sob. "Aaron's dead."

"I know, *figlia mia*."

"He loved me."

"I know."

Anthony brushed the tears from her cheeks and then wiped away his own as he whispered in a quaking voice, "When the doctor says you are able, you will come home, Sophia. Your mama wants you back. She asks you to forgive her, and I ask the same."

A spontaneous movement from behind Anthony drew Sophia's gaze to Lyle's suddenly tense expression. She saw the protest in his eyes and sensed the panic that welled inside him at her father's unexpected words. Her heart reached out to him even as she felt the weight of her father's gaze and realized there was only one response she could give.

"Oh, Papa, I can't come home."

"Can't come home?" Stricken, Anthony gripped her hand. "Why, *figlia mia?* It's where you belong."

"No, Papa. Not anymore." Aaron's face again appeared before her and Sophia pleaded, "Please try to understand, Papa. So much has happened. All my life I searched for that person inside me . . . that person I saw in my mind. When I left home, I tried to tell myself that I had found her with Aaron, but I knew somewhere deep inside that I hadn't. It was too late when I realized . . ."

Taking a deep breath, drawing strength from the growing light in Lyle's steady gaze, Sophia continued in a whisper. "Aaron loved me, but his love was selfish, Papa. It wasn't Aaron's fault. He didn't really know how to love until it was too late. But I did. I should've been able to teach him, but I couldn't somehow. I let him down, and there's nothing left now of what we shared but painful memories and some charred and tattered silk. There should've been more . . ."

Sophia halted, breathing deeply in an effort to go on. "I don't want that to happen again, Papa. I've failed one man I loved. I don't want to fail another."

The ambulance drew to a halt and Lyle moved back to her side. He addressed Anthony, his smoke-stained face unsmiling. "Sophia's trying to tell you that she's coming home with me. You don't have to worry about her, Mr. Marone. I'll take care of her."

"Sophia . . ."

Responding to her father's spontaneous appeal, Sophia forced back the emotion that tightened her throat. She clutched his calloused hand, her heart in the four short words she spoke.

"I love you, Papa."

Anthony's dark eyes locked with hers. Pain, then a reluctant understanding, dawned there in the moment before Lyle scooped her up into his arms, brushing aside the attendants who prepared to move her stretcher. Sophia leaned against Lyle as he carried her into the hospital, intently conscious of Anthony's lagging step as he walked behind them. Her father's sadness weighing heavily on her heart, Sophia drew from Lyle's strength as they moved into another room and the door closed behind them.

Leaning toward her in their momentary solitude, his expression solemn, Lyle whispered, "I meant what I said, Sophia. I'll take care of you."

"And I'll take care of you."

A hint of a smile touched Lyle's lips at her reply. He trailed his fingertips against her cheek, sobering. "I'll love you all my life."

"As I'll love you . . ."

His eyes moistening, Lyle continued in a breaking voice, "I'll make all your dreams come true, Sophia. I'll —"

Pressing a finger against his lips, Sophia whispered hoarsely, "Oh, Lyle, don't you see? I was searching in all the wrong places for the image of myself that I saw in my mind. What I was looking for was here all along, in your eyes. I see myself there now, as I always wanted to be. I'm beautiful. I'm respected. I'm loved. I have everything that's important, everything I couldn't have with anyone else but you because you're a part of me. The rest —" Sophia shrugged, a haze of tears returning with the image of Aaron's face, "The rest is gone in a wisp of smoke.

537

And if grief remains . . ." Sophia briefly closed her eyes as the searing pain rose once more. "I know I can only make it right by loving well this time, with all my heart."

"Sophia . . ." His gold eyes glowing with the consummate fire, Lyle whispered soft, unintelligible words against her lips, the need for words ceasing the moment his mouth closed over hers. Loving him, knowing he loved her, Sophia knew—oh yes, she knew—no other fire would ever burn so bright, nor so long, nor so true as the one between them.

Oh, yes, she knew . . .

Epilogue

A hairbrush in her hand, Sophia stood at her bedroom window, looking out onto the early-morning street. The sun danced on her bright hair, on the flawless sheen of her skin, and on her small, perfect features, which were seriously composed. Her active strokes had ceased as she had paused to survey the budding trees and new green of the grass in the field beyond. In the distance she could see the rise of the new city of Paterson, more handsome and active than before the great fire that had taken such a tremendous toll a year earlier, but Sophia knew in her heart that for many, the scars remained.

Aaron's image returned before her mind. It was a painful image in many ways, but Sophia kept tears at bay. She had come to terms with her dark memories by acknowledging the things that she could not change. Aaron was gone. No amount of regrets could negate the terrible tragedy of his death. Samuel Weiss had sold his mill shortly after the fire, and his wife and he had then moved out of the city.

She had made her peace with Mama in the time since the fire, but some things had not changed. The look in her eyes, the trace of resentment, occasionally returned. The reason for it was a mystery, a secret she supposed would never be revealed. As for Papa . . . Sophia smiled. Papa had remained close by until she recuperated from her ordeal a year earlier. He had supported her, smoothed the sharp edges that remained between Mama and her, and, understanding the grief that she concealed so well, he had soothed her aching heart. The sound of his voice had been balm to her wounds, and the words, *"figlia mia,"* lovingly spoken, were still among the sweetest she had ever heard.

An unexpected sound turned Sophia's head at the moment strong arms slipped around her waist from behind.

"Lyle . . ."

Sophia's smile of greeting was covered by his kiss and she indulged it, separating her lips in sweet intimacy, drinking deeply of the love that flowed between them. Tested under the harshest conditions, it had remained strong, invincible, growing deeper each day.

Lyle stroked the rise of her stomach. "You're getting lush and round, darling, like a ripe, warm melon."

"Ah, Lyle," Sophia laughed softly. "You flatter me so."

Leaning back against the muscled wall of Lyle's chest, Sophia allowed his warm strength to fill her once more. Yes, a new life healed . . . Its prospect had brought joy to Aunt Julia's eyes, and had even tempered the reluctance with which Matthew Kingston had accepted her marriage to Lyle, the son he had only recently acknowledged and his partner in the mill. As for Edith . . . her pale eyes remained cold. Sophia supposed the woman consoled herself that Paul, happy in Paris, was free to return to the business any time he wished, with a portion of the mill remaining his. A difficult woman, Edith would, Sophia feared, remain difficult to the end.

Anna . . . now so strong . . . and Rosalie, bright and quick as ever, had quietly rejoiced at their new relationship to the "boss" at the mill. Angela Moretti would never chase Rosalie, calling her names again.

Ah, yes . . . her Seasons of Silk . . . Sophia absent-mindedly fingered the silk dressing gown she wore, one of

540

her many creations that the wealthy of the city had eagerly sought after the fiery holocaust of a year earlier. Madame Tourneau had been quite happy to take her on again, in a capacity far above that in which she had formerly labored. After all, the wife and daughter-in-law of two of the most respected silk manufacturers in the city added a prestige on which the Frenchwoman could bank.

The city had healed. And except for occasional dark moments of sorrow and regret, *she* had healed.

Looking up at Lyle unexpectedly, Sophia saw an expression she had seen before, an uncertainty that tempered the glow of his eyes—a trace of pain.

Turning in his arms, Sophia touched his cleanly shaven cheek, fragrant with soap. She slid her fingers into his hair, thick and bright as the sun. She curled her hand around his neck, a possessive gesture she enjoyed and he indulged, but this time he didn't smile.

"What's wrong, darling?" Sophia searched his face, her obvious concern curving Lyle's lips with a smile.

"Nothing. It's nothing."

He brushed her mouth with a kiss that clung despite its brief intent until his arms were wrapped tight around her and she returned as he gave, loving and wanting.

Lying together later as the sun rose higher, casting its glow on their intimacy, Lyle caressed her cheek, but the shadows between them remained.

Unwilling to indulge them, Sophia whispered, "Tell me what's bothering you, *caro*. I want to know."

Lyle's reply was hesitant . . . reluctant as he searched her face. "It's just that sometimes I wonder what would've happened if Aaron hadn't been killed that day."

"I would still be here beside you, as I am now." Her gaze locking with his, her voice trembling with the sudden fervency of her words, Sophia whispered, "If you doubted that before, you must never doubt again. I knew that day

541

as I know now that *you* are the only man who touches my heart, the only man who speaks to my mind and to my soul, and the only man I have ever loved as I love you. And if I mourn for Aaron, I mourn the tragedy of waste, the pain of loss that for some will never cease, and the man he could never be."

Sophia searched Lyle's face, love in her eyes and in her voice as she whispered, "The truth is, my darling, that I was always yours."

Drinking her words with his kiss, Lyle took them deep inside him, loving her.